REINING IN
MURDER

REINING IN MURDER

Leigh Hearon

KENSINGTON BOOKS
http://www.kensingtonbooks.com

KENSINGTON BOOKS are published by

Kensington Publishing Corp.
119 West 40th Street
New York, NY 10018

All Kensington titles, imprints and distributed lines are available at special quantity discounts for bulk purchases for sales promotion, premiums, fund-raising, educational or institutional use. Special book excerpts or customized printings can also be created to fit specific needs. For details, write or phone the office of the Kensington Special Sales Manager: Kensington Publishing Corp., 119 West 40th Street, New York, NY, 10018. Attn. Special Sales Department. Phone: 1-800-221-2647.

Kensington and the K logo Reg. U.S. Pat. & TM Off.

ISBN-13: 978-1-4967-0033-9
ISBN-10: 1-4967-0033-3
First Kensington Mass Market Edition: April 2016

eISBN-13: 978-1-4967-0034-6
eISBN-10: 1-4967-0034-2
First Kensington Electronic Edition: April 2016

10 9 8 7 6 5 4 3 2

Printed in the United States of America

For Lorene

REINING IN
MURDER

CHAPTER I

She awoke suddenly out of a troubled sleep. The silence within her small bedroom felt deafening.

From across the hall in the kitchen, the Seth Thomas clock bonged the quarter hour. Annie Carson looked up. It was 3:15, a time all smart horsewomen should be asleep.

The clock that marked each quarter hour in slow, sonorous tones was a comfort. The vibrate mode on her cell phone was nothing but an irritant.

"Hell's bells." Annie sighed and picked up the offending item. She glanced at the caller ID and swung her legs out of bed. She knew she was going to get dressed, and warmly, too.

"Top o' the morning to you, Annie," came the voice on the other end. "We've got a live one on Highway 3, Milepost 11. Near rollover with a horse trailer."

Annie cringed. "How's the horse, Dan?"

"Scared. But no broken bones or blood—I think. It's a miracle, but he seems to have survived the crash. Can't say the same for the driver."

"I'll be there as soon as I can throw on some clothes."

"Appreciate that." Dan clicked off.

"And by the way," Annie said to the dead connection, "it's not the top o' the morning. It's the middle of the freakin' night."

Dan Stetson—aptly named, since his head was about as big as a ten-gallon hat—was the local sheriff in Suwana County. Annie was used to getting calls in the middle of the night from Dan, so it didn't take her long to pull on her work clothes, fire up her F250 with the three-stall horse trailer attached, and gulp down a cup of reheated coffee while she waited for the rig to warm up. She nodded to Wolf, a mangy Blue Heeler who had thoughtfully placed himself in front of the kitchen door in case Annie forgot he existed. He trotted behind her into the frigid air and leapt, in a single graceful bound, onto the back of the truck and into his open crate.

It might have been late February, but on the Olympic Peninsula the thermometer still dropped into the twenties at night, so *layering,* the euphemistic word Northwesterners used to describe heaping on silk underwear, insulated jeans, and a trio of ratty old Scandinavian sweaters, was still the current fashion trend in the dead of night. Annie double-checked her brake lights on the trailer and glanced up at the gun rack behind her. There was her trusty Winchester .30-30, never used on a human—yet.

Annie eased out the clutch, turned on the defroster full blast, and drove slowly to her property gate. She gazed in her rearview mirror for a few brief seconds to imagine her small herd of horses asleep in their stalls. Only Trotter, the donkey, who usually had more sense than the rest of them, was jogging back and forth against the paddock line, plaintively braying his displeasure at her departure.

"Don't worry, you old jackass," she muttered. "I'll be back in time to feed you."

The metal farm gate, as usual, was gaping open at the top of her driveway, and Annie cursed herself for once more failing to secure her property before retiring. At forty-three, she wasn't quite as spry as she'd been at thirty, capable of running an ax murderer off the farm if she'd ever encountered one. But after a lifetime of scrimping and careful saving, she just couldn't convince herself to spend the money on an electric gate, which would have made life immeasurably easier and safer.

Milepost 11 on Highway 3 was only three miles away, but it took Annie a cautious five minutes to navigate it. Fog patches unexpectedly appeared before her, spreading a thick gray spell across the road. Just past Milepost 10, the eeriness vanished. The roadway ahead of her was lit up like the Fourth of July, the whirling strobes and headlights from half of the Sheriff's Office patrol squad staked out in a semicircle in the middle of the highway. Glints of steel shimmered off the berm on the north side of the road. Even with all the traffic, Annie saw in an instant what had occurred.

A long double line of heavy skid marks swerved to the ditch off the right side of the road. At the end sat a Chevy Silverado, its rear end ridiculously suspended in midair. The vehicle apparently had caromed off the road, hit the steelpost fence beyond the ditch, and bounced back to rest. Meanwhile, the horse rig, a gooseneck two-horse slant load, was twisting perilously to the left, held up by only one wheel.

In the center of the semicircle of black-and-whites, Annie noticed an ambulance from the local medical clinic, its back doors ominously gaping open, waiting to receive the body. Two EMTs peered into the Silverado on the driver's side, while another tried to wrench open the battered passenger door, which gave no signs of cooperating. No doubt they were figuring how best to extract the driver, Annie thought. Outside the action sat the prized fire truck from the volunteer unit in nearby Oyster Bay. The two local boys inside the cab looked transparently disappointed that their services would not be needed. Annie had encountered these boys be-

fore on similar calls, and unabashedly liked them for their will-
ingness to come out in the dead of night to deal with misery
and tragedy on the local highways and farms. She suspected
they liked her, too, possibly for the same reasons. That, and
the fact that Annie paid one of them handsomely twice a
year to shear her sheep.

Annie brought her Ford and trailer to a crawl on the right
shoulder of the road. Before she could turn off the engine,
Dan Stetson was beside her window, gesturing her to crank
it down. Dan looked distraught—not a good sign. He was
also eager to talk.

"Don't know what exactly happened here, Annie," he said,
slightly out of breath. "It's the damnedest thing. Truck suddenly swerves off to the right, jackknifes, and the trailer almost
overturns. Neighbors back there"— Dan pointed somewhere
in the distance— "hear the sound of the truck's crashing into
their fence line and are on the phone pronto. We get out
here, and there's a horse—who seems to be okay," Dan said
in response to Annie's panic-stricken look. "I got to tell you,
Annie, our in-transit time was one of our personal best, but
nothing could have saved this guy. We found him slumped
dead over his air bag, which we assume inflated as soon as
he hit the Truebloods' fence posts." Dan pointed in the direction of the truck. "Didn't have a chance. Just glad we
could save the nag."

Annie's eyes followed Dan's outstretched hand.

"Let me park my rig and join you," she said. Carefully
noting where technicians had staked out the road, she eased
her truck and trailer onto an unused portion of the shoulder.
She could sense, rather than see, Wolf's excitement from his
vantage point in the truck bed.

"Okay, buddy. But don't go messing up any of the accident scene."

She unhooked the carrier, and Wolf obediently bounded

out to join his mistress on the ground. They walked over to Dan, who now was scratching his considerable head.

"Interesting that the horse survived, but not the driver," Dan continued. He looked at Annie, as if he expected her to give the definitive answer. Instead, she just stared back at him. The fact was she hadn't the slightest idea why the accident had occurred, although she'd never give him the satisfaction of telling him so.

"Seat belt on?" was her only comment.

"Yup."

"What about the horse?"

"He's out of the trailer, and Tony's handling him, just there, beyond the fence line." Dan pointed again.

Annie inwardly sighed a breath of relief. If Deputy Tony Elizalde had control over the animal, all would be well. Tony had grown up with parents who worked at a local race-track, and had it not been for a conscientious high-school counselor, chances are Tony would have entered the same trade—grooming, washing, and cleaning stalls. Instead, Tony went to college, took the test to become a deputy in the local county Sheriff's Office, passed with flying colors, and now was one of the steadiest members of the police team. He also knew horses front ways, sideways, and backward. If the horse that had tumbled on its side was now in Tony's care, Annie was content.

She glanced over to the left side of the road and saw Tony trying to calm a strikingly tall bay covered in sweat and skit-tishly dancing around him. Annie turned her mind to the more immediate problem.

"Who's the owner?"

"Who do you think, Annie?" Dan replied. "You're look-ing at $50,000 worth of horseflesh over there. Who in this godforsaken county can afford the care and feeding that nag requires?"

Annie's shoulders slumped. Who indeed. Hilda Colbert, that's who. Annie hated her. Well, to be honest, she didn't hate her; she just hated the way she treated her horses. Hilda was a relative newcomer to the area, a California transplant who had made millions in the software industry and now fully indulged her passion for raising and riding hunter jumpers and thoroughbreds. Although Annie wasn't sure it was a passion for horses or just a passion for control. She'd seen the way Hilda acted around her champion equines and it wasn't pretty. In fact, the only thing pretty around Hilda was the state-of-the-art riding complex she'd constructed in the valley. It truly was a thing of beauty. But inside were housed eighteen neurotic, overwrought horses that didn't know which command to follow any time Hilda was on one of their backs.

"I don't suppose you've called her," Annie said glumly.

Dan snorted. "Hell, no! I'm not waking up the queen. That's your job."

Annie sighed. "Who's the deceased? One of Hilda's underpaid minions?"

"Nope. A guy out of Wyoming. Professional hauler. Can't understand why he swerved, though. You'd think he'd know better than to try to clear a deer."

"So that's what you think?" Annie asked. "Just one of your typical caught-in-the-headlight accidents?"

"Won't know until the State Patrol gets here with the Total Station. But offhand, I can't think of any other reason. It's a straight stretch of road. Unless, of course, he had a heart attack or something."

Annie squinted through the blazing circle of lights and silently agreed. There was no good reason for anyone to go off the road here. "Odor of intoxicants?" she asked.

"Nope. Unless you count the distinctive odor of Calvin Klein."

Annie laughed. "Maybe he had a hot date with Hilda."

"I hope not. I had to break the news to his wife just a few minutes ago. Doubt she would have been very happy to know hubby was on his way to a dalliance."

Annie realized that to outsiders her banter might have been off-putting, but after working with Dan on a dozen or more accident scenes involving horses, she had picked up the gallows humor so often adopted by law enforcement as a way to cope with sudden death. But Dan's remark brought her back to reality. A man had died, his wife was now a widow, and the valuable horse he'd been transporting needed comfort and a warm stable.

"Keep me posted, will you, Dan?"

"Will do." Just then, Dan's radio squawked, and she heard him revert to his professional parlance.

The thoroughbred was a magnificent creature—sixteen hands or more, Annie guessed, with classic bay markings. Annie walked over to Tony, who stood beside the shuddering horse, stroking its neck and whispering sweet nothings. At least the horse wasn't moving its feet anymore. Annie extended her hand to the bay's nose by way of introduction. The horse nuzzled back, licking the salt and dirt off her hand.

"Aren't you a handsome fellow?" she whispered to him.

"He sure is," said Deputy Elizalde. Tony clearly was in love. It would be hard not to fall in love with this horse; he had pedigree written all over him, and his elegance, despite his nervousness, permeated the air.

"Well, time to get him back in a trailer," Annie said. "This could be tricky." She reluctantly withdrew her now-very-clean hand and walked back to her truck, where Wolf jumped into the driver's seat as soon as Annie cracked the door.

"You're too young to drive," Annie told him, and Wolf agreeably relinquished his spot for the passenger side.

Horses like terra firma, and convincing them to step onto a springy surface that moves can be a hard sell. This thoroughbred, Annie realized, probably had been loaded into a trailer dozens of times and was used to the experience. Nonetheless, it had just survived a terrifying encounter and emerged from a twisted crate of steel that must now be perceived as a claustrophobic nightmare. Horses remember through their senses, particularly visually, and Annie was afraid just the sight of her trailer would turn this proud animal into a quivering beast with one thought: to bolt, rear, strike out, and do anything but get back into the box that an hour ago had threatened its survival.

Annie backed up her trailer fifty feet away from the fence line. She made sure there was hay in the feeder and added a couple of carrots for good measure. With one eye on the bay at all times, she quietly swung open the hinges that unlocked the back doors.

Deputy Elizalde slowly slid his hand up the lead line and started the walk over. Annie watched the bay skitter its way through the blinking lights of the patrol vehicles, its eyes white with fright. Tony was doing a good job, Annie noticed—he had his hand solidly on the lead rope but wasn't gripping it so tightly that the bay felt it had its head in a noose. In her sleep-deprived state, Annie lazily began to think that everything was actually going to go all right.

She was wrong.

CHAPTER 2

ONE SECOND LATER

A piercing *whoop-whoop* split the air. Even Annie jumped at the sound of the fire truck, which slowly followed the ambulance, bearing the body of the dead Wyoming hauler, through the slalom course of accident markers strewn on the road.

The bay took a flying leap into the air, snapping the lead line out of the deputy's hands, and, riveting its body in straight alignment to the road, sped off at a full-flight gallop.

In the corner of her eye, Annie saw Tony sprawled on the ground, shaking his head. She didn't think; she simply reacted. Racing to the center of the road, she spread her body as widely as she could and slowly started waving her outstretched arms up and down. The bay continued hell-bent toward her. Annie willed herself not to jump out of the way.

Ten feet before certain collision, the horse suddenly veered to the right. Annie's heart sank but then lifted as she saw Tony beside her, mimicking her arm movements to keep the bay from getting by.

The bay reared within striking distance of both of them. It bolted to the left, but now Dan Stetson was on her other side, keeping the blockade intact.

The half-dozen remaining deputies seemed rooted to their spots, as they watched the bay twist, turn, rear, and buck, as it tried to find a safe passage away from its own private nightmare.

"Get your butts over here!" Dan yelled out to his mesmerized crew. "That damn Leif! He's just got to play cowboy with that horn. I'd rip his brain out if he had one!"

By now, the line holding the horse in check was secure, but the human corral only made the bay more frenzied. Giving up on trying to find a loose link, the bay began to circle before them, going faster and faster so that even Annie, standing still, felt dizzy from the horse's frantic exertion. The road was littered with flashlights, accident-scene tape, and other detritus from the site of the overturned trailer. The dangling lead rope from the horse's halter snaked on the ground. Annie prayed that the horse wouldn't stumble and fall, or worse, step on the halter and break its neck.

The horse was a blur as it hurtled past her, but as it swept to the other side of the circle, she saw, with alarm, that it was punctuating the air with short jabs from its hind hooves. This was not good. It was one thing to have a scared horse, but a scared and aggressive horse was a danger to everyone.

"Cover for me!" Annie shouted in Tony's ear. Tony nodded, and took a step to his left to fill her place. On Tony's right stood Deputy Williams, who immediately cinched up the line. Deputy Kim Williams was one of the few females and the only African-American officer on the force and worked out big-time. Annie felt an added sense of security knowing Kim was there as she walked into the center of the storm.

Once inside the circle of officers, Annie stood perfectly still, but even if she'd been doing jumping jacks, she doubted whether the horse would have noticed her presence as it whirled around her. She realized that the horse was in a zone all its own, one dominated by the right side of its brain, the side dedicated to survival instincts. Its ability to think, reason, and understand were gone. In its place was an animal instinct for just one thing: getting free, at any cost.

Annie remembered this as she forced herself to breathe in and out—long, slow breaths that belied how she felt. After counting to a hundred, she slowly turned her eyes toward the bay. Every time the horse passed by her, Annie focused on the same spot on the horse's hindquarters. She did not move. No one in the outer circle said a word.

What seemed like a thousand laps later, the bay's right ear made an infinitesimally small twitch toward her.

Annie immediately took a small step backward and cocked her head to the left. The bay wheeled around and came to a sliding stop. The change was so abrupt that everyone in the circle involuntarily took a step back.

Annie put up her hand to signal her need for silence. The bay remained still, shaking, his breathing heavy and ragged as sweat poured off his coat. Annie met his gaze for a good, long moment, then angled both her body and her outstretched arm to the left.

The bay half reared and lunged in the other direction, continuing its frantic race around the human fortress. Annie continued to stand motionless. This time, the cue that she was looking for took far less time. Again, the bay twitched its ear closest to her, and Annie responded with a quick cock of her head. The bay wheeled around and stood before her, as if waiting for its next instruction.

Once more, Annie stretched out her arm, which sent the animal back to circling inside the human wall. The bay was tiring, that much was obvious. But its desire to keep running seemed as strong as ever.

Again and again, Annie got the bay to stop, only to send him away. She realized that by now, most of the men keeping the bay hemmed in probably were wondering what the hell she thought she was doing.

Just trying to get through that magnificent, thick skull of his, she thought to herself.

The sixth time the bay stopped, he gave a big, shuddering sigh. Annie sighed back.

And then a miracle occurred. The bay took two tentative steps toward her.

Annie took two steps back.

Behind her, someone within the circle involuntarily groaned.

"Shut up, Jake," Dan Stetson hissed through his teeth. "She knows what she's doing."

Bolstered by this unexpected praise, Annie wanted to flash her appreciation toward her friend but dared not take her eyes off the bay. She waited. And breathed.

The bay took two more steps toward her, this time, with less trepidation. Annie promptly took two steps back.

Now silence reigned all around them. Only the soft breeze in the overcast February early morning sky accompanied the strange dance between Annie and the bay.

The next time the bay took two steps forward, Annie stood still. She waited to make sure the bay wasn't going to move, then slowly turned and began to walk away.

When she was within a few feet of the human circle, she stopped.

"Is he there, Dan?"

"Right behind you."

"Then open up, boys, because we're coming through."

The deputies in front of her promptly stepped back, causing the rest of the circle to do the same.

Annie calmly walked through the eight-foot space now given to her. When she'd gone a good twelve feet beyond the crowd, she stopped again. The slow clip-clop of horseshoes followed in her wake. When she could feel the bay's breath behind her, she slowly reached up and took the lead rope.

"Hello, beautiful," she said.

She stroked his shiny, wet neck a few moments, then said in an even voice, "Get someone to drive my rig back, would you, Dan?"

Annie then took hold of the lead rope and started walking.

"You're not going to walk that horse all the way back to your place, are you?" Dan sounded incredulous.

"Yup," Annie replied. "See you later."

The deputies watched Annie and the bay's backs as she and the horse continued down the country highway, past Annie's Ford, where Wolf stood up in the cab, dumbfounded that his mistress would leave without him, and into the fog.

"Oh, and wait about a half an hour, would you, Dan?" Annie's voice floated back to them. "I'd hate to have to do this all over again."

Overhead, a few light sprinkles began to fall. It was going to rain.

"Come on," Annie said to the bay, as she zipped up her parka. "It's time to get you home."

CHAPTER 3

MONDAY MORNING, FEB. 22ND

Something was tickling her nose. *Like a delicate feather,* Annie thought drowsily, before she got the full onslaught of tuna breath. She opened her eyes and found herself under the calm and steady gaze of Max, whose white whiskers brushed against her face.

"What's up, pussycat?" She clutched Max firmly to her chest. The black-and-white kitten melted in her arms and rewarded her with a deep, strong purr. Annie trained all her cats to be docile on command. Not exactly an easy task—in fact, starting a stallion was, in some ways, easier than getting a cat to snuggle at will. Smugness at her prowess as Cat Whisperer overtook Annie for one, small instant before she remembered the events of just a few hours before.

Tossing Max unceremoniously aside, Annie sat upright and looked at the bedside clock—9:00. Hell's bells! Had she been asleep that long? She leapt out of bed, ripped off her sleeping sweats, and stepped into her Lees. The clothes she'd worn earlier still lay in a wet heap on the bathroom floor. The sprinkle that had started Annie and the bay on their long walk home had turned into a downpour within minutes.

The only good thing about the rain, Annie had thought sourly at the time, was that it at least cooled down the bay's red-hot heat. The bay, in fact, seemed to like the spontaneous shower. Annie did not. It was pitch-black; dawn was still a good two hours away. The three-mile trudge home seemed endless. After telling the bay—whom, she noticed, was an exceptionally polite listener—her life story, Annie and the bay finally rounded the last bend, and her farmhouse was in sight.

So was her rig—Dan had taken the parallel road to her farm and neatly parked it in front of the stables. A light already was glowing from inside her kitchen, accompanied by Wolf's insistent barking that told her *his* feelings: it was high time she'd come home. Annie wasn't surprised Dan had managed to get Wolf inside the house; she kept a spare key in the most conspicuous place possible: under the doormat.

Annie had led the horse to one of her spare stalls, rubbed him down, applied Schreiner's, her tried-and-true herbal horse tonic, to the few nicks she saw, and was pleased to see that her observations during the walk home seemed to be accurate—the bay had walked away from disaster with hardly a scratch. She was also pleased to see the bay obediently lower his head so that she could put on a cooling-down blanket. By then, the first glimmer of light had made its way to the stable windows, so Annie decided to give everyone an early breakfast, starting with Trotter. So amazed that Annie had fed *him,* the superior member of the equine family, first, he practically forgot to bray.

Finally, Annie allowed herself to trudge back to the farmhouse, soak in a hot tub with a cup of tea, and fall into bed.

Had it been a few hours earlier, the tea would have been scotch.

When Annie had acquired her farm, she'd built her stables within easy viewing distance from her bedroom window. She liked falling asleep watching the horses standing in the paddock adjoining the stalls, knowing they would soon be inside, crunching on their last bits of hay. She never locked the herd in their stalls at night; despite Trotter's opinion of them, Annie knew her horses were smart enough to come in out of the rain should they so desire. By early morning, she knew she'd find them all in their stalls, anyway, for their requisite power nap. Annie envied her horses for a lot of reasons, but high among them was their ability to appear wide-awake and sassy every morning after only thirty minutes of REM sleep while properly lying down.

Now she saw all four of her horses and Trotter waiting impatiently at the paddock gate. Normally, Annie would have turned them out two hours before this.

Wading in fat wool socks to the kitchen door, she tugged on her muck boots and, with Wolf at her side, walked to the gate to let her horses out of captivity. Sam, her pinto, looked at her reproachfully as she came nearer.

"Oh, bite me. It's not *that* late."

Trotter brayed back. No interpretation needed. *Oh yes, it IS.*

Opening the gate to the first of two ten-acre pastures, Annie watched with pride, as she did every morning, at the five beautiful beasts that had entrusted her with their lives.

Bess, her ancient Morgan, was Annie's first horse, and was now entering an elegant maturity that Annie hoped to match when she was the same age. She'd taken in Bess after a childhood friend, thrilled about her acceptance to an East Coast university but distraught at the prospect of selling her horse, had begged Annie to care for the animal until she returned. That was fifteen years ago. The friend had never come back to the Olympic Peninsula, but Annie hadn't minded. She seldom rode Bess anymore, but when she did, Bess still had the heart, if not the stamina, of a yearling.

Sam, her pinto, was her working horse. With Annie on or off his back, the two of them had reached a level of equine-human telepathy that was uncanny.

She'd never forgotten the ad for Sam she'd found chalked on the Cenex board seven years before: "Free to good home: Gelded pinto, fifteen hands. If you don't take him, the glue factory will." Sam was eating her pasture grass by that evening. His previous owner had described Sam as aggressive and unpredictable. Annie was herding sheep with him within two months and loved him for his endearing and steadfast desire to perform for her.

Baby, her three-year-old saddlebred-in-training, had belonged to a local rancher, who thought she wasn't "pretty enough to keep." Annie thought the guy was nuts but refrained from saying so when she offered to "take the horse off his hands" for a few hundred dollars. Even her equine vet, Jessica Flynn, who wasn't easy to impress, had agreed.

"That horse is just criminally cute," Jessica had muttered the last time she'd administered vaccinations at the farm. The little horse knew her place in the herd—somewhere lower than Trotter—but she had plenty of spirit, and Annie was sure that she would be a superb trail horse in time.

And then there was Rover, so named because the quarter horse had an extraordinary mouth that could open a gate faster than a human. Usually, he went no farther than the nearest clump of fresh pasture grass, but it was a trait Annie wasn't sure other horse owners would love as much as she did.

Annie had adopted Rover three years ago during one of her jobs as part of the Horse Rescue Brigade in Suwana County. She and Dan Stetson had started the brigade twenty years ago, after Dan came across a farm near Squill River with four of the most despondent, malnourished horses Annie had ever seen. She and Dan had rounded them up over the indignant protestations of the owner, who put down his shotgun only after Dan threatened to arrest him for obstructing the course of justice if he so much as made a move past his front porch.

Years later, Rover had been part of another herd she and Dan had rescued from a derelict owner. Annie had vowed that as God was her witness, Rover would never go hungry again—as long as he didn't founder.

Trotter had been a gift from an old boyfriend. The boyfriend was long gone, but Annie was fully aware that she now had far more affection for the little burro than she'd ever mustered for the former beau.

Annie swung the paddock gate open, waited a moment to make sure all five pairs of eyes were on her, then nodded to let them know they were free to leave. It was a measure of respect Annie demanded from her herd. When she was eight, Annie had once opened the paddock gate for a friend's pony, which nearly ran her over in his desire to get to his pasture. She had never let that happen again.

Unlike the others, the bay had spent the night in its stall. The brief introduction she'd given last night of "Sam, meet the bay. Bay, meet Sam," hardly sufficed to ensure they'd all get along in a common paddock area. In fact, every horse

Annie had acquired spent its first week looking over a fence line at its new companions before exchanging muzzle handshakes.

She was curious to see how the bay was this morning. So after watching her herd gallop off toward its favorite grazing area, she turned to the stable and the bay's stall.

She heard the bay before she saw him, a low, worried nicker that told her he was unhappy about being separated from his new herd, even at this early stage of their friendship. Through the stall bars, Annie saw the bay pacing back and forth, its tail swishing. She could have sworn she saw the horse grimace.

"Easy, boy," Annie murmured to the bay. "You're okay."

Then she noticed the uneaten hay in the feeder, and beside it, the bucket of bran mash unceremoniously dumped on the floor.

"Horses all over the world whinny for that mash." Annie felt an unreasonable pang of hurt course through her, even while her rational brain told her the bay's lack of appetite had nothing to do with her culinary skill.

Taking a string halter by the stall, she slipped inside and waited for the horse to approach her. Again, she was delighted to see the bay politely lower its head for her. At least the trauma of last night had not left the bay a nervous wreck. Annie led the bay outside to the stall corridor, where the light was better.

Equine mouth inspections were one of her least favorite tasks—no one wanted one's fingers mistaken for a carrot. However, there were three healthy mounds of manure in the stall and the water bucket, filled last night, now was barely half-full, so the bay clearly wasn't colicking. The only other reason Annie could think of for the horse's poor appetite was its mouth.

She hauled over a mounting block, climbed on top, and started to run her fingers along the corner of the bay's mouth to see if it would open up. The bay abruptly tossed its head, narrowly missing Annie's own. She hurriedly removed her hand and got down from the block.

"And now, Plan B," she told the horse.

Tying the lead to a stall bar, Annie went into her tack room and retrieved a handful of carrots.

"How about these?" she asked. "They're organic, if you care."

The bay sniffed at the carrots, and snapped at the end of the one closest to him. He jawed uncomfortably for a few seconds, then spit out large chunks of bright orange and emitted a tortured whinny.

"Got it. Why don't you take a nice constitutional in the paddock while I make a call?"

She led the bay to the paddock, now deserted. As soon as the gate opened, the bay broke loose from the lead rope, broke into a gallop, and raced around the fence line, loudly conveying his desire to be with his companions, now out of sight. Annie raced after him and grabbed the end of the lead rope, snapping it to get the bay's attention.

Again, she saw that split second sliding stop. She walked slowly and deliberately up to the bay.

"That's the second time you've done that in less than six hours. Aren't you getting tired of repeating yourself?"

Annie quickly unloosed the string halter and stepped back. The bay resumed its race around the paddock, but steered clear of her.

"Well, at least I can report that his lower extremities are working fine," Annie muttered. Heading back to the tack room, she picked up the phone and called Jessica.

"Hi, Annie," Jessica said after Annie had said hello. "What's up?"

"I have a thoroughbred gelding rescued from a turnover last night who's shunning my world-famous bran mash."

A high-spirited laugh rippled through the phone line. "And you're calling me to see if I'll trade recipes?"

"I wish. I'm pretty sure it's something to do with his teeth. No external injuries. He's pooping and drinking—just not eating. And, for the record, he didn't like my farm-fresh carrots, either."

There was a silence on the other end. Annie knew that Jessica was consulting her electronic date book.

"Well, today isn't good, but then, it seldom is. Let's see, I think I could switch a barn call to later this afternoon and come by in an hour or so. Does that work?"

"Thanks, Jessica. He's a beauty. High-spirited, but a real looker."

"Just my type. See you in an hour or so."

Annie knew that the "or so" was the reason horse owners had a special name for veterinarian calls: "vet time." In Annie and most every other horse owner's opinion, vets worked at least twice as hard as human doctors and knew twice as much. They spent their lives on the road, driving from one barn to the next, never knowing exactly what lay before them on the other end. A simple checkup might morph into a lengthy diagnostic workup. The delivery of a foal might result in emergency surgery. Or worse.

Still, she had no doubt that Jessica would arrive as soon as she was able, but certainly not before Annie had time for a late breakfast. She had about an hour to stew about the unfairness of rescuing a horse that didn't like her cooking and was going to cost her, at least up front, a pile of money before being sent on its way.

"Come on, Wolf," she said. "Let's get some chow."

As Annie and Wolf strolled up the slope leading to her back door, she noticed a familiar Suwana County patrol vehicle parked in her driveway. Dan. She picked up her pace, anxious to hear the news and have the chance to kvetch to someone other than her dog about the bay's emergency care.

Wolf apparently was tired of her conversation, too, because he bounded away from her to greet Dan first.

"Morning, Annie," Dan said from the front seat of his car, where Wolf now had his big front paws on his lap. Dan tipped his hat at Annie. Dan insisted on tipping his hat to every woman he encountered. It was an endearment that never failed to charm the ladies—except Annie. She knew him too well.

"So what's the verdict?" Annie said. "Why'd the rig crash?"

Dan laughed. "Right down to business, as usual. Why, you haven't even offered me a cup of coffee yet."

"I haven't even made it yet, you big lug," Annie replied. "As you may recall, I had a rather full night last night, helping your sorry butt."

"And don't scrimp on telling us how you feel, either."

Annie relented. It wasn't Dan's fault that the driver had stopped for a deer and got himself killed, leaving a horse behind.

"Come on in, and I'll fix you some breakfast," Annie said. Watching Dan's eyes light up, she added, "Don't think it's special or anything. I was going to make it for myself, anyway."

"Perish the thought," Dan said as he stepped out of his car.

"First things first," Annie explained to Dan as she got a pot of coffee going. In the five minutes it took for the coffee to perk, Annie managed to assemble scrambled eggs, a thick slab of bacon, and fresh bagels on the table.

"You never cease to amaze me, Annie," Dan said. "With cooking skills like yours, it's a wonder some man hasn't capitalized on them by now."

Annie snorted. She'd tried marriage once, but her then-husband couldn't stand the competition, and Annie had offered him no real alternative. He'd hit the highway soon after he learned Annie would rather be straddling a horse than him.

Dan, on the other hand, had recently celebrated his twenty-fifth wedding anniversary to Dolores, who ran the Cut 'N Curl beauty salon in town, and just seen his first grandson born. He didn't always seem particularly happy, but, on the whole, appeared content.

Annie was kind enough to let Dan eat most of his eggs before bringing up the subject again.

"Did Mitch find anything?" she asked, in what she hoped was a polite and delicate manner. Mitch, she knew, was the only guy in the WA State Patrol within a hundred-mile radius who actually knew how to operate the Total Station, which electronically calculated data from crash sites to reconstruct how motor vehicle accidents occurred.

Now it was Dan's time to snort.

"He did and didn't," he said enigmatically. "What I mean is, we know what didn't cause the accident but still don't know what did."

"How fascinating."

"Go ahead, be sarcastic, but this case is turning out to be just a tad harder than what you might think. Mitch spent the rest of the night going over the accident scene and has it stored in the Total Station six ways from Sunday. But what he found still doesn't add up."

Annie got up and refilled Dan's cup to encourage him to continue.

"Deceased is Wayne Johnston. Like I said, he's from Wyoming. Has an excellent reputation for hauling. Doesn't drink, and from what everyone says, doesn't overcharge, even when he's hauling a high-priced stallion. In fact, his honesty is what made him one of the most-sought-after haulers in the West."

"And his driving skills?"

"Obviously he's got a clean record, or he wouldn't have had his job. We still don't know why he swerved—there were no deer grazing in the vicinity, and we've had no sightings of cougars and coyotes in that area for over a year now."

Annie knew that. Most cougars and coyotes had retreated to what little wilderness was left to them. Only occasionally, such as during a particularly bad winter, did they try to find prey as close as the farming community.

"But what we did find was interesting," Dan continued. "A set of tire tracks from probably a midsized SUV stretching from the road to about two hundred feet from the crash site."

"Where'd they stop?" Annie leaned forward.

"On the Truebloods' property. They started from the east gate, which Cal says is seldom used. They're fresh, all right. Neither Cal nor Mary have the slightest idea how they got there.

"Then there's two freshly dug post holes on the other side of the Truebloods' fence line. No one knows how they got there, either, or for what purpose."

Annie thought for a moment. "I don't recall seeing any cars or trucks on the road getting to you. But then, I could barely see in front of my face, what with the fog."

Dan nodded sadly. "We're poking around, but chances are no one's going to remember seeing a truck with mud-lined tires cruising the highway in the dead of night."

Annie silently agreed before she asked, "When was Wayne last seen alive?"

"According to his VISA receipts, about an hour before at the steak house in Garver's Corner. Wayne had himself a hefty T-bone, a diet Coke, paid his bill, then filled up his rig with gas at the local Shell. He got a bottled water to go and a candy bar. We found the empty wrapper on the floor of the cab."

"How about the rig? Everything in working order?"

"Yup. Lights, brakes, steering system, oil levels—everything checked out."

There was a companionable silence while Annie assimilated the information.

She looked up to see Dan staring at her. Slightly embarrassed, she blurted out, "You haven't even asked me about the horse yet."

"How's the horse?"

"Don't ask. He's got some kind of tooth problem—barely touched his hay last night and *completely* ignored my famous mash. At least he's drinking." Annie was still unreasonably upset that the bay hadn't eaten her trademark feed that nearly provoked a stampede when Baby, Bess, Sam, and Rover so much as smelled it.

"Tough luck. Is Jessica coming over?"

"Should be arriving anytime."

Dan cleared his throat.

"Have you called Hilda yet?"

Annie wheeled around from the kitchen sink, where she'd taken the breakfast dishes.

"No, I haven't, and I don't intend to until I know the state of her horse. I'm not having that woman tell me I caused her poor horse's toothache until I get a professional opinion."

The crunch of tires on the road outside distracted Annie from further diatribe.

"That must be Jessica," Annie said in surprise. "She's right on time."

"Well, will wonders never cease," Dan said. "Thanks for breakfast, Annie. I still say your skills are going to waste."

"They most certainly are not," Annie retorted. "*I* enjoy my cooking very much."

Dan laughed. "Autopsy's being done as we speak. I'll let you know when anything new turns up. In the meantime, don't let Hilda get to you."

"I'll try," Annie grumped. "But she just has a way about her."

"I know, I know. But the fact is she couldn't be luckier having you take care of a horse that's lucky to be alive at all. And you can tell her I said that."

For once, Annie was at a loss for words.

CHAPTER 4

Monday Afternoon, February 22ND

Annie would later reflect that her breakfast with Dan was the most enjoyable part of her day.

Now, however, she was chagrined to see the bay standing at the paddock gate and bellowing to the empty field. The vet followed with her portable kit.

Jessica whistled. "What a gorgeous guy. Who has the honor of riding him?"

"Hilda Colbert."

Annie heard a muffled groan.

"Why does that woman get all the best horses?"

"Money," Annie said flatly. "Pure and simple. Although I resent your suggestion that Rover is in any way inferior to that thoroughbred in front of you. He keeps the pasture mowed, and his bedside manner is impeccable."

Jessica laughed. "You are so right. Okay, let's have a look at the guy."

The bay's nervous whinnies echoed along the walkway as Annie led him to the tacking-up area in the barn. While

Jessica set up her equipment, Annie put the bay in cross ties. She decided to keep his halter on, so she'd have access to the lead rope.

"All right, sweetie, let's take a look at your mouth." Jessica rubbed the horse's forehead, moving gently down the sides of his face and around his mouth. She was rewarded with a sideswipe lick.

"He is a licker," Annie said. "I personally don't have to wash my hands for a week."

Jessica laughed softly. "Good boy." She went back to her truck and returned with a headstand, which she let the bay sniff before setting it in front of him. She then took out a large steel speculum and placed the halter section over the bay's head, while she continued to let him lick her open hand.

"So far, so good." Donning blue nitrate gloves, Jessica opened the tooth cups with one hand and gingerly placed her free thumb at the back of the bay's mouth, where lips met jaw. "Open up, that's a good boy."

The bay jerked his head up, half rearing before the cross ties brought his legs down with a resounding thud. A strangled whinny emanated within his chest.

"I should tell you, he's a tad sensitive about the inside of his mouth," said Annie.

"No kidding."

Jessica strapped a head lamp onto her head while critically examining the horse's jawline.

Annie was looking elsewhere. The bay was shaking, its eyes wide and wild. Annie had seen that look just a few hours before. She stroked the bay's neck as the vet again pressed her thumb on the same pressure point to encourage the bay to open its mouth.

"That's it, just open up. There's a good boy," Jessica crooned.

She was rewarded with a solid kick to her nether regions.

Jessica fell backward, her scream intermingling with a high-pitched squeal from the horse that reflected more rage than fear. The lead rope Annie had been clutching swished on the floor like a snake. She snatched it up again. The bay's head swiveled wildly around, snapping the cross ties back and forth. The barn roof was too high for the horse to hit its poll, but Annie was concerned that the strength of the bay's fury might take out the cross ties. She knew she couldn't hold him without that support.

Annie glanced at Jessica, sprawled on the stable floor, clutching her crotch as she wheezed out a string of curses.

"Don't worry about me," Jessica panted. "I'm past child-bearing age, anyway."

Annie couldn't answer. Nor could she stop the manic dance the bay was performing in its restricted space. She could barely hang on to the lead rope and try to avoid the bay's striking hooves.

And then it stopped. In the silence that followed, only the sound of Jessica and the bay's labored breathing filled the air.

Annie heard a small click. She knew that sound. Someone or something had opened her paddock gate. A familiar clip-clop clattered on the concrete floor.

"Trotter!"

The donkey poked his head around the corner and ambled down the aisleway, pausing to nibble at a bit of stray hay on the floor.

"What are *you* doing here?"

The bay gave a low-throated call. Trotter responded with an inquisitive hee-haw. Annie and Jessica stood still as Trotter walked up to the bay, where the two sniffed noses. Trotter nuzzled the bay's lower neck—the highest point he could reach—until the bay lowered its head and gently exhaled.

Then Trotter turned and continued his pursuit of stray hay on the floor.

Jessica scrambled up from the floor and gave Annie a hard look.

"Drugs," they said simultaneously.

Annie never liked to see a horse sedated although she knew the horse hated it even more than she did, deprived of its natural senses and therefore, in its mind, more vulnerable to unknown prey. And there was the fear that the twelve-hundred-pound swaying animal would actually fall while under the influence and not be able to get up.

Jessica knew all about Annie's fears and pooh-poohed the latter, insisting that if Annie would simply stop resting her butt on the bay's—which was heavily leaning into Annie's thigh at this point—all would be fine.

Annie politely thanked her for her opinion but didn't believe her.

Now, with the bay's eyelids dropping and its head lowered halfway to the ground, Jessica was able to delicately probe inside its mouth to her heart's content. She whistled an old Travis tune as she peered and poked.

"Oh, oh, oh."

"What do you mean, 'oh, oh, oh'?"

"Some yahoo took a power saw to his mouth and cut off his premolars to the bone."

Annie's mouth tingled. More silence.

"Yup—three-zero-six is cut right to the gum line. I'll bet my Tucker saddle we've got a tooth root abscess. And voilà"—Jessica fiddled a bit more inside the droopy bay's mouth—"an already fragile tooth has splintered into a jillion glittering little pieces." She stood up from her squatting position and stretched her back.

"One more time for the medically-challenged?" asked Annie.

Jessica sighed. "In recent years, motorized floating, rather than using the traditional rasp, has become all the rage. It's fine, and, in fact, quite efficient, as long as the user knows what he's doing. This vet obviously didn't. Young horses' teeth are changing all the time. They don't need much outside help."

"Jessica. The point—please."

"Judging by his mouth, I'd say this guy is only about three years old. You don't need to do much to a horse's mouth at that age—just make sure that any emerging points are taken off, and the mouth is developing nicely. There's nothing wrong with this fellow's mouth except an overindustrious vet who whittled away his surfacing teeth so much that bone infection may very well have set in.

"My guess is that when the trailer overturned, the horse clamped down and broke an already fragile tooth. It would have occurred anyway, sooner or later, although perhaps not this severely."

"What can you do?"

"Take some X-rays, find out the extent of the damage, and go from there."

An hour later, Annie was peering over shadowy images Jessica had produced from her portable digital X-ray machine.

"See that first check tooth?" Jessica pointed to an image on the screen. "Thanks to our saw-happy vet, the lamina dura is almost completely eroded."

Glancing at Annie's pleading look, Jessica smiled. "Annie, the bottom line is that the traumatized tooth lost its ligamentous attachment, which caused significant paradental disease. The infection has gone straight down to the root, and the broken tooth is wallowing in the pus."

Annie felt dizzy. Visits to the dentist were never high on her list, and when she did, she begged for massive doses of nitrous oxide.

"This is one of the teeth horses use most often to chew," Jessica continued. "Eating is a side to side motion. Trouble is, every time our guy takes a bite on the wrong side, he's in real pain."

"Jessica, what can you do?"

"Well, that's the good news. There's really only one alternative. Extract the tooth. We can't put it back together again."

"Camptown Ladies sing this song—Doo-Dah! Doo-Dah!"

The jovial chorus came from the tack room. Annie jumped. The bay did not, still lost in its own haze of equine dreams.

"My ringtone," Annie explained to Jessica, who looked askance. "It seemed a good idea at the time." She walked over to the tack room and picked up her cell phone.

"Annie speaking."

"Hilda Colbert."

Annie was silent.

"Ms. Carson? Are you there?"

"Yes, I'm here. And yes, your thoroughbred is currently stabled at my farm. You've heard about the accident, I presume?"

Annie seldom spoke so primly, but that's the kind of effect Hilda had on people. Proper English was a poor defense against Hilda's antagonistic nature, but it was the only one available to Annie right now.

"Yes, I have, and I wonder why I haven't heard from you before now. Do you realize it's two o'clock in the afternoon?"

Annie did not, but a quick glance at her watch proved it to be true.

"I apologize, Mrs. Colbert, but rescuing your horse took

most of the night, and I'm just now attending to your horse's care."

"Well, I don't care what time you got in. The question is, when are you going to transport my property to *my* care? I expected *my* thoroughbred to arrive by nine o'clock this morning."

A fine, pure rage surged through Annie.

"Mrs. Colbert, are you aware that your horse barely escaped sudden death—a fate your transporter did not avoid—after a horrendous accident on the way to your property last night? Your thoroughbred was lucky enough to escape with hardly a scratch, and it took most of the Sheriff's Office and me to ensure that he made it to my farm in one piece and without additional trauma."

There was a sputter on the other line. Annie ignored it and kept talking.

"I spent most of the night ensuring he was safe and healthy, and am now spending most of my *day* tending to a medical emergency concerning his teeth. I had every intention of calling you this morning, except that the matter of a broken tooth got in the way."

"What have you done to my horse?" Hilda shouted through the phone lines. "He was in perfect health when he left Tennessee three days ago!"

"That is not true," Annie shouted back, then lowered her voice. "Your horse has a significant problem with"—she glanced at Jessica, who mouthed the answer to her—"tooth three-zero-six, which was so diseased that it shattered on impact. We're about to remove the problem."

"Did I hear you right? Did you just say that you're going to remove one of my thoroughbred's teeth?"

"You did."

"Over my dead body."

"Just one moment, Mrs. Colbert. I'm sure you'd like to hear from the *professional*."

Jessica glared at Annie as she picked up the phone. Annie retreated to the bay, where she felt infinitely more loved.

Jessica clearly had more experience with irate horse owners because she kept her words to a minimum and her tone of voice neutral. Annie was impressed, and not a little ashamed at her own reaction. Oh, well.

"Yes, Mrs. Colbert. Your feelings are quite understandable." Jessica went silent as she listened, then said, "Texas A&M, with graduate studies at WSU in Pullman."

A pause.

"Yes, I'm sure University of Pennsylvania is a good school as well."

A longer pause.

"I'm not a qualified dressage instructor, but I'm sure your horse will learn to handle the bit without the tooth." More silence.

"Of course, that's up to you. But the horse is in no condition to be moved at present. He's still under sedation. He really should have time to rest and recover before he's transported again."

Annie stroked the bay, for whom she felt increasingly sorry. "Poor baby," she whispered. "We promise you'll have enough teeth left to bite her."

Jessica was speaking again.

"I'm sure Annie will be more than happy to accommodate your feed requirements, but please be aware that your horse will be on a restricted diet for the next few days, in any case, as he recovers from surgery."

Annie was humming "Camptown Races" and combing the bay's mane when Jessica gestured furiously at her.

"Let's address that issue after your horse's health is restored, Mrs. Colbert. And now I'm going to give you back to Annie."

Annie gingerly picked up the receiver, hot after the five minutes of chastising she was sure Jessica had just endured.

"Yes, Mrs. Colbert?"

"I'm sending my man, Todos, over this afternoon to make sure you're caring for the horse properly. Todos will inform you when the horse will be transported. Is that clear?"

"Yes, Mrs. Colbert." Annie felt she was in second grade again, answering Miss Paul's question of whether or not she knew when recess ended, which she had learned, to her great surprise, was a nonnegotiable subject.

"One more thing, Ms. Carson. My equine dentist floated the thoroughbred's teeth one week before he left Tennessee. Dr. Ted Barnes."

Annie had no idea who that was. Hilda Colbert continued. "I'm sure he did an impeccable job. I don't know what you and your friend think you're doing, but I am not at all convinced that this procedure is necessary. Therefore, until I learn otherwise, I assume that you will cover all the costs associated with this farm call."

"The hell I will!"

"Annie!" Jessica didn't waver from her studied gaze into the horse's mouth, but her voice conveyed her shock.

"Don't worry. The old bat hung up before I said it. By the way, it looks like I'm paying you."

"Let's talk about that later. Right now, I need your help."

Two hours later, Jessica tenderly packed the gaping hole where the bay's tooth had been and handed Annie enough bute to last through the morning.

"And NO HAY," she reminded Annie. "Nothing but water tonight. And tomorrow, watered-down pellets. I don't want to come back here because I hear the guy's choked."

"Got it," Annie said wearily, while she vigorously massaged her right hand. While Jessica had done the real work, she had been assigned the menial tasks of holding the bay's head while Jessica administered a nerve block, then the bay's tongue to one side so it wouldn't get in the way. It was now late afternoon, and the stalls still hadn't been mucked. The mere thought of wrapping her hand around the shavings fork made her fingers cramp.

But at least the bay now had his life force back. He wasn't going to run around any racetrack, but his head was upright, and his legs no longer worked like a drunken sailor's. Trotter, the bay's new best friend, had stood by during the entire operation and now was housed in the adjacent stall, where he contently munched on a flake of pasture hay. It was too bad Trotter ate while the bay couldn't, but Annie wanted to make sure the bay had company. For some reason, the little donkey had a soothing effect on the thoroughbred.

Rake in hand, Annie waved good-bye to Jessica from the stable entrance, then, with a sigh, turned, to the daily task in front of her. She wondered, for the millionth time, why she just didn't hire a horse-crazy teenager from one of the local 4-H clubs to do this odious, not to mention odiferous, job for her? In the early-morning hours after the horses had been turned out, it wasn't so bad. Rhythmically swinging "horse apples" into the cart as country-western music crackled on the radio behind her was a good way to stretch her muscles and give her time to think about her day.

Annie's steadfast belief that no one knew her horses and how to care for their health as well as she did was the real reason she wouldn't sub out this menial job. Bring a youngster into the mix and they might see the lack of poop in one horse's stall as a way to leave earlier, not as an early-warning sign of colic. Annie noticed these things—who was cribbing and needed more outdoor time, even if the wildest rainstorm was raging; who wasn't drinking enough water at night; and who was the most adept at using their lips to garner stray pieces of straw just under the stall door. At the moment, Rover and Trotter were in a dead heat.

Besides, she took utter heart-melting delight in seeing where each horse (and donkey) had laid its pretty head at night. The straw covering the mats clearly outlined each equine's position.

To prolong the inevitable job ahead of her, Annie checked the bay's bandage one more time to make sure the bleeding had stopped, gently rubbing his neck.

"You're a trooper," she said to the preternaturally quiet bay. "In fact, if you were mine, that's what I'd call you."

She quietly let herself out of the stall and pulled the mucking cart toward the front of the stable row, noting that a little oil on the axle wouldn't hurt. Well, all in good time. Right now, stalls needed mucking.

Annie had finished Trotter's stall and just begun Baby's when she heard the crunch of tires coming down the driveway. She was glad for the break; even in the dead of winter, she'd peeled down to just a turtleneck and was still sweating. She walked outside to see a tall, lanky cowboy leaning on the paddock fence, one boot hooked over the lowest stile.

"Nice place you got."

His aquiline features were picture-perfect, with a trace of either Hispanic or Native American heritage in them. Black hair fell almost to his shoulders. If not for a small permanent downturn of his mouth, like a perpetual sneer, the cowboy would have been handsome. And he was young, Annie realized. He couldn't be more than in his mid-twenties.

Turning his eyes over to Annie, he looked at her shrewdly. She felt slightly uncomfortable without knowing precisely why.

"How can I help you?"

"I'm here to look at Señora Colbert's *caballo*."

Of course. This must be Todos. Somehow, despite his name, Annie had expected a young Englishman in jodhpurs, who spoke with a clipped accent. Hilda's tastes did not run to rodeo events. Todos looked like he could be a champion roper.

"You must be Todos." She held out her hand.

He smiled slowly, saying nothing, and reluctantly gave her a limp handshake.

"Let me show you the bay." Annie waited until Todos made the first move toward the stable and followed him in. "He's in the last stall on the left."

Todos slipped into the stall and lightly and expertly ran his fingers over the bay's body, ending with his face.

"He's just come out of surgery, so I wouldn't touch him too much there."

Annie had recently touched him at that precise place, but now she didn't like the idea of anyone else doing so. The bay stood still, not moving.

"A bad tooth?" Todos's question sounded doubtful.

"Must have happened when the trailer flipped. The tooth was a goner, anyway."

Annie received another slow smile. "That so?"

Annie said nothing.

"Well, Señora Colbert wants her property home. As soon as possible."

Annie felt *very* defensive. "Vet's coming by in the morning. I'd wait until she checks in before making a decision on moving him."

"You need more boarding fees?"

Annie's gut boiled again. What was it about these people so that everything they said enraged her? But she was not going to lose it again.

"Just the time it takes to make sure the surgery's held, and he's ready to go . . . to go to his new home."

Todos nodded. "Of course. Señora Colbert will call you herself to set up a time. I think around nine. I hope your vet is here before then."

As if Jessica could rearrange her already-crammed work schedule to accommodate this bozo! In reality, Jessica probably would be here at seven-thirty, but Annie wasn't going to tell Todos that.

"I'll see what I can do." Annie's tone of voice implied that she would do nothing at all.

Todos slipped out of the stall as silently as he'd entered and walked back down the aisle. Annie noted that he hadn't given the bay a single pat or friendly gesture. He could have been examining a 4-H horse model.

Suddenly curious, Annie asked, "So what will he be used for?"

"Eventing. Jumping. That is, if he can compete without his full mouth."

"The vet doesn't think it would matter."

"*Bueno*. Because if a gelding cannot be ridden, there's not much reason for him to live, is there?"

Annie managed to keep an impassive face long enough for Todos to get in his truck and drive off the property, then plunked down on a hay bale, put her face in her hands, and sat, quivering, until her breath was under control.

"God damn that Hilda Colbert to hell," she muttered. "People like her don't deserve to *live*."

"Camptown Ladies sing this song—Doo-Dah! Doo-Dah!"

"Curse that ring tone, too," Annie grumbled, but managed to pick up the phone on the fourth chorus.

It was Tony Elizalde, a welcome voice.

"How's my beautiful horse?" he asked.

Annie laughed. Funny how everyone who encountered this hoof-stomping, head-rearing, time-consuming, money-eating beast wanted to take ownership of him.

She filled Tony in on the latest events, ending with Todos's visit.

"I've never met the guy, but he's supposed to be good at what he does," Tony told Annie. "I hear he's also the main attraction at the Roadside Tavern on Friday nights."

"Well, that may be, but he's got the personality of a slug. It's probably why Hilda hired him. Same bloodlines."

Tony chuckled. "I sure hope the big guy's going to be all right. If you need any help, just let me know."

Annie thanked him, then asked if there was any news on the accident.

"Wouldn't know," Tony said cheerfully. "That's the sheriff's job. I've spent the day holed up by the ferry dock, ticketing people who forget to buckle up driving off."

"Ah, our taxpayers' dollars at work," Annie murmured.

"Hey, someone's got to save them from themselves."

"I never got the chance to thank you for all your help last night."

"No problem. Glad I was around. Maybe I'll swing by tomorrow morning before work to look in on our wild beast."

"Please do. Just don't kiss him. His mouth's still a little tender."

"I'll try to control myself." A squawk emanated in the background. "Gotta go. Weaver on the road."

"See you tomorrow," Annie said into the disconnected line.

She sighed and turned back to the job at hand. By four-thirty, the shadows on the stable walls lengthened so that Annie was forced to turn on the overhead lights. The winter days were getting longer, but not by much.

When she finally emerged from the stable, a soft darkness filtered across the farm landscape. A long thread of horses outlined the paddock fence, ghostlike in the rising fog. Low-throated nickers told her they were ready for their evening meal.

"Come and get it, guys."

Suddenly a small, spritelike figure popped up amid the mist.

"Annie! Annie! Where's your new horse?"

Hannah Clare skipped forward and fluidly slid between the fence stiles. "I heard all about it, Annie! Where is he? Where is he?"

Eight-year-old Hannah was the eldest of five children who lived with her parents down the road. For reasons unknown to her, Annie had been adopted as Hannah's play aunt. It was not for Annie's massive efforts to be a Big Sister. Hannah had simply appeared one day and decided Annie was her new best adult friend. Annie hadn't said otherwise. From then on, Hannah was a frequent visitor to Annie's farm, showing up after school and sometimes buzzing in before breakfast.

Annie wasn't a patsy—she'd made sure that Hannah knew all about horse safety before letting her near the animals—but the little girl had proven to be a smart, savvy youngster to whom the horses naturally gravitated.

"He's back here, Hannah, but speak softly—he's just had a visit from the dentist."

"Ouch." Hannah instinctively brought her hand to her face, where new, pink braces recently had been installed.

Hannah tiptoed with great exaggeration to the bay's stall, where she stared at him with such intense longing that Annie couldn't help but fulfill the youngster's wish.

"Okay, Hannah, go on in. But no carrots. He's still finding his way around and can't eat just yet."

Hannah didn't wait for Annie to open the gate. With the enviable agility of a small child, she slipped through and crept toward the bay, which looked at her with curious interest.

"He's beautiful, Annie," Hannah breathed.

"Isn't he though."

They stood in companionable silence until Hannah tentatively, then eagerly, stroked his mane.

"Is he yours?"

Annie could hear the hopefulness in the child's voice. So far, Hannah had ridden Bess, Annie's ancient Morgan, but the languid stroll the horse produced was hardly up to Hannah's idea of cowgirl fun.

"No, Hannah, he's not," Annie said firmly. "He belongs to someone else. I'm just taking care of him right now until his owner can come get him."

Hannah's downcast face was palpable in its misery.

"And that's tomorrow," Annie added. "But I do think it's time you had a turn on Sam. Why don't you come back tomorrow afternoon, and we'll saddle up old Sam and see if he remembers how to trot?"

Hannah could barely contain herself. "*Really?*"

"Really. I'll have his saddle out by the time you get out of school, all ready for you."

"But, Annie!" Hannah was hopping on one foot with agitation. "You know I can't saddle a horse alone!"

"You want to ride Sam?"

Hannah nodded vigorously.

"Then you're going to have to figure out a way to saddle him. Of course, I'll help."

All this animated conversation had awakened the bay from the lingering effects of the anesthesia. A deep rumble rose from his chest, and he brushed his face across Hannah's chest.

"Oh, Annie! I love Sam, really I do! But I really, *really* want to ride this one!"

While shedding her barn clothes inside the farmhouse door, Annie was greeted by an exuberant Wolf, whose whole rear end seemed to shiver in delight. She ruffed up his fur, letting him slobber all over her. It was the least she could do for a dog who'd been cooped up all day to make sure a guest horse wasn't further traumatized. Glancing at her clock, Annie noted with surprise that it was close to eight. The horses had been fed, and the farm was ready to shut down for the night. Usually, this would have been accomplished two hours earlier.

Padding comfortably into the kitchen in her socks, Annie dumped Alpo into Wolf's bowl and headed to the kitchen cabinet, where her coveted Glenlivet was stored. After pouring herself a severe jigger, she headed to a rocking chair inside her small living room. She thought about turning on the news, then thought better of it. Better to inhale the fumes of single malt scotch and scratch Wolf's ears.

The landline beside her rang shrilly. Annie didn't have the benefit of changing this ring tone, but even if she had, she was sure she it would not be the rousing chorus of "Camptown Ladies."

She plucked up the phone, buoyed by the sudden warmth that good scotch had poured through her body. "Annie speaking."

"Sheriff Dan at your beck and call."

"Dan! My man! What's the news, oh arbiter of justice and shedder of light?" Annie realized she'd probably inhaled a little bit more scotch than she'd thought.

"Wish I was there, Annie, wish I was there. Is this the first jigger or the second?"

Annie sat up straight, any transient buzz gone. "What's the news?"

"Wayne Johnston got a major slug of GBH, otherwise known as the 'date rape drug,' within an hour of his death. There was no deer on the road. Just a man pulling a trailer who'd been doped out of his mind and crashed."

"So . . ."

"So we're classifying it as a homicide, Annie. And that horse you've been caring for is now considered a material witness."

CHAPTER 5

TUESDAY MORNING—WEDNESDAY AFTERNOON,
FEBRUARY 22ND AND FEBRUARY 23RD

Annie looked up from the bay's mouth, frosted with wet,
warm bran mash, as a fleet of cars rumbled into her driveway. Nudging the horse's mouth away, she placed the feed
tub on the stall floor. The bay's long neck followed in one
fluid motion with not a flicker of interest in Annie.

The quiet munch-munch of horses eating their morning
hay followed her as she walked to the stable door.

"Dan! Jessica! I don't think I've ever seen so many people at my house at once!"

"And I hate to break it to you, Annie, but we're not even
here to see *you*. It's that pile of horseflesh that interests us."

Annie laughed. "Better look quick, Dan, because Hilda's
minions are going to show up any moment and haul him
away."

"That's just what I'm counting on. I need to talk to both
her and her man."

Annie and the sheriff walked down to the bay's stall. Jessica, who had ignored all the banter, was already listening
carefully to the horse's gut with her stethoscope.

"He looks good, Annie."

"Yeah, and notice his appetite." Annie was unconscionably
pleased that the bay was straining to get to the uneaten portion
of her mash, now placed outside the stall door.

Annie and Dan fell silent as Jessica delicately placed her
finger in the back of the bay's mouth. This time, he willingly
opened up, and the vet peered inside, using her head lamp.

She dabbed a cotton patch on the side where the offending tooth had been removed. Examining the cotton, Jessica turned to Annie, a pleased smile on her face.

"When was the last time you checked him?"

"About nine last night. Just after I got a call from"—Annie felt, rather than saw Dan's sharp look at her—"from DISH, wanting to know if I wanted cable," she finished lamely.

Jessica didn't seem to notice the linguistic non sequitur.

"Well, he's doing just fine. See? Just a little old dried blood. He'd probably stopped bleeding by the time you saw him, Annie."

"Yeah, well, I didn't exactly look. I just made sure he was upright and his water bucket was full. I couldn't bear to look at the pleading look in his eyes too long."

"Everything looks as it should be, and there's no sign of infection. I'll just give him another dose of antibiotics to make sure he stays on the right path."

Jessica did this with dispatch, then retrieved the bran mash and placed it before the horse. The bay lunged at it.

"Speaking of pleading looks, Annie—" said Dan.

"Forget it! One breakfast a year is enough. I have things to do."

"And I don't? When's Hilda's man supposed to show up, anyway?"

"Crack of dawn, was how he put it yesterday. But he said Hilda would call first, and I haven't heard a peep from her since Todos left."

"What did you think of the guy?" Jessica seemed genuinely curious.

"Well, he did seem to know what he was doing." It practically killed Annie to admit this. "But he's as snobby as Hilda, just without the fine clothes. In fact, I thought he was a local cowboy."

"Yeah," Dan agreed. "He doesn't seem to fit into Hilda's usual assortment of dressage trainers. Well, no sense hanging around if he's not going to show anytime soon. I'm going to head down to Laurie's Café and get some grub. Annie, let me know when Todos shows up, will you? I want to talk to him *and* Hilda today if possible."

It occurred to Annie that Dan was just as capable of doing this job as she was, but if making a phone call got her out of making breakfast, she wasn't going to argue.

It was nine o'clock by the time both Dan and Jessica left, after admiring Baby's new spurt in growth and listening to Annie gush about her plans for her. Truth be known, it was Annie's way of getting everyone to leave so she could get on with her day.

The material witness did not want to be sequestered.

As soon as Annie opened the paddock gate, the bay let out a low, throaty bellow of protest. Trotter turned from the rest of the herd galloping out to the main pasture. He walked back inside the stable aisleway, squarely planted his four hooves, and gave a mournful, earsplitting hee-haw.

"Oh, fine. Go out with your buddy to the paddock. Just don't talk to him about the case."

All morning, Annie kept a close eye on the stable clock, watching the hours tick past. She was damned if she was going to call Hilda again—but what was taking her so long? She half expected Hilda to come swooping in with an entourage that included the revered Dr. Barnes. Or maybe her personal attorney. Or both. By the time Annie had finished mucking the stalls and set out Sam's tack for Hannah that afternoon, she had worked herself into a fine frenzy—and had told off Hilda at least six different ways in her head.

Noontime came and went, and with it, so did Annie's resolve. She trudged back to the farmhouse and dialed Hilda's number again. Her message this time was colder and more to the point. Just to put a little zing into the one-sided conversation, Annie tartly ended with, "And please call Sheriff Stetson immediately. He wants to talk with you *and* your barn manager. Today."

Still feeling peeved, Annie made two PB&Js—one for her and one for Hannah for later—then sat down at her computer and made out an invoice to Colbert Farm. She added Jessica's bills, stuck in a surcharge for the medicinal bran mash, then took it out. No sense in sinking to Hilda's level.

Her anger was not yet assuaged, but the PB&J made Annie feel marginally better. And when Hannah arrived, Annie forgot all about the rude and irritating behavior of stuck-up horse people. The little girl's thrill at riding a real working horse was so appealing that no one, especially Annie, could fail to be caught up in her enthusiasm.

Hannah proved to be just as adept on Sam as she had been on Bess. The old Morgan was healthy and perfectly capable of being ridden as long as her rider didn't weigh more than a hundred pounds. But at this stage in her life, Bess's gaits had dwindled down to one and a half: walk and a sort-of-trot. No amount of kicking, clucking, leaning forward, or whistling could disturb Bess's sureness of mind that the pace she provided was perfect.

With Sam, Hannah learned that a little nudge and "kiss" took him from a fast walk to a brisk trot. She squealed with pleasure as Sam bump-bumped her around the sixty-foot-round pen. Hannah had never trotted before and didn't seem to mind the jolting rhythm. Even so, she held on firmly to the saddle horn while Annie kept hold of the long lead line attached to Sam's bridle. By the time the other members of Annie's herd had gathered by the paddock in anticipation of their evening meal, Hannah had learned to relax into the trot and no longer looked like a puppet on a string.

"Please, please, can't I cluck next time?" Hannah wheedled as she carried the bridle while Annie lugged the saddle to the tack room. Hannah didn't have delusions of wanting to be a chicken; she'd learned that afternoon that while a kissing sound meant trot to Sam, a cluck meant canter. She was sure she was ready. Annie wasn't.

"First, you have to trot Sam around the pen five times without the lead rope," Annie reminded her. "And we have to make sure your parents agree that you're ready to try."

Watching the small child's face, Annie softened the blow. "But now you can help me bring in the horses and feed them."

Hannah raced off for the lead ropes and halters.

The bay apparently had enjoyed his time outside even if he had spent the day in a paddock with a donkey. He walked calmly and politely into his stall and waited patiently for his dinner—more hot mash, with a dash of watered-down hay. Annie wondered what the bay's life had been like before coming to the Olympic Peninsula. Had he been confined to a stall twenty-two hours a day, brought out only to exercise? So many thoroughbreds were, and it infuriated Annie to think of the boredom they must feel. She'd always thought owners who kept their horses stalled should be forced to live in a closet.

The answering machine light blinked when Annie entered her home that evening, but it was only Dan Stetson, asking if she'd relayed his message yet. After dinner, she tried Hilda's phone once again, but she didn't bother leaving a message this time. Nor did she have the energy to call Dan. Instead, she went to bed. In the sixty seconds it took her to fall asleep, Annie decide that the next morning she'd simply deliver the bay herself, phone call or not.

By midmorning, Hilda had still not called. And no one ever seemed to pick up the Colbert Farm phone line. Well, she might as well let Dan know what was going on with his precious witness. She called the County Office Building and got Esther, the county's sole dispatch operator who, on slow days, filled in as receptionist.

"Dan's in Tacoma, testifying in that meth-lab case," Esther informed Annie. "He's likely to be there most of the day. But I'll tell him you plan to haul the horse when he calls in. Funny how that woman doesn't seem to want to get her horse back, isn't it?"

Funny was one word Annie would not have thought of to describe the situation.

Annie wasn't looking forward to trying to trailer the bay again. But pride and sheer obstinacy wouldn't allow her to call Tony or anyone else who might help her.

She sighed, hooked up the trailer to her truck, and headed to the stables, dreading the task to come.

Then an epiphany struck, and Annie knew just how she would solve the little problem of loading.

First, she called Wolf, who bounded toward her, recognizing the trailer as an emblem of daring adventure about to begin.

Next, she asked Wolf to herd Trotter into the trailer. This was one of Wolf's favorite jobs. Anytime Annie and her friends went on an overnight trail ride where Trotter's packing ability was required, Wolf was asked to perform this critical task. In fact, he did it a lot better than most humans. Donkeys do not like to be herded using traditional methods. A dog yipping at your heels, urging you to go forward to the hay, proved a lot more effective.

Trotter skittered into the trailer with one sharp bark from Wolf and immediately began to eat the hay in the feeder strung up at the front. Annie quickly locked the slant gate to keep him there. Now the only hurdle was getting the sixteen-hand bay in with his new friend. She led the horse to the trailer door and gently tapped his rear end to step forward. The bay put one tentative hoof out, pawed the air for a minute, then stepped back. Annie waited a few seconds and tapped again. Now the bay extended his left front leg, snagged the end of the trailer floor with his hoof, and wavered. Annie could almost hear the horse's conflicting thoughts. *Should I go in with my friend? Or stay out where it's safe?*

Trotter's bray brought his indecision to a rapid conclusion. With one bound, the bay leapt into the trailer. Annie closed the slant gate one nanosecond later, then leaned on the door, marveling at her good luck.

Inside, the bay began a small tap dance, but Annie wasn't alarmed. The slant gate would keep him safe, and she quickly tied his lead rope to the inside tie to keep his head controlled. Now the bay had just enough room to duck his head into the hay feeder, but not enough to rear or lie down. As for Trotter, he knew trailering like the back of his hoof. Nothing the bay did would upset him.

Easing out the clutch, Annie started the climb out of her farm driveway and down to the valley where the bay's new home was located.

Shelby was about twenty miles away, and in a different country as far as Annie was concerned. Here, the dense Northwest forest gave way to miles of sparsely populated pine and deciduous trees. A few remaining dairy farms still eked out an existence, a sorry reminder of the thriving farms that once literally brought milk and butter to people's homes. Most of the land had been taken over by developers in the past twenty years, so that the landscape immediately preceding Annie's turnoff was wall-to-wall town homes, with convenient off-ramps to strip malls filled with commercial activity.

The ride had gone well. The bay had settled down after the first mile or so, and Annie kept a substantial distance between her rig and the drivers ahead to avoid any fast stops. She wished she could take a quick trip to the Thompson ranch, where her flock of ewes and solitary ram were now wintering, as it was right on the way. But the thought of stopping even for a few minutes and risk upsetting the rhythm of the so-far-peaceful journey quickly quashed that fleeting idea. She contented herself with a few quick glances over to the fields in which she knew the ewes were pasturing and made a mental note to check on their well-being when she had more time. Lambing season was just around the corner.

Turning west onto Myrtle Road, Annie drove down a quiet lane of modest homes, most of which had small horse farms literally in their backyards. This was where the brash new development had stopped—until Hilda Colbert's complex came into view.

A large electronic gate adorned with metal images of jumpers stopped all comers a quarter mile away. Annie got out and took a quick look at the bay and Trotter. The donkey still had his nose in the hay; the bay had barely touched his, and the look in his eyes could only be called apprehensive. *Time for this journey to end,* Annie decided. She got back into the rig and drove up to the gate, then pushed the intercom button to let the farm know a vehicle wanted to enter the property. No answer. This really was becoming a nuisance, Annie thought, as she saw a muck tractor coming out of a huge, twenty-horse stable on the rising slope. She squinted her eyes. She couldn't make out the driver but knew the John Deere wasn't driving itself.

"Hey! Over here!"

A small Hispanic man looked up.

"*¡Hola!*" Annie waved her arms. "*¡Aquí!* I have Señora Colbert's *caballo!*"

The man sat silent for a moment, then turned off the engine. "*¡Un momento!*" he called back.

Annie got back into the truck and waited.

Two minutes later, a long, grating buzz and loud click sounded and the large metal gate majestically swung open. Annie waited for the gate to fully extend, then slowly drove through and around to the back of the stable. A fleet of trailers emblazoned with the Colbert Farm logo met her.

"You'd think *one* of these could have collected the bay," Annie muttered as she got out of her truck. Her own rig looked dwarfish next to Hilda's procession.

The farmhand came around to greet her, a large German shepherd by his side. Wolf strained against his tether from the flatbed, anxiously barking.

"Shush." Annie undid the buckle, and Wolf leapt out, unmindful of the harness still on him. "And behave."

The dogs danced around each other, yelping exuberantly, then raced off down the slope.

Annie and the farmhand looked at each other and smiled. "Instant *amigos*," she said, and stuck out her hand. "I'm Annie Carson."

The little man seemed slightly unnerved at Annie's extension of friendship, but he took her hand and softly shook it.

"I'm here to deliver Mrs. Colbert's new horse. Is this a good place to unload?"

Annie got a blank stare in return.

Cursing herself for not taking Spanish in college, Annie frantically sought for a phrase that might make sense.

"¿Dónde está Señora Colbert?"

She got a shrug with widespread hands that intimated that Señora Colbert could be anywhere in this big, wide world.

"¿Dónde está Todos?"

"Todos? *Él consigue el heno.*"

Getting hay. Great.

"Quando . . . um . . . back?"

"Oh, *mucho mas tarde.*" Judging by his tone, Todos could be gone for days, months, perhaps years.

"Well, I need to get these guys out of the trailer," Annie said, realizing her actions from here on out would speak louder than her words. She motioned toward the back of the trailer and, using her hands, suggested that he unlock the paddle latches. The man nodded vigorously and began to pull up the latch on the left, behind Trotter.

"Wait! Stop! *¡Ahora!*" Annie ran over to the window grill, untied Trotter's lead rope from the tie, and threw it over his withers. "Okay!"

Annie's helper pulled up the latch and stepped aside. Trotter daintily stepped backward and expertly found his way to the ground. Annie took the lead rope and walked him away.

"Señora!"

Annie turned. The man's face was a mixture of horror and incredulity.

"*¡Es un burro!*"

Annie hooted with laughter. The idea that Hilda would buy a donkey was worth the price of admission to this fancified place.

Gesturing to the other trailer door, she said, "*There* is Señora Colbert's *caballo.*"

Her helper scurried to it and waited for Annie to give the signal to lift up the latch. This time, Annie stepped inside the trailer and stroked the bay's mane, now wet with perspiration, as she loosened the lead from the stall tie.

"Easy, boy," she whispered, as the latch lifted, and the back gate swung open. "Just one step at a time."

The bay took four quick steps backward until one hoof hit air. A split second later, he put it down. Annie threw the lead over his back and emerged outside just as the horse's four hooves met ground. Gathering up the lead line, she led him directly to Trotter, who was drinking deeply from a water trough.

"*¡Magnifico!*"

Annie had to agree, and not just about the gorgeous bay. Looking around for the first time, she saw perhaps eighteen other highly pedigreed horses, each in its own paddock, each eating from its customized hay feeder. They were all blanketed, some with hoods, and Annie realized that she'd never thought of doing this while the bay was at her place. But then, she never blanketed any of her own horses. They were perfectly capable of growing their own winter coats.

Yet the grandeur of Hilda's horses could not be obscured by their outerwear. Anyone with a modicum of horse savvy could see that Hilda had amassed a stunning collection of prime hunter jumpers—including a jet-black stud, Annie saw, housed in its own fifteen-foot-high paddock, far away from the mares. The stallion was pacing back and forth, tossing its head in utter frustration, and in doing so, had created a well-worn track around the perimeter of its personal cage, *Poor boy,* Annie thought to herself, *he's far too worked up for his own good.* She had never understood why so many breeders insisted on sequestering their stallions from the rest of the herd. She knew from experience that if handled correctly, stallions didn't have to turn into rapists. It just took time, training, and understanding.

Turning back to the bay, she noticed that the small Hispanic man was running his hands up and down the horse's legs, looking for possible travel injuries.

Again, Annie felt a small pang of guilt. She hadn't even thought of putting travel boots on the bay. She never did with her own, simply because she knew her horses were smart enough not to step on themselves.

But Hilda's minion seemed to be content with what he saw. He smiled at Annie, took the lead rope, and led the bay toward the massive stable. She watched him cross tie the bay in the washing-rack area. He twisted several knobs, and water from four overhead and two wall jet nozzles suddenly burst forth, lightly watering and massaging the horse. Apparently, this was the standard equine spa treatment around here.

"You've come to the right country club," she quietly told the bay.

While the stableman attended to the bay, Annie left Trotter by the water trough with a flake of hay to keep him happy, and called Wolf to her side. It was time to hunt down the deadbeat. Before she left, she was determined to get a signed receipt that she'd delivered the bay, along with a check for services rendered. Annie could well imagine Hilda claiming that she'd never received her prized thoroughbred and sending an avalanche of attorneys down on her.

Hilda lived in a Spanish-style hacienda with a top story that looked utterly out of place. It was completely out of sight of the stables. Unlike Annie, apparently Hilda didn't care if she was within earshot or eyesight of her horses. Of course, Todos presumably lived in a caretaker cabin, and the stableman she'd just met seemed to be a fixture on the place. But still. Annie's dislike of Hilda deepened.

A late-model Land Rover was in the front driveway. A good sign. Annie gave the doorbell one long buzz. *No use in being subtle now,* she thought.

The yelping of agitated dogs cut through the air. It seemed to come from around the back of the house. Wolf charged after the sound.

"Wolf!" The Blue Heeler knew better than to take off without Annie's express command. She strode after him, muttering at his misbehavior.

That emotion subsided when she saw the small kennel in the backyard, filled with two Belgian Tervuren pups, jumping over each other in their enthusiasm. Wolf had his nose stuck through the wire, and the pups were licking him with fierce intensity.

The kennel was saturated with the smell of urine and the sight of dog poop. The lone water dish hooked to one side was hanging at an angle, bone dry, which one pup licked in vain. The other pup was gnawing on what seemed to be a piece of paper. Annie did not see a scrap of dog food in the pen. The anger she'd felt for Wolf transferred to the pups' owner.

"You poor things!" Annie unlocked the kennel latch,

snatched the paper from the pup's mouth and wrestled the water dish from the other pup's mouth. Glancing around, she noticed an Olympic-sized pool to the left of her. There was no cover on it, and the water inside was steaming, wisps floating over and through the old-growth trees surrounding it.

Many Northwest natives had hot tubs on their properties; a soak in the tub was a welcome respite from a day out in the cold dank rain. Only the truly foolish and extremely rich installed swimming pools in their backyards for a swimming season that lasted perhaps sixty days. Apparently, Hilda was one of this group. A tennis court probably was over the next knoll.

Annie found a hose near the pool shed and, after a spurt of icy water rushed out, she was able to get enough flow to fill the water dish to the brim. The pups lapped it up before Annie had time to shut the kennel door. She filled the dish three times before the pups fully slaked their thirst.

And still no sign of Hilda.

The sound of pounding feet and ragged breath took Annie's attention from the pups she now cradled in her arms. She looked up, and saw Hilda's helper running over the crest of the hill, his chest heaving with exertion. He looked frantic.

Had something happened to the bay? Annie scrambled to her feet, still holding the pups to her chest.

"What's wrong?"

"No, no, Señora! You don't come here!"

Annie stopped, confused. You don't come here? She WAS here. No one seemed to mind before.

"No come to Señora Colbert's *casa! Muy malo.* Come, come away!"

So that was it. No one dare set foot on Hilda's property. Well, to hell with that.

"The hell with that," she told him. Carefully placing the

pups back in the kennel, she motioned for him to follow her. He seemed rooted to the spot. "Come away, Señora!" he hissed.

"Nonsense." Annie walked up to the long sliding glass door facing the backyard and rapped loudly on it.

"Mrs. Colbert! It's Annie Carson! Answer the door!"

She could hear the man whimpering in the background.

"Mrs. Colbert! I've brought your thoroughbred! Please answer the door!"

More silence. Annie peered inside the window, shading her eyes with one arm. In keeping with the exterior, Hilda obviously liked California-Spanish décor. The red-tiled floor was littered with Navajo rugs, a stark contrast to the white stucco walls, one with a huge mural of a black stallion. Two horseshoe arches shaped the room, which seemed to be divided between entertainment center and wet bar. A wrought-iron staircase banister in back of the arches led upstairs.

Annie jiggled the sliding-glass door handle. To her surprise, it wasn't locked.

Behind her, she heard moaning. "No, no, no, Señora. Please, come away."

Annie held her finger up to her lips and whispered, "Shhhh." The little man's frightened posture made her more resolved to confront Hilda on her own turf. Giving Wolf the silent command to stay, Annie slid the door open a good foot.

The stableman took off like a jackrabbit.

Once inside, Annie realized that this is where Hilda probably spent most of her time. A huge BOSE HDTV framed one side of the room, and the La-Z-Boy chair in front of it looked well used. On the coffee table were scattered various well-known horse magazines, mostly on dressage and jumping. Several issues of *People* magazine poked out behind the horse fodder. Beside the table lay an unopened UPS package.

Annie glanced at the return address. It was from a pharma-
ceutical company in New York. She wondered if the contents were for Hilda or her horses.

Glancing over to the wet bar, Annie was amazed to see
an espresso machine that took up almost the entire width of
the counter. It was a far cry from the Mr. Coffee drip in her
own kitchen, so stained by coffee grinds that it would never
be pearly white again.

As much as Annie normally would have liked to snoop, an
unnamed fear began to creep over her. She wasn't afraid of
confrontation, or even breaking or entering, which apparently
was what she was doing. But Hilda's silence made no sense.
The Land Rover in her driveway made it clear she was home,
but the piercing cries of her young dogs and Annie's own
yelling still didn't evoke a response.

She crept upstairs, unthinkingly putting her hand on the
grilled banister, then jerked it away. No sense in leaving
more of her carbon handprint than absolutely necessary.

"Mrs. Colbert! Anyone home?"

Annie emerged from the stairwell onto the main level of
the home, a massive living room with cathedral windows
that overlooked the valley.

It was very, very still. And there was a bad odor in the air.
Maybe Hilda had more neglected dogs in the house. Annie
tiptoed on the plush carpet through the living room and down
the hallway leading to what she assumed were the bedrooms.

The smell was getting worse now. Annie's heart began to
hammer in her chest.

The door at the end of the hallway was open a few inches.
Annie fumbled for her handkerchief and put it over her mouth
and nose. Using one finger, she gently nudged the door, causing it to slowly open two more inches.

Hilda Colbert was lying on her back on her king-sized
bed, her chin jutting up toward the ceiling at a curious angle.

She was dressed in full riding gear, down to her high rider dress boots and full seat breeches. But Hilda wouldn't be riding today, or any other day. The choker band of her show shirt was fully obscured with a thick, congealed mass of blood. And whatever had caused this bright red ribbon across her neck had left Hilda's head perilously close to leaving the rest of her body.

Annie sank to her knees. The stench of death was overwhelming, and she could barely process what she was seeing. Taking deep, gulping breaths under her handkerchief, she tried to think. She was a trained emergency technician. What should she do? Check for a pulse. Oh, God. Was it really necessary? Could she even stand?

She decided not to try. She tied her handkerchief in an old-fashioned rustler fashion knot and crawled on all fours to the bed. The river of blood that had begun at Hilda's neck continued across her eight-hundred-thread-count Egyptian sheets.

Annie slowly got to her feet and steeled herself to look at Hilda's body. There was too much blood to see the wound, but Annie knew that whoever had killed her had done a savage job. And Hilda, it appeared, did not see it coming. Her eyes were wide open. Her face held a surprised expression. Looking down, Annie saw that her fists were clenched. One held a shred of paper.

Gingerly, Annie reached for it, knowing that she shouldn't. But rigor mortis was either just coming on or fast receding, and Hilda willingly ceded the paper, something she probably never would have done when she was alive.

It was nothing—just the ragged edge of a sheaf of what obviously had been fine stationery at one time. There were no words scrawled on it, no treasure map—no clue that gave Annie any idea as to *who* had killed Hilda or *why* she had held the scrap so fiercely at the moment of her death.

Or did it? Slowly, Annie reached into her jeans pocket where she'd stuffed the tattered piece of paper she'd wrested from the pup's mouth just a few minutes before.

She awkwardly pieced them together. Despite the inroads made by the puppy, enough of the document remained to ensure its fit.

It was the bay's foal registration papers, with proof of filing with the Jockey Club. Annie's eyes swept through the complicated pedigree that had led to the gelding's birth until she found what she'd been looking for: "Trooping the Colour." The bay's name.

"I always thought you were a trooper," she said quietly. Then she dug out her cell to call 9-1-1.

CHAPTER 6

WEDNESDAY AFTERNOON, FEBRUARY 24TH

"One more time, Annie. Tell me what you saw, from start to finish."

Dan Stetson and Annie stood by the swimming pool, away from the medics and technicians who were in the process of transporting a black body bag into a nearby ambulance.

"I've already told you, Dan, from start to finish, about a jillion times. What else do you need to know? Am I a suspect? Should I be calling a lawyer?"

The events of the day had put Annie in understandably a sour mood. As soon as Dan and his gang arrived with their sirens blaring and swirling police lights going full tilt, she'd been shooed out of the house. She'd sat idly by for what seemed hours.

At first, she'd played with the puppies and considered transferring them to a fenced area in back of the pool, where they'd have room to play. But Dan probably would have considered that evidence tampering.

By now she'd fully recovered from the shock of finding the body. Her self-confidence also had returned after she saw two of Dan's deputies run stumbling out of the house to puke. At least she had better guts than that.

"Look, Annie, I know you've been through a lot." Dan said. "I just need to know exactly why you came up here, and all your movements from the time you entered the property."

"Jeez, Dan! Why did I come up here? I had a twelve-hundred-pound horse on my hands who doesn't belong to me and costs me more in two days than my mortgage is each month! I was taking him back to his owner, because he didn't . . . belong . . . to . . . me." Annie drew out the last words for emphasis. "Besides, I told Esther all this. Why don't you ask her?"

"You told Esther you were coming up here?"

Annie glared at him.

"Okay, calm down, Annie. I don't suspect you of anything but trying to do a good deed. But when I go back to my office tonight and have to write up a report, I want to make sure I've got my facts straight. That's two murders in Suwana County in three days—more serious crime than we've seen in two decades. I don't want the county commissioners to feel compelled to bring in outside help."

Annie caught the undercurrent of Dan's words. If the county commissioners felt Dan Stetson's law-enforcement team wasn't up to the job, they'd call in the neighboring force from Harrison County. Jim Bruscheau, the Harrison County sheriff, was everything Dan was not—overbearing, bombastic, and derisive of anyone who worked under him. If Dan had to play second fiddle to Bruscheau, his life would be a living hell, and his professional reputation would suffer.

"Why don't I just walk you through it, step by step?" Annie said.

Dan smiled. "Great idea. Just start from the time you came up to Hilda's place."

Annie walked around to the front door, Dan in tow. She felt slightly appeased. She also had the feeling she'd played right into Dan's hands.

"When I saw the Land Rover, I assumed Hilda was home. So I banged on the door, but that only got the attention of the pups around the corner. Wolf raced off. I followed him and saw the poor things. My first concern was getting water into their pitiful kennel. I don't mind saying I was ready to kill Hilda myself at that point."

Dan looked at her sharply.

"Okay, scratch that," Annie continued. "How about 'Ms. Colbert's apparent animal neglect affected my mood greatly'?"

Now, Annie was standing by the empty kennel. With Dan's permission, she had eventually moved them to the fenced-in yard, where they now sprawled over Wolf, fast asleep.

"Then the worker, who, by the way, I am sure is paid peanuts under the table, came racing up, all in a dither over my even being on Hilda's estate. I told him to get over it and knocked on the sliding glass door in back."

Annie was about to demonstrate when Dan caught her arm.

"We've just taken fingerprints of the entire plate, Annie. I believe you."

"I think I yelled out to Hilda to open the door. It was about that time that the farmhand took off, scared to death that Hilda would see him up here. Then I went inside. And yes, the latch was off. I didn't break and enter. I just entered."

"Remind me someday to acquaint you with the finer details of the revised code of Washington regarding burglary," Dan said. "I'm sure you were just concerned about the state of Ms. Colbert's health at this point."

"As I matter of fact, I was," Annie replied. "Here was all this ruckus, and yet Hilda didn't poke her head out to tell me to go away. It seemed strange."

Dan handed her a pair of disposable shoe covers and latex gloves.

"Put these on. What happened next?"

Annie struggled into her gloves and thought carefully.

"Well, I remember I only used one finger to try the patio latch and was surprised when it gave way. Then I tiptoed up the stairs, over there. I think I touched the banister. I probably was still calling for Hilda to come out and play."

Annie and Dan silently went up the stairwell.

"When I got up to the landing, that's when I smelled the odor. I also remember thinking what a fabulous view she had."

Annie walked up to the massive windows again. The Olympic Mountains looked so close, she thought, it was as if you could walk right up to them from the back door. She glanced around at the living room and couldn't help feeling a tad envious at Hilda's bank account, if not her taste in furniture.

"Ah. Look. Hilda's landline. It probably has all the nasty messages I left for her over the past two days."

Dan strode over and delicately picked up the phone with one of his gloved hands, then put it down.

"We'll have to get the password," he said. Leaning toward his squawk box on his shoulder, Dan bellowed, "Esther!"

From the other side came Esther's voice. "Yes, Sheriff?"

"We need to get the password to Hilda Colbert's voice mail. Write up a search warrant for me and get Judge Casper to okay it over the phone. We'll want all the messages, current and saved. I need the disk on my desk pronto."

"You got it, Sheriff." Another squawk signified the end of the call.

"You pay Esther to do that kind of work?" asked Annie.

Dan grinned. "She loves being asked to do things she usually only sees on *Law & Order.*"

"You sure about that?"

"Why, Annie. You're a good judge of character. Couldn't you feel the love in her voice?"

Annie decided not to dignify his question with an answer. "So anyway, then I just followed the odor." Annie glanced down the hallway, but neither she nor Dan made a step toward it. Bright yellow tape, labeled CRIME SCENE—DO NOT CROSS, barred their way.

"What did you do when you saw Mrs. Colbert?"

Annie fell silent. She hadn't yet told Dan that she'd pulled one scrap of registration papers out of Hilda's dead hands and the other out of a puppy's mouth. She just wanted the chance to first read them over in private. Then she'd turn them over. Somehow, she knew that this would not be considered good police form.

Fortunately, the good and bad angels flitting beside Annie's head got the chance to flee.

"Sheriff." The voice was metallic, coming from Dan's radio, but Annie recognized it as Deputy Williams's. There weren't that many female officers on the force, and Kim Williams's voice was eminently distinctive: low, husky, authoritative, and Annie suspected, extremely seductive in the right setting.

"Adolpho Todos has arrived at the scene. Should I send him up?"

Dan shifted his considerable weight and cocked his head.

"Nah, keep him at the stables. I'll be there in a jiffy. How's he seem?"

"Cranky. Busy unloading a truckload of hay."

"Said anything yet?"

"Nope. He's busy bossing the help around right now."

"Good. I'd hate to have him say anything without having his rights read to him first."

Annie stared at Dan.

"Todos? You think Todos did it?"

"How in the heck should I know, Annie? But you know as well as I do that everyone's a suspect until proven innocent."

Annie was bemused that now that Hilda was dead, Dan accorded her the courtesy of her surname, something he'd never done before.

"Gee, Dan, that's not how I remember Mr. Berber talking about Con Law in high school. But then, you never were a good student in that class, were you? Too busy trying to look up Dory Mason's skirt, as I recall."

Dan grinned but said, "Everyone's a suspect, Annie. Remember that."

Todos was angrily unloading bales of hay from the back of one of Hilda's two-ton pickups when Dan and Annie pulled up at the stables. The farmworker Annie had met earlier was the unfortunate recipient of Todos's aggression. He literally had to dodge the flying bales, set free by a wicked-looking hayfork, as he tried to assemble them onto a loading cart.

"Señor Todos."

Dan strode up to the barn manager and stuck out his hand. Todos took it with about as much enthusiasm as he'd taken Annie's a few days earlier.

"This must be quite a shock for you," Dan said.

Todos let a long stream of spit out of the side of his mouth and said nothing.

"Mind if we talk somewhere where it's quieter?"

Todos barked out a rapid-fire stream of orders in Spanish to the nearby worker, then turned back to Dan.

"We can meet in the tack room."

Annie trailed in behind Dan and Todos, trying to look as inconspicuous as possible. The two men sat down at a round table, scattered with dressage magazines, while Annie feigned interest in the blue ribbons and photos on the wall. Dan gave her a pointed look and nodded toward the door. Annie meekly went out just in time to hear the door shut firmly behind her.

Next to the tack room was a bathroom twice the size of Annie's at home. She discovered that if she opened a small bathroom window and crouched on the toilet seat beneath it, she could hear most of what was being said.

"Let's start with a few basic questions, shall we?"

Over the next twenty minutes, Annie learned that Todos had come from Mexico City to the Olympic Peninsula about six months ago. He'd heard that Señora Colbert was looking for a new manager and was hired on the spot. Todos had worked at racetracks since he was eight years old, first as a groom, then as a jockey. When he grew too tall for that role, he decided it was time to ply his skills in a country where he could make decent money in the horse trade. He was now twenty-four. He had come with superlative professional references. In fact, he was the best in the business when it came to training and riding thoroughbreds. It was common knowledge.

Annie noticed that Dan pointedly had not asked about Todos's green card status. Nice of him. *Too nice,* she thought. Todos continued.

Señora Colbert was very demanding, but then, so was he. Within a month, he and Señora Colbert had fired the entire work crew and hired new personnel—although, Todos implied, even this crew was barely functional and probably wouldn't have lasted much longer. When Todos wasn't bossing the crew, he was exercising the horses and managing Señora Colbert's eventing schedule. He often accompanied her on exhibition trips. She was a good rider, yes, but had a lot to learn. Todos implied that if she had used him, instead of her expensive trainers, she would have many more ribbons adorning her tack room and arena walls.

Señora Colbert was a very private woman. No one was allowed up at her house, even if one of the horses had fallen lame or ill. All communication had to be done by phone. Even Todos had never been as far as the front door. The one time that a worker had gone to Señora Colbert's home, he had been immediately sacked. This was before Todos's time. Workers from other ranches still talked about it.

It was not uncommon for Señora Colbert to visit her horses often. On the other hand, it was not uncommon for her to stay away for days at a time. No, Todos did not know what she did outside of the horse business. She seldom left the premises, and when she did, she took her Land Rover.

Every Monday morning, he and Señora Colbert met in Señora Colbert's office in the stables and decided what needed to be done in the week ahead. Unless Señora Colbert came to the stables to watch him exercise, or ask for one of the horses to be saddled for her own use, he had no reason to talk to her.

The last time he saw Señora Colbert was two days ago, after he'd returned from Annie's. He'd reported that the horse seemed to be sound although he suggested having Señora Colbert's sports-medicine vet evaluate the work done on the bay's mouth. He did not trust the job that "the woman" had done.

Señora Colbert said that she would contact Annie herself and let him know when the bay would be transported to her stables. She implied that it would be soon. When he didn't hear from her, he was surprised but not alarmed. Señora Colbert was a fine businesswoman, but, after all, she was a woman. She might have changed her mind about when she wanted the bay moved for no reason at all.

He had met Señor Colbert only once, and judging by Todos's tone of voice, he was not impressed with what he'd seen. Marcus Colbert worked in California and only came home a few weekends a month. He never talked to the man— what would he have to say to him? He knew nothing about horses. Nothing. And he disliked his wife living apart from him very much. He had heard loud arguments before in the arena.

"Arguments, you say? Did you witness these arguments? Hear any sounds of violence?" asked Dan.

Annie strained to hear the answer, but all she could glean from the other room was silence, for what seemed an excruciatingly long time. Finally, she heard Todos clear his throat. He had not actually *seen* Señor and Señora Colbert fighting, he told Dan. It was not his place to watch such things. But he had heard plenty of shouting, always about the horses. Señora Colbert would not obey her husband and return to California. And there was nothing Señor Colbert could do to change her mind.

Well, I'll give you that much for common sense, Annie silently told the dead woman.

As far as violence, well, it was possible. Once, when the husband was visiting, Todos had seen Señora Colbert with a badly bruised arm. But she said she had fallen off a horse and who was he to question? He also once had seen Señor Colbert with a black eye, but no explanation was given. Todos was certain it did not come from a horse. Señor Colbert would not know how to even mount a horse.

Even with a wall separating her, Annie could hear the sneer in Todos's voice. The clear implication was that Marcus probably didn't know how to mount anything, including his wife.

"Señor Todos," said Dan, "you're been very helpful and extremely thorough. And I know you've got a lot to do now that Mrs. Colbert is . . . well, is gone."

Dan was laying it on a bit thick, Annie thought.

"It make no difference," Todos said carelessly. "We do the work."

Annie heard Dan clear his throat. "Well, I know that. But I do have to ask you, Señor Todos, what you were doing from the time you last talked to Señora Colbert on Monday until four o'clock today, two days later."

"Oh, you need the alibi? Señora Colbert requires only the best hay for her animals. There is no such hay made here, and we have enough for only a week more. So I call a ranch in Eastern Washington and secure a load. Then I drive up to get it."

"When did you leave?"

"Tuesday morning. I get the hay, spend the night in a motel, and come back today."

From inside the bathroom, Annie involuntarily hooted in disbelief. Tuesday morning! She'd waited from six o'clock Tuesday morning until she'd locked the barn for the night for Todos to arrive. *And Hilda didn't even have the decency to call to let me know,* she thought. *Some people have all the nerve.*

Annie felt a sharp pang of remorse. *Had* the nerve. *Some people* were dead. Come to think of it, the last time Hilda probably had seen her horses was when she was ordering Todos to hit the road for hay. Hilda wasn't going to see her beautiful beasts again. Now *there* was a fate worse than death.

Annie heard the tack room door open. She quickly flushed the toilet and came outside.

"Annie!"

She walked up to Dan, straightening her clothes.

"Now that you're done listening in private, why don't you come in and join the party?"

Annie was happy to comply. Once they were seated at the table, Dan resumed his questions.

"Do you know how to reach Señor Colbert?" Dan asked Todos.

Todos tossed his head toward a printed phone list beside the tack room phone.

"He may be on the list. I never noticed."

"Well, that's that, I guess. I'll let you get back to your work."

Todos silently up and walked toward the door, making a point, Annie thought, of not looking at either her or Dan. Maybe he was an undocumented guy. If that was so, she couldn't blame him for wanting to say as little as possible.

"Oh, one more thing."

Todos slowly turned.

"Did Señora Colbert have any enemies? Anyone you know who might want to wish her harm?"

Todos allowed a small smile to touch his lips.

"Señora Colbert was, how you say, not a friendly person. She don't have enemies, but . . . she don't have friends."

Todos turned to leave.

"And one more thing," said Dan. "I'll need proof that you got that hay and spent the night in Eastern Washington. When you have time, of course."

Todos smiled again. Annie wondered if he was ever capable of injecting even a modicum of warmth into the act.

"*No problemo.* You can see for yourself, right now."

Todos pulled a crumpled motel bill and receipt for hay out of a pocket of his jeans. He handed them over to Dan, who looked at them and carefully placed both in a folder.

"Right. Thank you, Señor Todos. I'll let you go now. Take

my card. If you think of anything, you'll let me know, won't you?"

"Of course." Todos vanished.

"You didn't read him his rights," Annie said.

"Didn't need to. We'll check out his alibi, of course, but it seems pretty straightforward. Now I want to talk to the husband."

Marcus Colbert was second to the last on the phone list—just above the local plumber. Dan jotted down the phone numbers, then looked at Annie.

"I hate doing this," he said.

"I'll bet you do. That's why you get paid the big bucks."

Dan snorted and picked up the tack room phone. He called the first number listed for Mr. Colbert. A receptionist answered. Mr. Colbert was not in. Dan thanked her and said he'd try his cell.

Hilda's husband picked up on the first ring with an abrupt "Colbert" loud enough for even Annie to hear. Dan cleared his throat and plunged in.

"Mr. Colbert, this is Dan Stetson, sheriff of Suwana County. I'm afraid I have bad news for you."

As Annie listened to Dan flailing around for the right words to say, she realized there were no right words. How do you tell someone that his spouse has been brutally murdered?

All Annie could hear were Dan's responses, which sounded positively pathetic judging by the number of questions Mr. Colbert was spewing.

"Mr. Colbert, I know this is a tough thing for you to swallow right now. I'll keep you informed of our progress every step of the way. Right now, it doesn't look like there will be any until tomorrow, when we expect to get the results from the autopsy. And the reports from our evidence technicians."

"Ask HIM questions. You're getting murdered," she hissed at Dan.

Dan threw a pained look at Annie. He cleared his throat.

"But I need to know from you now: Did your wife have any enemies? Anyone who might want to hurt her?"

Another inaudible diatribe issued from the phone line. Annie impatiently tapped on Dan's shoulder.

"Ask him about the horse! Did he know about the accident?"

Dan put his hand over the mouthpiece and whispered back, "Why in the Sam Hill would I ask him that, Annie?"

"Hey, you're the one looking for suspects! If he knows about the hauler's murder, maybe he's connected to Hilda's murder, too!"

Dan rolled his eyes but asked, "Mr. Colbert, are you aware that your wife recently purchased a thoroughbred?"

This time, Dan held the phone at a cocked angle, so Annie could hear the response.

"Sheriff, if I kept track of every time my wife bought a new horse, I'd have nothing else to do with my time. If she did, it doesn't surprise me. Why are you asking?"

"Only because one of our local horse rescuers has been taking care of your wife's new thoroughbred for the past few days. The hauler had an accident on the way to your wife's farm three days ago, and the horse was injured."

Annie noticed that Dan adroitly avoided the news of the hauler's death.

"Well, I'm sorry to hear that. Is the horse going to be all right?"

"Why don't I let Annie Carson, the woman who's been tending to the horse, tell you herself?"

Dan thrust the phone into Annie's hands.

"Mr. Colbert. I'm terribly sorry to hear about your recent loss. Rest assured that your wife's horse is now in excellent health, and in fact, is here at the stables as we speak."

"Ms. Carson, I wish I could tell you that I really cared

about my late wife's most recent acquisition, but truly, I don't. The one time I rode a horse, it tried to buck me off, and I really don't even like to be close to the beasts. But I'm grateful to you for caring for the animal. Tell me—were you friends with my wife? She knew so few people in the community, it seemed."

For a recent widower, Annie thought, *he certainly is taking the loss of his wife well. Maybe too well. Then again, maybe losing Hilda is like losing a painful bunion.* Annie swallowed hard and crossed her fingers. "To be truthful, Mr. Colbert, we were only passing acquaintances. But I know that everyone who lives here greatly admired her facility and . . . and the magnificent hunters and jumpers she kept here."

There was a sigh on the other end of the phone.

"Ms. Carson, I appreciate your praise, but can't help but note it has nothing to do with my wife's personality. I know she was hard to get along with at times. She was a tough nut to crack, and believe me, I know it better than anyone. So I thank you doubly for caring for the horse. Would you mind terribly continuing until I get there?"

This would not be a good time to bring up the issue of the unpaid bill, Annie thought. And what could she say? She might as well continue to care for the bay until the issue of compensation had been resolved.

"I'd be happy to, Mr. Colbert," she said, and handed the phone back to Dan.

"Mr. Colbert, we're trying to trace some of the more recent phone calls made to your wife. You wouldn't know, by chance, the password to her home phone? Her birth date? Eight-six-seven-zero. Thank you so very much, Mr. Colbert. That helps us a lot. Otherwise, we'd have to do a lot of paperwork to get this information. When will you be flying up, sir?"

Annie winced as Dan signed off. It seemed she was doomed to have her messages to Hilda broadcast to the world, whether she liked it or not.

Dan turned to her.

"Can you believe the stupidity of some people? The password is Hilda's birthday."

"I heard." If Annie hadn't still had a 1990s model phone with a built-in answering machine, she probably would have used her birth date as a password, too.

It was now close to five. The evidence team had finally packed up and left. Annie suspected that Hilda's body had arrived at the medical examiner's office and was already being prepared for a thorough dissection. Dan called Esther to cancel the search warrant. Even Annie noticed that Esther seemed disappointed. Esther did perk up when Dan asked her to arrange for a Spanish interpreter for the next day; he intended to interview all of Hilda's other workers tomorrow, starting at eight in the morning.

Kim Williams was the only deputy left on the scene. She, Dan, and Annie returned to Hilda's residence to listen to her voice mails.

Kim got out her digital recorder and gave the okay to Dan to start playing the messages.

Annie kept her head down as the messages started rolling. Sure enough, Annie's voice was the first to be heard, loud and clear. After her second angry tirade had been publicly aired, she began to squirm in her chair. She thought she heard both Kim and Dan chuckling but didn't look up to find out.

But, to her surprise, Annie wasn't the only one who was being humiliated by the replaying of old messages. It appeared Hilda had been slow to pay her vendors. Interspersed with Annie's diatribes were increasingly angry rants from tack and feed stores, and one pleading one from a well-known sports equine vet. Annie felt slightly mollified. She certainly didn't have Hilda's wherewithal, but she did pay her bills on time. People in the country counted on that. A check that didn't arrive on time could mean you didn't eat, or pay your mortgage that month.

The machine announced the next call: "Monday, February 25 at 2:16 P.M. Caller unknown." A man with a deep and cultured voice began to speak. The words he spoke chilled Annie right down to her bones.

"I will destroy you. You will be a dead woman before you know it. Consider yourself warned."

Annie looked up and met Dan's gaze. The man's voice was unmistakable. It was Marcus Colbert.

CHAPTER 7

THURSDAY, FEBRUARY 25TH

Annie rested her muck rake on one elbow and picked up her ringing cell phone. Last night, after unloading Trooper and Trotter back in her barn, her first move had been to change her cell ring tone. She'd decided she'd had about as much of Stephen Foster as she could take. The new one sounded as if it came out of an old-fashioned, hand-cranked telephone box.

"Annie Carson speaking."

"Ms. Carson, this is Marcus Colbert."

Annie's throat closed. Nothing like talking to the number one murder suspect of the woman whose body you'd discovered to put a damper on your vocal cords.

"Ms. Carson? Are you there?"

"Yes, Mr. Colbert." Her voice squawked.

"Call me Marcus. Please."

I'll be calling you by your inmate number soon, Annie thought, but politely replied, "How are you?"

"I'm about as well as can be expected, I guess." A long sigh emanated from the other end of the line. "I hope you don't mind, but I got your number from Mr. Todos, Hilda's barn manager. I'm at the San Jose Airport, waiting to board a plane. I should be arriving in your area around eight tonight. I wondered if I could stop by for a moment before I head out to the ranch."

"Why?" Annie blurted out the question before she could think.

"Well, I realize you've been taking care of my wife's horse for an unconscionably long time. And I understand a vet bill is involved. I thought I could write you a check."

For a cold-blooded killer, he sounds quite reasonable, Annie thought. *And I might as well get paid before he goes to the pokey.*

"That's very thoughtful of you, Mr.—I mean, Marcus."

"Not a problem. In the past twenty-four hours, I've discovered that Hilda wasn't very good at paying her suppliers. I don't know why, since she had plenty in her bank account. I feel it's the least I can do."

This man is just too kind, Annie mused. *Maybe he hired a ruthless killer to whack Hilda.*

"Well, I appreciate your offer, and I'll take you up on it. Let me tell you how to find me."

As Annie gave Marcus directions to her farm, she mentally mapped out the conversation with Dan that would follow this one. Ha! Not only was she the one who'd first entertained the idea of Marcus as the killer, she would lead him straight into the sheriff's handcuffs.

Her next call was not quite as thrilling as she'd expected.

"Are you out of your Sam Hill mind, Annie? We know he's coming in on the 5:25 out of San Jose. Don't you think we boys work with our buddies out of state?"

The day before, Dan was worried that his "buddy" from the next county would butt in on his territory. Now that he had a suspect in mind, everyone was his friend, Annie thought sourly. And dollars to doughnuts it was Esther who'd been the one to find out that information.

"Well, I just thought you should know." Annie's tone was nothing if not haughty. "Just in case you come by and find a trail of blood leading to the bedroom."

"We'll be at your place no later than nineteen-hundred hours. And if you hear from him before then, give me a call, would you?"

"Oh, your *boys* will probably tell you as soon as he's dialing my number." Annie abruptly ended the call before Dan had a chance to answer.

Her mood improved a half hour later when she got a call from a friend a ferry ride away, pleading for help in teaching a young colt ground manners.

"He's a sweetheart, Annie, but he needs your magic touch." Samantha Higgins owned a boarding facility in Arndorp, a small Norwegian farming community just west of the Peninsula and about six miles from Annie's farm as the crow flies. Sam was a professional horsewoman, and, in fact, president of the Northwest Trailblazers, the local riding club, but she occasionally took in new horses to train. When she wasn't training animals, she invariably had her hands full teaching six-year-olds how to tack up a horse.

"You're in luck, Sam—I have exactly one stall left. You sound far away. Where are you calling from?"

"The Worden Canal Bridge. I'll be at your place in about fifteen minutes. With the horse."

As soon as the lead rope was untied from the hook inside the trailer, the "sweetheart" leapt a full 360 degrees and lunged out of the trailer. The diminutive Arab was soaked with sweat. He'd also been plenty jittery on the forty-five-minute ride over. Annie conservatively estimated it would take Sam a good hour to clean out the trailer bed.

"Whoa, Jeremy! Whoa there, boy!" Sam grabbed the trailing lead rope and tried to stop the colt's propulsion.

"In here." Annie stood by the wide-open paddock gate. In the remaining minutes before Sam's arrival, she'd emptied the last empty stall of winter vegetables and hustled Trooper and Trotter back into their own stalls, where they now stood, placated by unexpected midday hay.

With Marcus's imminent arrest, Annie realized that Trooper might continue to board with her for weeks or even months to come. If that were the case, then Trooper would have to learn how to acclimate with her other horses out in the pasture. But there was no sense in rushing the process, and right now the paddock had to be free for the new addition to Annie's equine family.

The colt rushed in, and Sam unsnapped the lead line seconds before being trampled underfoot. Annie swung the gate shut as Sam eased out of the paddock. For several minutes, the two women watched the colt race around the fence line without pause.

Annie spoke first. "Jeremy?"

"It wasn't my idea."

Another minute passed. The colt showed no sign of slowing down.

"Aside from having too much energy, what are his issues?"

"Oh, nothing that you can't cure, Annie. He's just turned three, and his owner has let him be a total baby his entire life. I've watched her feed him. She just brings out a bucket of grain and lets him put his face in it as she lugs it—and him—over to the feed bin. Jeremy thinks everyone is another colt to play with. He rears and bucks just to let you know he's happy to see you. Frankly, I'm surprised his owner is alive to tell me about it."

"Ever been under saddle?"

"I've barely gotten him under halter. His ground manners are nonexistent. He's a lot of work, Annie. I hope you have time to take him on."

Annie laughed. "So why'd you bring him out here without knowing the answer?"

"To tell you the truth, I'd loaded him this morning with every intention of taking him back to his owner. I was led to believe that all he needed was a little retraining. This is way too much for me to handle with everything else I do. Then, as I was waiting for the bridge to open, I thought of you and just decided to take the chance that you'd say yes."

"He looks like a lot of work."

"He is."

"It will take a lot of time. And money."

"That it will."

"My lambing season is a mere month away."

"I'll help."

The colt came to a sliding stop in front of Annie, reared up, and let out a deafening whinny.

"I'll have to rename him."

"Thanks, Annie. I knew you'd come through."

* * *

By suppertime, Jeremy had been renamed Geronimo, and was following Annie around the paddock as docilely as a well-fed cat. At first, he'd reared every time Annie turned her back, once even touching her shoulder blades with his hooves, but he quickly learned that every time his front feet left the ground, he was pushed back into the corner. Geronimo was never quite sure how he ended up there, but it occurred often enough that he decided rearing wasn't so much fun when it meant your butt got pushed against the rail.

Annie could guess at his thoughts. *This new human is nice, and she smells good, too. Once, she even fed me carrots out her pocket, and all I did was stand there. Now she's leaving, which means it's time to race around the paddock again. But wait! She's coming back, with a very strange horse.* Geronimo whinnied. The strange horse whinnied back, but it was like nothing the colt had ever heard in his life.

This is turning into a very interesting day.

Once Annie was sure that Trotter and Geronimo were going to get along, she set to work getting dinner ready for the horses. With the new addition, the issue of where to put Trooper during the day was paramount in her mind. Geronimo definitely was going to be in the paddock for the foreseeable future, and most likely along with Trotter. She couldn't risk putting the thoroughbred in with such a green horse, but the only alternative was the pasture with her other equines.

I need to remember to ask Marcus if that's okay, she thought to herself, before realizing that the only decision Marcus soon would be making would be which expensive criminal defense attorney to hire.

The feed bins filled, Annie walked up her driveway and across the street to the stretch of mailboxes. Opening her own battered box, she pulled out bills, bills, circular flyers, more bills—and one letter with distinctive flowery handwriting in, of all colors, magenta—and no return address. Annie sniffed the envelope. Lavender. It could mean only one thing.

Annie sat down inside her kitchen and poured herself a small scotch. Letters from her half sister Lavender always required the help of medicinal beverages. For the past fifteen years, she'd received quite a few epistles from her free-spirited, slightly offbeat half sister, and they all were precursors to the same thing: a visit, without a discernible end date.

Annie sighed as she ripped open the envelope and averted her head to avoid being overwhelmed by the fragrance inside. She picked up her glass, inhaled the fumes of her single malt, and, after a moment's hesitation, bolted down half the contents.

Dearest Sister, Annie read, and barked derisively. Lavender insisted on calling her "Sister" instead of her given name, which Annie chalked up to her having read too much Jane Austen when she was young. But not only was the sobriquet in itself appalling, it presumed far too much, in Annie's mind. There was nothing she could do about the fact that her father had run off with his secretary in his real-estate business when Annie was a gawky eleven-year-old. Nor could she do anything about the fact that said secretary promptly got pregnant and produced little Lavender. But it was too much to expect Annie to cotton to her unplanned and unwanted extended family with any real warmth or enthusiasm. Since most of her contact with her father consisted of stilted phone calls on birthdays and on Christmas, pretending to be nice wasn't that difficult. After Annie's mother died, the phone conversations stopped altogether, which was just fine with her. Unfortunately, Lavender felt an inordinate desire to keep in touch with a half sister she barely knew.

And Lavender was a lightweight; that's all there was to it. Probably her name didn't help, Annie thought. But since the age of three, all Lavender had wanted to do was to play Cinderella and practice how to look most adorable. With her long blond hair and perfect, small-boned features, it wasn't hard. Annie's father had been a pushover, she'd learned from Lavender's letters. What had been an extravagance in his former household, such as buying Annie a pony, became de rigueur in his new life. Ponies, dogs, cats, bunnies, and whatever other animal captured Lavender's curiosity for the moment were bestowed on her without a thought of what would happen to them once her enthusiasm faded. After the animal craze dwindled, Lavender took up lessons in hip-hop, pop singing, and other such pursuits, sure that she was meant to be the next Lady Gaga. The trouble was, Annie recalled, if anything took more than fifteen minutes of con-centration, Lavender quickly lost interest. Even a year in Switzerland—something Annie would have sold her soul for—left Lavender with an atrocious accent and a French vocabulary that any fifth-grade student could top.

Dearest Sister, Annie began again. She tossed back the rest of the scotch before continuing to read.

> *You will be DELIGHTED to know that I am going to be in your world SOON!!! As you know, I have worked hard these many years to develop my natural gifts as a psychic and am very attuned to what the universe tells me. The very clear message that I have gotten is that I should be with you!! Also, there is a very spiritual Native American elder nearby who teaches how to communicate with animals and ex-plore their previous lives. Isn't that PERFECT, Sister? I'll be helping you train horses by exploring their deepest thoughts and emotions. We will be SO GOOD together!! See you SOON!!*
> *Love, your sister Lavender.*

A poor imitation of a Celtic cross was inked in below her name.

Annie put down the letter and searched for her address book, pouring herself a hefty refill on the way. This little scheme had to be nipped in the bud. Immediately. Squinting at the many crossed-out numbers in her address book for Lavender, she finally selected the one that appeared most recent and dialed the number.

It was disconnected. Hell's bells. How could she head Lavender off at the pass?

As she avoided thinking of the obvious, she savagely parsed Lavender's letter. "Be in your world soon." *My ass,* Annie thought. *You're in outer space permanently.* "Natural gifts as a psychic." *Oh, yeah? Then hear this: STAY AWAY.*

Annie sighed and reached for the address book again, this time searching for her father's number. There was simply no one else to call who might know where Lavender was parked at present.

A female voice answered on the sixth ring, sounding breathless.

"Hello?"

"Is Douglas Carson in?"

"No, he's out sailing right now. Can I take a message?"

"No. Well, yes. Would you tell him his daughter Annie called and needs to get hold of Lavender right away?"

"He has *another* daughter?"

"Well, technically yes, but that's about as far as it goes," Annie replied. "Just who am I talking to, anyway?"

"I'm *Mrs.* Carson. The third." A small titter accompanied this information.

"Congratulations. You wouldn't happen to know where Lavender is, would you?"

"I'm afraid I don't. She left the day before we were married. I don't think she approved of me." Another titter.

"And how long ago was that?"

"Almost a week. Doug and I are celebrating our first-week anniversary tomorrow!"

"You wouldn't happen to know if Lavender was driving or flying, would you?"

"Well, she took the keys to Doug's Aston Martin, which didn't make him very happy, let me tell you."

"Great. Forget the message."

"I do hope we meet some time . . . what was your name again?"

"Carson. The same as yours."

Annie hung up the phone.

She reluctantly put her glass of scotch away and headed to the barn. With a six-day head start, Lavender could show up at any time. Of course, she probably would have forgotten how to find her, but anyone in a forty-mile radius could point her to Annie's farm. *This is not good.*

Thoroughly grumpy, Annie immersed herself in the business of feeding the horses and making sure their water buckets were full. Geronimo and Trotter were now best buds, grooming each other in the paddock. She decided to keep them in there for the night. No reason to make the colt feel more penned in than he already felt. Annie sensed that Trooper was a bit disquieted by his long-eared buddy's change of allegiance, so she moved him to the stall closest to the paddock, where he at least could keep an eye and an ear on his now-old friend.

Engrossed in her own thoughts of how to work the colt the next day, Annie didn't hear the stable door quietly open. The quiet "hello" that resonated a foot away caused Annie to shriek and drop the stable broom to the floor with a clatter.

"I'm so sorry. I didn't mean to startle you."

The man who'd uttered the words looked down at Annie, his keen blue eyes unhesitatingly bearing into hers. He was at least six inches taller than she and carried himself well.

The Armani suit didn't hurt, either, but Annie suspected that even if he'd been wearing overalls, Marcus would still look good.

And what was no less startling, Wolf was right by Marcus's heels, tail furiously wagging. It was obviously her Blue Heeler was dying to make friends with this stranger and, if he was lucky, convince him to throw him a stick.

Annie quickly glanced at her watch—6:00 P.M. Try as she might to feel concern over being in the same room as a cold-blooded wife killer, she couldn't. Marcus breathed civility and good breeding. Besides, Wolf had already given him the canine thumbs-up.

Marcus held out his hand, which was quite large, with carefully manicured fingernails.

"I know I'm early, but hoped to find you at home. At the last minute, the airlines bumped me up to first class on a nonstop flight. I guess it's one of the perks of owning one of the few Silicon Valley companies whose stock hasn't tanked."

He gave her a lopsided grin and did his best to look grateful. "I really wanted to thank you personally for caring for Hilda's horse, under the . . . circumstances."

Annie grinned back and stuck out her own hand, after wiping it on her jeans. "Pleased to meet you, Marcus. You're just in time to see your latest equine baby before he goes to sleep."

Walking over to Trooper's stall, Annie wondered how she could be so calm in the face of what surely was impending danger. She'd heard Marcus utter horrible words in his voice mails to Hilda, and as much as Annie disliked Hilda, she wouldn't want anyone to be the recipient of such hateful language. Now Marcus had shown up hours ahead of schedule, and ahead of Dan, too. Yet she wasn't looking for a way to get her shotgun. She was more interested in showing the man a horse. She glanced behind her. Marcus was calmly walking toward her, while Wolf did his best to lick his now-free hand.

The bay had been contentedly eating hay, but turned around to face them.

"Isn't he gorgeous?" Annie asked, looking at Marcus. She noticed that Hilda's husband had slightly graying temples on a full head of black hair and dark blue eyes that slanted downward, making his gaze look empathetic and a bit sad at the same time. *If I'd been Hilda,* she thought, *I wouldn't have let this guy spend most of his time in California. At least, not alone.*

Marcus tentatively put out one hand and lightly stroked Trooper's mane.

"He is beautiful, indeed."

He removed his hand and then looked critically around the stable, now filled with horses quietly eating the last of their dinners.

"What a lovely place you have."

Annie gave a half chuckle. "Compared to yours? How can you say that?" *My goodness,* Annie thought, *I might as well be in eighth grade again.*

Marcus turned and looked again at Annie. It was disconcerting just how far those eyes could look into another person's face, she thought.

"Yes, Hilda has a beautiful structure, too. But here, you see the ways in which you've crafted this place into your very own. It shows who you are. Hilda's was top-of-the-line, but it always seemed somewhat sterile to me, despite the millions of dollars that went into its construction."

Annie stared at him, dumbfounded. Who was this man? And why had he been with Hilda?

As if anticipating her question, Marcus gave a quirky half smile. "You're probably wondering how Hilda and I ended up together. Me, who doesn't know one end of a horse from

the other, for all practical purposes, and Hilda, who lives—
who lived and breathed horses as long as I've known her."

Annie cleared her throat. "Well, the question does come
to mind, yes."

"Hilda and I've known each other since we were children. I'm sorry. I have to remember to refer to her in the past
tense. It's not easy to do. Our families were very close; my
aunt was Hilda's godmother. After I graduated from Whar-
ton, we married because we liked each other a lot, and it was
the expected thing to do. But, as time went on, I rather feel
that I was supplanted by an ever-expanding herd of horseflesh."

Marcus spoke jokingly, but his words intimated a sense
of failure.

"And now this." Marcus spread his arms out to his sides.
"Hilda murdered. A terrible business. I can hardly believe it
even now, and I've had all night to wonder who would want
to do such a thing to my wife."

Annie watched his eyes fill with tears and restrained herself from flinging her arms around him in an attempt to comfort him. At least, that's what she told herself she'd be trying
to do. She felt distinctly guilty about the trap that had been
set for him.

"Do you have any ideas?" she asked.

The words sounded rude, even to Annie. Marcus quickly
turned to her and saw a deep blush spread up Annie's neck
and face.

"I'm sorry. That's none of my business."

"Don't be sorry. *I'm* the one who's sorry. After all, I've
been told you're the person who found Hilda's body. At
least I've been spared that agony. It must have been horrible
for you."

"It's just hard to believe someone . . . could be that violent." And suddenly Annie realized that she no longer asso-

ciated the brutality she'd seen in Hilda's bedroom with this man for reasons she couldn't begin to understand.

Marcus gently stroked Trooper's mane and looked down at Annie.

"It's impossible for me to think so, too. And to answer your question, no, I don't have a single idea as to who would so savagely kill my wife. But I intend to find out."

He leaned over to take in the bay's smell, thoroughly winning Annie's respect and, if she admitted it, her heart. She rested her check on the bay's withers to inhale the bay's good, strong unmistakable equine odor herself.

Annie heard the sound of tires crunching on gravel outside. Before she could think of an exit plan, Dan strode through the stable door. Both she and Marcus had involuntarily started as soon as the stable door slid open. Annie could see from Dan's expression that he assumed they'd been caught in a compromising position.

"Marcus Colbert. You are under arrest for the murder of your wife, Hilda Colbert. You have the right to remain silent. Anything you say can and will be used against you in the court of law."

As Dan recited the Miranda warning, he twisted Marcus's arms behind him and secured the handcuffs—rather tightly, Annie observed. Marcus looked astounded but said nothing.

"You have the right to speak to an attorney, and to have an attorney present during any questioning. If you cannot afford a lawyer, one will be provided for you at government expense."

As Annie watched, Dan frog-marched Marcus out of the stables and into the police vehicle waiting outside. Tony stood beside the patrol car, a set of keys in his hand. She watched him get into a black Mercedes, presumably Marcus's rental car. She could not look at him.

As the cars roared off, Annie was full of thoughts she did not have time to express. On the top of the list was to cry out to Dan, "Wait! You've got the wrong guy!" The second was, "The least you could have done is hold off until he'd written me a check!"

CHAPTER 8

FRIDAY, FEBRUARY 26TH

Annie attempted for the third time to ease her pickup truck into the last parking space for the Suwana County Courthouse, high on the hills of Port Chester, the county seat. Her hands were shaking. On the way into town, Dan had called her with the results of Hilda's autopsy.

"This is strictly off the record," he warned her. "You never heard this from me, remember."

For once, Annie didn't have a flip comeback. She was too curious to know what Dan had to say.

Hilda had died, Dan informed her, from a long, jagged gash to her neck that had severed her jugular vein and her right carotid artery. The good news was that the massive hemorrhaging instantly rendered her unconscious. The bad news was that there was a chance, just a small one, that if help had been immediately summoned, she might have survived. In Hilda's case, living in an isolated mansion had worked against her.

"What about the knife?" Annie had asked Dan.

"We don't know that it's a knife, Annie. No weapon was found at the scene." Dan had been uncharacteristically patient. "It could have been a ballpoint pen for all we know. What we do know is that whoever wielded the weapon used exceptional force. Which pretty much rules you out, strong as you are. Our killer was a one-man fighting machine—and he was mad as hell. Oh, and she'd been dead at least eighteen hours before you found her. Hank, the coroner, said it's real hard to tell once rigor starts to wear off. But he did say lividity was well set in."

Annie hadn't the slightest idea what lividity meant and certainly wasn't going to ask Dan for a definition. That's what Google was for. She silently counted backward, and realized, miserably, that Hilda probably had been murdered the day after their angry phone conversation. She then thought of Marcus's strong, well-manicured hands. It didn't seem possible that he used them for anything except signing merger agreements or opening up a good bottle of wine.

"Annie? You still there?"

"Yeah, Dan."

"We're still waiting for the blood tests and fingerprint analyses. I'll keep you informed. But remember, not a word to anyone, and that includes the stud we arrested yesterday. 'Course, we can't talk to him anyway since he's lawyered up." Dan sounded thoroughly disgusted.

After the call, Annie's thoughts flitted again to the registration papers that she'd pulled from Hilda's lifeless hands and, less easily, from the pup's hungry mouth. She'd thought of telling Dan about them, but the more time went on, the less appealing the idea became. While she didn't think Dan really would charge her with anything, she realized there were legal terms to describe what she'd done. "Obstruction of justice" and "evidence tampering" were the first that came to mind. Right now, the Scotch-taped papers were safely stored in a cardboard box under her bed, along with her birth certificate and Social Security card. She knew she'd have to deal with the issue sometime, but not giving the papers to Dan immediately made it more difficult to explain why they were still in her possession. She wasn't sure she even knew the answer to that. Besides, she couldn't think of any way the papers pointed to Marcus's guilt, and that was the whole reason she was here in town early on a Friday morning.

Annie took several deep breaths before getting out of her pickup to join the fray. She didn't often have cause to visit the courthouse or adjacent administrative building, but when she did, the walls echoed off her hollow footsteps as she walked down the silent halls.

Today, things were different. This was the day of reckoning for the unfortunate Suwana County residents (and visitors) who recently found themselves afoul of the law. At 9:00 A.M. sharp, Judge Casper would enter the courtroom and the process of sorting would begin. One by one, those charged with crimes would walk to the defense table, hear their crimes recited in open court, enter a plea, and, if they were lucky, be released on bail. Most of those approaching the bench would be clad in the county jail's pumpkin orange jumpsuits and flip-flops. Marcus would be one of those people.

As soon as she entered the courthouse, Annie was caught up in a swarm of lawyers and families, all jostling for space along the crowded hallways to talk before the court session began. Edging her way down the corridor to the county's sole courtroom for criminal cases, she noted that while all the lawyers looked pretty much alike, the families they represented were as diverse as the rows of tomato plants soon to be on sale at the local hardware store. The townies were instantly recognizable. They all were dressed in Northwest Classic, a mixture of Birkenstocks, L.L. Bean, and Lands' End, with a few retro hippie touches thrown in. County residents farther out sported a multitude of fashion statements, culled from the half-dozen secondhand stores in the area. There seemed to be an inordinate number of babies in the crowd. Having children could lead anyone to a life of crime, Annie thought, but this was downright appalling.

She squirmed her way through the courtroom doors, noting that there was hardly a seat left inside. Panicking, she looked around until she spotted six unused inches next to a massive woman who looked as if she could spread her girth along the entire bench if she exhaled. Annie walked over and politely gestured that she wished to sit down. The woman glared, but grudgingly moved her rump an infinitesimal space to the right. Annie smiled sweetly and plopped down. The woman quickly moved over even farther.

It suddenly dawned on Annie why the courtroom was filled to capacity on a day most people would rather be inside by the woodstove. *Of course.* It was Hilda's death and the arrest of her supposed murderer. Annie didn't watch TV. It wasn't that she had a political agenda that caused her to eschew the media; she simply didn't have time to watch. She had completely forgotten that the airwaves would be full of the news about Marcus's arrest and all the lurid details of Hilda's death.

Her heart sank. Slowly looking around, she saw the inevitable TV cameras and photographers staked out in one corner. Maybe Judge Casper would throw them out, though she doubted it. The judge was up for reelection in the fall, and he could use the publicity.

But Judge Casper pleasantly surprised Annie. He promptly dismissed the media with barely concealed distaste and started the docket agenda as if it were any other day in the life of his court. Marcus was the next-to-last inmate to be called. Annie's heart beat faster as he approached the bench with an attorney who clearly was from out of town. Marcus was still in the county-issued jumpsuit, but Annie noticed that the V in the top revealed a very athletic chest with a generous sprinkling of black chest hair. *Damn, the man was good-looking.* Annie looked down and squeezed her fists, then looked up as Marcus's attorney began to speak.

"Your Honor, I am the attorney of record for Mr. Colbert, and we intend to post bail in the amount of $100,000 immediately following this proceeding. Mr. Colbert is a very busy man who has businesses throughout Northern California. I would ask that the court allow Mr. Colbert to travel back to his primary residence and workplace so that he can continue his life as normally as possible while the investigation continues."

The judge had been scribbling on a notepad throughout this speech, but now looked up.

"Investigation continues? I was under the impression that Mr. Colbert had already been charged with first-degree murder."

A subdued wave of laughter wafted through the room until Judge Casper's gavel came crashing down.

Marcus's attorney cleared his throat.

"I am, of course, quite aware that Mr. Colbert has now been formally charged, but in the weeks ahead, we intend to prove that this charge was prematurely made and should be dismissed with prejudice in short order."

Annie glanced at the prosecutor, Judy Evans, who was impeccably attired in a business suit that looked every bit as expensive as the one Marcus had worn yesterday. Dan stood beside her, whispering furiously in her ear.

Without giving any indication of Dan's presence, Judy walked forward a few steps and stopped.

"Your Honor. We would not have brought this most serious charge of Homicide One if we did not firmly believe that we had brought the right man to justice. However, I look forward to seeing what Mr. . . ." She turned to Marcus's defense attorney.

"Fenton. James Addison Fenton III."

"What Mr. Fenton will provide us in the 'weeks ahead.' Our investigation is not yet closed, but I strongly believe that what the Sheriff's Office will uncover, based on tests and so forth already in the works, will only substantiate our claim that Mr. Colbert is responsible for his wife's death. Furthermore, we would object to Mr. Colbert's being released and able to return to California at this time. He is a man of considerable means and has the wherewithal to go anywhere in the world he so chooses. I consider him to be an extreme flight risk."

Judy Evans stepped back smartly and stood by the state's table.

Judge Casper glared at Marcus's attorney. "Mr. Fenton?"

"Your Honor, Mr. Colbert has absolutely no criminal record and is prepared, of course, to surrender his passport. The affidavit of probable cause is specious, at best. It links my client to the crime merely by the existence of a single phone message. We have not yet had time to analyze that message to see if, in fact, it is the voice of our client."

Mr. Fenton peered over his horn-rimmed glasses at the prosecutor.

"Neither, I suspect, has the state. In fact, Your Honor, the state informs me the discovery in this case amounts to a single three-page report written by"—Mr. Fenwick ruffled through his papers on the defense table—"by a Sheriff Dan Stetson. It is essentially a report of a death, Your Honor. A horrible death, we stipulate, but with not a single fact that points to my client as the responsible party.

"There were *more than six men* working on the property when Mr. Colbert's wife was killed. Yet not one of them has been interviewed. As far as I can see"—Mr. Fenton flipped through the flimsy sheriff's report—"only one worker *has* been interviewed to date, and he was off the property at the time of Mrs. Colbert's death. *As was my client.*"

The attorney turned and faced the judge.

"Your Honor, I know as an out-of-town attorney, I am persona non grata among many of the officials of the court. Yet, I feel compelled to tell you that in Santa Clara County, such a case would not even get to this stage. There is simply not one shred of evidence that ties Mr. Colbert to the crime. He is as heartbroken over his wife's death as anyone would be. It is inconceivable that he would become a fugitive. At the moment, he has the extremely distressing job of planning his wife's funeral and dealing with the grief attendant to that process."

Wheeling around, he glared at Judy Evans, who took an involuntary step backward and put one hand to her chest.

"Mr. Colbert is just as interested as the prosecution to find the perpetrator of this crime. I suggest she marshal her efforts in that direction rather than trying to pigeonhole my client into a premature posture of guilt."

There was a small intake of breath among the court audience, Annie included.

Judge Casper banged his gavel again.

"Ms. Evans!"

Judy Evans walked quickly up to the bench.

"Is Mr. Fenton correct? Is this report the sole basis of your decision to arrest this man?

Judy nervously fiddled with the chain of faux pearls around her neck.

"Well, Your Honor, as I said, we're in the middle of conducting a number of critical evidentiary tests, and you know how the crime lab is backed up just now. . . ."

"Well, in that case, I see no reason to make the defendant wait while the state finishes putting its case together. I'm going to release Mr. Colbert, with the stipulation that he post the appropriate bail, and allow him to return to California until such time that his presence is again required in court."

Mr. Fenton cleared his throat.

"Yes, Counselor?" Judge Casper clearly was not amused by the subtle interruption.

"While my client intends to return to California within a few days, he does need time to make arrangements for his wife's body. He also needs to talk to his late wife's staff and review her business records to make sure Mrs. Colbert's obligations are dealt with in a timely manner. This will require access to at least her business office, which I believe is located in the equestrian area and not the residence."

Mr. Fenton stepped back with a feigned air of modesty while Judge Casper decided how to respond.

Annie could see that the judge was fuming, but whether it was because of the incompetency of the Sheriff's Office or because of Mr. Fenton's requests, she couldn't tell. For a full minute, the judge did not take his eyes off Marcus's lawyer. Annie sat rapt, watching the stare-down. She was betting on the judge. In the end, it was a draw.

Still glaring at Mr. Fenton, Judge Casper demanded, "Ms. Evans? Is Mrs. Colbert's body ready to be released to the family?"

The prosecutor nodded curtly. "Yes, Your Honor."

"Then, Mr. Fenton, you can instruct your client that he may begin making arrangements for his wife's body as of today."

"Thank you, Your Honor." Mr. Fenton said it with feeling.

"However, Your Honor," Judy politely interjected, "the property is still a crime scene. Detectives are still gathering evidence. It's likely to remain so for several days, perhaps as long as a week."

Judge Casper looked pained.

"Ms. Evans, I don't want to dictate how the Sheriff's Office conducts its investigations, but it seems to me that under the circumstances, we could allow Mr. Colbert access to areas that have already been searched. Would that include his wife's office?"

Judy hurriedly put up one finger and trotted over to Dan. They whispered tersely to each other for more than a minute. Then Judy returned.

"Your Honor, we can grant Mr. Colbert access to the equestrian buildings, including Mrs. Colbert's office, as soon as this afternoon. However, we do request that sheriff's deputies be stationed in any room Mr. Colbert might enter. And we request that he take nothing from the premises with him."

"Your Honor." Annie thought Mr. Fenton sounded on the verge of a hissy fit.

The judge put up one of his large palms to silence him.

"Mr. Fenton, your client may access the areas Ms. Evans has outlined under the rules she has set forth."

Mr. Fenton gave a short yelp.

"*With* the exception of Ms. Evans's request not to take business files with him. Ms. Evans, your detectives have had sufficient time to search and seize anything they believe to be of evidentiary value. I am not going to prohibit Mr. Fenton from being able to take care of his wife's business simply because you want more time to probe. That time has come and gone, at least in reference to these buildings. Furthermore, Mr. Colbert will be allowed to talk to his wife's staff, in the presence of sheriff's deputies, about matters that concern the running of the ranch. Do I make myself clear?"

Both Judy and Mr. Fenton murmured assents. Annie thought that Marcus's attorney looked like a cat who'd just swallowed cream. Judy looked as if she wanted to scratch his eyes out.

Glaring at Marcus, Judge Casper continued. "You, sir, will keep in weekly contact with your attorney, who will report to the court on that basis your whereabouts and your

current address. Your passport will be confiscated until these
proceedings are over, *and,* should you be prosecuted, you
are found innocent. Next case."

As Annie struggled out of her pew, she felt her eyes filling with tears. Part of her felt sorry for Dan, who'd just been
humiliated in court over his paucity of evidence. But mostly,
she felt supremely happy that Marcus had been set free. For
now.

"Do NOT, I repeat, do NOT talk to that woman!"

Mr. Fenton, who had been so eloquent in court, was now
showing another side of his legal persona: that of a junkyard
dog. He stood in front of Marcus, who was again dressed in
his Armani suit, and glowered in Annie's direction.

Annie had squeezed by the Suwana County deputies
guarding the jail entrance from the swarm of reporters outside. She saw Tony in the crowd and gave him a nod. Tony
gave her a short nod back and looked straight ahead, his posture ramrod straight. He probably was just as ticked as Dan
Stetson about the Sheriff's Office being accused in open
court as having done a half-ass job on the case. Annie really
couldn't blame him for being loyal to his boss, but that was
no reason to eschew her overtures, she thought.

She'd hoped to be able to talk to Marcus before he left
with his attorney. But no sooner had the jailhouse door
clanged and Marcus emerged from the inmate exit than Mr.
Fenton leapt up, literally shielding his client from her approach.

"She tried to frame you, Marcus! Don't tell me she didn't!
The reason you spent a night in this despicable county jail is
because *she*"—and here, an accusing finger pointed directly
at her—"tipped off the local cops!"

Marcus gently pushed aside his attorney's arm.

"Jim, it doesn't matter if they found me at Annie's or at

the local roadside café. That sheriff was hot to arrest me. It was only a matter of time."

"I don't care! The fact is that this woman is NOT your friend. As your attorney, I instruct you not to speak to her."

"And as my attorney, and a very well-paid one, you will trust me to do what I think best," Marcus replied. "This woman saved the life of my wife's horse. She found Hilda's body. She's been through hell, and I won't have her blamed for the shenanigans of a couple of small-town cops. This will all blow over before you know it, Jim. In the meantime, I'd like Ms. Carson to take me to Hilda's ranch, if she would be so kind."

Mr. Fenton fumed, but he apparently knew his client well enough not to push when the cause was futile. He snapped his burgundy briefcase buckles shut and strode to the jail entrance, also surrounded by Suwana County deputies in uniform. As one of them politely opened the door for him, he turned, and yelled back, "Remember, Marcus, no talking about the case! If I see that woman's name in one more police report, I quit!"

The attorney rudely shouldered his way through the reporters amid high-pitched voices and raised microphones.

"What woman, sir? Who were you advising your client NOT to talk to?"

"Is it true that your client made a threatening phone call to his wife just before she died?"

"Was Marcus Colbert seeing another woman?"

The deputy, startled by the sudden onslaught of voices, hastily shut the door, but not before Annie faintly heard Mr. Fenton slam his car door, rev his engine, and roar off.

The deputy who'd just missed crushing the reporters' fingers turned to Annie.

"Ma'am? You're Annie Carson, aren't you? The woman who helps us on horse rescues?"

Annie turned toward the speaker. He was embarrassingly

young looking, eighteen or nineteen at most, although he must have been older, or he wouldn't be in uniform yet. He still had acne and an emerging Adam's apple. He looked appealingly innocent and eager to please.

Annie smiled and stuck out her hand. "Good memory, Deputy . . . Lindquist," she said, looking at his name tag. "What case did we work on together?"

"It was my first call, ma'am. Horses left to starve on Old Man Wilson's farm, up near Big Squill. They were awful thin. I remember you came in and rounded them up. I think they thought you were the best thing they'd seen since their last hay flake."

Annie remembered the case. It still made her sick to her stomach to think about the four emaciated horses, sunk to their pasterns in mud while their owner, Mack Wilson, drank his life away inside his dilapidated farmhouse. He hadn't even known the horses were leaving until Annie's trailer was backing out of the driveway and Dan was ordering Mack to put down his shotgun. Mack never saw his pitiful herd again.

"That was a tough one," she agreed. "You know, we had to put two down. They just weren't going to make it. But I found good homes for the other two, one of them, actually, on my place. You may remember him. It was the quarter horse."

"That's good, ma'am. You want some help getting out of here?"

"I sure do."

Deputy Lindquist told them that the only way to leave without having to deal with the media outside was the back route. The back route turned out to be a closeted stairwell that led to the underground sally. It was the entrance for inmates who had to be shackled from wrist to feet and were considered high-risk. It hadn't been used for years.

"What kind of truck do you drive, ma'am?"

"An F250. Blue."

"Hand me your keys, ma'am, and I'll bring it to you, then the two of you can just leave from here."

Annie thankfully obliged him.

A few minutes later, riding shotgun in Annie's pickup truck on Highway 101, Marcus fumbled in his coat pocket and drew out a pack of Nat Sherman cigarettes. He absent-mindedly tapped the end of the slender brown cigarette against the pack.

"Jim really shouldn't do that."

Annie started. "Do what?"

"Slam the door like that. His mechanic is on permanent retainer just to realign parts on his car. Jim has a bit of a temper, in case you didn't notice."

"I thought he was pretty darn wonderful in court."

Marcus laughed. "That's why I pay him the big bucks, although criminal law is hardly his bailiwick. I'm sure he'll refer me to a more specialized attorney once he gets back to his office."

Annie gave a sidelong quizzical glance at her companion. "You mean, he won't be able to defend you?"

"Wouldn't make sense. Jim's the go-to guy for corporate mergers and IPOs, and believe me, I know just how good he is. But his criminal law knowledge probably extends to knowing where to pay a traffic ticket."

"That's too bad. He speaks so eloquently. I could just imagine him in front of a jury, winning their hearts and minds."

"He does have a certain expressiveness about him, doesn't he? Back in Silicon Valley, he's known as the Smooth Operator. His competitors call him 'Smoothie' behind his back."

"Well, everything he told the judge was absolutely right. And, Marcus, he's also right about me." Annie looked down, then back at the road ahead of her. "It's true. I did tell Dan

Stetson that you'd be coming over. You see, I heard the voice message."

"I haven't, but I hear it's pretty gruesome. I don't blame you for jumping to conclusions. In fact, what surprises me now is that you've jumped in the other direction. Why do you believe I didn't kill Hilda?"

Annie thought for a moment, then smiled and glanced over at Hilda's widower.

"Quite frankly, it was part Wolf—that's my Blue Heeler— and the bay. Both of them trusted you instantly. If he'd thought you were dangerous, Wolf wouldn't have let you near me, and frankly, I don't want to think of how the bay would have reacted. In fact, Hilda's horse liked you a lot more than he probably would have liked your wife. And a horse never lies."

Marcus threw back his head and roared. "Poor Hilda! She really was a lovable person, you know. You just had to know her."

"I guess."

"Do you mind if I smoke?"

"If you do, I'll hit the eject button while we're going around the corner at sixty miles per hour."

"I take it that's a yes."

Todos might not have shown much respect for Marcus in front of Dan Stetson, but he was positively unctuous in front of the man himself. He swept off his cowboy hat as soon as Marcus emerged from Annie's truck and ducked his head deferentially when Marcus extended his hand. When Annie joined Marcus, Todos murmured, "*Buenos dias,* Señora Carson," in such a sincere tone that Annie looked hard at him, wondering if this was the same taciturn wrangler who'd summarily ignored her a few days before.

After a brief conversation about the horses, Todos showed

them into Hilda's stable office. A Suwana County deputy dutifully tagged behind them, but Marcus strode to Hilda's desk, completely ignoring the man, and Annie decided to do the same. Looking at the desk strewn with bills and unopened mail, Marcus gave a barely audible groan. At this, Todos politely took his leave to "take care of Señora Colbert's beautiful *caballos*." One of them, he said, had thrown a shoe and he must assist the farrier. Annie thought it more likely he didn't want to miss the opportunity to boss someone around but said nothing to Marcus.

Marcus strolled around the spacious office, idly picking up piles of envelopes, then placing them back down without reading them. He lit a Sherman, and, since Hilda wasn't around to object, Annie said nothing. In fact, she had been surprisingly silent for the rest of the journey out to the ranch and while Marcus and Todos had talked about the future care of the horses.

She wondered if she was right in her assessment of Marcus. Could he be Hilda's killer? God knew being around the woman could make anyone homicidal, given enough time with her. And it was true, Trooper had expressed no fear or hostility toward Marcus, even when Marcus had interrupted the bay's precious dinnertime, and Annie placed a great deal of faith in how horses, dogs, and most other animals, for that matter, intuitively responded to humans. But the digital recording was troubling, to say the least, even though Marcus seemed to make light of it. Nor had he said a single word as to why he thought someone would imitate his voice to try to cast him in the role of suspect. If it was not Marcus, who the hell was the person who'd voiced the threat to Hilda?

"A penny for your thoughts."

Annie looked up, realizing that she'd been staring at her cowboy boots for the past several minutes and now realized that they needed a shine.

Marcus absentmindedly straightened up a sheaf of papers. "I know, it's pretty depressing. Let's get out of here. All this paperwork is making me claustrophobic."

He walked to the door and opened it for Annie.

"I'll deal with all this later. There's too much on my brain right now to concentrate on anything, anyway. How about a walk? You know, I've never seen the whole place. When I've flown up, it's usually been for a long weekend, and there were times when I never even left the ranch house."

Was Hilda so good in bed that Marcus never wanted to leave? Annie felt a stab of jealousy and immediately felt guilty. She was alive. Hilda was not.

The two walked through the long stable hallway, Annie silently admiring the cedar siding on the inside stall walls while Marcus merely seemed intent to move forward. There were twenty stalls in the barn, all set in a circular fashion. In the middle was a competition-sized dressage arena. Large black numbers had been tacked up at various lengths against the inside wall. A sprinkler in the middle silently settled the dust.

Marcus made an abrupt right and headed toward the back of the building, near the road to the house. Annie had to trot to keep up with him, wondering what made him change his direction so quickly. Then she realized that the walls were strewn with photos of Hilda at jumping events. She glanced at the various medals festooned along the wall. Maybe Hilda had been a better rider than she thought. It was just a damn shame that she had to fight her horses every step of the way to compel obedience.

"I just remembered a gate I used to see out of our bedroom window, and always wondered where it went," Marcus told her. "Let's see if we can explore what's beyond it, shall we, without arousing the suspicions of the police."

Annie smiled and nodded her assent. Passing the hay room, she was overwhelmed with the smell of rich Timothy hay and fragrant alfalfa. The hay barn was fairly redolent with the aroma, and the bales stood neatly packed, from floor to ceiling, ready to be fed to a bevy of large performance horses. There was nothing like that smell, Annie thought to herself. That and the smell of horses. It was better than any perfume on the market.

They walked up the gravel road toward Hilda's house. Bright yellow crime-scene tape still draped the perimeter and across the door. A deputy, whom Annie didn't recognize, stood by the front door and nodded curtly at them as they walked by. Out of the corner of her eye, Annie saw him talk discreetly into his shoulder mike. She knew he was informing Dan of where they were going. A sense of annoyance swept through her. She didn't know whose intrusion she resented more—that of the police or the media. Didn't people have better things to do?

"Oh, the puppies!"

Annie started running toward the pen.

"Wait up, Annie! Wait up!"

Annie reached the pen, now empty, seconds before Marcus, who arrived, panting and catching his breath.

"What puppies?"

"Two little Belgians, that's what! They were here when I came by two days ago. Now where are they?"

Marcus squatted on his knees beside her. He spoke gently. "I don't know. I didn't know anything about any Belgians or any other dog on the premises. It's hard enough to wrap my head around being the executor for all these horses. But I'll find out, I promise you."

Annie sniffed. Her throat felt scratchy. She was close to tears, and she didn't want Marcus to know it. She stood up.

"Okay." Her voice was husky. She swallowed. "How about that walk?"

At the back of the Hilda's property, beyond the swimming pool and carefully manicured lawn, stood a lone stile gate, hanging forlornly by one hinge. Beyond lay an overgrown path that clearly had once been a back entrance to the property. Marcus gingerly prodded the top stile, and the gate silently swung open.

They walked through a volunteer forest of aspens, now shorn of leaves and giving light to the dull gray sky above. It was still winter, and Annie wished she'd worn her down parka rather than her corduroy blazer. As they crunched along the dead leaves, Marcus stuck his hands in his pocket and slowed his pace. It was a comfortable silence.

Then Marcus cleared his throat.

"Annie. I am touched by your instant loyalty to my cause, but I want you to know that I never would have harmed Hilda, as hard as she was to deal with at times.

"The truth is, we hadn't been getting along before her death. In fact, we had a big blowup just two weeks earlier. I'd given her an ultimatum: start coming home more often or the marriage was over. She demanded the same from me. The problem was, we were both talking about different homes."

Marcus stopped, reached in his pocket for another Sherman. His first exhale sounded like a sigh of defeat.

"That might work for a lot of my employees, but it's impossible in my position. I simply have to be a hands-on kind of guy. I tried to explain that to Hilda, but she just couldn't see it. Of course, she'd retired from the company years before, when it was still in its infancy. She made a killing on the initial IPO and didn't understand why I wouldn't cash in my share as well. But my life's work is with my company, not with a herd of four-footed friends. I was happy to continue working. That was *my* life."

It'll never work, Annie thought to herself. *I'd demand the same thing.*

"We last talked on Valentine's Day. The conversation did not go well, I can tell you that. Hilda hung up on me, and

I didn't try to call her back. To tell you the truth, if Hilda were still alive, I'm not sure where we'd be right now. But whatever happened in our relationship, I always assumed that she would still be among the living."

They'd reached the end of the path, which came out behind the sectioned horse pasture onto the local road leading to the highway. They stood together, looking at the elegantly blanketed horses, each quietly grazing in its allotted space.

"But I will tell you that I never, and I mean *never,* told Hilda that I'd kill her. I don't know what was in that message, or whose voice is on that recording, but they are not my thoughts, and it isn't my voice."

"I'm sorry, Marcus," Annie said. "I still believe you. But frankly, I can't see how this is going to help your case. The prosecutor is going to find out about your marital difficulties sooner or later."

"I know. But I wasn't here, and surely the tests that are being run will prove that."

"They'll say you hired a hit man."

"They can ransack my home and office as much as they want. They won't find anything."

"They're probably already at your front door."

"Well, then, let me write you a check before they freeze my accounts."

Driving home in the late-afternoon gloom, Annie felt her thoughts match the weather. There was a nip in the air. The forecast was for a few inches of snow. The horses would be hungry. And poor Wolf—he'd be wondering where his mistress had gone. She'd assured him she'd be back by noon. She popped a Patsy Cline recording into her CD player. It fit her mood.

Inside her jacket, her cell phone emitted its shrill, old-fashioned jangle. Annie fumbled to retrieve her earpiece while the phone continued to buzz away. She had never learned how to turn the thing on fast enough to intercept a call. In her rush, a piece of paper floated out of Annie's pocket. She managed to grab it before it fell and was lost in the detritus littering her truck's floor. Marcus had made sure that Annie had his cell phone number before she'd dropped him off at a Victorian B&B in Port Chester. She was heartened to know that he wasn't immediately leaving the area until he, as he'd put it, "sorted out Hilda's mess of a desk" and made arrangements for her body.

Finally, affixing the earpiece, she glanced down at her phone and instantly recognized the missed call on the screen as Dan's county number. She pulled over to the side of the road, adjusted the earpiece, and punched REDIAL.

"Stetson." Dan's voice was abrupt, and not very friendly.

"Dan, it's Annie. You called?"

"I saw you in court."

Annie said nothing.

"Well, I just want you to know that your precious Mr. Colbert is having an affair with one of his employees."

She could not, would not speak.

"Yeah, he's been after the head of corporate relations for quite a while now. Common knowledge at the firm. I'm flying down to San Jose tonight to get her statement."

"Well, bully for you, Dan. Is that all you have to tell me?"

"I also want to say that despite the performance that hot-shot city attorney gave today, we've got our man. Doesn't surprise me. The institution of marriage has gone to crap these days, anyway. Worth less than the piece of paper a license is printed on."

Now this was new. Annie had seen Dan in many guises, but bitterness was never part of his repertoire.

"Dan? Are you all right?"

"Oh, and Adolpho's alibi checked out. He picked up the hay and spent the night at the local HoJo. Left an empty six-pack in the room."

Annie was silent.

"I know you, Annie. You think Marcus is just too damn good-looking to have killed his wife. But let me tell you something. He's a killer, an adulterer, and I'm going to nail his ass if it's the last thing I do."

Annie drove the rest of the way home in silence.

CHAPTER 9

SATURDAY, FEBRUARY 27TH

The next morning, Annie awoke to four inches of freshly fallen snow. It was lovely, coating the entire farm with a white blanket that hid the imperfections so noticeable by day—her rusted tractor, the mud in the paddock, and the heap of junk that Annie had yet to haul out to the local recycling center. Today, all was pristine and good. And Marcus was out of jail.

For a moment, Annie's spirits were buoyed. Then she recalled her conversation with Dan last night.

"He's grasping at straws," she muttered to herself and hauled herself out of bed, made more difficult by a pile of down quilts, upon which placidly reposed one plump black-and-white kitten. Wolf sprawled on the rug below her feet.

"Come on. Let's get going," Annie said to her brood. "It's six-fifteen for heaven's sake. Time to move."

Max opened one eye and ignored her. Wolf leapt to his feet, trotted to the bedroom window, placed two large paws on the lower windowpane, and barked exuberantly.

"Yes, it's snow, get excited," Annie said good-naturedly.

Yet she, too, succumbed to the snow's infectious spell, whooping and throwing snowballs after Wolf as he loped down to the barn. She heaved open one of the stable door panels and was engulfed by the smell of horses. The nickering and low-throated murmurs around her acted as an instant balm. She fleetingly wondered if she just stayed here with her horses long enough, perhaps Lavender would never show up and Marcus's criminal charge would go away. It was a pleasurable if not very realistic thought.

After serving seven hot mash breakfasts, she watched her herd gallop into the pasture, a cloud of snowflakes in their wake. Trooper was again spending the day in the paddock with Trotter, but seemed content. If she was going to take care of the bay indefinitely, she knew she would have to assimilate him with the other horses, but for now, everyone was safe and getting along, which was the point.

"Wow. You sure have beautiful horses."

Annie whirled around and saw a man in an L.L. Bean jacket sitting on the rear bumper of a van, which, judging by the giant logo on each side, belonged to a local television station.

She stared at him without trying to hide her disgust.

"How'd you find me?"

"I saw you leaving the courthouse through the back way and got your license."

"*You ran my license?* I thought only cops could do that."

"Nope. You just have to know the right people."

"What do you want?"

The reporter got up from the bumper, dusted his rear, and stretched.

"Do you get up this early every day?"

"Today I slept in. What do you want?"

"Well, first let me introduce myself. I'm Rick Courtier, from KXTV in Seattle. We got the news of the Colbert murder off the police radio."

"You listen to police radios?"

Rick smiled. "Watch TV much?"

"Not at all. Does it show?"

"Afraid so. Anyway, we heard about the homicide, which is rare in your part of the world. We wanted to give our viewers the chance to hear about the discovery of the body from the person who found Mrs. Colbert herself."

"Well, your viewers will just have to be disappointed. I told what I saw to the police, and that's where it stops."

Rick did not seem at all affected by Annie's rejection.

"I understand that you also orchestrated the arrest of the man accused of murdering Mrs. Colbert."

"I was present when he was arrested. That's all I have to say."

"You know, it's cold out here. Why don't we go someplace where it's warm and we can talk better? I'd be happy to buy you a cup of coffee."

These guys are slick, Annie thought to herself, as Tony Elizalde's patrol car wheeled into her driveway. Rick wheeled around, then back to her.

"Now, Ms. Carson, was that really necessary? I'm just trying to get a story. I hope you understand that."

In fact, Annie had no idea why Tony was in her driveway, but she saw no reason to tell that to this predatory animal.

"I don't. I only understand that you're trespassing on my property and keeping me from my job." Annie spoke loudly, for Tony's benefit. Tony was now out of his car and coming toward them, his hand on his service weapon.

"What's the matter, Annie? Is this guy giving you trouble?"

"Only if he doesn't go away and never comes back."

Tony turned to Rick. "ID, please."

Rick sighed and reached for his wallet in the back of his pants.

"Stop, please, sir. I'll do that for you. Keep your arms at your sides."

Tony was really laying it on thick, Annie thought with bemusement, but she didn't mind. The guy deserved it.

Tony gingerly extracted the wallet and flipped it open. He pulled out a driver's license and a business card.

"Rick Courtier?" Tony pronounced it without the French accent.

"Courtie-ay, but close enough," Rick answered.

"Is there any reason for you to be on this property?"

"I just came to talk to Ms. Carson about what she knows about Hilda Colbert's murder."

"Well, Ms. Carson doesn't want to talk to you about Hilda Colbert's murder, do you, Annie?"

Annie shook her head.

"So I guess it's time for you to pack up and be on your way, isn't it?"

Rick sighed again, took the license and card proffered to him, and handed the card to Annie.

"If you change your mind."

Annie took the card but said, "I won't."

Annie and Tony watched silently as Rick got into his van, made a slow circle around the driveway, and eased up onto the highway.

"Vultures." Tony spit out the word, then on the ground.

This was new behavior. In fact, Annie was beginning to wonder whether she knew Tony or Dan well at all. Both were behaving in ways she had never experienced. It was as if Hilda's death had caused an imperceptible shift in the attitude of the local police force. It was making them cynical and mean. Yet these same men were her buddies. She counted them as not only working associates but as genuine friends. Now, the murder of an outsider—for that's what Hilda was, despite owning a large tract in the county—was causing all sorts of internal havoc, and Annie didn't like it. At all.

"Have you heard from Dan?"

Tony shook his head. "I've got my hands full today, and so does he. I've got to run down the evidence we pulled from Hilda's bedroom and home to the crime lab in Olympia, *and* I'm supposed to have a digital voice expert lined up by end of day. Which reminds me why I came by. Stop by the station the next time you're town so we can get a copy of your prints. We should have taken them the other day."

Annie looked askance. "Whatever for, Tony? I thought you'd ruled me out as a suspect. Or should I bring Wolf along so you can get a set of his paw prints, too?"

"Simmer down. It's because you're *not* a suspect that we need them. We have to be able to make comparisons as the crime lab processes the prints we took at the scene. I don't suppose you have a concealed weapons permit on file? That would save you a trip."

"I never conceal my shotgun. It's out in front of me at all times so everyone can see it."

"That's what I figured. Well, sorry for the inconvenience, Annie, but we need you to help us do our job."

This somewhat mollified her. "Have you heard from Dan?"

Tony groaned. "Dan's in San Jose, but he's not just interviewing the floozy Marcus was seeing. He's working with the San Jose cop shop, finding out as much as he can about the guy. And you have no idea what a hellish business that is. He was up half the night filling out sworn affidavits for search warrants on Marcus's home and business. Judge Casper was not amused to be awakened at 0500 hours to issue them over the phone."

Tony shook his head as if he wanted to clear the memory from his brain.

"And that's only the half of it. Now Dan's got to get *all* the warrants reissued by a judge in Santa Clara County before the local boys can even serve them." He sounded both indignant and incredulous over the lengthy process it apparently was going to take to delve into Marcus Colbert's personal and professional lives.

Annie wished she could feel sorry for Dan and Tony. But the truth was, she felt it only appropriate that after making Marcus's life a living hell over the past few days that Suwana County's own local boys had been forced to grow up and learn to play by the rules. She realized that Tony was still talking.

"And believe me, Dan won't come back until he's personally examined every scrap of paper and piece of evidence that comes in on the inventory lists. With any luck, the local deputies are executing the warrants as we speak."

Tony studiously watched the vestiges of the overnight snow flurry settle on the trees and ground as he delivered this last bit of news. Annie knew Tony as an exceptionally calm person—it was one of the reasons she trusted him around any horse—but she could tell that he was close to seething.

"Well, thanks for coming to my rescue." Annie didn't know what else to say. She hoped like hell nothing incriminating came from the searches.

"No problem. I'd better get going. But, Annie, remember, a good-looking horse doesn't always make the best ride. It might buck you off just as quickly as a rodeo nag."

Annie looked quickly at her friend. "Whatever do you mean?" Her tone was neutral.

"I mean that Marcus may dress better than any of us, but we're building a strong case against him, and the fact is, he'll be wearing prison garb for the rest of his life *if* he's lucky. Don't spend your time on someone who's ultimately going to let you down."

Annie felt a pang of fear, but said nothing. In the dark recesses of her brain, she reflected that it probably would behoove her to cash Marcus's check.

It also seemed like a good time to work with Geronimo.

The young colt had never seen the snow before, and it almost sent him over the edge with excitement. She led Geronimo into her sixty-foot-round pen, where he proceeded to lick, bite, and nuzzle the snowflakes still coming down while prancing around in the fluffy substance. He even made a horse angel.

Geronimo had come a long way in the last few days. He continued to follow Annie around like a dog, stopping when she did, and even backing up when she retraced her steps. And he had not reared again although Annie wasn't sure his boyish enthusiasm wouldn't get the best of him at some point. Now it was time to teach him to follow her direction. At the end of an hour, all Annie had to do was look hard at his rear quarters, and he scooted his butt around squarely to face her. She knew that the colt was trying hard to please and let him relax in a paddock adjacent to the one with Trotter and Trooper after he'd perfectly performed one last pirouette.

Annie had been aware that her landline had been ringing incessantly throughout the lesson. She could hear the shrill ring out in the crystalline air. Over a quick late breakfast, she punched the message button and was amazed to hear thirteen messages awaited her.

Most were from the media. Annie snorted as each articulate voice tried his or her best to make Annie grant an interview. She savagely punched ERASE after each one, and was just about to eliminate the rest on general principles when a familiar, well-modulated voice filled her kitchen. Annie sat back to listen.

"Annie, this is Marcus. I'm heading back down to California tomorrow but hoped to have a chance to talk to you before I go. Would you give me a call when you have a chance?"

Annie cleaned the stalls and fed the horses before giving in to the urge to return Marcus's call. Hard as it was to admit, she was still smarting from Dan's accusations of his infidelity the night before. True, no one would ever think that Annie and Marcus were in any way romantically involved, but then there was that telltale heart of hers, which beat like a rabbit's every time she happened to be around the man.

Mucking seven stalls was exhausting. It also infused an odor upon Annie that she did not wish to carry with her the remainder of the day. She took a quick shower, then trudged up the hill of her driveway to collect her mail.

Back in her farmhouse, she quickly sifted through the pile, looking for the florid violet handwriting and unmistakable odor of Lavender's scent. Nothing. Feeling slightly more hopeful, Annie finally picked up the phone and punched in Marcus's cell phone number.

"Colbert." The voice was as abrupt and authoritative as it had been the first time Annie had heard it in Hilda's tack room. She was momentarily jarred.

"Marcus, it's Annie," she finally said, quietly.

"Annie! How nice to hear your voice!" Marcus's tone instantly changed, now rich and warm. *Like night and day,* Annie thought, and wondered, for the hundredth time, if her instincts about Marcus's innocence were right.

"You asked me to call?" With an effort, Annie deliberately kept her tone of voice impersonal.

Marcus didn't seem to notice.

"Yes, I wanted to bring you up to date on those pups you'd said you'd found at the ranch. I tracked them down for you!" He sounded like a kid who'd finally won the big teddy bear for his girlfriend at the state fair.

Annie sat up, all pretense of being aloof forgotten.

"You did! Oh, Marcus, that's wonderful! Where are they? How did you do it?"

Marcus laughed, obviously pleased at his grateful audience.

"Elementary, my dear Watson. I asked Todos this morning. The fool had decided that the Belgians should be taken to the animal shelter. And that's being generous. I got the distinct impression from the other workers that if Todos had had his way, he would have given them a swimming lesson in the pool without their water wings."

Annie's yelp on the line apparently urged Marcus to finish the story.

"But they're fine, Annie. I called the shelter and the puppies are warm, fed, and happy. And I've just made a rather large donation in Hilda's name to the shelter to ensure their safety until we decide what to do with them. Have you . . . er, given that any thought?"

Living on a farm with animals great and small, Annie was accustomed to making split-second decisions. Events too often occurred that required choosing a course of action in a nonexistent time frame. In response to Marcus's question, Annie didn't even have to think.

"I'll take them. There's plenty of room in my house and

barn, and both are warm. I'll find good homes for them. Or maybe I'll keep one and give Wolf a companion. I'll deal with that later. But I am so grateful to you for rescuing them."

"My pleasure."

An awkward silence ensued.

"So . . . you're returning to California tomorrow?" She knew she sounded wistful.

There was a pause on the other end of the line before Marcus answered.

"Annie, is something wrong? I know I laid a lot on you yesterday, and realize you may still be reeling from too much information."

"It's not that. It's just . . . well, you're right. I'm getting too much information from a lot of people. It makes it hard to sort things out." *Lame, lame, lame,* Annie thought miserably to herself.

"Then that settles it," Marcus said briskly. "I can't leave with you still thinking I'm the bogeyman. I'd like to get together tonight, but I've still got six inches of paperwork that I've taken from Hilda's desk and need to sort through, and I have a feeling I'll be ordering in pizza by the time I'm done. Can we have dinner tomorrow evening? My flight doesn't leave until 11:00 P.M. You can ask me anything you want, and I promise to answer with the truth, the whole truth, and nothing but the truth."

"So help you God?"

"By the hairs of my wife's latest acquisition. What's his name, by the way?"

Annie gulped, thinking of the still-concealed paperwork that had revealed the bay's name. "I'm calling him Trooper."

"Trooper it is, then. How is the big guy, anyway?"

"Fat and sassy. Enjoying his time with the plebeians."

Again, Marcus's soft, low chuckle filled the phone line. Annie was feeling better. And she internally decided their meeting would be an excellent time to hand over the registration papers for the bay. After all, the horse now belonged to him. Marcus should have them to help settle up the estate.

Marcus was speaking again, interrupting her private thoughts. "I'll stop by around six, is that all right?"

"Could you make it six-thirty? That'll give me enough time to get the horses in for the night and shake off Eau De Equine."

"Sorry, couldn't hear that. Do you have another call coming in?"

Annie also heard the rude beep that told her someone else wanted her attention.

"It's probably just the media again, whom I'm assiduously trying to avoid."

"I know what you mean. Let's talk tomorrow."

Marcus clicked off and Annie pushed the CALL WAIT button on her phone.

"Annie?"

She didn't recognize the voice. It sounded as if someone was being strangled by Godzilla. She looked at her phone, thought of hanging up, but decided to be gracious for the first time that day.

"This is Annie. Who's speaking, please?"

"It's Dan. I'm calling from San Jose."

She hardly recognized his voice. It was thick and low, and his words were garbled.

"What's wrong, Dan?" *Oh, God, not more bad news about Marcus.*

"She's left me! Dory's left me!" The sentence was punctuated with a large hiccup and a wracking sob.

"What?"

"She told me in a text! Can you believe it? I knew something was going on. I could feel it. And . . . there's more, but I don't want to tell you over the phone. Annie, I don't know what to do!"

Those were words Annie had never expected to hear out

of Dan Stetson's mouth. He always knew what to do. It might not always be right, but lack of confidence was not one of Dan's weaknesses.

But this was her good friend, clearly in crisis, and far away from home.

"How can I help?"

"I don't know, Annie! It's just unbelievable. Twenty-five years we've been married. Twenty-five years! And now she's fallen for some hustler who puts Brylcreem in his hair."

Annie wanted to say that no one had used Brylcreem since their high school prom, but she could hear Dan's ragged breath over the phone. He suddenly started to sob. Loudly.

A numbness stole over Annie's body. There was nothing quite so shocking as hearing a man like Dan cry.

"Just talk to me, Dan. It'll be all right. When will you be home? Do you want me to talk to Dory?"

Talking to Dory was the last thing Annie wanted to do, and she regretted making the offer as soon as it came out of her mouth.

The doorbell rang. Hell's bells!

"Dan? Dan?"

Dan continued to bawl loudly into the phone.

"Dan, someone's at my door. It's probably a reporter, so I'll be back in a second. Hold on, okay?"

Dan muttered something unintelligible. Annie took this to mean he'd understood and she rushed to the door. Peeking through her kitchen window, she saw no media van or car in sight. Perhaps it was Hannah. *Was this her day to ride and I forgot?*

She opened the back door cautiously.

A slender reed of a woman stood on the doorstep. She was a good two inches taller than Annie and dressed in a peasant blouse, flowing, multicolored skirt, and, to Annie's horror—Birkenstock sandals. She didn't know which was more dazzling—the woman's beaming smile or the mass of bright pink hair above it. A bevy of bangles jangled as Annie's visitor flung out her arms toward her.

"Sister!"

CHAPTER 10

SATURDAY NIGHT, FEBRUARY 27TH— SUNDAY, FEBRUARY 28TH

Annie groaned. She had been standing in the center of her living room, still in shock from Lavender's appearance. Wolf, at her feet, emitted a small, inquisitive whine.

Lavender, however, seemed utterly pleased with her new situation. She'd plunked down her paisley satchel in Annie's guest bedroom without being asked and immediately set up her toiletries in the hall bathroom. A quavering soprano voice singing an old Dylan tune echoed off the bathroom tiles. The tinkling sound of glass hitting the floor interrupted the performance. "Oh, shoot," said the soprano, in a voice an octave lower.

"Kill me now," Annie muttered, and marched into the kitchen. It was definitely Glenlivet time.

Now sipping her scotch, she surveyed her half sister on the couch with a critical eye and asked, "How was your trip?"

"Oh, Sister! What a journey! I met *so* many interesting

people. Life changing, actually! You never really know where you're going to find your real family, do you?"

You certainly didn't have any trouble finding ME, Annie wanted to say. Instead, she remarked coolly, "Well, the family you left behind in Florida is wondering where their Aston Martin is. Did it arrive with you?"

Lavender made a face.

"That piece of junk. I traded it in Fort Worth for a bus ticket out here. It just stopped running one day."

Annie felt a very slight sympathetic pang for her father. She knew he loved that car more than his firstborn daughter.

"Did you try taking it to a shop?"

"Of course, Sister! But the engine was simply gone. I think they said something about the oil. Really, Father could have done a better job of making sure it was drivable. It wasn't my fault."

Of course not, thought Annie. *Nothing ever is.*

"So how'd you get here?"

"The nicest deputy, Sister! He was so handsome, too. When I got into town, I just went to the police station and asked for a ride. Tony said he was going your way, anyhow. Do you think he has a girlfriend?"

Tony Elizalde. Already Lavender had put him on a first-name basis, but then, she probably did that with everyone. Still, Tony shouldn't have aided and abetted Lavender's scheme. At the very least, he should have called to warn her the ditz was on the way.

"He has several girlfriends. All of whom know how to wield machetes."

Lavender's stricken face made it clear that she did not fully appreciate or comprehend Annie's sense of humor.

"Never mind. So, what are your plans now?" Annie sounded cross even to herself, but the pink apparition before her didn't seem to notice.

"Why, to help you, of course! Whatever I can do. You just say." Lavender sat back and looked quite pleased with herself.

"Great. We'll be up at six, then. You can help me feed the horses and muck the stalls. Consider this an easy introduction to farm life. In another month, you can help with the lambing."

Lavender looked horrified.

"Oh, no, Sister! I meant, whatever I can do using my special skills! You know, talking to your animals, helping you with your spiritual crises, empowering you to do the work of the Spirit—"

"I don't have any spiritual crises, Lavender," Annie interrupted. The words came out a tad louder than Annie would have wished. "And I'm perfectly capable of communicating with my horses."

The sight of Lavender's crestfallen face made Annie stop short. She sighed. It was her tenth audible sigh since Lavender had arrived a half hour before.

"Look, Lavender. I don't want to stop you from pursuing your dream, whatever it is. But you just can't go around assuming that other people need your help. If you don't want to help with the horses, at least you can help around the house. It hasn't been cleaned in years. And I'm prepared to let you stay for one month. But that's it."

Annie raised her hand as Lavender leaned forward and tried to speak.

"If you really want to stay in our community, I'm certain you'll find something to do," Annie continued. "And I'm sure you'll find many friends who are much better suited to your lifestyle than I am. Consider me a springboard into your great journey of life."

She spoke the last words sarcastically, but it was lost on Lavender.

"You're absolutely right, Sister. I know this is where I'm meant to be . . . in your community, I mean, not your house. Not forever, anyway."

"Great. Well, I'm going to bed. If you're hungry, feel free to rummage around in the kitchen."

"Good night, Sister. And thank you so much for the opportunity to work in your home. I didn't want to say it before, but you're right, there's a lot of bad karma here. I can cleanse that for you."

"Yeah, well, fine. Don't forget the dust while you're at it."

The following morning, Wolf was delighted to see his mistress out of bed and in the barn in record time. He'd never understood why Annie persisted in lolling around the kitchen, savoring a second cup of coffee, when the whole outdoors awaited them, fresh and new in whatever guise nature had bestowed upon it the night before. But today, it seemed that Annie understood the fierce pull to be outside. Wolf romped his way to the barn, with Annie in tow.

Annie's rapid departure had nothing to do with her desire to postpone her next encounter with Lavender, although admittedly, talking to her half sister wasn't something she looked forward to. The soft, steady snore emanating behind the guest room door assured her that Lavender was still safely in the arms of Morpheus. Annie made a mental bet with herself that she wouldn't arise before noon.

She was much more concerned about Dan, whose call she'd abruptly truncated when Lavender appeared. The line was dead when she got back from the door, and she'd run out of emotional fortitude for others after her talk with Lavender. Yet his behavior had been so uncharacteristic that Annie was genuinely concerned for her friend.

After the horses were fed, she settled in with a fresh cup

of coffee in the tack room and called him on his cell. It rang
for so long that Annie was preparing her message when Dan
picked up.

"Hello, Annie."

He had never sounded this defeated.

"I'm sorry, Dan." Annie rushed out her apology. "My
worthless half sister showed up just as you called and demanded all my attention. By the time I got her settled, you'd
hung up, and it was too late to call back." That was a lie, but
only a white one.

"I figured you had better stuff going on than to listen to
me whine."

Self-pity never sat well with Annie.

"Oh, bite me, you big lug. Believe me, I would much
rather have stayed on the line with you than listen to my
idiot half sister blather on about the state of the universe. I
was trapped. But I'm free now, so tell me what's happened.
You have my full attention."

Dan demurred, but Annie was determined to get it out of
him, and he finally gave in. It seemed that Dory had recon-
nected with an old classmate, Wally Torgeson. Annie remembered Wally. He was a running back on the football
team, openly smoked despite the coach's warnings, and did
indeed wear Brylcreem in his hair. Everyone tacitly knew
him as leader of the jocks. After graduation, Wally had
joined the Navy, done a couple of tours in the Persian Gulf,
and then stayed in the San Diego area. He'd been married
and divorced three times, because, as he told Dory, he'd
been waiting all his life for her, his one true love.

Dory had found Wally on Facebook. What the hell. Dan
didn't even know how to turn on a computer; he had Esther
for that. The two old classmates had been corresponding for
months. When Dan was down in Olympia testifying last
week, Dory had driven to Sea-Tac to meet Wally's plane.
The rest was history. Wally was everything Dan wasn't. He

owned a successful marine repair shop in Coronado and was making a killing with his Internet presence. He had what Dory called Real Money. He could still fit into his Navy uniform and worked out every day. Dory was packing up her belongings as they spoke and probably would be in San Diego by the time Dan got home tomorrow.

"I don't know what to say, Dan. I'm so sorry. Maybe this will all blow over in the next week or so. It seems pretty sudden."

"To hear Dory talk, our marriage has been a volcano about to blow for the past ten years. She says she only stayed together for the sake of the kids, and now that they're out of the house, she is, too. Says it's time for her to lead the life she's always wanted. And that's without me in it."

"What about her business?" Dory's salon, Cut 'N Curl, was the favored place for most of Suwana County's female population.

"Says she's going to let Shellie run it for now and decide whether to sell it or lease it later. Meanwhile, she's left a week's worth of casseroles in the freezer and says after that I'm on my own. If I live that long. According to Dory, I'm a heart attack waiting to happen." His voice trembled.

Dory was right, but Annie wasn't going to say so. She was stunned at the resolute methodology with which Dory had planned her departure. *Never underestimate the determined drive of a woman in love,* she thought ruefully. Poor Dan.

"How's the case going?" she asked cautiously. She really didn't want to hear any more bad news, but there wasn't more she could say to Dan without turning him into a completely maudlin sop again.

Dan's voice grew stronger.

"I know you still think Marcus is as pure as the driven snow, Annie, but we have got motive with a capital *M* locked up with what we've found down here. We got a digitally recorded statement from the woman he's been seeing, and it's pretty clear that Marcus was going to toss Hilda aside at the next opportunity. But it gets even better. Hilda must have known what was up because over the past two weeks, she and the family estate attorney were burning up the lines. We're getting a court order today to get at her revocable trust and see just what's been revoked. If Marcus thought he was going to kill his wife and benefit from it, he's going to be sadly mistaken."

Annie's insides felt leaden. Every time she talked with Marcus, her emotions flipped sideways and convinced her he had to be innocent of murdering Hilda. Unfortunately, the information that followed always implied that she was a total and delusional fool.

"How about opportunity? Doesn't he have an alibi?"

"We're working on that, checking every airline and rental car company in the area. But so far, no one's come forward to establish one, and, of course, since he's lawyered up, he's not talking."

Dan's tone of voice made it clear that he disapproved of a person's Fifth Amendment right to remain silent. Normally, Annie would have argued the point, but decided today Dan was too fragile to banter with.

"Tony tells me that he came to your rescue yesterday morning."

Annie started. "Oh. Yes, he did. In fact, he was pretty wonderful," then remembered how he'd been a lot less wonderful by driving Lavender straight to her home. Well, no point in burdening Dan with his deputy's lack of judgment. Unless he'd called Dan, and it was all Dan's idea. Annie willed herself not to go there.

"I had no idea that the media could be so disgusting," she said. "They've been trying to score an interview with me for the past forty-eight hours."

"And it's only going to get worse. We're expecting a dozen crime show production crews to camp out at the court-house when the trial rolls around. *If* it rolls around. Best thing that Marcus could do right now is to 'fess up and take his punishment. Easier for him that way and sure would save the county a ton of money. As it is, the county commission-ers already are trying to figure out how to pay for the inves-tigation."

Annie had heard enough.

"So what time does your flight get in tomorrow? If it's early enough, I'll buy you a beer."

"Aw, hell, Annie, you don't have to do that. I'll be fine. Least I got a case to keep my mind off things. But listen, Annie, you watch yourself. What you encountered yesterday will be magnified tenfold if you keep hanging out with that guy. And don't tell that sister of yours what I've just told you. What we say is between ourselves."

"She's my half sister, and don't worry. I won't even tell her where the spare key is."

Dan gave a half chuckle.

"Is she cute?"

"She has pink hair. Need I say more?"

Marcus called in the middle of Annie's morning stall cleaning to confirm their dinner engagement that evening. Annie had convinced Marcus not to pick her up; the last thing she wanted was for Marcus to encounter her pink-haired half-wit half sister.

"So then let's meet at Laurie's Café," said Marcus, "I'm about to check out but have a number of things to attend to this afternoon. Actually, I have to be in about five places at once, but I should be able to wrap things up by six-thirty."

"I'm impressed you even know about Laurie's Café,"

Annie replied. "I thought only the natives knew where to find the best liver and onions served this side of the Rockies."

Marcus chuckled. "Consider it a date, then. See you this evening."

A date. Annie's heart started unaccountably fluttering again. She was infinitely relieved that he would not be coming to her home. The thought of introducing Lavender to Marcus was anathema to her—she could too easily envision her wacky half sister insisting on reading his aura, or worse, trying to wrangle an invitation to join them, and Marcus, Annie feared, would be too much of a gentleman to refuse. Then there was the little problem of how to introduce Marcus. He was so clearly out of place in the community, and Annie had no desire to tell Lavender exactly why he was in town.

Annie also wondered briefly how she could keep Lavender from hearing about the recent deaths of Hilda Colbert and Wayne Johnston. But on that account, she needn't have worried. Trudging back up to the farmhouse after her stable chores, she could hear the blast of her ancient television before she reached the back door.

She found Lavender sitting entranced in front of the set in the living room, listening to the local news blare out the latest details in Hilda's murder case. Annie winced, strode over to the set, and turned it off.

"Sister! Why ever didn't you tell me? Finding a corpse all by yourself! And coming face-to-face with her murderer, too. No wonder your house is filled with bad karma! I'll get to work on it right away!"

Annie took a deep breath.

"Don't concern yourself, Lavender. This isn't something I really care to discuss with you, anyway."

Lavender gave her the same downcast expression she'd used the night before. She must have spent years practicing in front of a mirror, Annie mused.

"Look, it's not as if I don't want to," Annie lied. "It's just that it's an ongoing investigation. I'm not allowed to talk to anyone about it except the police. And frankly, I'd rather not do that, either."

"But I could use my psychic powers to help you!"

"I'll be sure to pass that on to Sheriff Stetson," Annie said drily. "But I need to get your promise, Lavender, that you won't talk to the media. They've already camped out on my doorstep once, and they may try to again. You don't know anything about the case so you have nothing to say. Is that clear?"

Annie felt as if she were speaking to a five-year-old, but she was damned if she was going to risk seeing Lavender on the five o'clock news prattling about her latest psychic insight about the case.

Lavender vigorously nodded up and down, her eyes wide and innocent. Annie didn't trust her for a second.

"Good. Now, I'll be in and out the rest of the day, so if you need anything, you can take my old Chevy pickup to town."

"Thank you."

Something about Lavender's demeanor gave her pause.

"You do have a license, don't you?"

"Well, I don't have a Washington license yet, of course."

Annie studied Lavender, who was busy picking up the laundry she'd been folding in front of the television set.

"How about any old driver's license?"

"Well, I did, back in Florida, but then it got taken away."

"It got taken away? By whom?"

Lavender scrambled to her feet with her clothing.

"It was all a big mistake. I smashed my car, then forgot to show up in court. I guess the judge decided to take away my license. That's what the letter said, anyway."

"You *forgot* to show up in court?" Annie's words were

mocking in the extreme. "Did your psychic powers fail you?"

Lavender faced Annie, her face blotched with anger.

"You and Daddy! That's just what *he* said! But you just don't understand! Ever since that woman came into Daddy's life, it's been impossible to live with them! She's tried to turn Daddy against me. I was a nervous wreck, just trying to second-guess how to act around them. I was lucky I wasn't killed in the accident. Not that anyone would care, of course," she ended bitterly.

This conversation is going nowhere, Annie thought to herself, with a sinking feeling that any subsequent attempts to communicate with Lavender would not go any better.

"Okay, drop it. But you can't drive, and I can't take you anywhere today. We've got a fairly decent bus system in the county, and there's a bus stop just a short walk from the house. I'll pick up a bus schedule for you, and you should be able to get to wherever you want to go."

"Fine." Lavender's feelings clearly were still hurt. Annie didn't care.

"And you might check up on your court case back in Florida. I'd hate for Sheriff Stetson to have to arrest you on a failure to appear."

Lavender's horrified look was worth the price of her admission into Annie's home.

Annie was uncharacteristically at odds with herself the rest of the afternoon. She thought about working with Geronimo, then decided to give him a day off. It was for her sake, really. She simply didn't have the emotional energy to deal with his exuberant strength. Instead, she puttered around the tack room, setting up the horses' evening feed an hour early. She was anxious to see and talk to Marcus and impatiently waited for the winter sun to sink behind the mountains, the horses' cue to come to the fence line.

The only bright spot in Annie's day was her call to the Suwana Humane Society to arrange to pick up the Belgian Tervurens the next day. Hannah was due for her next lesson, and Annie knew the sight of the pups would give her little friend no end of delight. The woman who answered the phone was warm and deferential. Marcus must have given the shelter a significant donation, Annie thought. If the shelter director realized they'd just received money from a man accused of murdering his wife, that hideous realization wasn't reflected in her vocal delivery. The pups were ready to leave the shelter anytime, the woman gently suggested, but Annie wasn't about to leave them with her half-brained half sister, even for the hour she'd be spending with Marcus that evening.

As she fed the horses, Annie continued to wonder whether she'd made a huge mistake in trusting Marcus. In her gut, she felt certain that she was right about his innocence—but to listen to Dan and Tony talk, the evidence was overwhelming, and all that was needed was for Marcus to plead guilty and be done with it. Yet . . . something nagged at the back of Annie's brain, and wouldn't let go. She tried to tell herself it wasn't her hormones.

The one issue Annie didn't struggle over was her decision to give Marcus the registration papers for the bay. She'd already decided that she would simply tell him the truth. Okay, maybe not all of it, but most of it. He knew she'd discovered the puppies. So she could honestly tell him that she'd rescued one piece of paper out of a puppy's mouth. He also knew she'd discovered Hilda's body. She'd simply tell him she'd snatched up the paper in her hand without thinking while she was calling 9-1-1, stuffed it in her back pocket, and forgotten all about them until she did the laundry and then literally put the two together. Marcus didn't have to know that she'd just wanted to savor the papers before giving them to the police and then, too much time passed to make it plausible. He probably would encourage her to go to the police with what she knew, but then, he was leaving that night on a plane back to San Jose. Whatever she decided to do after he left was her own business.

She was simply relieved to get the registration papers out of her hands. They already were stored in the glove compartment of her truck. Just getting them out of the house had relieved it of bad karma. Whatever Lavender allegedly did was lagniappe.

Mental anxiety did wonders for Annie's work ethic. The horses were fed, watered, and tucked in their stalls in record time. By 6:10 P.M., she was on the road.

Two eagles circled high above her truck as she made the left turn into town. Annie had never set much store by omens, but today, the sight of the birds made Annie inwardly cringe. If she wasn't careful, she'd soon be buying into Lavender's spiel and planting a ceramic Buddha in the front yard.

The lineup of battered old pickup trucks in front of Laurie's Café brought Annie's thoughts back to her familiar reality. Laurie's Café had been a fixture in Suwana County for the past sixty years and the décor, inside and out, hadn't changed much during that time. It was a place where local farmers congregated to eat, swap stories, and start or end their day with meals that definitely were not on the Surgeon General's recommended list. The food wasn't fancy, but it was good, and there was plenty of it.

Annie left Wolf in the front seat, promising him all her leftovers when she returned. She cast her eye around the parking lot for an unfamiliar car and realized that she had no idea what Marcus would be driving. Annie stepped inside the café and breathed in a mixture of warm apple pie, meat loaf, and the irresistible smell of deep-frying fat. No Marcus. Well, he would arrive soon; she was sure of it. She intu-

Leigh Hearon

ited that this was a man to whom punctuality was a given, and she was five minutes early. She helped herself to a corner booth that she knew afforded some privacy, ordered coffee, and surveyed the customer base this evening. It was the usual assortment of country folk, most of whom she knew by sight. It was still too early for the real tourist season.

And Marcus would stick out in this crowd like a sore thumb. She wondered if it was wise for him to have chosen a place where they both might be known. Even now, she saw a few of the locals giving her the once-over. Annie had never been one to make anything of herself outside her own small world, but now she assumed her face had appeared on TV, and her name had made it into the local newspaper. She wished she'd been smart enough to buy a newspaper just to check. Copies of the local rag and *Little Nickel* were stacked right outside the entrance, but Annie didn't want to walk across the dining room again.

Inside her parka, her cell phone gave off its old-fashioned ring tone, and Annie gave an involuntary jump in her seat. She searched for her cell frantically before finding it in the most obvious place, her outside front pocket. By that time, the phone had stopped making noise and more than one eye was on her in the crowded dining area.

Annie put a five-dollar bill on the tabletop and, with as much dignity as she could muster, walked outside, and got back into her truck. Wolf's initial happiness at seeing her faded when he realized she was not carrying his dinner.

Annie was in no mood for sympathy. Pushing Wolf over to his side of the front seat, she locked the door and pressed for voice mail. She knew who it would be before the voice started speaking.

"Hi, Annie. It's Marcus. I'll be there soon. I promise. One last business meeting just took longer than I expected. Why I ever agreed to it is beyond me, but there you have it." There was that soft chuckle that made Annie's heart melt.

"Go ahead and order one of your local famous oyster burgers for me. I'm less than a half hour away." There was a click on the other end of the line.

Annie sighed and settled back in the car. She had no intention of going back into Laurie's Café with or without Marcus. She'd simply wait for him outside, and the two of them could find a quiet place to talk, perhaps back at her place. *Oh hell.* Not with Lavender there. Well, they could go out past the reservoir to talk. It was a favorite spot for teenagers to go and neck, at least in Annie's day. God knows what they did there now. She giggled. The thought of kissing Marcus in her truck had certain desirable aspects to it. She drew Wolf nearer to her and hunkered down to wait.

Four hours later, Annie was abruptly awakened by the sound of a large truck peeling out. She glanced up, unsure of her surroundings, then remembered where she was. *Where is Marcus? Did I miss his call?* Annie grabbed her cell and stared at it. Nothing. She sat up and hurriedly found the last number called and punched it in. It rang four times, then clicked over to voice mail.

"Hello, you've reached Marcus Colbert. Please leave your message at the tone."

Annie clicked off without doing so. Her heart began to hammer. There was no good reason for Marcus not to be here by now. And no good reason for him not to tell her if there was. Something was wrong.

She absentmindedly petted Wolf and reached to turn on the ignition. Then she realized what else was wrong, and what had been nagging at her subconscious for the past two days. *If Marcus had left that horrible, awful message for Hilda, why had he given Hilda's voice mail password to Dan so readily? Why would you give the police information that would turn you into an obvious suspect?* It didn't make sense. But neither did Marcus's no-show. Grimly, she took her cell phone once again and punched in Dan's cell number. She might be waking him at a very bad time, but he needed to know that his prime suspect was now a missing person.

CHAPTER 11

MONDAY, FEBRUARY 29TH—TUESDAY, MARCH 1ST

Annie crouched near the kitchen woodstove, her chest nearly touching her bent knees. Her hands idly fingered a bit of cedar kindling, as if she were gravely contemplating its worth as potential fuel for her fire. Annie's hair, uncharacteristically hanging down, swept the floor with long, tangled trellises.

The door to the woodstove stood wide open, but no roar issued from within. The house was cold, and Annie's heart was the coldest thing in it.

Drawing a ragged breath, she reached without looking for a piece of the local paper, stacked neatly behind her. She crushed the sports section and tossed it into the woodstove. It was a dejected throw. She sighed deeply.

Annie later realized she'd been asleep in her truck a solid four hours the night before. She'd awakened Dan from his own sound sleep. Not surprisingly, her pleadings to start the search for Marcus *right now* were rudely dismissed.

"Hell, Annie! If I started searching for everyone who

ever broke a date, I'd be backlogged from here to eternity," he'd grumbled.

Annie had squelched her sudden anger.

"He called me when he was on his way," she insisted. "He said he had one short meeting and would meet me at Laurie's Café. If something else had come up, he would have called."

Dan had balked, cursed, then resigned himself to following police protocol.

"He probably had a meeting with the guy who sold him a new passport. In fact, he's probably on his way to Ecuador as we speak," he told Annie, who'd bitten her lip so many times during the conversation that it now dripped blood.

But Dan had agreed to send someone out to the B&B where Marcus had been staying and to Hilda's ranch to see if there was any sign of him. And he promised Annie he would put out an APB if, and only if, Judy Evans agreed it was necessary.

"Better cash that check of his now," was his parting shot. "Although I wouldn't be surprised if his accounts are already drained." Annie had feverishly punched "disconnect" several times and snapped the lid of her cell phone shut, sorry that mobiles were not constructed to properly convey an angry hang-up with a resounding bang. What she didn't realize until later was that she'd also erased Marcus's voice message to her.

That was eight hours ago, and since then, Dan had called twice. The first time was to tell Annie that Marcus had checked out of his B&B at 10:00 A.M. the day before and had not been sighted anywhere on the Olympic Peninsula. The second time was to let her know he'd talked to Marcus's attorney, who denied hearing from his client, and then had informed the prosecutor of Marcus's disappearance. Judy Evans was even less than sympathetic than Dan; she'd told him to lose no time tracking down the missing suspect and assured him that she'd issue a warrant for Marcus's arrest if he hadn't surfaced by the end of the week, his first check-in deadline.

It seemed that no one within the judicial system believed that Marcus was in danger. They all thought the worst of him, which made it even harder for Annie to bear. Now she feared that if Marcus were found, some overly eager deputy would shoot to kill. Dan still had a few good ol' boys in his posse.

An hour ago, Esther had called on Dan's behalf to let her know that all points of entry in and out of Washington were now being searched by every available law enforcement agency. Esther sounded mildly sympathetic, which Annie appreciated.

Despite the all-out search for Marcus Colbert, Annie had never felt so hopeless and bereft of spirit in her life. The more the hours slipped away, the more desperate Annie's thoughts became. She wished for the thousandth time that she'd saved Marcus's last message to her, so she could prove to Dan that his disappearance was not of his own doing.

Annie also wished she'd saved the message so she could hear Marcus's voice once more. Somewhere, deep down in her gut, she had the miserable feeling that she'd never hear Marcus speak to her again. She hoped he *had* taken a flight to Ecuador. At least then she could be sure that he was safe. At this moment, she was terribly afraid of what she didn't know.

She straightened up, putting her hand on the small of her back, now sore from prolonged bending over, and nearly jumped when she saw Lavender placidly looking at her from the kitchen door, wearing one of Annie's flannel night-gowns.

Naturally, Lavender hadn't brought any warm clothes with her.

"Jesus, you nearly scared me to death," Annie said crossly, wiping her face with the back of her arm and knowing she couldn't hide her distressed state.

"What's wrong, Sister?" Lavender spoke quietly, without her usual exhilaration.

Annie glared at her. "None of your business."

"You got home late last night."

"It's my life. I can do what I want."

Lavender walked over and awkwardly tried to hug Annie, who ducked and wrapped her arms protectively around her midriff.

"A friend is missing, okay? I'm just upset about that. I didn't mean to snap at you."

"I know," came the calm answer.

"Come here, and learn how to make a fire." Annie's tone was brusque, but she didn't care. Lavender had to learn how to live in this house, too, even if it was only for twenty-eight more days and counting.

The morning brought no more news on Marcus's whereabouts, but it did bring a little joy to Annie's life, in the form of two fat, soft, and sweet-smelling Belgian Tervuren pups. Earlier, she'd arranged to take Hannah and her siblings to the Humane Society to pick them up, but when Hannah's mother, Judith, had come to the door and seen Annie, she'd immediately offered to take the kids herself. Annie was immensely relieved. She was in perpetual awe of Judith's seeming unflappability when surrounded by her brood of children, who usually were simultaneously talking and climbing over themselves when Annie appeared on the scene.

She cheered up enough to make oatmeal for herself and Lavender, then take the truck into town to buy puppy chow and teeth chews. To her astonishment, Lavender offered to clean out the pantry, the pups' sleeping quarters for the time

being. There was no way Wolf would allow the pups anywhere near his domain at night, which was at the foot of
Annie's bed, or anywhere else in the room he deigned to
sleep.

*She probably just wants to make sure the dogs don't bed
down with her,* Annie thought to herself, then felt ashamed
at her suspicions toward her half sister's first true act of
kindness while in her home.

Annie's mood was somewhat marred at the bank, where
she presented Marcus's check and was regretfully told that
there would be a ten-day hold on the check until it cleared
from its point of origin in California. Yet the mere act of depositing the check made her feel that she was doing something in the effort to find Marcus. If the check cleared, she
thought, then presumably Marcus was alive. Or maybe not.

The arrival of the puppies brought much-needed laughter
into Annie's home. The entire Clare clan was enchanted with
the little pups, and Annie took deep satisfaction at watching
the children happily play with them. She joined in the excited discussion of what to name them, and good-naturedly
withdrew her suggestion of "Mutt" and "Jeff" when a loud
chorus of "Noooos" followed her contribution. Only when it
was clear that downtime was necessary for both pups and
kids if the world was going to continue to revolve on its axis
did she remember that Marcus was still missing. She helped
usher the children out the door, promised they could come
back tomorrow, promised that she would not name them
without their knowledge—before turning her thoughts in-
ward again. Lavender escaped to her room for a nap.

Annie went outside to the stables to think. As always,
mucking stalls was a catalyst in the process.

She finished the stables in near record time and was
heading over to Trooper's quarters when the phone rang.
Annie dropped the mucking fork and ran back to the tack

room. She noticed that her hands were shaking as she picked up the phone.

"Annie? We have some news. Sea-Tac police found Marcus's car in the long-term parking lot this afternoon. Car's locked; no one's inside. Doesn't look like anything else is inside, either, although the windows are tinted so damn dark that it's hard to tell.

"Annie?" Dan sounded concerned.

She realized she hadn't said anything back. She wanted to hear everything he had to say, first.

"Sorry, Dan. That sounds like good news."

"I hope so. So far, we haven't found any evidence that Marcus boarded a plane, domestic or international. But we won't know for sure for a day or two. He could have boarded under another name. We've asked Homeland Security to look through all the videos, starting from 1400 hours yesterday, and that's going to take some time."

"What are you going to do with the car?"

"We're having it hauled as we speak to the Seattle PD impound lot to look it over. We'll secure it as evidence, then head back later tonight. I'd like to stop by when I hit God's green earth again, Annie. As of now, you were the last person to talk to Marcus. I need to get your statement."

"Fine. I'll be here." Annie would have done almost anything to keep in the loop of the investigation. If giving her statement gave her more information, she was happy to do it. "But you'll probably have to meet Lavender."

"Your pink-haired sister? Can't wait."

"Half sister," Annie corrected him, but Dan had already hung up the phone.

Annie got one more phone call that afternoon, and it was not a pleasant one.

"Is Anne Marie Carson home?" It was a male voice, one she didn't recognize.

"Speaking."

"Ms. Carson, I understand that you have a real valuable piece of horseflesh on your property." The vernacular placed the speaker as a born-and-bred local. Annie's heart thudded, but she was silent. The voice went on.

"So, the way I heard it, the horse's owner is dead and the man who killed her is a fugitive from justice. Am I getting it right, *Ms*. Carson?"

"Who is this?"

"Oh, just a friend of a friend."

"What, too scared to tell me your name?" Annie's body was on high alert, but unlike her equines, who would have been ready to flee, Annie was poised to stand and fight.

"Not important. But my friend wants you to know something. He said to tell you maybe you can handle the horse you got now, but Marcus Colbert is one stallion you don't want to mess with."

"Who are you?"

"As I said, it's not important. Just pay attention to what my friend says. He'd hate for you to get into trouble."

Annie banged down the phone, her heart pounding.

The puppies were fast asleep in their new bed, and the house was filled with the all-encompassing warmth of a good woodstove fire when Dan arrived later that evening. Annie had told Lavender that the sheriff would be making a house call, and apparently her previous warning that she could be arrested for not appearing in a Florida court had been taken seriously. Lavender had fled to her bedroom immediately after dinner and shut the door. Musky incense began to waft through the house, intermingling not unpleasantly with the cedar fire.

Dan sniffed the air suspiciously as he removed his gloves, tipped his sheriff's hat, then tossed it onto one of Annie's chairs.

"You aren't going all woo-woo on me, are you, Annie?" His tone was dubious.

"Hell, no. The aroma is gratis of my new boarder. You know perfectly well I prefer the smell of horse manure and fresh hay."

"Well, that's a relief." Dan peered through the open kitchen door. "Where is she, anyway?"

"Hiding in her room. I told her you were mean and ugly."

"Aw, Annie. You always were the flatterer."

Reverting to her usual banter with Dan raised Annie's spirits. If she could joke, she could get up tomorrow. She could cope with life again.

"You got any of that single malt on the shelf?"

Annie arched one eyebrow but dutifully pulled down the Glenlivet and poured hefty slugs into two shot glasses. She was more than happy to empty the bottle if it got Dan to talk about what he'd learned.

The sheriff eased his body into one of Annie's small kitchen chairs and flung one meaty arm over the back. He took the proffered glass from Annie and drained it in a single gulp. Annie stared at him, momentarily stunned. Then she refilled his glass and demurely sat down next to him and waited for Dan to speak.

He cleared his throat gruffly, looked at his nails critically, then sighed.

"Well, Annie, I hate to say this, but it looks like you were right."

Annie stopped herself just in time from making a predictable sarcastic reply.

"In what way?"

"There's no sign that Marcus ever boarded a plane, under his name or any other. We'll know definitely later tonight.

My money still would be on his being a fugitive from justice except for the car."

"What about the car?" Annie's throat tightened.

Dan sighed and shifted his weight from one leg to another.

"It's clean. *Too* clean. Everything's been wiped down. Can't find a single usable print on the entire vehicle."

Annie privately thought that if Marcus were to abscond, he might very well have thought of doing that precise thing, but she said nothing to Dan. She sipped her scotch thoughtfully and waited for the next tidbit of information.

"Of course, Marcus might have thought of doing that, too," Dan said, deflating Annie's thought of herself as budding detective. "But we found one piece of evidence that shouldn't have been there. Marcus's briefcase, full of business papers from the ranch. It was wedged way back into the trunk. Almost missed it when we cleaned it out. That has Marcus's prints all over it. Now why would he leave that behind? Seems like it'd be the first and only thing he'd take— other than his money, of course—if he'd really fled the country."

Annie's heart sank. "But surely there are video cameras in the airport, aren't there, Dan? If Marcus wasn't in the car, couldn't the cameras tell us who was?"

"You'd think so. There should have been. But the airport security cameras are run by humans, not computers."

"I don't understand."

"Every floor of the airport is monitored at a dozen different angles. Problem is, those monitors are manned by airport security, so when you get tired of watching one area, you can flick to a new vantage point. It's your call. In this case, we've got Marcus's car arriving at the airport at 22:43 hours, but with the tinted windows, you can't tell who's driving. We next see the car go all the way up to the twelfth floor—

that's the open-air deck—but no one on shift at the time bothers to do any surveillance up there. So there's no visual record of anyone getting out of Marcus's car. "

"How about the exits?"

"No video in the elevators. Apparently our great state of Washington believes it's an invasion of privacy."

Annie thought about that for a moment. Then she leaned forward and topped off Dan's glass, almost empty.

"I got an anonymous call today." She said it reluctantly. Earlier, she'd decided she wasn't going to tell Dan, but considering that Marcus was now halfway off the suspect list, she figured she could risk it.

"What kind of call?"

"Oh, just some local yokel who said he was 'a friend of a friend,' who wanted me to know that he knew I had Hilda's horse."

"Why would that be news?"

"Well, he also warned me off Marcus. Said he was someone I shouldn't mess with." Annie had no intention of telling Dan the man had described Marcus as a stallion.

"Well, a day ago, I would have agreed with your anonymous caller. Now, I'm not so sure."

"So what do you think, Dan? Are you convinced now that something happened to Marcus? "

"I think it's looking mighty suspicious. All of Marcus's accounts are intact, although of course, every single one of them will be frozen as of this Friday if he doesn't appear."

"Damn it, Dan! I just deposited Marcus's check and it'll take ten days to clear!"

"Sorry about that, Annie. It had to be done. There is one bright spot, though. I talked with Hilda's man, Todos, on the way back to the Peninsula. He assured me that he was more than willing to stay on and take care of the horses, with or without money. Quite the guy, that Todos. They don't make much more dedicated employees than that, these days."

Annie was so livid that the only thing she could do was pour herself another belt of scotch.

"You call me immediately if this anonymous caller ever contacts you again," Dan added.

She didn't hear a word he said.

The next morning dragged on, much as the one before, broken up only by the welcome onslaught of Clare children coming to visit the puppies. They were even more exuberant than usual, and it took five minutes for Annie to figure out that their parents had discussed the situation and decided that they could, indeed, take one puppy home. Not today, unfortunately, nor tomorrow, but when Annie decreed that the time was right.

"But don't you think we should take both of them?" Hannah looked anxiously at Annie. "I mean, they're brother and sister. They might miss each other."

Annie was on the living room floor, trying to extract one of the pups from underneath the sofa, where for some reason it felt safer. Annie was sympathetic with the dog, but she also didn't want to find pee saturating her furniture before she had a chance to shove some newspaper underneath him.

"Well, Hannah," she said, turning toward the youngster, "did you miss your brothers when you went off to horse camp last summer?"

Hannah thought about it.

"Not exactly."

"Besides, you've already got two cats to keep the pup company. And you know you can bring him—"

"Or her. We might take her."

"—or her over here anytime you want for a play date. In fact, we could train the dogs to go with us on trail rides."

Hannah brightened at this and, problem resolved, turned back to the puppies, both of whom were now scrambling over each other and licking any scrap of human skin in sight.

Annie was waiting in line at the local Cenex store when she overheard two locals talking behind her back about the case.

"Good thing elections are coming up this fall," a fat man in overalls muttered to his companion, a thin, spindly farmer who was missing most of his lower teeth.

"True enough." The farmer carefully spit into a nearby wastebasket, put there precisely for customers such as him.

"Two murders and one escaped convict, all within two weeks! Jesus God, what the hell is Dan Stetson doing about it? Nothing, absolutely nothing."

Annie's anger started to rise, but she kept still, wanting to hear more.

"When someone hits a deer out on the highway, he's Johnny on the spot. Someone's bike gets stolen, he's right there taking down a report like it's a matter of life and death. But when something real happens, he's plain over his head."

"Yeah, and that's one big head to get over."

The two men chortled at their fine sense of humor.

"Did you hear the widder of the truck driver's in town? She's mad as hell and making a big stink. Here her husband dies, and nobody cares about him. It's all about Miss Fancy Pants in her rarefied horse farm. Like that was a death to be mourned."

"My boy tells me the widder's talking to the local newspaper. She says if she can't get the attention of those TV cameras, she'll talk to whomsoever will listen."

Annie was glad, for once, that the men at the counter were taking their sweet time filling orders. Usually, she waited impatiently as a customer discussed the merits of placing donkeys versus mules in the herd as the best deterrent against cougar attacks against their livestock. The conversation could last ten minutes, all for the price of a bag of chicken feed. The cashiers never seemed to mind.

If I spent half my day talking about matters that didn't concern me, I'd never get anything done, was Annie's usual unspoken thought. But today, she was glad that the line was moving even more slowly than usual. She picked up a book—*Birds of the Pacific Northwest*—in a kiosk next to her and idly thumbed through it while she continued to listen. The pages were well-worn. Apparently, other bored people in line had preceded her.

"So who's thinking of running against him? Deadline for applying is coming up pretty quick, I reckon."

"Next, please."

Annie reluctantly put back the book and approached the cashier stand and gave her order. The men in back of her hushed up. Apparently, they didn't want to give any secrets away so close to the counter.

While watching the well-muscled crew load horse feed and a mega bag of puppy chow in her F250, Annie came to a decision. She might not have been happy with the way Dan had handled Marcus's arrest, but it wasn't fair that he get slaughtered by the local populace simply because he was overloaded and stretched thin. So, instead of heading back to the farm, she eased her truck onto the highway and headed into town. If Dan wasn't around, then surely Tony or Kim Williams would be within calling distance. Someone needed to tell them that a little PR was required to ensure Dan would continue to run unopposed, as he had for the past twelve years. Besides, she had to hand over her mitts for fingerprinting.

* * *

"Like you're telling us something we don't already know?" was Tony's unusually sarcastic reply. Annie, perched on a hard metallic chair in Tony's cramped and very messy office, had just poured out the conversation she'd overheard in the feed store, and now was staring incredulously back at the deputy.

"We're getting a dozen calls every day from concerned citizens," he said, in a more reasonable tone. "We've been told the entire force should be fired, the FBI should be brought in, and Dan Stetson should resign immediately. And those are the nice callers."

Annie unconsciously ran her hands, still inky from being fingerprinted earlier, down the front of her jeans. "So what can be done? You can't let people think that Dan and everyone else on the force are incompetent."

"Annie, the best—and only—thing we can do is our job, which is to find out who killed Wayne Johnston, who killed Hilda Colbert, and what the hell happened to her husband. That's more than a full-time job, as you well know."

"Yes, but—"

"Besides, we're getting heat from all sides from folks that really matter. Dan was in a closed session with the county commissioners last night until eight o'clock. The P.C. mayor is sending us e-mails daily, asking for updates, as if he has a right to know what's going on."

Tony snorted. His reference to "the P.C. mayor" didn't, Annie knew, refer to hizzoner's political correctness. It was simply local verbal shorthand for the mayor of Port Chester, the only hamlet in Suwana County with the funds for this part-time position.

"And, just between you, me, and these four walls, we're dangerously close to the FBI's descending on us, whether we want their help or not. One of our less-than-bright commissioners is trying to convince us that Johnston's murder falls under a Federal code for violent crimes against interstate travelers. Last night, she threatened to call the Seattle FBI office unless we solve the case within the next forty-eight hours. And you know where that could lead. Before long, Dan and I would be relegated to fetching coffee for a bunch of suits who don't have a clue as to where to look."

Any hope that Annie had of being reassured by Tony that what she'd heard was just an aberration had just been extinguished. Things were even worse than she thought. She made a decision and reached into her old saddlebag, which served as her purse, and brought out two envelopes. She handed the first to Tony.

"This is my statement. Dan asked me to write it last night, but I thought it might be better to do it with a clear head this morning."

"Glenlivet time, I take it?"

"I wasn't the one who asked to have it poured. I merely served as the bartender."

Tony grinned, reached over, and retrieved the envelope. He quickly scanned what Annie had written out about her last conversation with Marcus, folded the paper carefully, and put it back into the envelope.

"I'll make sure Dan sees this as soon as he gets back."

"But doesn't it seem odd to you? I mean, why would Marcus say he was running late, then not show up?"

"Cold feet? A business emergency back home? I can think of a dozen different reasons, all perfectly innocent, and some not so innocent, as to why Marcus would break a date. Besides, Laurie's Café isn't exactly haute cuisine."

"Be serious, Tony! Something happened to Marcus, and you know it."

"Something happened to a lot of people around here in the last ten days. Marcus's disappearance is troubling, but the facts are we've got two murders to solve, and they take priority. The best we can do on the second Colbert case is hope that someone finds him, dead or alive, in the next few days. He's out of our jurisdiction."

"Well, how about this? There's nothing you can do for Wayne Johnston or Hilda Colbert right now, except find their killers. Marcus Colbert may still be alive. Maybe you should spend time on *his* case on the chance that you can still save a life."

Annie knew she was being unreasonable and didn't care.

"We could," said Tony, "but Marcus still has three days to check in with his attorney. Yes, I know"—Tony raised a hand as Annie began to squawk her rebuttal —"his car at Sea-Tac does look suspicious. And *if* he doesn't call in this Friday, and *if* he's still alive, which I seriously doubt, he'll be heading straight back to jail. There's no way a judge would let him out on bail, even if we don't have all the pieces from the crime lab in yet. And if he's found alive by the time the digital voice expert's report comes in and what we expect to find in his bank records, he can kiss his freedom good-bye."

Clearly, Tony was still smarting from the humiliating court hearing a few days ago.

"What's in the second envelope?" he asked.

Annie swallowed hard. This had been a tough call. By rights, Marcus should now be in possession of what was legally his property—the registration papers for the bay, aka Trooping the Colour. She wished, not for the first time, that she'd just left the paper in Hilda's cold, dead hands and tossed the chewed-up one. But she hadn't, and the thought of holding on to them now, even for one second longer, was anathema to her.

She reluctantly handed over the second envelope, saying nothing.

Tony looked inside, then inquisitively at Annie.

"Where did this come from? And why is it in two pieces?"

"I found them the day I found Hilda's body."

"Then why are you giving them to me now?"

"I thought . . . I realized . . . well, they're evidence, aren't they?"

"Undoubtedly," Tony said drily. "But you still haven't answered my question. Why are you handing over evidence in a murder case six days after they came into your possession?"

Annie had thought about how she would answer this question. She'd decided to try the first story she'd thought about telling Marcus, before opting to tell him the truth. Somehow, she didn't think the truth would elicit the same slow grin on Tony's face that she'd envisioned seeing on Marcus's.

"They were in Hilda's bedroom . . . or outside, I can't remember which. I was in such a state, finding the body that I must have snatched them up without thinking. I forgot all about them until I did my laundry this morning. They were stuck in the jean jacket I was wearing that day. I thought they should go to you."

Tony gazed at her for a full five seconds before answering.

"That is the lamest, most miserable explanation I've heard the entire ten years I've been with the Sheriff's Office."

She smiled weakly.

"However, I'm not going to ask you how you really got those papers, or where you really found them. I'll leave that to others." His tone was grim.

"Fine. I just came by to try to help. If this is what it gets me, I'll take my sorry ass home."

Tony sighed, rose to his feet, and stretched.

"Look, Annie, we're all under the gun right now. Tempers are short, and whatever patience any of us had at the beginning is long gone. Dan's got more to do than any man's got a right to, plus he's dealing with Dory's running off on him. We appreciate your help, we really do, but you have to understand that any scrap of information you might have that will help us solve these cases we needed yesterday. So just get off your high horse for one second and look at things our way. Every day that goes by, the trail gets colder and we get more heat from the county commissioners. In fact, things really couldn't get much worse."

Annie felt slightly mollified as she left the Sheriff's Office, but only slightly. Mostly she just felt relief that the registration papers were out of her hands. What she hadn't told Tony was that before handing them over, she'd made a copy for herself. For some reason, it seemed important to her.

And Tony was wrong about things not getting worse. Annie returned home to find Lavender, sitting on the living room floor, her eyes once more glued to the television set. From the volume, Annie realized that the lead story centered on Marcus's sudden disappearance.

"Sister! Why didn't you tell me? I have to hear it on the news how you snuck out of the courtroom with Marcus and now you're hiding him in the Cayman Islands? Honestly, Sister, isn't that against the law?"

Annie strode over to her enthralled half sister, snatched the remote out of her hand, and turned the TV off. She flung her mail down on the couch and left the room.

"Twenty-five days, Lavender! That's how long you have before you're history here. Do you understand?"

She didn't feel any better when she heard Lavender burst into tears and run to her bedroom.

Annie felt like crying herself.

CHAPTER 12

WEDNESDAY EVENING, MARCH 2ND— THURSDAY, MARCH 3RD

From: Dan Stetson d.stetson@wa.suwana.gov
Date: Wednesday, March 2, 2016 6:00 P.M.
To: Annie Carson annie.carson@olypeninsula.net
          and ten other undisclosed recipients.
Subject: MISSION ACCOMPLISHED, THANKS TO YOU

Dear Suwana County Search and Rescue team:

Thank you for the long hours you spent today to help find little Peggy Laughton. Her parents are very relieved that their five-year-old was only lost and not abducted or worse. It's the tremendous hard work of search and rescue members like yourself who are willing to drop everything to help us in emergencies that that make Suwana County a safer place to live.

On behalf of the entire Suwana County Sheriff's Office, thank you for your great work today.

Best regards,
Sheriff Dan Stetson
Suwana County Sheriff's Office
"Making Suwana County safe since 1943."

From: Annie Carson annie.carson@olypeninsula.net
Date: Wednesday, March 2, 2016 6:33 P.M.
To: Dan Stetson d.stetson@wa.suwana.gov
Subject: HOW DARE YOU!!!!!!!!!!

I left my house at 8:08 A.M. today to help find little Peggy Sue and came home to find the calling cards of two of your deputies on my dining room table, proof that they gained ILLEGAL access to MY HOME as if it were another crime scene. I find two TRAUMATIZED puppies who peed all over my good rug and my house in complete disarray.

What the hell, Dan? Since when is searching my house more important than finding a missing five-year-old? I gave you my statement. I have fully cooperated with you throughout this investigation. Yet you're treating ME like a criminal. You also appear to be quashing my Constitutional rights like a June bug. Ever hear of the Fourth Amendment, Dan? I'm calling a lawyer.

Annie

P.S. I hope you found what you were looking for: NOTHING.

From: Dan Stetson d.stetson@wa.suwana.gov
Date: Wednesday, March 2, 2016 6:58 P.M.
To: Annie Carson annie.carson@olypeninsula.net
Subject: Re: HOW DARE YOU!!!!!!!!!!

If you picked up your cell phone once in a while, we might have avoided all this. Tony showed me what you brought in yesterday, and frankly you're lucky we didn't bring a warrant for your arrest along with the search warrant. Which we didn't need because your wacky sister voluntarily gave us permission to enter. Nice hair. Looks like something my soon-to-be-ex-wife would have done. If you'd looked at the inventory list we left, you'd realize we found squat. Happy now?

Dan

P.S. You don't know any attorneys.
P.P.S. Thanks again for your help today.

From: Annie Carson annie.carson@olypeninsula.net
Date: Wednesday, March 2, 2016 7:01 P.M.
To: Dan Stetson d.stetson@wa.suwana.gov
Subject: Re: Re: HOW DARE YOU!!!!!!!!!!

No, I am NOT happy, and I know how to pick up a phone book and look in "A." Come to think of it, ACLU sounds like a winner.

Lavender had no right to let you in. THIS IS NOT HER HOME. Not that this little fact apparently would have stopped you. I resent like hell your unnecessary intrusion into my personal life. The bar is permanently closed to you. The next time I see you on my property, I will ask you politely to leave as I'm loading my Winchester.

Ms. Anne Marie Carson

P.S. My cell battery was dead.

The conversation between Annie and her half sister earlier on Wednesday evening had not been a pleasant one.

After a grueling day of looking for the missing Peggy Sue, both Annie and Wolf were cold, tired, and hungry. For Wolf, none of these conditions seriously affected his outward demeanor—after all, Alpo was but a scoop away—but Annie's threshold for tolerating any more bad news was dangerously low. After seeing the deputies' cards on the table, her wrath reached a plateau Lavender had never seen before. Unfortunately, none of the ploys Annie's half sister typically used to placate people she routinely upset seemed to work. Lavender had cried, sulked, and was on the verge of hysteria until Annie told her she'd smack her into the next county if she didn't shut up.

"I thought they were coming to arrest *me,*" Lavender had whined to Annie in a voice muffled by several Kleenex.

"They should have," Annie said darkly.

"But they seemed so *nice,*" Lavender wailed back. "That tall guy, Detective Tony, told me you've been friends for years and years, and he helped save that big horse you've got in your barn."

"He's not a detective," Annie said through clenched teeth. "He's a deputy. And he had no right to insinuate that any friendship he *might* have had with me was reason enough for you to let him inside."

"You see, Sister?" Lavender tried to look her most pleading over red-rimmed eyes and a thoroughly dripping nose, without succeeding very well. Annie was sure that at age ten, that look had worked like a charm. Now, twenty-some years later, the charm had worn off. "It wasn't my fault. They *used* me. They took *advantage* of me. How was I to know?"

"Oh, bite me," Annie muttered and stomped off to her room, slamming her door behind her. She had come out once to retrieve her bottle of Glenlivet, only to belatedly remember that she had killed what little remained the night Dan had paid a visit. She slammed her door again, but not quite as loudly. It was hard to replicate the original sound with a large bag of Doritos in one hand and Oreos in the other.

Annie's missives to Dan Stetson had been created with orange-stained hands and a mouth smeared with vanilla cream and chocolate crumbs. She had paced up and down her small bedroom for a half hour after her last riposte, unaware that Wolf was looking inquiringly at her with puzzled eyes. Anger, he had seen. But he'd never known his mistress to stay inside when she was upset. Usually, she whistled to him, and they went down to the horses, where soon everything was right again.

It was only when Wolf gently sighed and put his head between his paws that Annie looked down and saw that her pent-up fury had affected one of the things she loved most. Turning to Wolf, Annie gave him a nod and pulled on her worn, wool-lined jacket. It might be cold and dark, but it wasn't snowing. It was time to give Geronimo a little training on how to navigate in the dark.

The next morning, Annie had arisen at her usual early hour, plugged in the coffee, and taken a long, hot shower, deliberately using up most of the small water tank as she did so. A cold stream of water was exactly what Lavender deserved. Of course, by the time her half sister actually got out of bed, the hot water undoubtedly would once again be up to full capacity. Damn.

She was still feeling residual resentment at her unasked-for guest, but refused to let it ruin her day. She cranked up the radio, poured herself a cup of coffee, and knocked on Lavender's door to tell her she could come out now without fear of being bitten.

But there was no answer. *The heck with this,* Annie thought. *It's my own home.* She opened the door. Lavender was gone. Her things were still there, in piles on the floor, dresser top, and everywhere except in their appointed places. But the woman had vanished.

Annie thought for a moment. Had she heard the sounds of anyone's quietly walking through the house last night? A door softly close? No, but then she had spent a good two hours with Geronimo, her hand lightly on the halter rope, letting him feel his way around the round pen, then outside until he learned to trust Annie's hand movements and not jump at the sound of an unseen noise. He really was coming along very nicely, Annie mused. And to think only a week ago all the little guy could do was run around in a circle. Too bad her training skills didn't extend to humans.

Lavender must have left while Annie had been taking a shower. Well, she was technically a grown-up and could fend for herself. Annie peered outside and looked at the sky. It was definitely warming up. What little snow remained on the ground would be history by noon. It was time to start her day.

For the first time in a week, the phone did not ring. The media circus seemed to have folded up their tents and left town. The strain of having to avoid talking to the press had taken its toll on Annie, but she also realized that by focusing her attention on the events around her, she had neatly side-stepped the issue of worrying—and grieving, if that was the right word—for Marcus, of whom there was still no news. Now, with the phones silent, and even her chatterbox half sister gone, temporarily, at least, Annie felt lonely. She didn't often feel lonely; she was comfortable in her own skin most of the time. And she was usually perfectly content to let her assorted four-legged friends provide all the conversation.

But at 1:00 P.M., when the phone shrilled for the first time that day, Annie leapt for it, not caring whether it was a wrong number or a time share marketer trying to sell her on a free weekend in Vegas.

It was neither. It was James Fenton, Marcus's lawyer, who gave the impression that he wasn't especially happy to talk to her but knew he had to make the professional call.

"Ms. Carson?" Fenton really couldn't have sounded less uninterested in her name.

"Speaking." Annie knew who it was but didn't feel like giving him the satisfaction. She still remembered how Fenton had described her the day Marcus was sprung from jail.

"James Fenton here." There was a slight cough. "Excuse me. Spring allergies."

Annie made a small, sympathetic noise, while her heart pounded. Did Fenton know something that Dan Stetson didn't?

Apparently not. At least, in the important sense, which was where on God's green earth Marcus was. That, Fenton did not know. But he definitely had new information.

In the last days leading up to his disappearance, Marcus had directed his attorney to give Annie power of attorney to divest Hilda's ranch of horses and equipment, which was to be done as her time permitted. When Annie had gasped, Fenton had rushed to assure her that this was a paying job, at least on paper. Marcus had authorized $50,000 out of his accounts to cover Annie's immediate time and out-of-pocket costs. When this amount had been expended, Annie had only to let Fenton know, and more funds would be forthcoming.

Unfortunately, with Marcus's disappearance, this plan was no longer viable. At least, on Marcus's part. Fenton informed her that sadly, all of Marcus's funds had just been frozen. It was precisely one week from Marcus's arrest and the court had made good on its threat. Annie had the distinct impression that Fenton was keenly aware that this meant his own invoices would go unpaid for the time being.

"It's a mess," he sighed into the phone. "Hilda's estate won't be probated for months, at the very least, and until there's a certificate of death made out for Marcus, his estate is in limbo, as well."

"What's happening to Marcus's company?" Annie asked. She wondered if his high-tech company was in a shambles, along with everything else.

"Ah. Well, there, we do have a glimmer of hope. Marcus structured his company so that there was always a successor, and, of course, there is a highly competent board of directors. So while Marcus's disappearance isn't exactly helping the stock price at the moment, it appears that the company is perfectly capable of continuing to do business."

Marcus was such a planner, Annie thought. Quite the opposite of Hilda, who apparently couldn't even pay her vet bills on time. No wonder Marcus had been so surprised and upset to find his wife's business affairs in such disarray. So did Marcus's well-honed organizational skills really mean, as Dan was certain, that Marcus had carefully planned his own escape?

As much as Annie loathed Fenton, she had to ask.

"So what do you think has happened to Marcus?" She tried to keep her voice objective and noncommittal.

"Frankly, I don't want to think about it," Fenton replied. He sounded weary. "I've known Marcus Colbert for twenty years. He's one of the most scrupulously honest people I've ever done business with. Used to irritate me no end. I just can't see Marcus fleeing his responsibilities like this. The evidence against him for Hilda's death was weak, and he knew it. I think he was genuinely upset about her death and wanted to see her killer brought to justice. We'd even talked about setting up a reward fund. That's impossible now, of course."

Annie felt marginally better, knowing that Marcus's attorney, slimeball that he was, harbored the same doubts that she had. Her mind was made up.

"How about the staff?"

"I beg your pardon?"

"I mean, how about the ranch workers? Mr. Fenton, I believe Marcus is totally innocent, and I just hope he isn't the third victim in this tragedy. If there's anything I can do to help out until Marcus is . . . is . . . found, then I will. I don't care about the money. I just want to do what's right. But I do need to know how to deal with the staffing issues."

"You mean, is Todos still in charge?" Fenton sounded drily amused.

"Precisely."

"Yes, Todos is still in charge, and his job now includes trying to keep workers on the ranch who don't believe in ghosts and curses. It isn't easy. He's also got a salary that's going unpaid for the time being. He's my next call. I don't know if he'll be as *magnanimous* as you seem to be."

The way Fenton had dragged out *magnanimous* made Annie's temper, never far from the surface, rise. She swallowed hard.

"Well, let me know. I need to know if I have to insert feeding eighteen thoroughbreds into my morning and evening schedule."

"Well, it's actually not as bleak as all that. I'm petitioning the court next week for release of funds to take care of the immediate needs of Hilda's animals. I'm not sure the judge will authorize the entire 50K Marcus wanted you to have, but I'm sure it'll be enough to keep the ranch adequately staffed."

In the air-space that followed, Annie heard what Fenton hadn't said. *"But there's no way I can expect to get compensated anytime soon."*

"Good luck with that." Suddenly, Annie was tired of James Fenton and everyone allegedly concerned with the well-being of Marcus Colbert. Dan would be content to find a body—or a plane ticket to Switzerland. Fenton would be content with a check. And what would she be content with?

That Marcus was all right.

Fenton coughed discreetly again.

"There's one more thing, Ms. Carson."

"Oh? What's that?"

"Marcus also deeded you full ownership of that horse you rescued. Of course, it's not yours, yet—not until Marcus is officially not a suspect, or is officially declared dead, *and* Hilda's estate is sorted out. But I thought you'd want to know at least Marcus's intent."

He'd given her Trooping the Colour. Marcus might not have known a lot about horses, but apparently he knew a lot about Annie Carson.

All of the snow had vanished by early afternoon, There was still no sign of Lavender, but Annie continued to not let her sister's absence bother her. She spent a relatively enjoyable rest of the day with her animals. She'd decided to put Geronimo under saddle for the first time. She had no intention of riding him today. She just wanted him to feel comfortable with fourteen pounds of leather on his back.

Getting Geronimo into the round pen in the middle of the day was easy since Trotter insisted on following them back. In fact, so did the rest of the horses. They probably assumed they were going to get an afternoon snack, Annie thought with amusement. When they realized they weren't being led into their stalls, the horses gathered around the corral fence, noses peering in. Apparently, they were willing to settle for a little live entertainment.

Once in the corral, Geronimo stood obediently as Annie left and returned with one of her working saddles. She walked up to him slowly and let him sniff it. Geronimo inquisitively switched his nose around the leather and licked the felt seat. Annie put the saddle on the ground and let the horse examine it to his heart's content. When she was sure Geronimo had thoroughly decided the object was not a predator or something to be feared, she picked it up and began to rub his back with it.

From long experience, Annie knew that getting a horse under saddle involved a huge act of trust between horse and rider. As a prey animal, an equine always was fearful of a predator landing on its back or ripping open its stomach. To willingly accept a saddle on its back meant that the horse trusted that its human companion had its best interests in mind.

Within a half hour, Annie had successfully placed a saddle blanket on Geronimo's back and now was feeding him baby carrots out of her hand. This was the easy part. She walked slowly away from the horse, who followed her with the bright expectation of more treats.

She picked up the saddle and moved slowly toward Geronimo's back, continuing to let him sniff the leather. As she lifted it toward his back, she heard a horse wheeze.

The sound didn't bother Geronimo, but it discombobulated his trainer. She walked over to the fence line to see which of her horses had made the unexpected sound. Bess, Baby, and Sam all looked fine. Rover had abandoned watching some minutes ago to forage for pasture grass—one had to have priorities, after all, and a once-starved horse knew exactly what those were. Trooper, however, was definitely off. Mucus was dribbling from both eyes, and his watery eyes drooped. To someone who didn't know horses, one would have thought Trooper was weeping over some unknown tragedy in his life.

Hell's bells. Had Trooper somehow gotten a cold? Horses weren't prone to getting them, being used to living in the outdoors and all—but Trooper wasn't an ordinary horse. He'd been used to blankets and heated stables and regulated temperatures all of his short life. A few days ago, Trooper had joined the rest of the herd and everyone seemed to be getting along just fine. Had Annie inadvertently precipitated an illness, simply by letting him be one of the gang?

She quickly turned out Geronimo, praising him for his good work with a few more carrots. After swinging the saddle and blanket back onto its appointed space in the tack room, she called Jessica.

An hour later, Jessica came roaring onto the farm, her compact vet van screeching to a halt in front of the stables.

Annie stood up and instinctively placed a hand on Trooper's shoulder. He'd jerked up his head as soon as he heard the furious crunch of tires outside. Both he and Trotter were in the stable, awaiting Jessica's arrival. Annie had been trying to fasten very rusty leg straps attached to a very old horse blanket, which she'd finally located in her tack room attic. It wasn't working very well.

"Where is he?"

Jessica rushed in, looking more concerned and, yes, frightened, than Annie had ever seen her.

"He's right here," Annie said more calmly than she felt. "What's going on?"

Jessica sat down on a hay bale to catch her breath.

"Sorry, Annie. But I've been living in fear for the past two months that EHV would make its way to our rural community."

Annie stared blankly at Jessica.

"Equine herpesvirus, Annie."

Oh, *that*. Annie knew all about that. It had started on the East Coast a few years ago and made its way to the West Coast through an infected horse at a Utah horse show. The virus spread quickly among horses and could be fatal. And it often started with coldlike symptoms. Annie felt an unnamed dread steal through her body.

"Wouldn't the horse have been tested for that before leaving Tennessee?" she asked.

"Not necessarily," Jessica said. "The epidemic was too new for regulated testing of horses being transported across state lines. We're *asking* horse owners to keep their animals at home and to avoid transporting them to areas where the virus has cropped up. But how and when the virus spreads or is contained is based solely on goodwill and common sense."

Annie digested this before asking, "So how will we know?"

"I'll have to test him. What are you calling him, anyway? And how did he end up with you? I know Hilda is dead, but why isn't her star manager taking care of the horse?"

Annie blushed, something she didn't often do.

"It's a long story. But the short answer is I'm calling him Trooper, which is short for his real name, Trooping the Colour."

Jessica shot Annie a hard, questioning stare.

"Didn't Hilda's husband come to your place about a week ago to look at the bay? Wasn't he a suspect or something?"

Trust Jessica to have only a modicum of the so-called facts that had been displayed on national television. She was the only other person in Annie's circle who knew as little about the outside world as she did. They were just too busy to keep up.

"Yes, and no. Could we stick to the subject at hand, Jessica? I mean, I'd love to fill you in on everything that *People* magazine left out, but at the moment I'd like to know if my entire herd is contaminated with an incurable virus."

She sounded a little sharper than she felt. Jessica's questions were perfectly legitimate, considering all that had transpired in the ten days since Trooper had had his tooth pulled.

Jessica drew up herself with dignity and a degree of elegance that Annie secretly envied.

"I'm sorry, Jessica."

"It's okay, Annie. I'd feel the same way myself if it were my herd. Let's get it over with."

* * *

In the end, Jessica had taken more blood from Trooper than just for the EHV test. She'd also given him a thorough physical examination, taken nose and throat swabs, fecal samples, and drawn enough blood to test for a variety of possible illnesses, including parasites, allergies, and rare forms of equine cancers.

Annie could see her entire bank account vanishing with another vet bill but said nothing as Jessica continued her thorough work. As usual, Trooper was . . . well, a trooper about being poked and prodded. Apparently, about the only thing that he reacted badly to was almost being turned over in a locked horse trailer traveling at a high speed. This seemed reasonable to Annie.

By now, the sun was waning, the air was chilly even inside the stable, and Annie wearily realized that it was just about feeding time. She helped Jessica load her equipment into the van and stood by the vet van while Jessica typed up her notes on her small laptop.

"I know you can't really give me a prognosis, but tell me anyway what you think."

Jessica finished an entry and turned to her friend.

"I'm cautiously optimistic, Annie. Trooper doesn't show every classic textbook symptom of EHV, but then, we're just starting to really learn about the disease, thanks to the new epidemic. In truth, it could be anything—worms, parasites, allergies, or yes, EHV. The one thing it isn't is a cold."

Annie visibly relaxed as Jessica said this.

"It's not your fault, Annie. There's definitely something going on with Trooper that we need to fix, but it's nothing that was caused by your care. Trust me on that."

"Should I segregate Trooper from the rest of the herd?"

"How long have they been sharing the same pasture and living area?"

"More than a week in the stables. Ever since I picked up

the bay, in fact. He's never spent the night anywhere since. And he's been out to pasture with the herd since Monday."

"Well, if it is EHV, it's probably too late now. I'll rush this sample to the lab, and we should get the results back by tomorrow. If it's positive, of course, then I'll have to test all the other animals and report my findings to the state."

"Of course." Annie's throat felt tight.

"But please try not to worry about that until you have to. I mean, *unless* you have to, Annie. Meanwhile, I'd just wash out Trooper's eyes and make sure he's comfortable. And don't worry about blanketing him. A week in the rugged Northwest has already started to pull up a new coat on him. He's plenty tough enough to stand our climate."

Everyone got hot mashes that night. It seemed the least Annie could do, considering that her most beloved companions were now waiting to hear their fate. She knew she should call Samantha and let her know that Geronimo was at risk, but she just couldn't face it right now. She'd know the truth soon enough, anyhow.

As she made her way up to her farmhouse, she noticed a light on in the kitchen and the shadow of someone moving around in it. Lavender. She'd returned. Funny—Annie didn't feel the same resentment that she'd felt almost every day her half sister had been with her. She didn't exactly welcome seeing Lavender again, but she didn't really mind that much, either. It was strange.

Opening up the back door, Annie did find one thing to welcome her: a fifth of Glenlivet, along with one of Dan Stetson's business cards. On the back, he'd scrawled, "To your good health and to good friends." *Aw. That was nice of Dan.* He hadn't had to do that. Well, yes, he had, but Annie gave him points for making the gesture.

She set the bottle on the kitchen table as Lavender turned

from the oven with a mitted hand. She had on an apron and her pink hair stuck out in bunches. Her face was hot and sweaty. She looked ebullient.

"Sister! I hope you don't mind, but I've made dinner. And all from local products, too!"

She brought out a casserole that looked suspiciously healthful but gave off an aroma that was not entirely displeasing, especially considering Annie hadn't eaten in eight hours.

Well, one healthy thing was enough. Annie got out two small glasses and unscrewed the cap on the single malt.

"Care to join me in a predinner drink, Lavender?"

CHAPTER 13

FRIDAY, MARCH 4TH

The Northwest lived up to its reputation the next day. Rain streamed remorselessly from the sky, and the forecast was for more of the same all weekend. Annie wrapped herself into her full-length slicker before heading out to the barn to feed the horses. First stop was Trooper's stall. He was standing, pooping, and interested in eating—all of which Jessica had assured her were good signs—but his eyes still ran, and he wheezed twice while she prepared the morning mashes.

She called Jessica's cell phone from the stable, but only got the vet's voice mail. Knowing Jessica, Annie assumed the hardworking large animal doctor had risen earlier than she and had been on the road since dawn. She decided not to leave a message. Her caller ID would tell what was on her mind. And, bless her friend, Jessica called Annie a scant twenty minutes later to let her know that the diagnostic lab had just received Trooper's vials of blood and other draws and promised results by end of day.

"So try not to worry, okay, Annie?" were Jessica's parting words.

Right.

She returned to the farmhouse to enjoy a solitary breakfast. Last night had been less hideous than she'd envisioned. It was a grudging admission. Lavender had been so proud of her casserole of quinoa, a grain Annie had never heard of, but apparently it was rich in protein and good for you, too. It certainly tasted that way. But Annie had been grateful for Lavender's efforts and, to be honest, her company that night. It was easier to feign interest in her half sister's prattling news of the day than think of her own equine issues.

Lavender, it turned out, *had* left under the cloak of darkness, but only an hour before Annie had arisen. She'd caught a bus into town and spent an enjoyable day acquainting herself with the locals. She'd gone to the community farmer's market, under cover of a tent this time of year, introduced herself to all the neighborhood merchants who specialized in what Annie called "woo-woo stuff," and even signed up for a library card. This last adventure floored Annie. Judging by the letter she'd received from her half sister, she wouldn't have thought Lavender had any interest in literature. Her instinct proved correct when Lavender proudly displayed what she'd checked out: *Northwest Native American Symbolism for Dummies.* Annie choked back her response.

Instead, she asked, casually, she hoped, "Any luck hooking up with your Native American elder?" The quicker

Lavender found employment, or at least a new hobby, the sooner she might vacate Annie's home.

"I tried, Sister," was the morose reply. "But no one's seen Soaring Eagle for several months. We think he's on a spiritual journey in Alaska someplace. When three crows circle overhead, we'll know he's coming back."

Annie decided not to ask who the "we" were. But she allowed herself a bit of secret hope. The sight of three crows circling in Suwana County was something you could pretty much bank on whenever roadkill surfaced. At that rate, Soaring Eagle could be back any day now.

Bolstered by several shots of Glenlivet the night before, Lavender miraculously had agreed with Annie's suggestion to continue her exploration of the great Northwest the next day. Annie made sure the decision still held that morning. She handed Lavender a twenty-dollar bill, telling her she could buy whatever groceries she needed to make dinner that evening. Despite her half sister's earnest promise to help out, the house remained as dirty and even more cluttered than ever. And Annie certainly didn't see much evidence that any bad karma had dissipated.

Happy as she was to see Lavender depart, Annie had been loath to turn out the herd after feeding. Between the torrential rain and the horses' questionable health status, it seemed wiser to keep them within eyesight. She gave them access to the paddock, but everyone seemed content to stay inside the stable and munch on Timothy without getting soaked.

Annie next headed into town, to the feed and farm supply shop just outside of Shelby, not far from the scene of Hilda's murder. She eased out of the Cenex parking lot and onto the road that led to a switchback to the major highway.

A few seconds later, she spotted the silent flashers of a patrol vehicle behind her. She obediently pulled over, thinking the deputy was on his way to an accident up ahead. God knows, this was the weather for cars to slip and slide into each other.

But instead, the patrol vehicle slid in behind her. Hell's bells! What had she done wrong? Headlights were on. Safety belt fastened. She couldn't be tagged simply because she hadn't signaled her way out of the parking lot, could she?

If she could have actually *seen* the lumbering figure get out of the patrol car, Annie would have known his identity in an instant. But blinding, sideways rain prohibited distinguishing anything more than a few feet in front and virtually nothing to the rear. It was only when a beefy arm landed on her rolled-down window that she recognized the officer who'd pulled her over.

"Sorry, Annie, but I couldn't get your attention any other way," Dan told her. "I tried honking, tried yelling, but this dad-burn rain drowned me out." He paused. "Sure hope the river doesn't rise."

Annie wondered if Dan's curious change of subject only meant he was still trying to gauge just how angry she remained at him.

"Thanks for the scotch." She meant it.

Dan slapped his hefty paw on the window, inadvertently sending a spray of water right into her face. She winced.

"Glad to do it, Annie." Dan sounded like his typical jovial self again. What a relief. His wife of twenty-five years might have left him in the midst of more unsolved homicides than he'd faced in his entire law-enforcement career, but Dan was intrinsically an upbeat kind of guy. It occurred to Annie that Dan's depressed state had affected her, as well.

Dan cleared his throat and peered into the car, seeking

out Annie's face. His trooper's hat obediently slid a plethora of raindrops into Annie's lap.

"I owe you an explanation. How about if I do it over lunch?"

"Anywhere except here. You're bringing the rain inside, and my neighbors are going to think you've pulled me over on a DUI if we stay here much longer."

"Meet you at Laurie's Café?"

Annie's heart sank. Laurie's Café was where she and Marcus were supposed to have met just five days earlier. Well, it was the closest restaurant in the area. She'd just have to get over it.

She smiled up at Dan. "You're buying, of course."

Once ensconced in the furthermost booth from the front door, two steaming mugs of coffee in front of them, Annie began to truly relax. This was like old times. She almost wished it *was* old times—before Hilda's death, before Marcus arrived, before Trooper came into her life. Especially before Lavender had come into her life. Had life really been that simple and uncomplicated a few weeks ago? Would it ever be that way again?

She took a deep draught of overbrewed coffee and peered inside the mug. Maybe the remaining coffee grinds would give her insight. She looked up at Dan.

"You first. I mean, I've got a few things to share with you, too, but I know you know a lot more than I do."

Dan sighed. "It's unbelievable, Annie. Hilda's murder is making people disappear like flies. I mean it. First Marcus, and no, I still haven't ruled him out as Hilda's killer, but I do acknowledge that a few holes are beginning to appear in that theory."

Annie glanced up with surprise at the sheriff, who was looking slightly embarrassed.

"I might have exaggerated some of the stuff we uncovered in California."

Dan sounded distinctly uncomfortable. In response, Annie arched one eyebrow, a skill she'd learned at sixteen and one that never failed to come in handy on the rare occasions it was required.

"Well, jeez, Annie, Dory had just dropped her bombshell, and I was in a take-no-prisoners kind of mood. It's true, Marcus was pretty tight with his Human Resources director, and frankly, I could see why."

Annie instantly envisioned a tall, reed-thin blonde with perfectly manicured nails, perfectly coiffed hair, wearing clothes from Neiman Marcus that showed off an impeccable figure that reflected daily sessions with her personal trainer.

Annie came back to reality with these reassuring words. "But it turns out that nothing was really going on."

"In fact, she admitted that she was the one who was pursuing Marcus, not the other way around. Figured with his wife safely in another state, he was fair game. Only, I guess Marcus really did love his wife . . . or at least honored the marriage vow. The last time the gal spoke to him, he pretty much laid it on the line. Told her if she couldn't get over it, she'd have to find another job. That was one good-looking blond babe, let me tell you."

Blond. Annie silently gave herself one point.

"Well, maybe *she* killed Hilda, if she was so hot to get into Marcus's pants."

"Believe me, Annie, the same thought occurred to us. But her alibi checked out."

"Maybe she got someone to cover for her."

"She was the guest speaker at a fund-raising dinner. Four hundred people have her back."

"Maybe she hired a hit man."

"Maybe you watch too much television."

Their food arrived, putting an end to an incipient squabble. Yes, things definitely were getting back to normal.

Dan was mopping up gravy with the last slice of bread from his roast beef sandwich when Annie decided it was time to continue the conversation. Glancing around the café and noting with satisfaction that most diners had left, she threw her paper napkin on the table. It was a gauntlet that Dan recognized. He leaned back, waiting for Annie's first question.

"Okay, shoot," she said. "Who's disappeared now?"

"Juan."

Annie gave Dan a quizzical look.

"The stable hand who tried to prevent you from going up to Hilda's castle."

"Oh. Well, maybe he just couldn't take Todos's tyrannical methods of getting people to work."

Dan sighed. "I know. I'd hate to be under his thumb, too. Then there's the 'curse of Hilda' still hanging around the place. In the last week, more than half the workers have given notice right after they packed their bags. But Juan just . . . disappeared. At six yesterday morning, he's feeding the horses like usual. At ten, he's gone. Left all his stuff behind in the bunkhouse, by the looks of it. Todos called us as soon as he found out. We've searched the property, and every patrol officer has his description, but it's like he just vanished."

"Well, what of it? The guy was clearly terrified of Hilda and probably jumped whenever Todos turned the corner and saw him. From what I observed, he's just a little mousy kind of guy. Surely you don't think Juan is involved in Hilda's death or Marcus's disappearance."

Dan observed Annie for a few seconds, his eyes focused and shrewd.

"Did it ever occur to you that the reason Juan was so scared when you were up to the house was because he'd just slit his boss's throat?"

It had not. Annie thought about it for a moment.

"He's too small. I can't believe he could overpower Hilda, even on a good day." She absentmindedly massaged her left wrist.

"Almost anyone, if they're worked up enough, has the power to cause serious physical damage to another human being, Annie. You'd be surprised what I've seen over the years."

Considering that the typical assault case in Suwana County consisted of a short-lived fight in a tavern parking lot where the loser ended up with nothing worse than a black eye or broken nose, Annie thought Dan was overstating his experience. But she held her tongue. She wanted to know more.

"Well, what does the all-knowing, omniscient Adolpho Todos have to say? He should know Juan and all the workers better than anyone."

"He's been extremely cooperative."

Annie snorted. "Sure, now that he's off the suspect list."

"Hold on, now, Annie. Todos doesn't have to stick around, either, but he's doing it just to keep the ranch together until the estate is settled. He made it possible for us to interview every single worker on the ranch the day after you found Hilda's body. He may not be the easiest guy to talk to, but I can't fault him for his work ethic or the way he's accommodated us on the property."

"So, you talked to Juan. What did you learn? What did you learn from *any* of Hilda's minions?"

"Nada. It's the recurring theme in these homicides. No one saw anything, no one knows anything, and no one can think of anyone who would want to kill the boss lady."

"Which reminds me." Annie had had about enough of

hearing about Todos's exemplary qualities. "I got a call from James Fenton yesterday."

Her pronouncement had the desired effect.

"What did he want? And why didn't you call me immediately?"

Annie glared at Dan.

"If he'd told me where Marcus was, of course I would have shared that information. But he doesn't have a clue as to where his client is."

Dan snickered.

"No, really, Dan. It's driving him crazy. Until Marcus is found, the estate is frozen, as you well know. Which means he doesn't get paid."

Dan grinned. "Well, there's a silver lining in every—"

Annie cut in. "Yeah, spare me your humanitarian views. But apparently a few days before he disappeared, Marcus designated *me* as the person to find new homes for Hilda's animals. And he's given me Trooper," she added hastily, as Dan sputtered over his coffee, and brown drops dotted her flannel shirt. Really, Annie was getting wetter talking to the sheriff than she would have just standing in the rain.

"Well, we'll see about that."

"What do you mean, *we'll* see about that? Doesn't seem to me that what Marcus decides to do with his wife's estate has any bearing on *your* work."

"Welcome to Criminal Justice 101, Annie. It has everything to do with my case. Marcus can't divest himself of anything of Hilda's because: A, he's a suspect in Hilda's and possibly Wayne Johnston's deaths; B, he's missing; and C, judging by the late-night calls to her estate attorney, his late wife may have revised her trust so that Marcus was cut off at the knees. You must know that the Colbert marriage was pretty rocky when Hilda was murdered. Seems to *me* that Hilda may have been doing a bit of advance preparation for the impending divorce."

Annie hated it when Dan was right, which, since his poor performance in the courtroom, was becoming far more frequent.

"Well, be that as it may, the horses need to be looked after."

"Todos is doing a fine job."

"I mean, beyond their day-to-day needs. They need to be exercised."

"As you may recall, Todos is a former jockey. I'm sure he can take care of that."

"Allegedly a former jockey."

"No, really a former jockey. Do you think we just take people's words at face value, Annie? Todos is a card-carrying member of the Jockey Club of Mexico. He got rave reviews from owners who race their thoroughbreds in Mexico City. When Hilda hired him, she knew what she was doing. She hired the best in the business."

Annie silently fumed. It was infuriating to learn that Todos was the real deal. She'd wanted him so badly to be a fake.

"Oh, and he's got a permanent green card, too. What's wrong with your arm?" Dan asked.

Annie looked down, and realized she'd been furiously kneading her left wrist.

"Oh, nothing. I was cleaning Baby's hooves, and she decided we were done a tad before I could put her hoof down. I got swiped with the hoof pick."

Dan bent over the table and solicitously looked at the angry red mark on Annie's wrist.

"Be careful, Annie. You got nicked a few centimeters left of a major artery. I don't want to have to find you dead on your place from bleeding out."

"You know me, Dan. I'm too ornery to die."

* * *

When Annie got back to her car after running errands all afternoon, she realized she'd received a phone call from Dan a few minutes before. The sound of rain pounding on her truck roof must have drowned out the ring tone. She pulled into the parking lot to hear the message.

"Annie, I wanted you to know that Judy Evans is going to call Fenton to confirm Marcus's intention to give you the executive authority to divest Hilda's animals. It won't change a thing"—he seemed inordinately quick to caution her—"but if Fenton verifies this is what Marcus wanted, we've agreed to let you onto the ranch *under supervision*"—as Dan enunciated each syllable, Annie rolled her eyes—"so you can go through the office and make copies of anything you think you might need should you eventually get that role. Happy now?"

Annie quickly punched redial, but Dan apparently was off doing business in the service of justice. She left a message for him to call her. On the hour drive up the coast to the only feed store on the Peninsula that sold her horses' favorite stall treats, she'd remembered what she'd forgotten to ask Dan at lunch.

At five, she stepped in her farmhouse to find the two Belgian pups still by the woodstove but now encircled under Wolf's massive paws. It was an adorable sight. *If only humans could get along as well as canines,* she thought to herself, and, stripping herself of her soaked jacket, headed toward the kitchen. Lavender was chopping onions on the sideboard, singing completely off-tune, and completely oblivious to the rest of the world. *I could be an ax murderer,* Annie thought. But instead of angrily reminding her sister to lock the door when she was home alone, she thought of the pups nestled by Wolf, and instead, asked how her day was. She immediately regretted it.

"Sister! What an *amazing* day! I met the most wonderful people. One of them lives just right down the road. . . ."

Annie tuned her out to respond to the clang of her cell phone. It was Dan. She ducked out of the kitchen for her bedroom.

"What's up, Annie?"

"I got your message. How soon can I come out to Hilda's ranch?" Annie didn't know exactly why, but she felt the sooner she was able to put her own footprint down on Hilda's place, the better. It was a symbolic way of showing allegiance to Marcus.

"Fenton confirmed with Judy this afternoon, so tomorrow, if you'd like," was Dan's response. "We just got the search warrant to look for Marcus's body on-site. The county commissioners aren't too happy about having to pay overtime on a Saturday, but a week's up and the guy's still AWOL."

Tell me about it, Annie thought morosely. Then her brain clicked in. *Look for Marcus's body on-site? At Hilda's place?*

"It'll be a mudfest with all the rain," Dan continued, "but we'll just have to work with it."

"Are you serious? You think one of the workers *is* responsible?"

"Hard to say. But Hilda's ranch has enough places to hide a dozen bodies. We just want to make sure we don't overlook anything in our search. It's about all we can do on the county's side. Anyway, the place will be crawling with deputies, so it's an ideal time for you to come out and go through the office. We'll put one of our junior members at the door. I promise no one will look over your shoulder if you promise that you'll make copies of anything you want and leave the originals."

Annie fervently hoped that she wouldn't be present if Marcus's body was actually buried on Hilda's property, but she couldn't see any way of turning down Dan's rather generous offer.

"What time should I be there?"

"How about ten? That should give us enough time to get organized on our end."

"Thanks, Dan. And, by the way, I meant to ask you—what's happening with Wayne's death? It's the one I always seem to forget about."

"Well, believe me, I haven't, and enough angry relatives of the deceased are making sure I don't. What is clear to us now is that Wayne Johnston's and Hilda's murders are related."

"You mean the same person killed both of them?"

"No, I just mean they're related. Someone didn't want Wayne to deliver that horse you're caring for. And Hilda knew something about the horse that we still don't. Your belated delivery of the thoroughbred's papers pretty much sealed that deal. If Hilda hadn't been found with them, they might have been two unrelated events. Just where did you say you found them?"

Annie hadn't, but she realized that the time for dancing around the truth was over.

"Well . . . one part was in Hilda's hand and the other . . ."

"In Hilda's hand! You understand now how withholding that little piece of evidence held up our investigation?"

Annie did, indeed. And the only way she could make herself marginally feel better was to go out to the friends who never let her down and feed them dinner. Then she would dutifully go back to the kitchen and hear more about Lavender's fun-filled day. The latter was penance, pure and simple. But she deserved it.

Yet even the cloud that hung over Annie's head that day dispelled much of its grayness that evening. As she ladled the last of the mashes into the horse stalls, Jessica came roaring up in her vet van and burst through the door.

"Good news, Annie! It's not EHV! The bay's just allergic to practically everything in your pasture, paddock, and tack room, including straw bedding!"

Some people might have taken this as bad news. But Annie and Jessica squealed like they were teenage girls again, hugged each other, and whirled around the stable like two ecstatic dervishes.

The horses thought the two humans were nuts.

CHAPTER 14

SATURDAY, MARCH 5TH

With an ice pick in her hand, Annie was aware that she looked a tad menacing. She didn't care. She turned to the object in front of her, raised her arm, and swung down using her full strength. A satisfying *ker-runch* resounded throughout the room. Ah. Progress at last.

Turning, Annie saw her half sister in front of her, clutching a hairbrush—*my hairbrush,* she noted. It would make, she thought, a totally ineffectual weapon.

She hoisted the ice pick again.

"*Thwack!*"

Lavender jumped, her nightgown billowing around her, and emitted a small whimper.

Annie smiled.

"And, this, dear Sister, is how we defrost the freezer."

After two nights of vegetarian fare, Annie had decided it was time to reclaim her carnivorous roots. Quinoa and pinto beans were all very well in moderation. But if one more grain-based casserole appeared in front of her tonight, she figured she might as well bed down with the horses and share their oats and hay.

The freezer, she knew, contained long forgotten morsels of pork chops, hamburger, and even a steak or two. When you lived alone, it was easy to buy in bulk and freeze the rest. It was time to find out what nestled among the sharp shards of ice that lay within her retro refrigerator, manufactured long before automatic defrosting was the norm.

Poking around, Annie espied a long, fat item wrapped in aluminum foil. Sausages! Fat, yummy sausages, made from parts of animals she didn't want to know about but wouldn't stop her from eating them. She pulled out the rock-hard package and reverently placed it on the kitchen counter. Surely it would thaw by dinner. She could already taste the greasy juices.

Lavender stared in horror.

"What?" Annie asked, with no little irritation.

"My God, Sister! Now I understand why your home is filled with bad karma. How can you fill your refrigerator with the sacrificed flesh of our fellow creatures?"

"Easily, Lavender. One shrink-wrapped package at a time."

Annie had been up since before dawn and already put in almost a full day's work. At half past four, she'd tiptoed into the stables where the horses were still sleeping, made their mashes, and prodded them into the pasture a full two hours ahead of schedule. What grass remained in March was still encrusted with crisp frost, but it couldn't be helped. She needed the time to strip the stalls of straw and take out every offending morsel. Straw, she'd learned the previous evening, was one of the worst allergens the bay had inherited.

She'd dumped wheelbarrow after wheelbarrow far behind the stables in the area reserved for horse poop. Jessica had assured her that it would make dandy compost that would be ready in time for next year's spring garden planting.

"He's also allergic to fescue, velvet grass, bayberry, and pine," Jessica had cheerfully told Annie the night before. "And forget about beet pulp. Flaxseed is also a no-no. Did I mention that alder is borderline?"

Annie groaned. Most of the items the bay couldn't tolerate weren't indigenous to the Northwest. Sure, there was plenty of pine in these here woods, but it was mostly at a higher elevation. But alder? Volunteer alder was everywhere, and sprouted freely on the ten acres that the horses called their playground.

"What'll I do?" she'd wailed, after the first euphoria from realizing her horses didn't have a dreaded, potentially fatal disease had faded. "I can change the bedding. That's easy. But do I have to cut down every single alder on the damn place? You know they'll reappear just when I've put the chain saw away."

Jessica had assured Annie that the alder issue could be controlled with a homeopathic medicine, which she'd order today.

"It's primarily the straw, Annie. Just change the bedding to cedar chips, and Trooper will be back to normal in no time. *But no pine chips.* You're just asking for the same problem if you do."

So Annie had resolutely risen from her bed the following morning to perform the first half of the job. She could order cedar chips from the local Cenex en route to Hilda's ranch and have them delivered while she was gone. In the meantime, there was the small issue of nicely telling Lavender that meat had to appear on the family table at least five times a week.

Annie smiled sweetly at her sister. At least, she thought she did.

"Lavender, I know you've got your heart set on going into town today, but I need you here at home."

Lavender started to pout, an instant irritant to her older sister. Would the woman ever realize that wiles that had worked in her youth were now simply embarrassingly transparent?

"But, Sister, I have things to do. I promised Martha I'd help her."

Martha? Who was Martha? After forty-three years of living in the same community, Annie assumed she knew everyone in town, not to mention the outlying areas. But apparently Lavender already moved in circles outside her own. Annie was pretty sure those circles were outside her own comfort zone.

"Sorry, Lavender. But as a nonpaying member of this household for only twenty-one more days, you have to expect to pitch in a little." Annie tried not to sound as annoyed as she felt.

A single tear slid down Lavender's cheek.

Damn, she's good, Annie thought. She sighed. "Can't your new friend Martha come here?"

"No, she can't! And I wouldn't want her to! I wouldn't want *anyone* to come here until the house is cleansed!"

Annie glanced around her kitchen, dishes still piled high in the sink from last night's dinner. "Cleanse away, dear sister. I'm not stopping you."

"Not that kind of cleansing! I mean a spiritual cleansing. Smudging."

Annie stifled a giggle. "Smudging? I've heard of a lot of folk remedies for hard to remove spots, but I never knew that *smudging* got rid of red wine stains."

"Oh, you think you're so smart!" Lavender flounced over

to the woodstove and knelt by the Belgian pups, who had claimed this spot when they weren't tearing up the house. The Belgians eagerly began to lick Lavender's hands. She looked up, and to Annie's surprise, saw something like real anger flash in her sister's eyes.

"You create a place for all these wonderful creatures yet bring in dead animals for us to eat. You're going against the laws of the natural universe. It's put your whole karmic cycle out of whack. No wonder you're finding dead bodies and everyone you associate with disappears. And until I can go out"—here, Lavender gave a half sob and gulped—"and find the sage I need to yes, *smudge,* your home, the negative cycle will never end."

Oh, *that* smudging. A faint memory filtered through Annie's brain. She'd read about this ceremony before. And Lavender undoubtedly had read about it in *Northwest Native American Spiritualism for Dummies*. Honestly, if her sister didn't sound so ridiculous, she could have been upset. She glanced at her watch: 9:30. It was time to go.

"Ah, Lavender? Can you use anything besides sage?"

After a few seconds, the muffled reply came. "Well, cedar is used a lot, too."

"Well, you're in luck. Cedar trees abound throughout my property. You can walk outside and gather as much as you want within twenty feet. But, Lavender, listen to me. I really do need you home today."

Lavender merely sniffed. *Oh, hell's bells.* Annie decided to give her sister a subtle lesson into how big girls got their way.

"Frankly, Lavender, I don't know what I'd do without you right now. I'm expecting a big load from Cenex. They're delivering bedding supplies that are *critical* to the horses' health. I need someone to be here to sign for them and make sure the workers put them in the right place."

She had Lavender's attention. She could sense it.

"Here I have to go out on business, yet it's vitally important that I get this new bedding for the horses by tonight. Why, if you weren't here, I'd be lost."

Lavender's face immediately changed. She stood up and wiped her hands on her nightgown, which now showed, Annie noticed, significant evidence of puppy drool.

"Why, of course, Sister. You just tell me what to do."

Like taking candy from a baby, Annie thought. *She simply wants to feel needed.*

"Just tell the men to stack the bags of cedar chips by the Timothy in the tack room, Lavender. And make sure they do it right, so one won't come tumbling down on our heads when we least expect it. I'll call Cenex and tell them to put your name on the account so you can sign for them."

Her half sister was actually preening, Annie realized. And putting her name on the account surely wouldn't do any harm. She couldn't imagine Lavender going crazy buying up what Cenex had to offer.

"Oh, and I won't have time to shop before coming home. So we'll have the meat that's thawing tonight."

"Meat, Sister? I told you I was a vegetarian."

"Well, I'm not. But you can give a shamanic blessing over it before we tuck in."

Turning into the lane that took her to Hilda's ranch, Annie could hear the activity before she saw it. A long, low grumble of machinery permeated the air around her. In her mind, she imagined ancient dinosaurs rising from the earth and voicing their displeasure at what they'd found upon reentry.

What she saw as she approached the electronic gate bore more than a small resemblance to the creatures that had emanated from the primordial ooze. The pelting rain that obscured her windshield made her fantasy more plausible. In the distance, she saw the outlines of a Kubota backhoe, carefully swinging a load of dirt high into the air, then angling it off to the side and unceremoniously dumping it onto a mound already the height of a draft horse. Twenty feet to the south, a bulldozer stolidly made its way through the underbrush, clearing the way for further excavation. Surrounding these machines were a dozen hot, sweaty deputies, covered in rain gear already flecked with mud and grime. Most of them held shovels in their hands. More than a few were leaning on them, clearly exhausted.

She hadn't realized she'd been idling the truck for so long until a sharp *tap-tap* on her window brought her back to reality.

"Excuse me? Ms. Carson? Is that you?"

It was the same young deputy who'd helped her and Marcus out of the jail last week, a short passage of time that now seemed a lifetime ago.

Annie rolled down her window and smiled. "Deputy Lindquist. How nice to see you again. Couldn't you find a job that kept you out of the rain?"

Deputy Lindquist's face took on a very serious look, or, at least, as serious a look as a twenty-year-old rookie could manage under the circumstances. He was drenched. With his clothes sticking to him, he looked as if he weighed ninety-five pounds.

"No, ma'am. Well, actually, yes, ma'am. I've been assigned to watch you. Well, not watch you, exactly. To *accompany* you to Mrs. Colbert's office, I mean."

Deputy Lindquist's face turned a bright red as he spoke, and Annie wondered if he'd been given the task because someone had found out about his mission of mercy at the jail. Well, if so, at least he'd have a chance to warm up. Annie intended to keep the thermostat as high as it could go in the tack room office.

"Fabulous. Want to hop in?" Annie started to move the

assorted magazines, coffee cups, and other debris from her front passenger seat.

Deputy Lindquist looked shocked.

"Oh, no, ma'am. Let me first get you to sign in here, then I'll open the gate. Wait for me to get in my vehicle, and I'll escort you in. I've been told to tell you to park right next to me and to lock your vehicle and give me your keys while you're working inside."

He thrust a clipboard inside the window, and Annie complied, fuming at all the unnecessary regulations. Jeez. Just because she was a tad late in handing over a couple of little pieces of paper. But there was no sense in taking it out on this poor guy, who was just trying to do his job.

"Here you go, Deputy." Annie spoke with an enthusiasm she didn't feel. She had the feeling this was going to be a very tedious morning.

Annie didn't anticipate the acute sadness she felt upon entering the office. She quietly took off her coat and sat down in the chair where she'd last seen Marcus. It seemed so unfair, she thought, as she pulled the first stack of papers on the desk in toward her. The man who should have been attending to this business now could be buried within eyesight of her. She quickly got up and pulled down the blinds.

"Would you like some coffee, Ms. Carson? Sheriff Stetson said to make sure you were comfortable."

Annie felt marginally better at Dan's thoughtfulness. "I'd love some, Deputy. I don't suppose Dan remembered to bring any doughnuts?"

"I believe he did, ma'am. I believe he did."

"Then I'd like two, please. Three, if they have chocolate on them."

Two hours later, Annie's head hurt. After locking the

doors to the office, Deputy Lindquist had unobtrusively sit-
uated himself in a corner and was now reading a law-
enforcement manual. *Probably studying up to become the
sheriff when Dan retires,* Annie thought. He was so quiet
that Annie forgot he was even there most of the time.

No one else had popped in, either. Apparently the work
outside was so all-consuming that no one cared what Annie
was finding, or attempting to find, in Hilda's office. Annie
was grateful that Marcus had at least been able to spend a
few hours here. The mounds of paper that had littered the
desk when they had first walked in were neatly organized in
piles. She'd initially thought this would make her job of re-
searching Hilda's stable fairly straightforward.

But it hadn't been that easy. Annie considered herself a
highly competent, knowledgeable horsewoman. But apparently her skills and training only went as far as the needs of
her own environment on the Olympic Peninsula. Sure, she
knew how to gentle horses, get them under saddle, and become willing, agreeable companions for their owners. She
even knew how to rope and barrel race, thanks to ten years
in the local 4-H while growing up.

But the equestrian world that Hilda lived in was another
country to Annie. She'd found the files on all eighteen
horses that were stabled here, and learned, to her surprise,
that Hilda owned five other horses who were boarded elsewhere and had been on the cusp of bidding on an "in utero"
breed when she died.

Good Lord, Annie thought. *How many horses can one
woman ride at once?* It had become clear that Hilda was
heavily into eventing competitions and participated in every
category: dressage, cross-country, and show jumping. That
explained, in part, the significant number of horses she kept
at the ready. After all, horses who excelled in dressage and
also happened to be champion jumpers were rare. But the

sheer cost of housing, training, and transporting all these animals staggered Annie's imagination. Which made Hilda's
reticence to pay her vendors on time either completely understandable or completely nuts, depending on the health of
her bank account.

Glancing up at Deputy Lindquist, who still seemed glued
to his manual, Annie spent a furtive ten minutes looking for
Hilda's financial records in the desk drawers. She came up
with zip. Either Marcus had transferred them to the briefcase
found in his car or, more likely, they'd been tagged by the
Sheriff's Office as soon as Judge Casper signed a search warrant for the premises. Either way, Annie thought, they now
were part of the inventory accumulating in Hilda's murder
case.

Still, what remained made fascinating reading. It was a
glimpse into Hilda's life that Annie had never known about
and probably never would have if Hilda hadn't, as old-
timers liked to say, "bought the farm." Annie wasn't sure she'd
ever want to share in that life. But it didn't stop her from eagerly poring through Hilda's files. After all, she'd been given
the job of determining where these beautiful, finely tuned
equine athletes would go from here. She needed to know all
she could about Hilda's "children."

She was so engrossed in the file on "Knight in Armor," a
17.2-hand Danish Warmblood with "big bold gaits and
tremendous suspension" that she didn't even hear the soft
knock on the inside door. Deputy Lindquist leapt to his feet,
sprinted to the other side of the room, and slipped outside,
closing the door behind him before Annie could barely register the fact that he was gone. She heard the remnants of a
low conversation, then the squawk of a radio. A few moments later, Deputy Lindquist stepped back inside the room.

"Ms. Carson? Adolpho Todos is here and wondered if he
could be of any assistance."

Annie rolled her eyes, then nodded at the deputy.

"Might as well. He's got to know what's going on, sooner or later."

Deputy Lindquist let Todos in, who, to her astonishment, removed his cowboy hat and approached Hilda's desk with a small smile.

"Señora Carlson, it is nice of you to come out and help us today."

What the hell? Had Todos had a frontal lobotomy? He couldn't even remember her name. Still, he was being way too polite. She understood his obsequious behavior around Marcus, but to have it extend to her? Well, at least it was easier to talk to someone who didn't put on the silent, stoic cowhand act all the time.

"My pleasure. Why don't you sit down? How's the search going?" Annie wasn't sure she wanted to know, but felt she had to ask.

Todos pulled up a chair and carefully sat down.

"I am having enough trouble keeping the horses calm. All this noise does not make for good digestion. If one of them colics, well, it will not be my fault."

Annie understood. Horses could colic, she often told new horse owners, if the moon was misaligned or you looked at them the wrong way. But the truth was that an equine's small intestine ran as long as seventy feet, and it didn't take much of a minor disturbance to upset its ability to function as required. All the strange activity and noise on the ranch today could easily provoke a colic attack in a sensitive horse.

"But I don't think they have found anything," Todos continued. "Unless you count an old tractor, buried far, far below the ground."

"Well, that's good news." Annie's relief was palpable.

Todos looked up at her quizzically.

"Perhaps."

"*Perhaps?* Don't you *want* Señor Colbert to be found alive?"

"If he is responsible for Señora Colbert's death, then finding him buried would be a blessing."

"We like to think our justice system is capable of dealing with murderers in a more civilized way, Mr. Todos." The voice came from the back of the room. To her surprise, Deputy Lindquist's voice had taken on a distinctly law enforcement tone. *Well, bully for him.*

Todos turned and gave the deputy an obsequious smile. "As you say."

Annie decided it was time to start the conversation over.

"Señor Todos, you've worked here long enough to know these horses quite well."

Todos permitted himself a modest smile of assent.

"How many of them arrived after you came on board?"

"A few."

"A few. Well, do you know if any of *the few* could possibly be sold back to the original owners?"

Todos looked at her as if she were a small child who had asked an idiotic question.

"Is not possible, Señora."

"Why is that?"

"Because the bills of sales are final. Once the horses leave the property, they no longer have the consideration of those who once owned them."

"Where did Hilda acquire her lists of prospective buyers?"

"Everywhere. If you are in the business, you know." Todos smiled at Annie. She felt his condescension practically dripping off his face.

"Well, you may know that Señor Colbert had asked me to find new homes for Hilda's stable," she said stiffly. "If you have any ideas of prospective buyers, I would like to hear about them."

"I will do so," Todos said. He shifted in his chair. "And how is the bay? Would you not like to return him to his home? We can easily accommodate him here. You must admit, Señora Carlson, that his living quarters would be much improved."

She was so angry that she didn't stop to think.

"I think not. Señor Colbert specifically hired me to take care of Trooper, and until he tells me not to, that's exactly what I'm going to do."

"Trooper? You know the horse's name?"

Annie froze. Would Todos know that she had confessed about taking the papers from Hilda's dead hands? No, there was no way Dan or Tony would have shared that bit of information outside the office.

"I read it in his file."

"Aha. I think for a minute that you have seen his papers. Did you know we are missing his papers, Señora Carlson?"

Annie felt a cold sweat rise up underneath her farm shirt.

"Really? Well, I'm sure Sheriff Stetson will be able to find them."

"And who will ride him? Are you exercising him, Señora Carlson? He needs to be ridden on a regular basis, you know, or he will not be so valuable when it comes time to sell him." Todos looked genuinely concerned for the horse's physical regime.

Annie bit her lip. Todos was right. Trooper did need regular exercise. She vowed she would start riding him, immediately. But she also vowed she would *not* tell Todos that Marcus had deeded Trooper to her.

"The bay is doing fine. But thanks for expressing your concern." She could not have sounded icier if she'd been Hilda's twin sister.

Todos got up from his chair and went to the door.

"Please let me know if I can be of assistance in any way, Señora Carlson." Todos again sounded excruciatingly polite. "Perhaps it would be easier for you if I take on the task of selling the horses. I have done so, many times. You need only ask."

It was all she could do not to hurl the Remington statue paperweight on Hilda's desk after him. If Deputy Lindquist hadn't been in the process of relocking the door, she just might have.

Annie stared at the stacks of paper in front of her, but the files on Hilda's exquisite herd no longer interested her. Now that she'd been unmasked as a complete ignoramus when it came to the "business" of horses, horses that had been entrusted to her care, she felt like hiding underneath the table rather than continuing her education. But she owed it to Marcus, who foolishly thought she'd been up to the task of making sure the horses went to good homes. She couldn't stop now. Her pride was at stake. What was left of it, anyway.

She stood up, stretched her back, and walked over to the credenza in the back of the room. Deputy Lindquist was once again hunched over his reading material. She squatted, opened the first drawer in front of her, and resolutely got to work.

An hour later, Deputy Lindquist informed her that her time was up. She docilely followed him out of Hilda's office, meekly accepted the keys to her truck he handed her, and drove slowly off the property. She regretted not taking the time to find Dan to have him confirm that no news was good news, but there were more important things to do now.

She eased down the highway, driving a steady fifty miles an hour, until she reached the bend in the road that signified the hind end of the Thompsons' farm, where her sheep were temporarily pastured. The Thompsons raised root crops, all of which had long been harvested, but the rich soil and re-

maining nutrients were exactly what her small flock needed
before lambing season. Johan Thompson appreciated having
his land "rototilled" before spring; Annie was delighted that
her own sheep pasture had the winter months to green up
and be ready for the burgeoning brood that would be born
just a few weeks hence. She parked her truck on the side of
the road and sat for a few minutes, her eyes straining to see
the flock that somewhere was feeding on the tail ends of
turnips, beets, and rutabagas. Failing to see a fluffy tail in
sight, she dug underneath her seat until she unearthed a pair
of binoculars. It took a few minutes, but she eventually espied the not-so-pristine white coats of the Rambouillets.
They were clustered together, heads intent on cropping nutrients from the ground, and looked healthy and content. None
of them were bending at the knees yet—a sure sign that
birthing was imminent.

But she realized it was getting to the time to start preparing for their reentry onto her farm, not to mention readying
and mending the birthing pens. And that was only one of
many tasks ahead. Shearing still had to take place, and after
that, skirting the fleece—the process of removing dung tags
left near the tail and other extraneous matter by hand.

She sighed, replaced the binoculars in their case, and calculated in her head how much board she'd need to buy from
Cenex. And what wiles it would take to get Lavender to
help. That is, if Lavender's month wasn't up by the time the
lambs were born.

Now that she was assured of her sheep's good health,
Annie pulled out the manila file she'd stuffed inside her own
sheep-lined coat. She gave an unnecessary furtive look around
her to make sure she was alone. Lavender had developed an
irritating habit of frequently and thoughtlessly rummaging
through Annie's clothes and bathroom supplies to find whatever she needed. It reinforced Annie's resolve that no other
human's presence would interfere with her ability now to

fully savor what she'd found in the last drawer of the credenza, underneath a stack of old horse magazines. She'd only had time to scan the correspondence that lay within, but it was enough to tell her that she was on to something.

She sped read what she'd found and she'd been right. The letter exchange inside the folder was a gold mine, and had to be a significant clue into Hilda's death. The exchange began back in 2010, when Travis Latham, a well-to-do investment banker in the county, had made what he considered a successful bid on the property Hilda had ended up buying. According to Latham, the offer had been accepted and he'd already secured financing for the balance of the selling price. A week later, Hilda countered at double the price. The owners, naturally, had accepted her offer. Latham's real-estate agent had raised quite a ruckus—in fact, half the letters to Hilda came from the agency, the other half from Latham—but the owners and Hilda had stood firm. The owners, apparently, had never signed on the dotted line, or if they had, no one was able to establish that they did. In every letter, Latham threatened to sue. Hilda's lawyers, all out-of-state, Annie noticed, threatened to countersue. But what Annie found most interesting was the last letter in the file, in which Latham threatened unspecified ways to do damage to Hilda if she didn't withdraw her bid immediately:

"If you continue to ignore the real-estate laws that exist in the state of Washington, I will destroy you," read Latham's letter. "Your business will be dead before it starts. I will see to it that no horse makes its way onto your property. Consider yourself properly warned."

Annie read the letter three times. Something was stirring inside her brain. What was it? What seemed so familiar? She strained but couldn't make a connection. Giving up, she turned the key in the truck's ignition and headed for home.

It was only when she'd consumed her second sausage that evening, under the distinctly disapproving eyes of Lavender, that it suddenly made sense. Latham had used much of the same language that Marcus had used in his last voice message to Hilda.

But was this good news? Latham might have followed through on his threat and been responsible for Hilda's death. But the similarity between his letter and the words on the digital voice message were too close for comfort. Had Marcus known Latham? Had they worked together, and Latham had then killed Marcus because he knew too much?

It was too much for Annie's brain to take in. She mentally added another question to the ones she wished she could ask Marcus. Then she reached for another sausage.

CHAPTER 15

SUNDAY, MARCH 6TH

Gazing at the pelting rain in her pasture, Annie wondered how Judith Clare possibly survived these kinds of days. With five children under the age of ten, Judith must use every ounce of ingenuity to keep her family entertained inside without losing her cool. Annie wasn't doing as well. All she had were two puppies, one dog, one kitten, a half-witted half sister, and she was ready to go ballistic.

"Stop harassing the puppies!"

Lavender looked up, bewildered. "I'm only playing with them, Sister. They need attention from humans, you know."

"Well, one has just vomited all over the floor, in case you

hadn't noticed. Try not to get them so excited. Puppy chow isn't cheap."

Lavender turned back to her charges with a childish pout. Wolf, Annie noticed, was hiding in the corner, looking, as only a dog can, thoroughly disgusted. Max, the kitten, was conspicuously absent. Annie knew he would emerge if, and only if, the house subsided into relative calm.

Midmorning, Annie had finally announced she would be in her room, where she intended to work undisturbed. It was a lie. The only work she possibly could have done in her bedroom was to clean up the clothes strewn on the floor from the past week and take a well-oiled cloth to her dusty bureau and bedstand. Both were admirable rainy-day activities, but Annie was not the least bit interested. Instead, she read through the Latham/Colbert correspondence for the fifth time. She'd practically memorized the letters, which was a good thing, because she realized she shouldn't have them in the first place.

In the middle of the night, she'd awakened with the sinking feeling that once again, she had screwed up. Dan's words came floating through her brain: "I promise no one will look over your shoulder if you promise that you'll make copies of anything you want and leave the originals."

Well, Deputy Lindquist had certainly fulfilled his end of the bargain. She, on the other hand, had furtively—and stupidly—simply pocketed the file and left with it. *But it wasn't my fault,* the evil-twin side of her brain insisted. *I was getting the bum's rush to leave. Nonsense,* the rational, mature side of her brain responded. *All you had to do was ask for two more minutes to make copies. Get real.*

Annie sighed. Good Angel's logic notwithstanding, she'd be hanged if she was going to 'fess up to Dan Stetson. She would simply have to find a way to undo the damage.

Reaching for the phone, she resolutely punched in Dan's cell phone number. She was prepared to be totally obsequious in order to gain access again to Hilda's ranch. She imagined Dan there now, covered in mud and soaked to the bone, barking out orders to deputies who probably looked like tin hats building trenches in preparation for the Battle of the Somme.

Instead, she heard the distant roar of a sports game and an announcer's excited pronouncements after Dan picked up the phone.

"What's up, Annie?" Dan sounded surprisingly peaceful.

"Some weather we're having, huh?" Annie regretted using such a trite opening, but having caught Dan at home, she wasn't sure how to begin.

"Yup. Makes me glad the county decided not to pay for more overtime. Supposed to let up by Monday. But I hear on the news that the Big Squill River is rising and might flood the folks down near Garver's Corner before end of day. In which case, I'll be pulling on my boots and hauling sandbags with the rest of them. But you didn't call me to ask about the weather, did you, Annie?

"No."

"To answer your question, we haven't found a body on Hilda's ranch. But we're not done looking."

"How much longer do you think it'll take to search?" Annie could hear the tension in her voice. She hoped Dan didn't.

"One more good day. I still maintain it's a long shot, but it had to be done. We're trying to level the areas we've dug, but we can only do so much on our meager budget. Too bad Hilda isn't still around. We've already dug the foundation for that tennis court she probably wanted."

Annie laughed. "Why, Dan Stetson! I believe you're getting back your sense of humor."

"Here I sit, feet up in my easy chair watching the game, a bowl of chips in one hand and a beer in the other. You know what Dory would say if she could see me now?"

"I can only imagine."

"I'm happy as a pig in a poke. This bachelor life is growing on me. If I could just train the dog to do the dishes."

"That's why God made dishwashers, Dan."

"Yeah. I'm going to have to figure out how to use it one of these days."

Annie fleetingly felt a small pang of sympathy for Dory Stetson even while acknowledging how badly she'd behaved exiting the marriage. Taking care of Dan could not have been easy. Or particularly fun over time, once the honeymoon was over.

"Uh, Dan? My work at the ranch isn't quite over yet, either. I didn't have time to make copies of the horses' files, which I'll need if I'm to find new owners for them."

"What's the hurry? It'll take months to settle Hilda's estate, and that won't even start until we get a copy of her revocable trust. Hell, the coroner only declared her officially dead last Thursday."

"I know, but eventually her estate will settle, and I need to be on top of the game."

In the background, Annie heard the doorbell ring.

"Hold on, Annie. Someone's at the door. If it's the Girl Scouts, I'm buying six boxes of the caramel kind. Hold on."

Annie waited patiently until Dan got back. She heard a ragged sigh as he again picked up the phone.

"Per usual, her timing is perfect."

"What are you talking about, Dan?"

"I've just been served. With divorce papers. Right in the middle of the Lakers game. If that don't beat all. She planned this."

He was going to cry, Annie thought. She'd heard the preemptive noises before.

"I'm so sorry, Dan. Do you want me to come over?"

"Nah, I'll be fine. And if you want to come out again on

Monday, be my guest. Just let me know what you're copying."

She heard a muffled sniff as he hung up.

Now Annie felt thoroughly guilty and frustrated. She'd misled Dan again, the second time in the past two weeks she'd ever acted anything less than honorably toward him. That was bad enough. But now she had to wait an entire day to rectify matters.

She glanced at the clothes on the bedroom floor that badly needed to be washed and the horse magazines on her bedstand that had yet to be read. She wavered for a moment; maybe housework would get rid of her funk. Suddenly, she was aware that the house was strangely silent. This could not be good.

She found the two Belgian pups once again ensconced under the kitchen woodstove and Wolf snoozing nearby. Lavender was at the counter, tunelessly humming as usual, both hands immersed in Annie's pot roaster. Surely she wasn't concocting yet another vegetarian casserole. Annie thought she'd made herself quite clear the previous day. No, the smell was too pungent. Lavender's casseroles, she'd noticed, erred on the side of healthful blandness.

"What's for lunch, Lavender? Tree bark?" Being a Bad Girl had put her in a bad mood.

"Very funny." Lavender's humming stopped.

"Sorry," Annie said, almost sounding as if she meant it. She walked over to the counter. "Smells like cedar."

"It *is* cedar."

"Oh." Something stirred in Annie's memory.

"Um, you're not going to spread that stuff around the house, are you, Lavender?"

Lavender turned to her and gave an exasperated sigh.

"Of *course* I am. It's part of the smudging ceremony."

"Great. I'll be following you with the fire extinguisher."

"I'm just *releasing* the smoke, for heaven's sake, not scattering burning needles. The only thing I'll be spreading in our home is cornmeal."

"Cornmeal? In *our* house?" Annie was so flabbergasted that she momentarily forgot to correct Lavender's presumptive remark. She glared at her half sister. "We *both* live here, as you well know. But the last time *I* looked, Anne Marie Carson was the only person on the property title."

"Oh, for heaven's sake, Sister. I didn't travel all across the country to watch your life disintegrate because unwanted spirits have taken up residence in your home. I am trying to get rid of all the negative energy. I'm trying to help you. Don't you get it?"

The only unwanted spirit who'd taken up residence that Annie could see was standing right in front of her. She silently counted backward from twenty, the days remaining when her half sister's lease ran out. Lavender serenely continued to bundle sprigs of cedar with twine she'd obviously found in Annie's all-purpose tool drawer.

For a brief moment, Annie envied her half sister's oblivious disconnect with reality. The moment passed. It was time to get Lavender in sync with the real world.

"Okay, Lavender. Here's the deal. You can smudge my house. But first you have to help me outside with the horses."

"Isn't that your job?"

"No, Lavender, it's *our* job," Annie replied. She didn't bother hiding her irritation. "Since you consider this *our* home, then all the animals that live at *our* home are your concern, too. Look outside. It's been pouring for the last three days. The pasture is a soggy mess. The horses have been standing in water for days now, and I'm concerned about their hooves. This is the perfect time for thrush."

"Thrush? I thought they didn't show up until the spring."

Annie burst out laughing, but abruptly stopped when she

saw Lavender's face crumple. "Sorry, Lavender, there's no reason you should know. Thrush is bacteria that grow on horses' frogs—not the kind you find on lily pads," she hastened to add. "Frog is what we call the triangular patch on the bottom of their hoof. It sort of acts as a shock absorber."

"So why do horses get this thrush?"

"Mud. Still water. Dirty stalls. I can clean the stalls, but there's not much I can do about the rain and the muck. That's why I need to check the horses' hooves and make sure no one's in trouble."

"But, Sister, I don't know anything about taking care of horses. Daddy always called the vet when Flicka was sick."

Flicka was the pony Annie never had.

"Well, there's a first time for everything. The horses should still be in their stalls munching hay, but put on boots and a slicker, anyway. One of them might decide to duck into the paddock before we have time to close the stall doors."

"I don't have a slicker. Or boots."

"Of course you don't. Well, grab what you can off the coatrack. Oh, and Lavender," Annie said, glancing at her sister's Birkenstocks, "don't forget to put on a pair of socks. I don't have a remedy for thrush that works on people."

As Annie anticipated, Lavender was more hindrance than help, and in truth, she hardly needed a second pair of hands. All of Annie's horses, including Trooper, showed no intention of venturing outside until the last blade of hay in their feeders was consumed, so confining the horses to their individual stalls, as Annie had expected, was a nonissue.

By the time Annie had examined Trotter and the bay, Lavender had succeeded in putting a string halter on Rover and had learned how to hold the halter rope so that she had control yet didn't apply undue pressure to the horse and thereby irritate him. Haltering the horses wasn't at all necessary; every horse, Baby included, knew to stand still and obediently comply when Annie asked for one of its hooves. But Annie decided it was high time that Lavender learned a few rudimentary skills when it came to equine care. How to halter and safely lead a horse was the first lesson in Horse Ed 101.

She was surprised at how reticent Lavender had first behaved around her large animals. Her half sister, Annie sourly reminded herself, had owned a pony for several years as a small child, yet she seemed totally intimidated by the horses she met today. Proud mother notwithstanding, Annie knew her horses were among the most gentle and forgiving animals in Western Washington. She'd trained them to trust any human being that Annie trusted to be around them, and to assume that any human's intent was good.

Old-timers referred to Annie's training as "sacking-out," an exercise in which owners whooshed plastic bags on a stick around horses' bodies until the animals learned that they had nothing to fear from the strange noise or movements. But Annie's training had gone much further than that. She could mount each horse from either side and dismount in every direction except over the horse's head. She could walk underneath and around them without the least fear of a sudden skittish movement or, worse, a kick. The John Deere tractors that occasionally drove through Annie's pasture drew no more interest from them than a flick of an ear. The only thing that aroused the horses' concern and could still set them into instant flight mode was the scent or sight of a predator. For that, Annie had her .30-.30 Winchester.

Lavender, Annie noticed, did not suffer from lack of pride about her meager accomplishments. Once she'd mastered haltering and leading, she relaxed considerably and began to stroke the horses while Annie worked, whispering to them what "darling little horses they were" until Annie secretly wanted to throw up. Lavender had about one-fifth the horse sense of eight-year-old Hannah, Annie thought, but give her another decade, and she might catch up.

Fortunately, all the horses' hooves showed no sign of thrush, but for good measure, Annie scrubbed each hoof with disinfectant and applied an iodine mix that would help thwart any unwanted germs. She was relieved that none of the horses required anything but maintenance care, because Lavender's incessant chatter would have made it difficult to concentrate on anything except the mundane task she'd set out to do.

It had started out innocently enough.

"So how do you like our Northwest weather, Lavender? Must be a big change from Florida."

"Florida! I couldn't wait to leave that place. Boca Raton is the absolute pits. Most of the people who live there look like they're ready to die, and the ones who are still breathing are absolute phonies."

Annie bit her tongue.

"I mean, no one, not even at my high school, had the slightest interest in anything except boys, cars, and waiting to tap into their trust funds. What's wrong, Sister?"

Annie was coughing violently.

"Nothing, Lavender. Must have got some hay up my nose."

"Anyway, I told Daddy that I was simply not going to come out, and that was that. Boy, did that cause a big stink."

Come out? Was Lavender a lesbian?

"Ah, what do you mean, 'come out'? Come out of where?"

"Come out as a deb, silly."

Annie stared at her, clueless.

"A deb-u-tante, Sister." Lavender looked at Annie as if she were the village idiot. "It's the big deal at our school. The senior prom is just practice. The real event is the coming-out ball. The closest is the one in St. Petersburg. It's held in December. Daddy said he didn't spend six years sending me to cotillion not to see me come out."

"Wow. What did you learn in cotillion?"

"Oh, just a lot of outdated dances. You know, how to waltz, foxtrot, tango. We even learned a totally antique dance called the Lindy. At least that was kind of fun."

"Well, it actually sounds like a pretty useless waste of time."

"Believe me, it was. And then I had to spend two whole summers during high school at finishing and charm schools to prepare for the great event."

The only thing Annie had finished during her high-school summers off was putting maraschino cherries on DQ banana splits.

"It wasn't all bad. I did learn how to drink Jell-O shots and not throw up. That was after class, of course. And our cotillion society had to do volunteer work at a local non-profit. It was part of our credo. Naturally, all the sisters decided to volunteer at the local art museum. The art museum, for God's sake! Where all you see are your friends and neighbors, anyway. I mean, we could have been feeding the homeless or walking dogs in shelters."

Annie's respect for her half sister went up one barely discernible notch.

"So why didn't you want to go through it? It sounds like the rite of passage in Boca Raton."

"Well, as it turns out, I couldn't have come out if I wanted to. When Daddy put his foot down, I went and talked to Mummy about it. And what she told me made it like so clear there was no way I'd be invited to *any* debutante ball in my lifetime."

Annie had forgotten about Lavender's mother—her father's secretary, who'd broken up Annie's own parents' marriage. She couldn't even remember what the woman had looked like. She'd been either too young or too traumatized to register such things. What she mostly remembered was her own mother, crying late into the night. Well, that was hardly Lavender's fault.

"How is your mom, anyway?"

"Fine. I guess. She and Daddy divorced when I was four, you know."

"I'd forgotten about that."

"All they did was fight, anyway. I was really young, but it was obvious that my parents hated each other."

That, Annie mused, was a comforting thought.

"Mummy remarried pretty soon afterward. She and Don moved to Gainesville. Don's a big corporate lawyer up there."

"So what was the big secret? Why were you all of a sudden not debutante material?"

"Because Mummy was pregnant with me when she married Daddy. And even back then, that was a big no-no."

Annie let go of Rover's hoof with a tad less care than normal, then instantly rubbed his pastern as if to say, "I'm sorry."

She'd had no idea that Lavender's mother was pregnant before they wed. True, it made her father's rapid flight from his marriage to her mother more understandable, if not respectable. But still.

"So what did you do?"

"I went back to Boca and told Daddy. He tried to talk the debutante advisory board into letting me in, but it didn't work. Then I got arrested for shoplifting, and that put the end to that."

Lavender said this lightly, as if she were describing her recent shopping exploits at the Gap.

"I guess so." Annie scooped up her tack box and gave Rover a treat from her pocket. "Okay, on to Baby. You can untie him now."

Lavender obediently unloosed the halter and followed Annie into the next stall.

"Anyway, Daddy wanted me to go to a school in Switzerland, where no one would know the big bad secret of my birth, so that's where I headed next."

"Well, at least you got to learn French."

"Yeah. Kind of. Only, everyone made fun of my accent. I think the Swiss were snootier than the girls back home."

"Halter, please."

Annie waited patiently while Lavender figured out which way was up. Baby wasn't going anyplace with fresh Timothy in front of her.

"So what happened after Switzerland?"

"I came home, but everything had changed. Daddy had always had a lot of girlfriends, but now, I guess because I was so grown-up, I was cramping his style. I don't think he knew what to do with me."

He and I both, thought Annie.

"I think I'd become an embarrassment to him. And it wasn't even my fault! I mean, I didn't *ask* to be born."

Oh, for God's sake, thought Annie. *I thought kids stopped saying that in junior high.* Only, in Lavender's case, her complaint actually made a modicum of sense.

"So I moved out and tried to get a job . . . but my temperament really doesn't fit into the nine-to-five scene. That's what my therapist said, and she was right. Daddy didn't mind supporting me. I think it was easier for him to write a check than have me move back home."

"How about your mom? Couldn't you have stayed with her?"

"Mummy might have said okay, but Don wouldn't let her. He said they already had two teenagers, and he didn't want to take care of a third."

That must have hurt, Annie thought. She remembered what it was like being pushed aside in favor of a new sibling. It amused her that Lavender and she actually had one thing in common.

"So I just started hanging out in Boca. I got into the Goth thing for a while, but it got old wearing black all the time and really, that era like really was done. So I started to get tattoos but when Daddy found out he made me go in and have them all taken off. *That* hurt more than getting them in the first place. Then, last summer, I hitchhiked with a friend to Sedona and got in touch with my spiritual side. It was a turning point in my life. That's when I knew I'd found my true calling."

Here we go again, Annie thought.

Fortunately, at that moment, a reprieve arrived in the form of an eight-year-old child who, despite the torrent of rain outside, had not forgotten that this was her day to ride.

"Hannah!" Annie had never been so happy to see the child.

"Annie! Mom says we can take the puppy home today! If that's okay with you, that is."

"That's fine, Hannah. He's ready to go to his new home. Hannah, meet my half sister, Lavender. Lavender, meet Hannah."

Hannah looked at Lavender with a mixture of awe and incredulity.

"Is that your real hair?"

Annie didn't know who was happier: Lavender, who got to escape to the farmhouse and prepare for her smudging ceremony, or Hannah, who got to help Annie examine Trooper's hooves and anoint them with medicine. Trooper, Annie was relieved to see, was doing much better. His eyes were clear, and only a few residual water lines from his tear ducts remained on his handsome face.

And if it was raining buckets outside, Hannah didn't seem to notice. Annie decided to turn today's lesson into a "walking through puddles day." It was clear that Hannah would much rather let Sam hop over the puddles. She gave a squeal of delight every time he did so, but Annie insisted that she make the pinto calmly and deliberately walk through the water instead.

"It won't hurt him, Hannah," she reminded her. "Remember, horses used to swim across rivers to bring pioneers out west. This is just a baby lake."

When Hannah successfully persuaded Sam to walk through five puddles without pause, Annie agreed to let the child trot Sam around the round pen. Annie hooked Sam's halter to the lunge line again, just in case the horse decided to break into a canter, but it was a safeguard that proved unneeded. Hannah had absorbed all she'd learned from the first time on Sam's back and easily found her seat as Sam quickly paced around the pen. They practiced going from a walk to a trot and back to a walk again with hardly a hitch.

"I know exactly when he's going to trot, Annie! I can hear his heart begin to beat!"

Annie couldn't have been prouder.

After scraping the water off Sam and layering him with Annie's one fleece cooler, the two walked back to the farmhouse for hot cocoa. They found Lavender in the living room, adorned in a flowing caftan, about to light a sheaf of cedar branches with a match. A trail of cornmeal already lined the four corners of the room. *If the house didn't have any mice,* Annie thought morosely, *it would tonight.* She hoped Max would emerge in time for the feast.

"What's she doing?" whispered Hannah, holding on to Annie's hand.

Lavender turned and beamed. "You're just in time, Sister! I didn't want to start the ceremony without you. Come over here so I can smudge you."

Annie rolled her eyes, then bent down to talk to Hannah at her height.

"Why don't you go into the kitchen and play with your puppy? I'll be there in just a minute."

Hannah solemnly nodded and fled the room. Annie suspected the child thought her half sister was as loony as she did.

She reluctantly walked up to Lavender, who fumbled with the matches until the sharp smell of smoldering cedar filled the room. Gazing deeply into Annie's eyes, Lavender raised the branch and began to fan the cedar around Annie's face.

"Stop coughing! I'm trying to smudge you."

"I can't help it! I feel as if I'm in a burning house!"

Throwing her a dirty look, Lavender raised the cedar above her head and began to recite: "We welcome the energy of the rising sun at the beginning of the day and the light of illumination. Welcome Eagle, flying nearest the heavens, with the clearest of vision. I welcome the energies and spirits of the East. HO!"

Out of the corner of her eye, Annie could see Hannah peering around the kitchen door.

"Are we done yet?"

"No. That was the prayer to the East. There are three more."

"You're facing west. I have to go. You're on your own."

An hour later, Annie and Hannah tiptoed out of the house with Barkus, the name the Clares had chosen for their new puppy, in his new dog carrier. By now, Lavender had migrated to Annie's bedroom, where they could hear her chanting in a high-pitched voice that Annie only could hope appealed to the Native spirit world.

Annie had insisted upon tiptoeing, and not just to avoid further contact with Lavender. They'd left the remaining pup asleep, wrapped around Wolf's front paws, and Annie wanted to make the separation of the canine siblings as easy as possible.

"Ummm! Your house smells good, Annie! Just like Christmas!" said Hannah.

"Right. It's been Christmas every day ever since Lavender arrived."

Hannah gave Annie a quizzical glance.

"That's a joke, Hannah. A bad one. Actually, the house does smell good, doesn't it?"

The reception of Barkus at the Clare household was predictably joyful, chaotic, and enthusiastic. Annie observed the Clares' two cats slink away in disgust, but she had no doubt they would return in good time, ready to teach the new kid on the block how to show proper respect to his superiors. Annie delayed her departure as long as she could, hoping to avoid seeing the rest of Lavender's work-in-progress. The last thing she shouted to the Clares, as she drove off in the now gloaming darkness, was "Remember! Barkus likes to eat MEAT!"

CHAPTER 16

MONDAY, MARCH 7TH

"Well, if that don't beat all."

Dan absentmindedly scratched his receding hairline and handed the manila folder back to Annie.

"Don't know how we missed this in the search," he went on. "It's important evidence, Annie, and I appreciative your bringing it to our attention so promptly."

Annie gave Dan a halfhearted smile. She still felt immensely guilty over the way she'd covered her second sleight of hand with Hilda's murder case file. At 8:00 A.M. on Monday, she'd arrived at the ranch and, after a few words with Dan, had slipped into Hilda's office, this time alone.

"I can't spare a single deputy to babysit you, Annie," the sheriff told her. "Deputy Lindquist is en route to the King County jail as we speak. Couple of miscreants got into a brawl at the Roadside last night. Someone called nine-one-one, and wouldn't you know, when Lindquist came calling, he found out they both had outstanding warrants on the mainland. I figured since he'd made the collar, he deserved the pleasure of bringing them in."

The rest of the "excavating crew," as Dan called them, were busy cranking up the machines that had been left out in the rain since Saturday.

"So you're working on your own recognizance," Dan told her sternly. "Don't take this personally, but don't let me down."

Annie nodded meekly and sent up a silent prayer of thanks to the unnamed brawlers, whose perfect timing had put them in the pokey but placed her in the position to remedy her own crime.

At least the downpour had finally ceased. The bone-chilling dampness that had permeated Annie's skin the past three days was gone, along with most of the overcast sky. The sun was starting to play around the edges of the clouds, and although the temperature wasn't much above forty, Annie felt that the weather was positively balmy compared to the last few days' onslaught. That, and being able to hand over the original Latham/Colbert correspondence to Dan made her feel fairly buoyant.

On the other hand, Dan looked tired beyond his years. Annie badly wanted to ask him what Dory was asking for in the divorce papers, but she knew it was none of her business. Instead, she asked him what he intended to do about the papers she'd uncovered, and that had presumably been left in situ over the weekend.

"Talk to Latham, of course," was his predictable answer. "Although this fellow Juan is still a viable suspect. We've tracked down the four other workers who skedaddled after Hilda's murder. But they've all just taken up working at neighboring farms. They said they didn't like the vibes around this place, and I can't say I blame them. But Juan seems to have vanished into thin air."

Annie had carefully prepared for this conversation. She'd hurriedly replaced the Latham/Colbert correspondence in its original drawer, then tossed the horse files on Hilda's desk and began to methodically make the copies she'd told Dan she needed. It had taken her the better part of the morning, and she'd cursed the scourge of technology more than once whenever Hilda's copier machine jammed, ran out of paper, and once, God forbid, required a new toner cartridge. Fortunately, she'd found a new one in the credenza, and aside from ruining her sweatshirt with black ink smears that she was certain would never come out, she'd managed to complete the job before he'd come in to check her progress. Besides, finding the toner in the credenza gave her the viable excuse for "uncovering" the Latham/Colbert correspondence.

The tedious task of photocopying Jockey Club records, pedigree histories, and various other documents had given Annie plenty of time to think. And the more she thought about Latham's not-so-veiled threats, the more likely it seemed that he was responsible for Hilda's death—and Wayne Johnston's, as well. Hadn't Latham said that he would make sure no horse made it onto Hilda's property? Well, by derailing Wayne's trailer, that's exactly what he might have attempted to do—although why wait until now, when eighteen horses already were on the ranch? The curious part was the similarity in Latham's writing style with the threatening voice mail. Dan might not make the connection now, but eventually he, or some other sharp deputy in the Sheriff's Office, would.

But even if Marcus had actually *said* those words to Hilda—which Annie still refused to believe, although she acknowledged that the voice *was* a dead ringer for Hilda's husband's—why would Marcus parrot the language used by a rival for Hilda's ranch? It simply didn't make sense. Except . . . Marcus had told Annie that he'd wanted Hilda to start spending more time with him in California. In fact, if she remembered correctly, he'd described it as "an ultimatum." But who would resort to murdering his wife simply because she wanted to spend time with her horses more than she did with him? *Plenty of people,* she could hear Dan saying. *Nonsense,* Annie silently responded. Annie's short-lived marriage had revolved around the same issue. Her husband had merely walked out and never looked back. The last she'd heard, he was living in Eugene with his new wife and four kids. Annie couldn't have been happier for him. If Hilda had refused to start commuting more to San Jose, Marcus would have simply filed for divorce.

Besides, how had Marcus ended that conversation? Annie thought back and remembered, *"To tell you the truth, if Hilda were still alive, I'm not sure where we'd be right now. But whatever happened in our relationship, I always assumed that she would still be among the living."* There. Did that sound like someone who'd kill his wife? Sure, she could hear Dan telling her, if he'd already done it and wanted to convince someone he was innocent. Well, she didn't buy it.

After Dan had left, she'd had just about as much paperwork as she could handle for the moment. Carefully locking the office door behind her, she whistled for Wolf, who had been patiently waiting in the back of her truck, and took off for a walk around the property, far away from the grinding noise of the machines that were still so methodically looking for what would only be a gruesome treasure.

She started up the hill that she and Marcus had once walked, a walk that now seemed to have occurred a lifetime ago. There was the same small, rusted gate that led to the overgrown road that obviously hadn't been used in more than twenty years. She stood by it, thinking about her last conversation with Marcus. Wolf, on the other hand, had no appetite for ruminating about the past. He rushed by her and pushed his way through the hanging gate.

Annie gave a small jump as he flew onto the overgrown trail beyond. She hadn't seen Wolf take off, but more to the point, the gate hinges hadn't made a sound. Odd. Most rusted gates creaked. This one didn't. Annie examined it more closely. Clearly, someone had recently oiled it. In fact, it had probably been oiled on the day she and Marcus had first walked through it. She distinctly remembered Marcus's opening the gate for her, gentleman that he was, but try as she might, she couldn't recall its making a single begrudging squeak.

But who would have oiled the gate, and why? At the time, neither Marcus nor Annie had thought anything of it. Both were too intent on Marcus's predicament, and in Annie's case, hearing Marcus explain his relationship with his deceased wife. But now, without Marcus to distract her, Annie knew she must tell Dan.

Calling for Wolf, she retreated down the hill and found Dan deep in conversation with Tony, who was relating the efforts being made to locate the missing stable hand. Annie stood by quietly and listened.

To Annie's practical brain, Juan as a viable suspect made even less sense than Marcus. After all, she'd seen the guy quiver by Hilda's home, and Dan hadn't. Juan didn't have the gumption to tackle Hilda, whether it was in her house or in the dressage arena. She'd also seen how lovingly and carefully he'd inspected the bay after its arrival. He'd unabashedly doted on the animal as soon as it stepped out of her trailer. There was no way he could be involved in murder. Why couldn't Dan see that? Latham had to be his guy. As soon as Dan talked to him, he'd realize that he'd imitated Marcus's voice and left the message for Hilda. Somewhere down the line, Latham must have met Marcus and realized the Colbert marriage was going south. Why not make the husband the fall guy for his murders? It was the only logical conclusion. She had to make Dan believe this.

"Juan's probably in Eastern Washington right now, waiting for the apple-picking season to begin," Tony was saying to Dan as she walked over. "He's an illegal immigrant, right? Why should he hang around to be a witness in a murder case, then get deported for his trouble?"

"Maybe," said Dan. "We've reached out to every law enforcement agency in the state, and no one's seen hide nor hair of him. We've even got INS working on his family back in Mexico. They haven't heard from him, either."

An uneasy silence passed among them. All of them, Annie knew, were wondering if Juan would end up being the fourth victim in this unholy mess of a crime. As she pondered Juan's whereabouts, Annie's curious tale of the non-squeaking gate went right out of her head.

With Dan in tow, Annie returned to Hilda's office and loaded the copies she'd made of all the horse files into an empty box. She did not ask to make a copy of the Latham/ Colbert file. Dan wouldn't have given it to her, and besides, she'd already jotted down Latham's address and phone number from his personalized stationery and tucked the note into her saddlebag purse. *It's okay, Annie. Dan didn't say you couldn't copy down information and take it with you,* her Bad Angel reminded her. The Good Angel declined to comment.

"Hold on, Annie."

She had just grabbed the knob of the door leading outside when she heard Dan's voice.

"Did you happen to see this note in the file?"

What note? Had she forgotten to put Latham's information in her bag? She clutched it closer to her.

"What note, Dan?"

"Looks like it might be from Marcus. Can't be from Hilda; it's dated after her death. And to my knowledge, no one else worked here, unless it was Todos."

Annie was at Dan's side before she knew how she got there.

"What? What is it?"

"Don't know. It just fluttered out when you put down a file. Do you recognize the handwriting? As I recall, the man wrote you a check."

Annie glared at him, willing herself not to remind him he knew full well the check would not be honored as long as Marcus's bank accounts remained frozen. Then she attempted to grab what Dan was holding.

"Not so fast, Annie. You can look, but don't touch. This is going to the crime lab."

Annie noticed that Dan was holding the note by its edge and was wearing his thick work gloves. She peered over his swathed paw. It looked like Marcus's handwriting, all right. It contained the same big block letters that Marcus had used when he wrote down his hotel and cell number the day they'd walked around the ranch. Annie's heart melted as she saw the precise way in which he'd jotted down his thoughts. On the top of the notepad was the date—March 3—the Sunday Marcus had disappeared. The rest of the note read:

DINNER WITH ANNIE
ASK ABOUT HAY
LATCH??
PAPER TRAIL

"Aww. Ain't that sweet," Dan said when they were both done reading.

"Spare me, Dan. You see? Marcus *was* going to have dinner with me that night! He didn't skip out. Something happened to him."

"A reasonable assumption; otherwise, we wouldn't be tearing up Hilda's property looking for the man."

Annie felt sick.

The brightness of the day was gone, even though the sun had finished its battle with the clouds and was shining brightly overhead. Annie crawled into her truck, eschewing Dan's offer to drive her home. She felt mortified beyond belief. Only a week ago, she'd scoffed at the deputies who'd hurried out of Hilda's house, upchucking over seeing a dead body. Now, it only took a mere note written by a missing man to make her queasy. She was losing her grip.

She drove home slowly, deciding to forgo her visit to Johan Thompson to talk about an exit date for her Rambouillets. She could do that by phone, although by rights she should be looking at her ewes and gauging for herself how long it would be before they would lamb, as well as checking for any potential issues.

No, that task would have to wait a day or two. Right now, she could only think about the possible meanings behind Marcus's short but poignant checklist. She wished like hell that she'd been the one to discover it, then retracted the thought. It would have been difficult to turn over that little item to Dan, especially since she was still kicking herself for deleting Marcus's last voice message to her more than a week ago. Better that it remained in the hands of the county. Certainly there was nothing incriminating about any of the items, although "Dinner with Annie" was sure to be titillating gossip throughout the Sheriff's Office before nightfall.

The other items had her stumped. *Ask about hay?* As far as she could see, Hilda's horses dined on the best money could buy. Hilda had probably pulled strings and managed to obtain the Eastern Washington Timothy and alfalfa that now, regrettably for local ranchers, was largely being compressed and sold to Asian markets. *Latch?* Now that was a clue that resonated with her. *Damn!* How could she have forgotten to tell Dan? Although knowing the sheriff, he'd probably have tried to convince her that one of Hilda's workers probably oiled all the gates once a week and not to worry her silly little pea brain over the trifling matter. *Au contraire,* Annie thought. *I just know it has something to do with Hilda's murder. But what?*

Paper trail. Now that was fraught with possibilities. Most likely, it referred to the Latham/Colbert correspondence since the note was found in the file. But it could refer to the so-called changes to Hilda's estate that Dan kept alluding to as the key to finding Hilda's murderer. Or it might have something to do with the sale of Trooper to Hilda. Annie was thankful that she'd used the ruse of making copies of all the horses' files to return to the ranch, so she could now peruse Trooper's file at leisure.

It was altogether frustrating. Annie felt as if Marcus was giving her obvious clues, but, as her ignorance of thoroughbred sales with Todos had revealed, she was just not smart enough to put them together and ferret out what he was trying to tell her. Annie didn't like to feel frustrated. But she felt an inordinate pull to do something that connected her with Marcus. And the only thing she could think of was to spend time with Trooper. As much as she hated to admit it, Todos was right. The horse did need to be exercised. His tooth problem had fully resolved a week ago, and there was nothing to stop her from working with him.

She arrived home and went straight to the tack room. What could Trooper possibly use for a saddle? He was two hands higher than her biggest mount, Rover, and no doubt was accustomed to being under English saddle. Annie had none. Well, she would have to ride bareback, that was all. If she decided to ride at all, she reminded herself. A lot had to happen on the ground before she would ever ask Trooper to allow her on his back.

One of the most satisfying moments of Annie's summer days was calling for her horses at the end of the long twilights the Northwest is famous for. During these heavenly months, the sun seldom set before 9:00 P.M. and Annie, who liked to be an indulgent mother when she could, allowed her horses to stay outside as long as possible. On long summer evenings, it took just one ear-piercing whistle to bring the whole herd galloping up to the fence. Now, during the winter months, the vocal cue was hardly necessary. At 5:00 P.M. sharp, she could count on seeing all the horses lined up along the fence line, waiting for their suppers in their clean, warm stalls. But now it was just a little past two, hours before they would appear. So Annie stood by the gate and gave her world-famous whistle to bring them in. Sure enough, they cantered in together, ears forward, eager to see what their favorite human had in store.

Stepping into the pasture, she quickly caressed each horse's mane in turn before quickly slipping a string halter on Trooper. She led him into the round pen, where he stood docilely in front of her, obviously waiting for her instruction. This was clearly a horse that knew he had been born for a specific purpose. He was so unlike the other young horses that had come under Annie's care, which thought behaving like a horse was their only job, and a fine one, too. It was only through Annie's patient, gentle guidance that each learned that he or she still could be a horse with a human by its side or on its back.

Annie put Trooper through her usual warm-up phases, starting with rubbing his body over and under until he low-ered his head and gave a big sigh. Annie knew this was Trooper's way of telling the world he was relaxed and ready for whatever came next. She then spent a half hour practic-ing his ability to move in all directions. She was curious to know how he'd been trained to yield.

For a horse, yielding to a human is counterintuitive. Put a constraint on a horse, and it will want to pull against it. Annie's job, as is the job of all good horse trainers, was to convince the horse to give in to the pressure. Hannah knew this as well as Annie. She knew that if she pressed her left heel against Bess's rib cage, the horse would move to the right. If Bess was in one of her stodgy moods and refused to move, Hannah would increase the pressure until Bess grudg-ingly gave in. There was a silver lining to cooperating, which Bess knew full well, because as soon as she moved to the right, Hannah stopped bugging her.

Similarly, if Hannah arced the reins to the left and Bess resisted moving in that direction, Hannah simply would continue to keep the pressure on and wait for the horse to accede to her request. Bess and all of Annie's horses knew that when they gave in to pressure, they would be rewarded by its removal. What was essential was the rider's ability to instantly acknowledge when the horse had given in to the "ask," and just as instantly release the pressure. It was a nuanced game that took all of the rider's attention to perform well, and the game rules varied according to each horse's temperament. Annie was curious to see how Trooper would respond to her own cues.

Within an hour, she declared him a prince, an absolute prince. Trooper might not have been taught to respond precisely to the same stimuli that Annie routinely used, but his desire to please was evident, and Annie was soon able to ask Trooper to move forward, backward, and sideways with a mere flick of her hand. When she was able to move his hindquarters and forequarters with a gentle laying on of hands, she knew she was ready for the next test.

Annie was fully aware of Trooper's lunging capabilities; his performance the night she'd met him proved that he could move at a full gallop around a circle without seeming to tire. But she was curious to know how he moved at different paces.

She attached a long lunge line to the string halter and stood in the center of the round pen. Trooper wanted to follow her and nuzzle her neck, but Annie asked him with her open arm to go back to his seat, and Trooper politely complied. As she expected, when she first asked him to circle, he broke into an all-out gallop. Annie could hardly blame him. After all, this is what Trooper had been bred and trained to do.

She gently jiggled the lunge line to get the bay's attention. Trooper ignored her; he obviously was programmed to think that when asked to move, he had one gait: run, and as fast as possible. But Annie's constant, rhythmic jiggling did not escape Trooper's notice. So he stopped. Annie went up to him and praised him. Then she asked him to circle again but did so with a languid movement with her left arm. The bay looked at Annie and walked off instead of running. Annie let him walk around the circle twice before jiggling him to stop and face her. To his utter surprise, she walked up to him and showered him with praise.

"No one's ever asked me to walk before!" Annie could almost hear the bay whinny the words.

By the time the sun began to sink over the Olympics, Annie had successfully gotten Trooper to walk and slow trot in a circle several times in a row. Anytime he'd started to break into a canter or a gallop, she'd immediately asked him to stop. When Annie asked him to stop for the last time, Trooper turned and licked his lips. Annie knew this was the bay's way of telling her that he was thinking about what he'd just learned and would remember it. Her lessons were sinking in.

Won't Hannah be surprised, was Annie's amused thought. *Getting Bess out of a walk is practically an act of God. With Trooper, teaching him* just *to walk is a whole new education.*

She glanced over to the house and realized that it was high time to let the pup out for its constitutional. Even the most well-trained puppy could only hold its bladder for so long. But even as she was thinking that, her brain was telling her to register another fact.

Her truck was gone.

It had been there, just an hour or so before, parked right in front of the house, where it always was. Had she left the keys in the ignition? Of course, she had; she usually did unless she needed them to get into her farmhouse. Annie groaned. Car thefts weren't unheard of in Suwana County, but in broad daylight? On her own property?

Unless the person who took the car happened to think

that this was *her* property, too. In which case, Annie's truck probably was being driven by an uninsured, unlicensed driver who happened to be related—remotely, but related, nonetheless, to her.

Trying to restrain her anger, knowing that the horses would sense her emotions, she quickly rubbed down Trooper and sent him out to play with his mates in the pasture. Then she strode up to the house. It was locked. And her house key was on her chain of keys that had rested in the ignition.

Fortunately, Annie's spare was within easy reach, and once inside her home, she found precisely what she'd expected: no Lavender, and a very wet Belgian pup. At least the pup looked guilty.

"It's okay, buddy," Annie said, scooping up the warm ball of fur. "It's not your fault you have a babysitter with an underdeveloped brain. She probably was dropped on her head when she was young. Let's go for a walk."

Annie hitched the puppy to its leash, which it had now known for a total of forty-eight hours, and it enthusiastically followed Annie and Wolf out to the tack room, where Annie started prepping the horses' dinners.

She'd just settled down to a solitary dinner of one large, very rare rib-eye steak, when a set of familiar police lights came floating down her driveway. She watched from the kitchen window as Dan got out of the driver's side, then politely opened the door to the rear seat. He tipped his hat as Lavender emerged, looking as hangdog as Annie had ever seen her. Annie sighed and walked out to greet them.

"I believe this belongs to you?"

"For a brief moment in time."

"Well, I found her going fifty-five in a school zone. I would have ticketed her on the spot, but she didn't have any identification. So we went back to the station, where we had a nice little discussion. Turns out little missy here doesn't have a license. Or insurance."

"I'm aware of that," Annie answered drily. "That's why I gave her a bus schedule."

"They weren't running when I needed them," came Lavender's muffled response.

Dan and Annie looked at each other.

"Well, I'd like to let her off with a warning, seeing how she's your relation and all, but you know how the state feels about school-zone violations."

Lavender looked pleadingly at Dan, who ignored her.

"And, of course she's got a couple of other criminal traffic charges in Florida to deal with, as well."

"Thanks for not letting her spend the night in jail," Annie said tonelessly. In her opinion, a night in jail was precisely what Lavender needed.

"Don't mention it. Your help on the case today was, shall we say, a mitigating factor. Well, Betty Sue's got all the paperwork. She can tell you when her first court date is. Oh, and she might think about getting a lawyer. Unless she wants to throw herself on the mercy of the court."

"Betty Sue? Who's she?"

"Why, your sister, of course. Elizabeth Susan Carson, according to the Florida Department of Motor Vehicles. But everyone calls her Betty Sue, isn't that right?"

Betty Sue Lavender fled into the house.

Annie laughed so hard and for so long that she began to hiccup. Dan shifted from one foot to the other, and finally began to awkwardly pat her on the back.

"Glad to see you're feeling better, Annie."

"Betty Sue! You've just made my day!"

"Well, I'm afraid I'm going to about unmake it. You'll be glad to know that we didn't find a trace of anybody on Hilda's ranch. Marcus is still AWOL, though, so we're not closing the case on him. In fact, it just got a bit stronger. We got the report back from the crime lab digital expert this afternoon. He's compared the phone calls Marcus made from the jail with what's on Hilda's voice mail. It's a match, Annie. Marcus left that message."

Annie didn't remember saying good-bye to Dan. She only knew that somehow she managed to say good night and close the door. The only thing she remembered that evening was walking into the kitchen and seeing her half sister devouring the rest of her steak.

Apparently, Betty Sue ate red meat after all.

CHAPTER 17

TUESDAY, MARCH 8TH

Not for the first time, Annie thought about how she and her half sister were polar opposites. The first and most obvious difference was the time each of them chose to rise and greet the day. Annie kicked off the covers by six each morning, no matter what the season. Daylight savings time, Christmas, Thanksgiving, federal holidays, and Sundays when humans wanted to sleep in weren't part of an equine's knowledge set. Getting breakfast at reasonably the same time every morning was.

Betty Sue Lavender (as Annie now secretly called her) had no perception of horses' dietary requirements and thought she either needed or deserved as much beauty sleep as she could get. Also, she snored. Annie was sure that she, herself, did not.

What's more, Annie thought gleefully as she sailed down the highway, *she could drive, and Betty Sue Lavender was grounded for a very, very long time.* A few minutes before Dan had departed last evening, Tony had driven in with her truck and silently handed her the keys without saying a word. Annie had nodded her thanks. She'd checked the truck for damage this morning but fortunately found only a nearly empty tank, which was soon remedied.

Betty Sue Lavender had stumbled out of the bedroom just as Annie was leaving. She'd decided she needed to get out of the house and take Wolf with her, even if she had no particular destination.

"Please make sure the puppy gets out again before noon," was Annie's parting remark. "He needs to go outside every four hours, and he was last let out at eight."

Betty Sue Lavender scowled at her, shaking her pink hair out of her face. Annie noticed the pink strands were now growing out at the roots, revealing mousy brown hair underneath.

"Coffee's still on. And there are cinnamon rolls on the counter."

Lavender stomped off to the bathroom and slammed the door.

Annie quietly slipped out of the house, Wolf discretely walking by her side. It appeared that Wolf needed a break from the puppy as much as Annie needed a break from Lavender. It took all her self-control not to suggest to her half sister that perhaps what she needed was a good smudging.

Now, on the road, Annie allowed her thoughts to drift back to the previous night's conversation . . .

"Why did you take the truck, Betty Sue?"

"Don't call me that!"

"Well, it is your name, isn't it?"

"I haven't been called that since I was six. Mummy and Daddy respected my decision to change it."

"Well, why didn't you get it legally changed?"

"I didn't know I could. I didn't think I needed to."

"Jeez, Lavender. Who did *Daddy* make the checks out to all those years he supported you?"

Lavender looked down and clutched the Belgian puppy she'd been holding ever since Annie strode into the house after saying good night to Dan. "That was different."

"Different? In what way? The distinction somehow eludes me."

"Elizabeth Susan is just my legal name. But I've been Lavender as long as I can remember."

Annie sighed. The conversation was getting off track, something, she noticed, Betty Sue Lavender seemed particularly adroit at bringing about. In fact, it was one of her better skills.

"Okay, *Lavender*. So why did you take the truck?"

"I needed it."

"For what?"

"To see a friend."

"A friend? You have *friends?*"

Betty Sue Lavender burst into tears.

"Yes, I do! More than you think."

"Ah. So since you have all these friends, why did you decide to grace my home with your presence?"

"They're new friends. I didn't know them when I came here."

Annie sighed again. Should she ask who these new friends were? They probably were a bunch of space cadets, the kind who came to the Peninsula to find enlightenment. Whether they found it or not, they seemed to never leave. She decided not to delve into the topic.

"So what are you going to do about this legal mess you're in?"

"I don't know. Call Daddy, I guess."

"Good idea. Don't forget to tell him what happened to the Aston Martin."

Lavender wailed anew into the Belgian puppy's neck, who squirmed to get down, but Lavender only drew her tighter to her.

Annie critically surveyed her sister. Her hair was in disarray, her face a blotchy mess, and her peasant clothes looked as if they hadn't been washed for a week. *It was a good thing my own life is in such apple-pie order,* she reflected, heading out the door.

Annie had no place to go and a dog that wanted to go anywhere. Back in her truck, she pulled out her frayed county map and perused the possibilities. Well, there was always the long-put-off conversation with Johan Thompson about when to bring the Rambouillets home. Annie perused the map. A mere twenty-two miles beyond the Thompson farm was a short trail to a year-round waterfall, one that Annie hadn't visited since she was in her thirties. Surely she had time to take a quick break and be back at the Thompsons before dark.

"Do you want to go on a hike?" she asked her companion.

The responding bark was in the affirmative.

Shoshona Falls was at the end of the cutoff road to Forks, a town Annie had visited once, long ago, and despite the fame that teenage vampire tales had brought to the place, she had no desire to return to it—even less, in fact. She was

quite content to take the road less traveled, without the fear
of encountering fangs.

And she'd forgotten how much snow still existed at even
this slightly higher elevation. The majestic prominence of
the white-covered mountains formed a stunning backdrop to
the valley that led up to the trailhead. While there was no
snow on the road, Annie could feel the nip in the air even
before she set foot on the ground. After parking at the ranger
station, she pulled out a wool hat and mittens from her glove
compartment and zipped up her parka. Wolf hurtled himself
out of the truck in a near frenzy, and the two headed up the
path to the waterfall. It was an exhilarating day for a short
hike, and the cold only sparked Annie's enthusiasm. As she
watched Wolf bound up the trail, her thought was the same
one she always had upon entering the local library: *Why
don't I do this more often?*

Old-growth firs flanked the trail, and Annie could hear
Wolf crashing through the underbrush as she continued her
slow and definitely more contiguous climb up to the sum-
mit. She wished her decade-old cell phone had a camera; at
every turn, she saw a photo in the making. A half hour later,
stepping over the stones in the creek that had transported
thousands of visitors to the waterfall site, she whistled for
Wolf. But, as usual, he'd preceded her arrival. She jumped
onto the bank that afforded an up-close and personal view of
the waterfall and found him standing on full alert, tail out
and ears forward.

"What's up, Wolfie?" Annie picked up a stick and threw
it into the small pool in front of the dog. Wolf didn't move a
muscle.

"C'mon, boy! Let's play!" Annie grabbed another stick
and dangled it in front of his face, a guaranteed method of
getting Wolf to snatch it from her hands and play tug-of-
war. But today, Wolf was more interested in watching the
waterfall. *Well, I always knew he had a strong aesthetic sense,*

Annie thought. She sat down beside him and watched the water tumble over the rocks above.

Annie had never been up here at the tail end of winter; before, she'd always visited in summer months, when the creek was small and placid and the waterfall pool an ideal place to swim. But today, she witnessed the full strength of the cascade, brought on by months of rain and the slow but inexorable trickle of melting snow. She was amazed at the sheer and unrelenting power of the white sheets that surged down to the pool, which then quickly spread to the thousand-year-old rivulets bordering the sandy bank on which she sat. *This is a force to be reckoned with,* she thought. *Wolf must recognize it, too.*

Out of the corner of her eye, she saw a flash of red. Damn! She'd left her binoculars in the car. Perhaps it was a purple finch, although weren't they uncommon in wooded areas? She scrambled to her feet, dusting the detritus of the bank from her pants. Taking a few steps forward, she peered again. The bird was sitting still on a branch halfway up the waterfall. And it appeared to be fluttering its wings. Was it injured? The only birds that held still and fluttered their wings were hummingbirds, and Annie knew enough about Northwest birds to realize there wasn't even a remote possibility that a hummingbird would nest here.

"Stay," she ordered Wolf, then leapt over rocks in the stream. When she'd gone as far as she felt safe, she looked again. No, this wasn't an injured bird. It was simply a piece of fabric. How had it ended up there? She looked over at Wolf and gave him the nod that told him he could join her. Wolf responded with such alacrity that she realized that this was what he'd been watching so intently when she arrived. Nature lover that he was, Wolf obviously was an even better champion spotter of things. And he was inordinately anxious to get to whatever he'd seen.

She gave him his cue. Wolf bounded up the wall of rock

with amazing ease and, with a single yank, retrieved the red fabric. Turning carefully, he slithered back down the jagged scarp to Annie, where he obediently laid the object at her feet.

It was Marcus's necktie, the red Armani tie she'd seen him wear the first time she met him, and the second time, too, when he'd emerged from the county jail.

There was no cell phone reception at the falls, and later, Annie realized it wouldn't have mattered if there had been. She doubted she would have been able to hear herself talk over the roar of the water. When she'd been able to compose herself, she'd tenderly folded the tie and tucked it into an inner pocket of her parka. Wolf had been at his most compassionate. He whimpered and put his paw on her hand as tears ran down her face. She'd praised him for his braveness and hugged him because she loved him. Then the two set off for the ranger station.

Dan and Tony had met her there. Tony had carefully extracted the tie from Annie's pocket and placed it in an evidence bag. Both of their faces were grim.

"We'll talk later, Annie," were Dan's only words.

"You okay?" Tony added.

"I'm fine," was her steady reply.

It had taken the detective and deputy more than an hour to get to the ranger station, plenty of time for Annie to recover her usual demeanor. She'd gratefully accepted the use of the women's restroom to wash her face as well as the cup of hot cocoa the resident ranger had offered her.

"You're practically the first person I've seen this year," the ranger said by way of conversation.

"Oh? Who else has been here?" Annie realized she'd appeared too eager and tried to regroup. "Well, you know us rugged Northwesterners. Even if it's raining, we have to get our exercise."

The ranger laughed. "That's the truth."

"Is that your guest book over there?"

"It is, and you're free to take a look although it's hardly accurate. A lot of people don't bother signing in even though they're supposed to."

Annie realized with a pang that she was one of those people. Sure enough, the latest entry in the book was for Maggie and Bill Hammerstein, both from Fond du Lac, Wisconsin, dated November 3 from the year before.

She drove home slowly with Wolf by her side, once more passing Johan Thompson's place, now without a shred of desire to stop by and check in. But the thought of facing Lavender's sullen face back at home was also anathema to her. She decided to kill time in the local minimart, snatching up six items she knew would appall her half sister. Without pausing to put them in the refrigerator, she headed straight to the barn to set up the horses' evening meals. When the herd was contently chomping away, she reluctantly dragged herself out of the tack room chair and called for Wolf to follow.

The house was swathed in darkness. *What, was Lavender now holding a wake for herself?* Annie broke into a jog, twisting the knob on the back door and turning on the kitchen light in a single fluid motion. She glanced wildly around her. No bodies in sight. She tiptoed to Lavender's room, knocked hesitantly once, then firmly grasped the doorknob and twisted it.

Lavender was gone—this time seemingly for good. All of her clothes, normally scattered on the floor and on bureau tops, had disappeared. The incense, candles, and New Age posters that had once adorned the walls were nowhere in sight. The bed was stripped of its sheets, now lying neatly in a pile by the closet. Annie stared for a long minute before finally, gently, closing the bedroom door. She went to the kitchen to pour herself a drink, one that, of all those in recent days, she felt she richly deserved. But before she could take down the single malt from the shelf, she saw an envelope addressed to her tipped next to it. The handwriting was childish and in purple ink.

"Oh, Lavender. Was it something I said?"

You know darn well it was, Annie's Good Angel said.

Annie sighed, poured herself a double, and sat down at the kitchen table to read the letter's contents.

> *Dearest Sister,*
>
> *I know that I have been a grate disappointment to you, and to be absolutely honest, I am not very happy with myself.*
>
> *I thought that it would be good for you to have me in your house, but you really don't need me at all. I have tried to help but I guess I have tried to help you in ways that don't fit your needs. I am sorry.*
>
> *But, Sister, I have recently met someone who does need my help. I know what you are thinking. It's not a guy; it's a woman who needs me in the ways you don't. So I have gone to live with her. She has asked me to.*
>
> *So I have left and hope that someday we can meet again and be freinds. The kind of freinds that I always hoped we could be.*
>
> *Love,*
> *Lavender*
>
> *P.S. I have taken the puppy. I hope you don't mind. He will be good company for my freind.*
>
> *P.P.S. And the puppy chow. Wolf doesn't need it.*

P.P.S.S. I have left a casserole for you in the freezer. I hope you enjoy it.

P.P.P.S.S. I promise to take care of my traffic stuff.

Annie didn't know whether to laugh or cry, so she did a little of both.

Annie belatedly brought in her groceries from the car. Fortunately, the ice cream hadn't completely melted. Outside it was below freezing, unseasonably cold for the time of year. Just as she was finishing, Dan called.

"Well, Annie, I guess this puts a lid on it."

"Direct as usual, Dan. Puts a lid on what?" Annie had consumed her first glass of single malt and was now on her second. Her mood had improved only imperceptibly.

"The case, Annie. What do you think? All of them."

"Oh, really? Do tell."

"Annie, I know this is tough for you to swallow—"

She snorted into her cell phone.

"—but Marcus has been our man all along."

"You find his tie, and all of a sudden he's a serial murderer?"

"Be reasonable, Annie. Tony, Kim, and I have been chewing on this all afternoon and evening, and we're of the same mind. Marcus killed himself. First, he killed Wayne, then Hilda, maybe even Juan, then couldn't take it and threw himself over the waterfall. If we're lucky, we'll find his body, or what's left of it, next spring. But if it goes into the bay, we probably won't even find his bleached white bones."

A bit of single malt came up in Annie's throat. She poured the rest of the glass down the sink.

"What about finding his car at the airport?"

"Oh, Marcus drove it there all right. He wanted us to think

he was absconding. I don't think he necessarily wanted the world to know he'd taken the easy way out. Somehow he got back to the Peninsula to do the deed. Or he had someone else drive his car to Sea-Tac for him. We'll find out."

"What about the car being wiped clean? And finding his briefcase still in the trunk?"

"Again, just a ruse. He must have overlooked the briefcase. Why not? With what he was planning, he knew he wouldn't need it."

"So why'd he kill Wayne? As far as I know, he didn't even know who he was."

"I don't think Marcus intended to kill him. He just wanted to kill the horse. Marcus was probably sick and tired of supporting his wife's expensive hobby."

Dan spoke in an exceptionally patient voice. Annie felt like a ten-year-old being told all the reasons why she had to go to bed at eight. It was infuriating.

"Well, what about the mysterious holes and tire tracks on the Truebloods' property?

"As far as the damage on Cal and Mary's property, we think that's just the work of some campaign volunteer who put up a political sign without the owner's permission. Probably that woman who tried to worm her way onto the city council last fall."

"But who drugged Wayne Johnston?" Annie realized she was shouting into the phone. She cleared her voice and spoke with an uneasy quietude. "Did Marcus fly up from San Jose to drug Wayne, then fly back again to kill Hilda?"

There was a pause.

"Point well taken. We still have to tidy up that loose end. Marcus had to have had a partner in crime. Probably the same person who drove his car to Sea-Tac. But don't worry. We're confident we've found the primary killer."

Annie tried to count to ten and got to three before replying.

"Dan, I know you want this to be wrapped up in one neat and tidy bundle, but it just doesn't work. You read Latham's letters to Hilda. What about him? Have you investigated him at all?"

"Haven't had time. Your little adventure took up the rest of our day. But don't worry. We will. He very well might be the guy we're looking for—the guy who helped Marcus on this side of the water. It makes perfect sense. With Hilda out of the way, Marcus could have sold the ranch to Latham, which Latham wanted in the first place. Everyone would have been happy."

"So why did Marcus kill himself?"

Annie realized that Dan normally would have been shouting back at her in the phone. But apparently he was so pleased with himself and the way he'd suddenly "solved" the case that nothing could shake his contented mood. Finally, he'd decided, the axis of the world was spinning the right way in the life of Dan Stetson.

"No need to shout, Annie. I know you're distressed. You seem to have become more involved in this case than any private citizen should. And we've appreciated your help. Even if some of it came a little after the fact."

Dan paused, and then spoke with unmistakable certainty. "It's very simple. Marcus wasn't born to be a killer. And when he came to be one, he just couldn't take the pressure."

Annie said nothing. She decided it would be futile, not to mention humiliating, to mention the small matter of the oiled gate on Hilda's ranch. And what Dan had told her made a modicum of sense, she had to admit. But only a modicum, and that was a long way from it being the truth.

Yanking open the freezer door, Annie looked mournfully at the casserole Lavender had left for her. She sighed. She

felt just like Dan after Dory had made her dramatic departure: alone and unwanted. Not to mention misunderstood.

Later that night, as she dug into the bowl of ice cream
that served as her dinner, she decided she wouldn't tolerate
feeling that way any longer. Dan, Tony, even Kim could go
on believing that Marcus was responsible for every single
homicide in Suwana County over the past decade. But she
would not. If no one else wanted to investigate Marcus's
disappearance, she would.

Lost in thought, she let the spoon drop down to her side
as she started thinking of what she could do first. Wolf, who'd
already found one item of interest today, now found another
in Annie's hand.

CHAPTER 18

WEDNESDAY, MARCH 9TH

The next morning, after a strenuous hour of cleaning
stalls, Annie had done a tidy job in her head of figuring out
how to tackle the job of clearing Marcus. She'd silently re-
viewed everything she knew the Sheriff's Office already
had done. She realized Dan probably hadn't told her everything that he knew about the case—not by a long shot.
Annie reasoned if she went over some of the same ground
Dan had, she'd at least be on the same page. She'd already
decided she would present herself honestly: just an innocent
citizen asking innocent questions. Nancy Drew had always

gotten people to open up about themselves, and Annie had read every single one of the books in her youth, along with the entire set of Hardy Boy mysteries.

Might as well start at the beginning, she'd thought as she hung up her mucking rake and began to premeasure the grain for the horses' evening meal. That meant going back to the scene of the original crime, or, more precisely, the last place where Wayne Johnston had been seen alive—the Garver's Corner steakhouse. Maybe, just maybe, she could glean something there that had escaped the notice of her law-enforcement friends.

Annie pulled her rig into the steakhouse at 4:00 P.M. Even on a weeknight, the place already was hopping. A long string of Harleys festooned the front lot, and Annie could hear the plink of the jukebox from inside without even rolling down her window. The rest of the parking lot was filled with industrial-strength pickup trucks, with a few beaters wedged in among the shiny chrome. Wolf, who'd been confined to his crate in the flatbed, now hopped into the front seat, drool already dripping from his open mouth. The smell of charbroiled beef was unmistakable and deliriously alluring.

Calling to Wolf to stay, Annie pushed open the entrance door, a bell overhead clanging to herald her arrival. Just like the parking lot, the place was packed, and the noise from the customers and music was overwhelming. One foot inside, she nearly ran into a stooped man in overalls with bright red suspenders standing by the counter. His white hair was pulled back in a ponytail, and Annie suspected it hung longer than her own brown braid. At Annie's mumbled, "Excuse me," he turned toward her, his light blue eyes crinkling into a smile.

"Haven't see you here before. New in town?"

Annie wasn't used to strangers striking up conversations with her, but she remembered she was here for information. She squelched the brusque reply rising in her throat and smiled back.

"Hardly. I live just twenty miles up the road. But I happened to be in the area and thought I could use a beer."

"You came to the right place. I've been having a beer here every night for forty-five years. I turn seventy next week, so it must be good for me."

Annie appraised the man, noting the faint spider-thin lines that etched his face and the red farmer's tan emerging from his white shirt. His overalls were bulky, but she could see he was still fit and fairly trim, without the bowling ball gut that so many locals produced after a lifetime of eating too much and drinking hard.

His blue eyes followed hers, not trying to conceal their amusement.

"So?"

"I think you should keep up the regime. It seems to be working for you."

He stuck out his hand, rough and gnarled, but, Annie noticed, exceptionally clean.

"Bill Sorensen. Pleased to meet you."

"Annie Carson. Likewise."

"Care to share the counter with me? I usually sit over there." Bill pointed with one bony finger down to the end, where the old-fashioned jukebox was parked.

"Ah. The optimal spot to play DJ, I see."

"The best spot to hold back the girls who insist on listening to hip-hop. If it ain't good old country twang, I ain't interested in hearing it."

"Bill here's been playing jukebox police for as long as I can remember," a voice said behind her. "But don't let him bother you, hon. You want something romantic, I'm sure he'll give you a pass. As long as you buy him a beer."

Annie turned and saw a tall, thin woman in a frilly white apron she hadn't seen sported by waitresses since she was a child. A pencil was stuck behind one ear and she carried a cartload of oversized menus in one hand while balancing a tray laden with burgers and French fries in the other.

"Now, Millie. Don't be giving away my secrets. I was hoping to teach her the ways of Garver's Corner's finest—"

"And only," Millie stuck in.

"—steakhouse myself. No, don't bother." Bill put up a deprecating hand. "We'll seat ourselves. Follow me, Annie. And don't believe a word this ornery woman has to say."

Annie meekly threaded her way through the crowd vying for attention at the bar and sat down on the stool Bill had saved for her. Her heart felt surprisingly light. Whether it was hearing the good-natured banter between Millie and Bill, or just indulging in a social activity for the first time since Marcus disappeared, she couldn't tell. All she knew was that she liked where she was, and she sent up a silent prayer of thanks to our Goddess of Serendipity that she'd stumbled across a longtime regular without even trying.

Bill pulled out a pile of quarters from his overall side pocket, tugging down so deeply that it seemed his coins had collected near knee level. He slapped them on the counter.

"There. That ought a keep us in country songs for a while."

Millie appeared at their side.

"What'll it be, hon? I know what this old codger drinks."

"Um . . . do you have any pale ale?"

"We have Sierra Nevada. Will that do for you?"

Annie nodded and turned her attention to Bill, who was studiously flipping through the jukebox selections in front of him.

"Dang! I swear there's less of George Jones every time I come in here. Millie, who's in charge of your music selection?"

But Millie was now at the other side of the room, taking orders from a table of bikers. She was laughing at something one of them had said, and swatted her hand at the nearest biker in a mock "I declare."

"My favorite country crooner is Patsy Cline," Annie told Bill. "My mother used to play it all the time." She didn't add, "And even more after my father left us."

"Well, your mother had good taste. Let's see. I believe I can still see a few remnants left of the Queen of Country in here."

"Queen of Country? I thought Reba McEntire was the Queen of Country."

"Hon, she learned everything she knew from Patsy and would be the first to admit it," said Millie, swooping in behind them with Annie's Sierra Nevada and a Bud Light for Bill.

Annie nodded, realizing this was not the time to argue country-music preferences. She turned to Bill as the first heartrending bars of "Crazy" floated over them.

"So how did you first discover this place?"

"Easy. Back in the late sixties, this was the only watering hole within thirty miles. At least, the only one that didn't have a sideline of renting out the ladies in the back room. I was just starting my farm back then. My wife and I would work twelve-hour days, and when the day was done, I'd be hankering for something that would wet my whistle and allow me to talk to someone else other than my steers. I started heading down here after work and never stopped. Sometimes, the missus would join me. Of course, that was before the kids were born."

Bill took a long pull on his beer, draining it. Annie looked around, caught Millie's eye, and signaled for a refill.

Bill and Annie both started talking at the same time, Bill beginning with "Do you have any kids?" and Annie plunging into the opening she'd rehearsed while driving here.

They both laughed, then Bill said, "You first. If a pretty woman wants to ask me questions, I'm sure not going to stop her."

She was blushing, she realized, to her annoyance, but not out of annoyance at Bill.

"I actually stopped by for a reason," she started, adding "besides the chance to meet you, of course."

"Flattery will get you everywhere, Annie. Continue."

"Well, I'm taking care of a horse right now that was in a near-rollover accident a few weeks ago. The hauler stopped here for dinner right before it happened. I was just wondering whether you or anyone else might have remembered seeing him here."

Bill took another long drink off his beer, which magically had appeared in front of him.

"You're thinking he was drunk?"

"Actually, no. I mean, we know he wasn't drunk. He had a steak dinner and a diet Coke. Then he filled up his tank and hit the road. It wasn't long afterward that his rig swerved off the road and hit a fence post. The hauler died, but the horse lived."

"Damaged?"

Annie assumed he was referring to the horse, not the truck. "Thankfully, no. The trailer never flipped, and the police were able to get him out before he tried to kick the doors down. I'm part of the local search and rescue, so I got the job of stabling him until . . . well, until his owner was located."

"I take it you're still taking care of the nag?"

"As a matter of fact, I am. His owner was found dead a few days later." Annie decided not to tell Bill that she'd been the one to discover Hilda's body. She wasn't sure it was privileged information, since it had hit the news practically upon impact, but she did know she didn't want to relive that scene any more than she had to.

"You think the two are related?"

Annie nodded. "Seems pretty clear. I imagine the police have already talked to everyone here, but I thought I'd just double-check. And I was in the area."

"Playing Nancy Drew, are you?"

To her extreme discomfort, Annie felt herself again blushing. But Bill didn't seem to notice, or perhaps was simply too polite.

"Let me see now. That would have been, what? Back in February?"

"It was a Sunday, the second-to-last one that month."

"Well, I would have been here. What did the fella look like?"

Annie tried to recall the grainy photos that had appeared in the local newspaper.

"He was a big guy, over six feet tall, I'd guess, and had a big cowboy build. I assume he would have been eating alone. It would have been around midnight, I imagine."

"That's way past my bedtime. But maybe Millie remembers." Bill turned around and hollered above the barroom noise. "Millie! Get your skinny white butt over here!"

To Annie's surprise, Millie promptly skittered over and, by the expression of her face, seemed to take Bill's description of her as a compliment. Around here, Bill obviously was the unmarried, divorced, or widowed woman's dreamboat. Go figure.

"Millie, Miss Annie here wants to know if you remember seeing a big, beefy cowboy eating a steak dinner here on a Sunday night back in February."

"Late February? Close to closing?"

Annie felt her heart pick up a beat.

"That's right. It would have been February 21st, the one before the leap day weekend."

"Why, I sure do. He was the cutest thing. So polite, and he left a tip bigger than anything you've ever tossed my way, Bill."

Bill snorted.

"I predicate my tips on the service received." He sounded as if he was reciting the Gettysburg Address.

"Hogwash. You predicate your tips on the number of quarters left on the table. But anyway, this guy was real nice. As I said, we were about to close the kitchen, but he said he'd been traveling all day and still needed to get to his destination that night. He said he'd got hung up on some road construction down south and already was behind schedule, but sure would like a real meal before he got back on the road."

"Apparently he charmed the shoes right off Millie here." Bill obviously was unimpressed. Millie appeared just as unimpressed by his comment.

"I talked him into getting our T-bone special. He must have liked it, because I remember handing the plate to our dishwasher when he was done and telling him he just might as well put it up with the dried set."

Annie interjected. "Did he make any phone calls while he was here?"

"Why, yes, he did. It was right at the end of his meal. He'd just been talking to another customer when his cell phone lit up. He stepped outside to take the call. I remember that. The manager thought he was about to stiff us for the bill, but I knew he'd be back. And he was."

Annie's head was swimming. "He was talking to someone in here? Did he appear to know who it was, or was it a stranger?"

"He was a stranger to me, I know that. I'd never seen him before. He'd come in a couple of hours before this guy and had been nursing beers all evening. Then he went over to the truck driver, and I assume asked him a question. It wasn't ten seconds later that the driver's cell phone rang."

"What did he look like? The other man, I mean?"

"Oh, now let me think. All our beer bums look alike to

me by now." Millie squinted her eyes and was silent. "He
was skinny, I know that."

"How tall? Was he short or tall?"

"Oh, he was lanky, all right. Not much more than five-
eleven, I'd guess, but definitely not a shorty. More like a
string bean."

That described about half of Suwana County's farming
community.

"Anything else? Hair color, tattoos, scars, clothing?"

Millie looked closely at Annie.

"Are you the police or something?"

"No, not at all. But as I was telling Bill here, the man who
came in for dinner was in a highway accident after he left,
and I'm taking care of the horse he was hauling. I'm just trying to figure out why he swerved in the middle of the road."

"Now, isn't that too bad. I didn't know that. I work so
much here that I'm too tired to click on the TV when I get
home. The only death I've heard about recently was that fancy-
pants horse owner who lived up north. Didn't she get hacked
to death or something?"

"Annie?" Bill's voice sounded worried. "Is that horse
you're taking care of . . . did it belong to her?"

Annie had the good sense not to answer but apparently
her face gave the answer. *Damn,* she thought, I never was
good at poker.

Millie looked pale. She abruptly sat down on a stool and
held one shaking arm out in front of her.

"You mean the man sitting right at that table was hauling
a horse to the woman who was murdered?"

"I'm afraid so." Annie was beginning to be sorry she'd
told Bill so much of the story.

"Do you think he killed her? Was I serving dinner to a . . .
a homicidal killer?"

"Not a chance. The driver was killed in a truck accident
within thirty minutes of leaving the steakhouse."

"But Annie thinks they're connected." There was Bill, helpful as ever.

"Did anyone ever talk to you? I mean, from the police?" Annie couldn't believe that this piece of information had escaped Dan's notice.

"I was off the next week. My daughter's grandchild was being born in Bellingham, and I was gone until the next weekend. Stan—that's the manager—told me a Suwana County sheriff's deputy had been by, but he didn't say nothing about wanting to talk to me."

Suwana's Finest at work, Annie thought sourly.

"So what happened after the truck driver took the phone call?"

"Well, he came in, paid his bill, and left."

"Did he say anything to you about the phone call?"

"I don't think so. Oh, wait. He did say something. What was it?" Millie tapped her fingers on her chin. "He said something about it being a 'funny' call. He kind of chuckled. He didn't seem upset about it or nothing."

"Did he stick around, or was he done eating at that point?"

"Hon, when he left to take his call, there wasn't enough meat left on that steak to feed a cat. I think he took one last pull on his diet Coke and just picked up the check."

"What about the guy who came over to talk to him?"

"Oh, he just went back to his stool and nursed another beer."

"Have you ever seen him again?"

"Not on my watch. But I could ask the other girls."

Annie dug into her saddlebag and pulled out a piece of paper. She scrawled her name and phone number on it.

"Would you mind? It may mean nothing, but if you do see him again, I expect the sheriff will want to talk to him."

"But you're not a cop?"

"Nope. I'm a friend of the sheriff's. I'm just trying to help out in any way I can."

Driving home, Annie knew full well that Dan definitely
did not want any more of her help, but that was his problem.
And Millie had added one more piece of information as
Annie was leaving that also piqued Annie's interest. The
beer bum who'd come up to Wayne had eyebrows that grew
together. That definitely narrowed the field. But how to find
that field was another matter. If only Dan could tap into a
database that magically identified every man in Suwana
County with that particular facial feature. Fat chance of that
occurring.

But the fact remained that she'd just uncovered another
clue that had slid right by everyone else. How this one, along
with the oiled gate, tied together escaped her for the time
being. But she was sure she would figure it out.

CHAPTER 19

THURSDAY, MARCH 10TH

Annie retired that night feeling thoroughly grumpy. It had
started when Wolf and Max abruptly turned up their noses at
Lavender's defrosted casserole, which promptly made its way
to Annie's compost bucket. If her animals couldn't stomach
her half sister's cooking, then she certainly couldn't. She'd
tried to spend the few hours left of her short evening making
sense of what Millie had related about the mysterious man
who'd approached Wayne. But even then, irritating thoughts

of Lavender kept creeping into her brain. Where was the woman? She'd frankly expected to hear from her before now. And there was no one to call, unless, of course, you counted their father-in-common, who probably knew less than she did and might or might not have wanted to know more. She went to bed feeling irrationally upset at Lavender's extreme thoughtlessness, and the gaping chasm in their respective levels of maturity.

At 5:00 A.M., Annie arose to a gray, overcast day that belied the fact that spring was officially only ten days away. It was still pitch-dark, and looking out her kitchen door, she could discern no movement from the stable or paddock area. The horses were all probably asleep in their stalls, taking their thirty-minute lie-downs before light would slowly begin to emerge from behind the mountains. But the anger she'd felt the night before at Lavender's disappearance was now replaced by another feeling—relief at her restored solitude.

She padded around in her kitchen, marveling at the silence from Lavender's absence, not to mention the two pups. Tossing Wolf and Max's breakfasts in their respective bowls—all meat—she retreated to the kitchen sink, where she stood nearly motionless, thoughtfully sipping from her mug of coffee. An hour later, she reluctantly gave up her post and pulled on her rain gear. It was time to feed the horses, then to ramp up the next stage of her investigation.

Annie had just nudged into the last parking place among the six allotted for the Suwana County Sheriff's Office when she saw Dan and Deputy Kim Williams striding out of the building. She honked her horn.

"Dan! Wait up!" She quickly jumped out of her truck and began running in his direction.

"What's up?"

Annie halted, momentarily flummoxed. She couldn't remember Dan's ever greeting her so perfunctorily. True, their last conversation had not ended particularly well. Annie had been left sputtering on the phone after Dan had done his best to destroy every last doubt in her mind about Marcus's guilt. She didn't quite remember what she'd said before hanging up, but she was pretty sure it wasn't nice. Still. She and Dan had been bantering and exchanging insults since the high school prom.

Even Kim looked exceptionally serious. She stood a respectful three feet to Dan's right, her legs slightly apart and her right hand dangling by her side, within easy grasp of her service revolver. She looks as if she was guarding an especially dangerous suspect, Annie thought, before she turned toward Dan.

"I've got something to tell you."

"Sorry, Annie. Don't have time right now. Police business. Bound to take us the rest of the afternoon. Whatever you have to say, you can say it to the desk."

Astounded, Annie watched Dan and Kim resolutely walk away and get into Dan's police vehicle. She watched the car circle around the driveway leading into the county buildings and head left, toward the highway. She noted that Dan hadn't put on his turn signal or his seat belt, for that matter. What was it about police officers that made them scorn the laws they were sworn to uphold?

Well, fine. Here she was, good little Ms. Citizen, but if that was how she was going to be treated, she'd just keep her new information to herself. She turned to go, but then remembered that Esther, Suwana County Sheriff's Office's oldest employee in both senses of the word, was probably on duty. Annie liked Esther. And Esther, when found alone, which was most of the time, was always a good source of information. Swallowing her indignation, Annie entered the department and, a few minutes later, was told to go back to the 9-1-1 operator's command post.

"I'm not interrupting anything, am I?" she said politely as she entered the eight-by-eight cubicle that served as the county's sole office for registering residents' complaints and crime reports.

Esther slipped off her earpiece and gave a high, trilling laugh.

"Hardly. Unless you count a stolen bicycle from the high school which, by the way, didn't even have a lock on it."

Annie gingerly sat down on the one unused chair the cubicle could accommodate.

"Well, you've probably had enough calls this past month to make up for the downtime. I'd be happy just to sit here and do the crossword puzzle."

Esther scowled, or attempted to. She was seventy-five years old if she was a day, Annie thought, and looked more like someone's beloved great-aunt who'd just baked your favorite cookies whenever you turned up at the door. Her snow-white hair was short but professionally done, and her face remarkably unlined for her years and for all the horror stories she'd undoubtedly had to listen to while on watch. Esther was wearing her usual uniform: Alfred Dunner slacks and a pullover sweater. Today, her sweater sported one large yellow fuchsia on the front. Most of her sweaters were adorned with some flower or another. Annie thought it was cute.

"What? You don't like crossword puzzles?" Annie was trying to be diplomatic and gauge Esther's mood. She'd decided upon entering the building that she had one very big favor to ask of her.

"Annie, I'm so good at crossword puzzles that even the *New York Times'* Saturday one doesn't take me past my first coffee break. But that's the problem. Haven't you heard what they're trying to do to me?"

"No, I haven't. What's going on?"

"In their ongoing quest to get me to retire, the commissioners are now suggesting that I be replaced by a computer."

"A what? Esther, you can't be serious."

"I am. The idea was brought up at the last board meeting, and apparently there was quite a bit of enthusiasm for the idea."

"I don't get it. How could a computer possibly do your job?"

"Quite easily, it seems." Esther's voice was uncharacteristically brittle. Put her on the phone with the parent of a runaway kid and she sounded like milk and honey.

"It's been tried in a couple of other small communities and while the results aren't in, nothing tragic has happened. Yet." This was delivered in a particularly ominous tone. "You got a problem? Just log on to the sheriff's Web site and send us an e-mail. When someone gets around to reading what you had to say, maybe you'll get a response."

"That's absurd! What about crimes in progress?".

"Oh, they'll go through the regular switchboard. But the bulk of the calls are supposed to go through the computer system. They want to knock my workday back to a few hours at night, when most of the calls for immediate response come in."

Annie snorted. Esther plowed ahead in her diatribe. Now that she'd found a ready listener, it would have been difficult to get her to stop.

"So don't plan on getting murdered in the middle of the day. Or pass out from lack of blood before you can reach your computer to let us know that you've been stabbed to death. I honestly wonder, what are they thinking? All it will take is one fiasco when the sheriff's deputies don't arrive in time, and this will all be on the commissioners' heads. Not a one of them could be elected dogcatcher afterward."

Annie silently agreed.

"The commissioner who made the suggestion was such a nice little boy, too. One of the best students in my class."

Annie had forgotten that Esther had once been an elementary-school teacher and had taught most of Suwana's citizens now over the age of forty. But when her husband died unexpectedly of a brain hemorrhage in his late thirties, Esther had accepted the job as dispatch operator. Her excuse was that she didn't like being alone at night, now that Walter was gone.

"Well, it's just ridiculous. No one could ever replace you, Esther. Why, you solve half the crimes in Suwana County before the police ever arrive on the scene. No one can get information out of people better than you."

Esther visibly preened. She gave Annie a smile, the first Annie realized she'd seen on anyone's face since she had pulled into the County Sheriff's Office.

"Oh, I don't know," Esther said, patting her hair. "It's just that it's good to be able to talk to a real person when you're in trouble. I've been told that time and time again."

"That's right," Annie said authoritatively. "And no one's going to let you retire or go sideways in the system. That commissioner may have his pet project, but it's not going to fly when the public gets wind of it. The commissioners will back down in a heartbeat. You'll see."

Esther gave Annie another smile, this one a bit tired.

"I hope you're right, Annie. I hope you're right."

A red light lit up on the console.

"Excuse me, Annie. Nine-one-one speaking. How can I help you?"

Esther listened intently and her fingers quickly flew over the pocket-sized keyboard on her desk.

"I see. How do you spell your last name? Yes, I'll tell the sheriff. Yes, I have your phone number. If he needs to talk to you, he knows how to reach you."

Esther unhooked her earpiece and shook her head in disbelief.

"They're still coming in. It's unbelievable."

"What are?"

"Calls from psychics. I don't know what it is about this triple-homicide, but it's generated more phone calls from nutcases than I can ever remember. I've heard them all. Of course, none of them make any sense."

Annie inwardly winced at the way Esther so cavalierly threw "triple homicide" into her conversation—after all, Marcus hadn't officially been declared dead yet, had he? But she kept her discomfort to herself.

"Well, if you get a call from my sister, Lavender, let me know. I'll take care of it personally."

As Esther plowed into her next pet topic, the state of Dan Stetson's personal and professional life, Annie relaxed and waited for her opening.

"I'm not saying it's all Dan's fault," Esther had told her. "Dory could have her moments, too. Hair-trigger temper, that woman. And you know Dan. He wouldn't raise his voice to an ax murderer if he knew he could get a confession otherwise."

Annie made a small murmur of assent although she acutely remembered Dan's curtness to her just an hour before.

"But after the boys left home, and Dory cut back at her hair salon, no pun intended, she started spending *way* too much time on the Internet. And that's what got her in trouble. Dan would go home and find Dory glued to her computer, breakfast dishes still in the sink and dinner nowhere in sight."

Esther had shaken her head disapprovingly. Apparently Walter had never known a missed meal prepared by his bride, even after a long day with rambunctious first graders. Annie nodded sadly in agreement. A meal not served on time was a serious crime to Suwana's well-nourished sheriff.

"But when she left, and all these horrible deaths came right after the other, he changed." Esther was emphatic. "Why, he'd come in here and practically snap my head off for no reason at all. And I wasn't the only one. He even laid into Deputy Elizalde one day so bad that I thought that the deputy was going to resign right then and there—or slug him."

"Maybe slugging him would have been the right way to go," was Annie's thoroughly unhelpful answer. "Dan's not exactly been sweetness and light to me, either."

"Well, he likes you, so you know it'll all blow over once this case is resolved. But that's the problem. Dan's dying to close it out, but the prosecutor won't let him. Says he hasn't turned over every stone yet. The fact is, we've already been made a laughingstock on national TV once, and Ms. Prissy Evans isn't about to let it happen again. So she's sending Dan out on wild-goose chases just to make sure every lead is taken 'to its natural conclusion,' according to her. It's driving Dan nuts."

It was the opening Annie had been waiting for.

"Maybe I can help."

Esther looked at her askance.

"Annie, I know you're involved in this case and all, but what do you think you could possibly do?"

"Maybe more than a man could. Or a computer."

Twenty minutes later, Annie emerged from the county building with a small bundle tucked into her inside jacket pocket. She was thankful that the Sheriff's Office didn't have the money to install metal detectors, because even though the package she carried wouldn't technically set off any alarms, she wasn't sure she could have passed the security guard without signs of guilt clearly evident on her face.

Once inside her truck, she patted her pocket just to make sure it had arrived intact from the twenty-foot walk to her truck. Yup, it was still there: a digital copy of Marcus's phone call to Hilda, the one in which he threatened to kill her. It also contained all the other phone messages, including her own and those from disgruntled vendors, but Annie wasn't interested in them. She'd never understood how Marcus could have uttered those words—they were so unlike the man she knew. Had known. Knew. She was determined to listen to them again and again until they made sense, or at least made sense to the case.

All guilt was replaced with mild euphoria five miles out of town. Her success in snaring the tape had bolstered her confidence, and the wariness she had felt that morning about independently contacting Travis Latham had dissipated along with the rain clouds that had threatened to spill this morning. But first, she had a stop to make. Latham's property was only a mile or two from Hilda's compound, a fact that had struck Dan as highly significant when she'd turned over the Colbert/Latham correspondence to him. But so was Johan Thompson's farm. And it was more than time that she looked in on her Rambouillets. They weren't ready to lamb, she knew—she'd have heard from Johann in a jiffy if that were the case—but they couldn't be far off from motherhood.

She pulled into the Thompson farm a little after noon. She half expected to find Johan and his wife, Hester, in the farmhouse for a midday meal, but she espied the craggy old farmer tending to his vintage International Harvester tractor. It was parked by his toolshed, a sagging wood building that looked like a junkman's cave to the rest of civilization but, Annie knew, contained a nut, bolt, wire, and engine part to fit any farm machine made since 1946 and could solve any mechanical emergency. At least twice a year, Annie listened to Hester Thompson threaten to haul the whole place to the dump, but Johan simply smiled on each occasion and Hester would never dare follow through. She'd told Annie she knew darn well where her canning jars disappeared to; she'd found every last one of the them in Johan's shed, serving as new homes for wayward machine parts.

"And he might as well keep them," she'd told Annie. "I wouldn't put so much as a cherry in one of those things now, not after all that grease and grime."

A rough wool blanket was spread on the ground, and all Annie could see were steel-toed boots and oil-spotted overalls, but she would have recognized the farmer anywhere. She knew his curses.

"Dad burn machine! I plugged you up a month ago. Where in tarnation are you hiding that leak?"

Johan spoke to all his machines that way. In fact, Annie suspected, he talked more to his farm equipment than he did to his wife.

"Johan! It's Annie. I came to check on my sheep."

She spoke loudly and from across the lawn in front of the farmhouse to give him plenty of warning. The last thing she wanted was to quietly walk up and watch Johan clunk his head on the tractor chassis in surprise. Annie figured it would hurt as much as having your head connect with that of a horse. This, she knew from experience, was painful.

Johan's rant against the offending tractor abruptly stopped. He scooted out from under the tractor with surprising agility and scrambled to his feet, thrusting a greasy hand toward her.

"Well, how-do, Miss Annie. I expected to see you long before this. Fact is, I was just about to call you."

"Is everything okay? I know I should have come by two weeks ago."

"Oh, everything's right as rain, which we've been having a lot of lately, in case you hadn't noticed. The girls are looking right plump although they're still eating good, and no one's hips have hollowed out. But you usually have them sheared before lambing time, and that can't be far off."

"No, I'm sure lambing season is right around the corner.

I've just had an out-of-town visitor and a lot on my plate. But I'll call Leif this afternoon and ask him to make my sheep a priority."

"That's what I was going to call you about. Leif stopped by yesterday and noticed the same thing. He said he could come out this Saturday if it suits your needs. He said you needn't be here if you're busy. Leif said his cousin's staying with him for the moment and is acting as his unpaid assistant."

Annie considered this. Leif was the volunteer fireman who'd blasted the fire engine siren on his way out of the accident scene on Highway 3 almost three weeks ago. He knew darn well what it had taken Annie to get the bay calmed down after that incident. If, by way of atonement, he wanted to spare her a day of herding and holding distraught ewes who didn't have the good sense to realize haircuts would make them immeasurably more comfortable that summer, she wasn't about to dissuade him.

"Great," she told Johan. "I'll plan on coming by mid-afternoon to see how he's doing and to settle up, but it'll be nice not to have to go home smelling of lanolin. I've got a lot of work to do on the birthing pens, anyway."

"Need anything?" There was a gleam in Johan's eye. Nothing pleased the man more than being asked to rummage through his eclectic collection of bolts to find the one missing piece that salvaged an otherwise useless farm tool.

Annie smiled. "I think all I'll need is a hammer and a box of nails. But if I run out of cedar planks for the temporary gates, I'll let you know."

An hour later, Annie was on her way to Travis Latham's, well fed from a lunch made and served by Hester.

Annie had gratefully accepted a doggy bag of stew for Wolf, who was waiting patiently by the truck, then bid her hosts adieu. As she watched her beloved Blue Heeler inhale his unexpected treat, she knew that he would be as hungry as ever for his dinner that night. Pulling out of the Thompsons' driveway, she wondered lazily if she'd ever feel the need to eat again.

Annie had never been down the winding country road that led to the Latham spread. That wasn't unusual; even life-long county residents such as she found it impossible to know all the back roads with inconspicuous driveways that often led to a community that didn't want to be found.

Travis Latham obviously wasn't among the segment of society that wished to be anonymous for reasons best kept to themselves. A prominent and well-built sign on Chesapeake Road heralded the Latham name and pointed the direction to the man's residence. Annie quickly realized the good sense in erecting the sign. Latham might not have wanted to shield his identity, but he sure didn't want to live close to his neighbors; Annie had driven a good quarter mile, and still there was no house in sight.

Nor, apparently, did he want to interact with them. She uneasily noted that several prominent NO TRESPASSING signs adorned the fir trees flanking the drive. She hoped they only applied to religious fanatics and ex-mothers-in-law.

Annie clocked another quarter mile on her odometer before she saw the beginnings of a long circular driveway and the smoke from a woodstove circling the air above. She instinctively reached overhead to check the presence of her Winchester .30-.30, then absently patted Wolf, seated beside her.

"Don't know what we'll find, buddy," she told her companion. "Let's just take it one step at a time." Wolf panted enthusiastically in response, his breath reeking of meat and onion.

Taking one step at a time was what the white-haired man she saw peering into the mailbox outside a six-foot steel gate was apparently doing as well. His shoulders rested on two forearm crutches, making him seem shriveled and smaller than he actually was. She watched as he awkwardly transferred the mail into a shoulder bag hanging off one arm handle and shakily closed the mailbox flap. Annie was still twenty feet away, but she could see the fragility inherent in his actions. Her desire to help overrode her fear of reprisal from being on the property, and she slid out of the truck, Wolf in tow.

"Can I help you?" she shouted.

The old man slowly turned, waving a mail flyer in a motion that said, "No, I'm fine." He shifted up on his crutches, which emphasized his rounding shoulders, and squinted toward her.

"Seems to me I ought to be asking you the same thing." His voice was mild, and there was a hint of amusement in his words. He did not sound at all threatening. And how could he be? Wolf could have knocked him over in a single bound.

Annie gave the old man her most winning smile while giving Wolf a nonverbal command to sit.

"You're absolutely right. I hope you don't mind my intruding on you like this. My name's Annie Carson. This is Wolf," she said, gesturing to the Blue Heeler, who now was on the ground, his paws in front of him, the image of perfect submission. "I wanted to talk to you. Is now a good time?"

"It's as good a time as any," he said, using his crutches to transfer his weight from one foot to the other. "Although I've had more visitors today than I have all month. I'll open up the gate so you can bring your rig inside. It's hard to turn around if I don't."

Probably on purpose, Annie thought as she flashed him a grin and she and Wolf climbed back up into her truck. She watched the person she assumed was Travis Latham painfully unlock the gate and pull it to one side, then slowly nosed her truck inside the property.

It was magnificent. Latham had created a home that made Hilda Colbert's house look like a bad knockoff of the Ewings' TV home on *Dallas*. The three-story farmhouse was newly built, but it retained all the charm of the century-old structures Annie saw dotting the landscape in her own neighborhood, with all the meticulous care that they lacked. A gleaming white wraparound porch set off the hunter green exterior of the rest of the structure. Colorful flowerbeds, many with plants exotic for the Northwest, bordered the entire home, except for one side entrance that had a ramp leading to what was probably the kitchen door. But that was the only evidence that the home had been remodeled to fit the owner's own limitations. There were eight long steps leading up to the front entrance, and the man slowly and laboriously mastered all of them without looking behind to see if Annie was in tow.

"You can bring your dog if you want."

Annie was slowly and silently walking behind him. She knew better than to ask if he wanted help again.

"Thank you," she said, meaning it, and whispered, "Heel" fiercely to Wolf as he started to bound toward the steps. She didn't want anything to upset the old man.

Once inside the house, Annie again marveled at the grandeur in front of her. Thick lush rugs carpeted the front hall and a living room she could see on the right. Annie didn't know good art from bad, but she suspected that what she was seeing now fell in the former category, judging by the frames and the individual lights perched over them, casting their glow on the images below. Old-fashioned lampshades adorning lamps with gleaming bases sat on mahogany tables. She could hear the solemn tick-tock of a grandfather clock somewhere in the distance.

"I used to have dogs," the old man was telling her. "After my stroke, I couldn't keep them anymore. Figured it wasn't fair to them if I couldn't walk them. You look like you've got a good boy."

"He is," Annie said, adding, "I really don't know what I'd do without him." *Damn! That was a stupid thing to say.* But the old man simply smiled ruefully and gestured toward the living room.

"Why don't you make yourself at home? I'll be with you in a few minutes."

Annie complied and sat gingerly on an overstuffed couch near a bay window. She ordered Wolf to sit, then waited primly, her hands on her lap, not daring to do more than glance at the big art book in front of her. She'd come to Latham's home expecting to be intimidated, but not precisely in this manner.

After what seemed to be an interminable time, the man slowly entered the room, bringing a glass of water with him. He carefully put it down in front of Annie, then made his way to a high-backed chair a few feet away. *It must be his chair,* she thought, *the one he can get in and out of it easily, unlike the rest of the overstuffed furniture in the room.*

Slowly placing his crutches on the floor, the man sat back, giving Annie the first good look she'd had of his face. The lines on his neck showed his age, which must have hovered somewhere in the late seventies, and one side of his face drooped more than the other, no doubt the effect of the stroke he'd mentioned. But it was a noble face, surprisingly clear of wrinkles, and the gray eyes that looked out under white eyebrows were clear, direct, and surprisingly warm.

"There are coasters in that side drawer. If you wouldn't mind."

Annie leapt to fulfill his request, then obediently took a sip of water.

"Now, what can I do for you? I've just seen the back of

Suwana County's Finest, so I'm going to assume that you may be asking me the same sorts of questions."

Dan had been here? So that's why he'd been so abrupt with her earlier. If she'd never told him about Latham's fight to get Hilda's property, he wouldn't have had to make the effort to investigate a lead he obviously thought was a dead end. *Well, tough darts,* she thought. *Sheriffs are supposed to investigate.* Although now, after actually seeing Travis Latham, she wondered how logical it was to think that he had anything to do with Hilda's and Wayne Johnston's deaths.

"You are Travis Latham, aren't you?" she asked tentatively.

"Last time I looked at my birth certificate," was his dry reply.

"I'm sorry to bother you like this, especially if Sheriff Stetson has already interrupted your day."

"But not so sorry that you're still here." Again, the words were said lightly, without provocation, but Annie got the message. This was a man who preferred directness over diplomacy. In fact, if she'd stopped to think about it, that's what was so apparent in his correspondence with Hilda. Annie immediately changed tactics.

"Point taken. So, Mr. Latham, let me try to explain why I wanted to see you."

Mr. Latham leaned back in his chair and waited. Annie took a big breath.

"I don't know if Dan—Sheriff Stetson—told you, but I'm the person who found Hilda Colbert's body."

If Annie was expecting to shock Latham, she didn't succeed. His facial expression was as impassive as ever. *Strange,* she thought. Perhaps it was because of the stroke he'd mentioned. Or perhaps he just was impervious to hearing about homicides of people he knew.

"I'm also the person who discovered the letters between

you and your real-estate agent to Hilda Colbert around the time when she purchased the property."

"Ah. So I have you to thank for the visit from the Sheriff's Office."

"I'm afraid so. And obviously I'm not here in any official capacity. And if I'd known that Dan—I mean Sheriff Stetson— had already visited you, I wouldn't have bothered you."

"You mean you would have just badgered the good sheriff for information?"

Annie blushed. "Well, if Sheriff Stetson had told me talking to you didn't help the investigation at all, I would have accepted that."

"Would you?"

They were only two words, but with a slight emphasis on the first. They caught Annie by surprise, and she thought a moment before responding.

"No, probably not. That is, if, not if I could come to that same conclusion myself."

"Ms. . . . Carson, is it? Ms. Carson, do you suspect me of killing Hilda Colbert?"

"No, not at all."

"But you did before coming here."

"I didn't know. Honestly. I just read the correspondence between the two of you, and it was clear you and Hilda had come to loggerheads over the property. Also . . ." Annie fell silent. She wasn't sure she wanted to tell Latham that what he'd written and what Marcus had said sounded awfully similar.

"Also . . . what else, Ms. Carson?"

"Nothing. The fact is, the Sheriff's Office is pinning Hilda's death on her ex-husband, and I'm just not convinced they're right."

"Where do I come in? I can tell you the same things I told the sheriff and his redoubtable deputy, Ms. Williams. I live alone. I no longer drive. My overly caring daughter-in-law comes over around six o'clock every night to deliver groceries and make sure I have everything I need for the day ahead. She leaves around eight, and I retire around ten. Aside from Melinda's recollection, there's no way to prove I'm telling the truth, but quite frankly, Ms. Carson, there are a lot of reasons that make it hard to put me at the scene of the crime."

"I believe you, Mr. Latham. But that's not really why I came," Annie lied. "I'm really interested in getting your opinion on something else altogether."

"Ask away. I hope your questions will be fractionally more interesting than those of the sheriff."

She couldn't stop a half laugh from emerging and to her surprise, Travis Latham gave a small chuckle himself.

"At this point in my life, I'm not too worried about going to jail. So if I'm being viewed as a possible suspect in a homicide, I'd rather have everything out in the open."

"Okay. Well, to begin with, did you ever meet Hilda?"

"Never had the pleasure. Only heard about her from a few friends. It was enough to make me want to avoid her company if I could help it."

"How about her husband, Marcus Colbert?"

"Didn't even know she was married. In fact, if I'd been asked to bet on it, I would have said she was single. I'm only going by her reputation, of course, not from personal knowledge. I've done a lot of real-estate transactions in my career, but I don't think I've ever come across anyone who was as merciless and unyielding as Ms. Colbert. I'm surprised she didn't die before she did. It was my mistaken belief that one had to have a heart to live."

Annie considered that. "So I know this is none of my business. But why, Mr. Latham, did you want to buy the property? I mean, I understand why you were upset about Hilda's swooping in with a ridiculously high offer and getting the real-estate agent to accept it. But you have a gor-

geous property already. Why did you want to acquire more
land? It was land, wasn't it? There weren't any buildings already there?"

Mr. Latham was silent for a long time.

"I must give you credit," he finally said. "You asked a
question that eluded the police. No, it doesn't make me cul-
pable of murder. But the answer does show just how heart-
less my opponent is, or was."

He closed his eyes and gave a long sigh.

"Seven years ago, my only grandson was brutally murdered by his peers, for no reason at all. Alex apparently had
some kind of phone that the other boys coveted, and he
wouldn't give it up on demand. He was pummeled to death.
He lay at death's door for three weeks before his parents—
my son and daughter-in-law—made the decision no parent
should have to make in their lifetime. They let him go. He
was never going to get better. He was never going to be the
boy we all knew and loved so much."

Mr. Latham put a hand over his face. His mouth was
working. Annie silently swallowed and was silent. Wolf put
his head on his paws and gazed sorrowfully up at the man.

"There's not a day that goes by when we don't wonder
whether we did the right thing. Or why this had to happen to
such a beautiful boy. For a year, I was so angry that I couldn't
see straight. The boys who were responsible were sent away,
but they'll be out of juvenile detention in just a few years.
They'll have lives as adults, something that Alex never will
have."

Wolf slowly got up and padded over to Mr. Latham,
dropping by his chair. Mr. Latham reached out and unconsciously began to stroke his fur.

"Then I heard about the property in Shelby, forty glorious acres that had never been developed and were ripe for
the picking. I got a brainstorm about how I might honor

Alex's memory and perhaps ensure that this kind of sense-less murder never happened again, at least in our own back-yard.

"I planned to start a ranch, a place where boys who had nothing and had little hope for their own futures could come and learn the basic skills of how to get along with other peo-ple. Taking care of dogs, chickens, pigs, and yes, horses, I presumed was a good start. I thought if I could teach these boys how to respect animals, to respect each other, and gain the kind of confidence they needed so they wouldn't feel compelled to bully others for elusive things that wouldn't make a damn bit of difference in their own lives, I might save another boy's life down the road."

"Did Hilda know of your intentions?" This came after a long pause, when Annie was sure that Mr. Latham was done speaking.

"She did, and she couldn't have cared less. All she cared about were her own precious horses. It was a complete and utter waste of a resource that could have done so much good."

Annie hesitated, but then asked what she wanted to ask.

"The language you used in your last letter was . . . pretty strong."

"I admit it. It was strong, but I still don't regret a word of it, even if the woman is now dead. My real-estate agent and my son both cautioned me against it. My son's an attorney and was afraid of a countersuit. I was at the point where I wanted her to bring it on. But she never did. She got what she wanted, and it was as if Alex had never existed."

Annie didn't know what to say. But then Mr. Latham took up the thread again.

"Six months later, I had my stroke. And that put an end to all my plans. Now I just exist in this house and accept the kindnesses of others."

"Mr. Latham, is there anyone else you can think of who hated Hilda Colbert? Anyone else you can think of who might have wanted to kill her?"

"As I said, I never met the woman. I know there were other people interested in the property, but I don't know if anyone felt as strongly about acquiring it as I did. And Ms. Carson, I must disagree with you on one small point. I don't hate Hilda Colbert. I pity her. She never knew what it was like truly to love another person. I did. And even though loving Alex breaks my heart every day, I still cherish my ability to do so."

As Annie drove home late that afternoon, she thought about Marcus and Hilda's relationship and wondered if Travis (as he now insisted she call him) was right. Had Hilda ever loved Marcus? Marcus certainly seemed to have loved his wife while she lived, as exasperating as she evidently could be. But if you loved someone, and strongly, too, couldn't those feelings turn to hate? Enough hate to say horrible things on the phone to them the week before they died? Enough hate to kill the person you once loved?

Before she went to bed, Annie stowed the DVD of Marcus's voice in the shoebox underneath her bed. She wanted to listen to it. She yearned to listen to it, to catch some nuance that would explain everything to her in a way that made sense. But not tonight. Tonight, she would think of Alex, and horses, and a wonderful Blue Heeler named Wolf, who understood human suffering better than most people.

CHAPTER 20

FRIDAY, MARCH 11TH

"Suwana County officials now suspect the death of Marcus Colbert was a suicide. Colbert was the husband of well-known equestrian Hilda Colbert, whose body was discovered more than two weeks ago in her home in Shelby. Police initially said Marcus Colbert was responsible for his wife's death, although he died before being brought to trial. Meanwhile, Sheriff Stetson has identified Juan Salazar as a person of interest in the case. Salazar was employed by Hilda Colbert on her ranch but has not been seen for several days. More on this story at the hour."

Annie's hand sent the radio alarm clock crashing to the floor. It had done its work, which was to rouse her to wakefulness, but the way in which it performed its job had put her in a thoroughly foul mood.

Stomping off to the kitchen for her first cup of coffee, Annie wondered angrily why people were so quick to rush to judgment. Marcus's body hadn't shown up, only his tie. He was a missing person, that was all. A missing person on whom the police were quick to place the blame for every homicide in Suwana County they couldn't solve.

Her cell phone emitted its old-fashioned trill. Annie grabbed it and noticed the blocked caller ID. It had to be Dan, she thought sourly, who blocked his identity every time he was on sneaky squirrel patrol. Sighing, she flipped the lid and said in her most perky voice, "Annie speaking."

"Annie, it's Dan. Sorry I was a little gruff with you yesterday. Just had a few things to take care of that couldn't wait."

Good old Dan. A pain in the butt one day, an apologetic little puppy the next.

"Did you accomplish what you intended to do?" Annie tried hard not to sound sarcastic and failed.

"Oh, yeah. Talked to that Latham guy you turned us onto. A harmless old geezer who just got his nose out of joint over Hilda's bulldozing her way onto the property. That report's been filed and buried."

"You don't think he had a motive for killing Hilda?"

"Motive, yes. Means, no. Opportunity, unlikely. Unless he called our county senior van and asked the driver to take him to Hilda's and back. The guy can barely walk, let alone wield a knife."

"So it *was* a knife that killed her?" Annie distinctly recalled Dan painstakingly telling her the murder weapon was unknown.

"Knife, penknife, whatever it was, believe me when I say Hilda would have turned it on him in a second, and you would have been looking at a different body altogether when you came along."

"Well, congratulations. And I hate to do this to you, but I've got another little lead that you might want to know about."

"Blast it, Annie! What in the Sam Hill are you doing? Aren't a dozen horses and seventy-five ewes enough to keep you out of trouble?"

"It's six horses at the moment, and you forgot the donkey. But never mind. I happened to be in the Garver's Corner steakhouse a few days ago and talked to the waitress who waited on Wayne Johnston."

Silence reigned on the other end of the line.

"And she said that a complete stranger approached Wayne just at the end of his meal. Then Wayne got a phone call and took it outside. He called it 'a funny' kind of call. Then he left the tavern—oh, after taking a last sip of his drink, but I guess the stranger stuck around awhile longer."

Annie thought she'd done a superb job of assimilating and conveying the facts. She was unprepared, therefore, for Dan's retort.

"And what was the stranger's name?" His tone was silky smooth.

"Well, how should I know? He was a *stranger,* according to Millie. That's the waitress. Didn't you talk to her?"

That last remark was a cheap shot, but Annie didn't care.

"I thought we had. What time did Millie say Wayne walked into the joint?"

"Close to closing. She had to tell the kitchen not to close yet, 'cause Millie, in her usual manner, convinced the man he wanted the T-bone special."

A prolonged sigh flowed into Annie's ear. "All right. We'll check him out. Does Millie remember what this 'stranger' looked like?"

"Enough for a police sketch, I would think. His most compelling attributes are eyebrows that grow together."

"Terrific. Well, thanks for planning my day. Don't know what I'd do without you."

"Oh, and you might want to look at Wayne's cell phone records, if you haven't already. And before I forget, ask me about Hilda's not-so rusty gate."

She was speaking to an empty line.

The phone calls continued to come while Annie was feeding the horses. Cursing the blasted device, she methodically went about her work and ignored the shrill tone. It was only when she shrugged off her stable jacket and procured another cup of coffee in her kitchen that she deigned to see who wanted to speak to her. Quite a few people, it turned out.

The first call was from Rick Courtier, the reporter whom Tony had tossed off her farm a few weeks earlier, and was proving, with this phone message, that he failed to understand that "no means no." Annie listened to ten seconds of his unctuous overtures before hitting the delete button.

The next message was from James Fenton, who merely asked Annie to call him. This she did at once, feverishly punching in the numbers as she sank into a chair by her kitchen table. She endured only a few seconds of staccato-like Baroque music before Fenton picked up the line.

"Good morning, Ms. Carson." He always sounded so bored at the prospect of having to talk to her, Annie thought. She wished the feeling were mutual.

"Mr. Fenton, what news do you have?"

"Against my strong objections, Marcus's disappearance has been classified as a suicide . . . although my guess is it'll take a year or more for the death certificate to be issued. The good news is that this determination will allow the process of settling the estate to begin. I've petitioned the court to release certain funds immediately, which means they could be available as soon as the end of next week. I just wanted you to know that the monies Marcus authorized for you to divest Hilda's horse property should soon be in your hands."

Horse property? Annie thought she'd only been given instructions to find homes for Hilda's horses. Oh, *that's* what Fenton meant. Being an ignorant, arrogant attorney, he could only think of them as things, not animals.

Annie didn't care about Marcus's money. "You know, they're still trying to pin Hilda's death on Marcus. Wayne Johnston's, too."

"I know, I know." Fenton sighed. "Believe me, it's been a real challenge dealing with these backwoods law-and-order types. My worst nightmare is if they manage to convince the prosecutor that Marcus is a serial murderer *and* he's found alive. At that point, Marcus's bail will be revoked and no amount of money will get him out of jail before trial. Make that plural. *Trials.* The Johnston family will sue, of course. That's why I'm trying to release as much of his funds now, before all hell breaks loose."

And you can get paid, Annie thought, but she said nothing. At least she and Fenton were on the same page regarding Marcus's innocence, even if for polar opposite reasons.

The last phone call was from Jessica, who, bless her soul, merely wanted to know how Trooper was doing.

"Great," Annie assured the vet. "I've hopped on his back a few times in the round pen and can hardly wait to get him under saddle and on the open road. I think he's enjoying his new life among the commoners."

"Delighted to hear it. Thanks to all the cold rain and new grass, I've had a higher-than-average number of colic and founder cases already this year. I just wanted to make sure Trooper's delicate system was handling his new environment okay."

"Eating like a horse. Pooping like a horse. All systems go. Oh, and Jessica, there's a good chance that I'll be able to pay off your bill in the next couple of weeks. Keep your fingers crossed."

"I will. Although I know you're good for it, Annie. But I never turn down money when offered."

As Annie said good-bye, she thought Jessica had a point. Marcus was not dead—she'd believed this, ever since she'd discovered his tie—but whether she was right or wrong, he did want her to have the money he'd left her. *And* Trooping the Colour.

She was out of food. She didn't know how it happened, even though it happened more often than she would have liked to admit. Horse, dog, and cat comestibles were in plentiful supply. Life would not have been worth living had they not been. But the stuff that propelled the mistress of the farm throughout the day was in pitiful, short supply. Even the freezer had been denuded.

Rummaging in the aisle that promoted unhealthy chips and dips, Annie heard a shriek behind her. She wheeled around, expecting to see a gallon of sickeningly sweet fruit juice on the floor or a child being yanked away from a row of candy bars. Instead, she saw a young woman with long brunette plaits hurtling her way toward her.

Annie tried to step out of the way but the woman was too fast. The next thing she knew, she was held captive in the arms of a stranger. She struggled to get free of the clearly disturbed inmate unloosed from the asylum until a piercing cry rang out across the entire store.

"Sister!"

It was Lavender, although Annie could barely see the resemblance to the woman who had shown up at her door a mere two weeks ago. This Lavender seemed, well, normal. The absence of pink hair got a lot of the credit. And the hippy peasant look was gone, too, replaced by jeans and a battered sweatshirt. But there was something else that was different about the woman who stood beaming in front of her. It was in her demeanor. The ephemeral gaze was gone. She looked, well, just plain normal.

"Lavender, where have you *been?*"

She didn't mean for her first sentence to come out this way. But then, she hadn't realized until now how genuinely worried she was about her half sister's well-being.

"Let me start again. Lavender, you look wonderful. Where have you been keeping yourself?"

Lavender laughed, and her blue eyes crinkled, making her look not only normal but downright pretty. *A few days out of my presence,* Annie thought, *and dead people come back to life.*

"I told you, Annie! I'm living with my new friend, Martha. Martha, where are you? I want you to meet my sister. The one I've been telling you about."

A tiny wisp of an elderly woman shyly standing behind Lavender took a few dainty steps forward and gave Annie a lovely smile.

"So you're Annie. I'm very glad to make your acquaintance. I'm Martha Sanderson. I've been enjoying your sister's company so much these past few days. I do hope you don't mind sharing her."

Not at all. The pleasure's all mine.

"Well, I've been a bit worried about her. But I'm glad to see that she's all right. Do you live nearby?"

"Martha lives right on the bus route, don't you, Martha? We met on the bus last week. She lives in the cutest house, and all alone. Well, until now, that is."

Martha put a gentle hand on Lavender's arm which surprisingly made Annie's half sister fall silent.

"I live in the robin blue cottage just about a mile from your place, Annie, near the turn-in to that new cider business. Lavender saw me struggling with my groceries on the bus about a week ago and was kind enough to help me. Since then, we've become fast friends. When she told me that . . . she thought you might . . . well, to make a long story short, I have a guest bedroom, and I invited Lavender to stay with me."

"And I love it, Annie! Martha's so nice, and we get along just like sisters!"

Something hard pierced Annie's heart. She didn't think Lavender had any idea of what she'd just said, but regardless, it was true. Martha obviously enjoyed Lavender's company far more than Annie ever would, and the pouting, disgruntled Lavender she'd seen in her own home had vanished. Maybe Annie just wasn't meant to be around people and should stick to animals. Annie pushed down the lump in her chest and smiled back.

"That's wonderful, Lavender. I'm so happy for you."

Lavender turned excitedly to Martha.

"Oh, Martha! Let's have Annie over for tea! I'd love for her to taste those scones you made this morning."

Annie immediately made noises of doing no such thing, but Martha took it all in stride. ·

"Of course, dear child. Annie, we'd be delighted to have you over. Can you come after you've finished your shopping? Do you think you can find the place?"

Annie already had pictured Martha's house in her mind's eye. She knew exactly where it was and what it looked like. It was one of the original farmhouses in the valley, noted for the pink and white rosebushes that graced the walkway leading to the home. It was adorable. Annie had always wondered who took such tender care of the fragile flowers, and now she knew.

"I've often seen your place from the road, and yes, I'd be delighted."

"Wonderful!" This was from Lavender. "Oh, but, Annie, you don't really want those chips, do you? Let me show you where the gluten-free section is. It's amazing what this store stocks for people who care about their health."

Seated in Martha Sanderson's parlor—there was no other name for it that fit—Annie looked around and made a mental comparison of the lavish home she'd been in just yesterday. Travis Latham undoubtedly had more expensive furnishings, but both homes exuded warmth and the personality of their occupants. In Martha's case, this meant an old-fashioned upright in one corner with a book of hymns laid open, and on the windowsills, rows and rows of antique Dresden dolls with matching crocheted doilies underneath. In the back of the room was a well-used fireplace with a mantel adorned with more than a dozen family photos. Larger framed ones hung on either side, some of which looked as if they dated back to the nineteenth century. Annie had no doubt that the entire Sanderson family tree was displayed in the room.

She wondered idly if Travis Latham and Martha Sanderson could ever be a couple. But then, Travis would have to adopt Lavender. She nixed that idea.

Lavender tripped into the room, bearing a tray of warm scones and a bone china tea set. She carefully set it down on the piano bench and left, flashing Annie a beatific smile.

"There's someone else I know you want to see," she said cryptically as she left the room.

A moment later, a small Belgian puppy came racing into the parlor. Annie scooped him up and hugged her. "How are you, kiddo? Are they treating you okay in this prison?"

"I hope so," said Martha, who appeared with napkins and small spoons. "In addition to the puppy chow Lavender brought, she's been eating a bit of raw steak every night. I'm afraid that's my fault. I hope that's all right for her."

"If her tummy can accommodate it, then I think it's fine. Although you are spoiling her, you know."

"My dear, I don't know how much longer the good Lord is giving me on earth. I intend to spoil as many people and animals as I can before I go."

Annie was amused to see Lavender resort to her finishing-school manners in front of her. She poured the tea as if she were serving the Queen of England and presented the scones as if they were a rare French delicacy. Annie did her best to mimic her sister's good manners for Martha's sake, and adroitly fed the small crumbles from her scone to the puppy hovering at her feet.

"I've admired your roses for so many years now. When did you first plant them?" Annie asked Martha politely after accepting her third cup of tea.

"Oh, honey, since I was twenty-one and a blushing bride. My husband, Fred, and I moved over here in 1952, when Fred took a job as a research chemist for the local lumber company. We met at the University of Washington. There weren't many women attending college in those days, and even fewer majoring in chemistry. The war had just ended, and veterans were going back to college in spades. I had my choice of men, I can tell you! But Fred caught my eye in our chem lab sixty-five years ago, and I've never looked anywhere else since."

"The valley must have looked a lot different back then."

"You'd hardly recognize it. Miles and miles of pristine forest, with just a sprinkling of houses hither and yon. Most everyone was involved in the timber business back then, in one way or the other. I wanted to go out and make my mark on the world, too, except that there wasn't anything for me to do. Women didn't take professional jobs back then, not if they didn't have to. Fred and I were never blessed with children, so I just devoted myself to my roses. When people would ask me how I grew them so healthy, I'd just tell them that's where my chemistry degree came in."

Martha's eyes were twinkling as she said this. Annie was amazed. Here was an intelligent, educated woman whose skills had been ignored and unwanted in a rural community, yet she showed no resentment at her lot in life. Fred must have been a wonderful husband, she thought.

As if reading her mind, Martha added, "Of course, I had my wonderful husband, up until 1998. We never lacked for intellectual conversation. And we tried to stay current with what was going on in the city. Don't get me wrong—we loved living here, every minute, but both of us needed to hear good music, see good art, and keep our brains stimulated. At the same time, we were happy to embrace what the Peninsula offered. We'd often go to a hoedown on Saturday night and hear the Seattle Symphony the next afternoon."

"You must know most of the families in the valley."

"Oh my, yes. You couldn't help it. You saw them at church every Sunday and at the Grange every other day of the week. I know all the 'first families' here, along with their grandchildren and great-grandchildren."

Annie was intrigued. She'd grown up in Port Chester, the biggest town in the area, and only moved to the country after she'd purchased her small farm. It had been important to her mother for Annie to attend the best schools the county had to offer, and they were in town. Her mother's job with the county also made living in town a necessity.

"Do you know the Truebloods?" she asked Martha. Like every other longtime native, Annie knew that the Truebloods were among the first families to own a lumber and paper mill in the area. And now she knew that Wayne Johnston had plowed his rig into their fence line on his zoned-out trip from Garver's Corner. The Truebloods were on her list of people to talk to, Dan be damned, and she wondered if Martha could shed any insights that might help her introduction.

"They were our first and best friends," came Martha's prompt reply. "John and Louise were just the nicest people. They welcomed everyone into their home. We spent many a Saturday night playing bridge and charades in their parlor. And the parties they'd hold! They were wonderful hosts, just wonderful."

"They had children, didn't they?"

"Six of them, as I recall."

Glancing at Annie's appalled face, Martha added, "It was the done thing in those days, dear. You needed sons and daughters to help out at home."

Which is probably why Martha and Fred never got a home bigger than this, Annie thought to herself.

"Did the children go into the family business?"

"Some did, some didn't. One of the boys, I believe, was killed in the Vietnam conflict. And the girls, of course, moved away after they were married, although I think one of them moved back here a few years ago. But it was Cal, the oldest son—he married Mary Darnell, another local gem— who truly stepped up to the plate after John retired. Of course, the timber business changed after his father got out. A combination of federal mandates and dwindling forests, I'd say. But the Truebloods still own most of the timber in this county. And they've been wise stewards of the environment, despite all the negative press that the timber industry has received."

Annie digested this. "So Cal and Mary's children may not automatically have a family business to inherit, it seems."

"Well, it's a blessing in some ways. They only had two children, a boy and a girl. The girl became a lawyer, and I believe is practicing environmental law in Washington, D.C., now. I don't know if she ever married. I don't believe so. I think she's a lesbian."

Annie started at Martha's casual declaration.

"Oh, don't look at me like that, dear. Believe it or not, we had gay people even back when I was born. We just didn't know it, and we certainly didn't call them that. I'm just glad that the world's advanced enough to recognize gay people and to stop paying so much attention to their sexual orientation."

Annie was beginning to like Martha more and more.

"How about the boy? The son?"

"Now that's a sad story. Eddie was always a bit of an outcast, even in his own family. He didn't take to school, and he got into a bit of trouble when he was a teenager. For the past three generations, every boy in the family had trotted off to the same Ivy League college, but Eddie couldn't even get into his father's alma mater with his grades, juvenile pranks, and yes, criminal record. He tried to start a couple of businesses, all with his father's money, of course, but couldn't seem to make a go of anything he tried. The last I heard, he wanted to buy farmland and start raising llamas, not that Eddie knows anything about llamas. But that's Eddie. He gets an idea in his head, and there's no stopping him until he's tried it and failed miserably. Unfortunately, everything he wants to do takes money, and I suspect Cal is about ready to stop supporting his half-baked endeavors."

Annie did her best to look sympathetic. She was sure Martha had spent countless hours comforting Louise Trueblood over her grandson's peccadilloes. Personally, Annie was just glad that she and Eddie had never crossed paths in high school.

At the end of the afternoon, Annie had convinced Lavender that the puppy should return to her home, at least for the next month or two.

"He needs to be trained, Lavender. And no one's a better dog trainer than an older, wiser dog like Wolf. Belgians are highly intelligent, but also highly energetic animals. They need a job. At my place, the puppy can learn from Wolf how to herd and be a good watchdog to my sheep. Here, you're going to have to walk him six times a day just to keep him from tearing up the house."

"Annie's right," Martha added gently. "Remember how the puppy chewed up all your clothes the first night you were here?"

Lavender nodded glumly. *Aha!* Annie thought. So that explains the change in style. The Peninsula-style chic Lavender had adopted had been born out of necessity. Well, she could only hope that Lavender realized her new apparel was more practical and more appealing. Annie had no doubt that Martha had been instrumental in persuading Lavender to go for a more natural hair color.

Annie and the puppy departed just as the sun began sink over the Olympic Mountains. From her truck, she waved the puppy's paw good-bye. Martha and Lavender waved back, a striking silhouette against the rosebushes, still stark from the winter months, but with the promise of blooms showing in every bud.

Just like Lavender, Annie thought as she drove home with the pup on her lap, conscious that she was breaking the law but unwilling to put the pup in an unfamiliar crate in her flatbed. *A bud just waiting to open to its full glory. And Martha, bless her heart, was just the woman to cultivate that process.*

For a dog, Wolf was fairly charitable about receiving the young upstart Belgian back into the home. He didn't snarl, and he didn't growl. He simply ignored him. Annie was content. Bolstered by the tea and scones she'd just consumed, she went out to tend to her horses' evening meal. It was almost seven-thirty before she returned to the house. The assessment she'd given Jessica of Trooper's health really had been right on, she told herself. The horse had ravenously consumed his mash and looked bright, alert, yet relaxed. She decided to take him out for a ride the next day if the weather permitted.

Now she made herself a pot of tea and sat at her kitchen table, willing herself to put down on paper what had been swirling in her brain for days. She reached for her collection of sharpened pencils and began to write. On the top of the sheet, she put in big block letters "MEANS," "MOTIVE," "OPPORTUNITY," and "ALIBI." On the left-hand side, she listed all the suspects to date. She began with her personal favorite: Todos.

She'd never forgotten his remark about what happened to geldings who were unable to compete or show. She didn't care if he was the hardest unpaid worker on Hilda's place. Or had the reputation as the most skillful trainer to the rarefied sector of the equine world. Any man who could destroy a horse for such a paltry reason would never rank above snake level in her book.

Did Todos have the means to kill Hilda? Absolutely—he had the run of the ranch and, Annie assumed, lived on-site. Motive? That was unclear. Todos undoubtedly was the highest-paid hand on the place, and Hilda was probably a cash cow compared to every other horse owner in the county. Opportunity? Again, he had more contact with Hilda than any other employee. Alibi? Ah, there was the rub. Todos had an airtight alibi. Damn.

Moving on, Annie considered Juan. Poor little, meek, underpaid, unappreciated Juan. Like Todos, he had the means and opportunity. Although he probably lived in some horrid little hovel on the ranch, not a caretaker cabin that she assumed Todos had been allotted. Motive? Who wouldn't want to see Hilda dead? If she'd reamed him out over some perceived failure or threatened to fire him, it might have been enough to set him off. Alibi? Who knows? Juan had taken off before anyone had the chance to ask him. But Annie couldn't forget her memory of him quaking beside her as she stood on the brink of entering Hilda's golden palace. Dan might think he'd been quivering with fear that Annie would discover the body that he already knew was there, but Annie still didn't buy it. He was just plain scared of a very mean woman.

Next was Latham. Although Annie had left Travis's property utterly convinced that he, too, was just another victim of Hilda's downright evilness, she now thought of several small details that had escaped her at the time. Such as his impassive face when she'd told him she had been the one to discover Hilda's body. Was this the natural reaction of someone given startling news? Unless it wasn't startling news.

Annie fleetingly wished she watched television so she knew what *CSI* detectives would think. And what about means? Travis certainly appeared to be a physical wreck, but who tended his garden? He said he lived alone. If Travis were capable of wielding a trowel or a hand weeder, he might be capable of sticking it into Hilda's neck. Motive? Travis reeked of motive. True, killing Hilda wouldn't bring back his grandson, Alex. And several years had passed since Hilda had usurped the property from him. But hadn't some famous person said "revenge is a dish best served cold"? She moved onto "opportunity." Not on his own. He'd have to have a confederate, and she refused to believe that it was Marcus, as Dan had suggested. Alibi? His word only. Poor Travis didn't even have a dog to back up his story. If Travis was innocent, Annie vowed to train the Belgian pup to be his companion. When the pup reached maturity, of course.

Next on the list was the mysterious stranger. Here, Annie put in a long string of question marks under each category. All she knew was that the stranger somehow was involved in Wayne Johnston's death. She was certain he was the one who had spiked his Coke. But again, even the stranger needed a confederate to make the call, so Wayne would go outside long enough for him to put the drug into the drink. Could it have been Latham? Todos? Or . . . Marcus?

Marcus, who was last on her list. Annie thought it was only fair. So she was dismayed to find that in doing so, she'd just painted herself into a corner. Means? Marcus was strong enough to kill Hilda, yes. Motive? Hilda was making impossible demands on Marcus; their marriage was all but over by the time she died. Opportunity? Annie wasn't sure, but she suspected it wouldn't be hard to fly in and out of the Olympic Peninsula on a private jet without submitting a flight plan. Or would it? After 9/11, life had changed for everyone, especially pilots. A quick search on her laptop informed her that as long as the pilot landed within the lower forty-eight and could fly without depending on instrumentation, no flight plan was necessary. Annie sighed. Suwana County had an airport. Nothing like Sea-Tac, of course, but big enough to be called "international" simply because private planes took off for British Columbia from its field. Alibi? To her knowledge, still unproven. And then there was that damn voice mail. She sighed again.

Tossing aside the paper, Annie headed for bed. There was still work to do. She just didn't know what it was.

CHAPTER 21

SATURDAY, MARCH 12TH

Annie leaned down and gently eased open the round-pen gate. Even at five-eight, she had to stretch the full length of her back to do so. But it was worth it. The view from Trooper's back was marvelous, if a bit daunting. She couldn't ever remember being on a horse so tall. In the saddle, she estimated that the bay stood closer to seventeen hands, and made a mental note to let Hannah figure it out the next time she came over to ride. On the mounting block, Hannah should be able to reach Trooper's withers with the measuring tape.

Saturday morning had dawned clear but cold, yet after her warm-up session with Trooper, Annie was ready to shed her sheepskin jacket. All week, the bay had behaved beautifully in the round pen at walk, trot, and canter. Now came the acid test. It was time to take him out on the trail. Annie had no intention of making Trooper one of her workhorses; he was simply too much fun to ride. But she was anxious to take a look at her sheep pasture and thought a nice quiet stroll along the fence line was just the ticket to test Trooper's comfort level in the great outdoors.

Besides, he was inoculated against the million and one things to which he apparently was allergic. Jessica had stopped by early this morning with small flasks of homeopathic medicine, which she guaranteed would inhibit his reaction to pine, alder, and practically every other indigenous plant in the region.

"It looks like eye of newt," Annie had dubiously told Jessica.

"Probably is. See, they're color-coded. So you can't make a mistake. Start him on the yellow flask, once a week, and work up to the blue and red bottles. In six weeks, he'll be on a maintenance program, and you'll only have to do this once a month."

Annie had obediently applied the first subcutaneous dose under Jessica's supervision and placed the rest of the medicine in her small tack room refrigerator.

"Not necessary, Annie. In fact, it's probably not good. Just store them at room temperature."

Annie had placed the flasks on her medicine shelf, looked at the latest bill for her very expensive hobby, and decided, then and there, that it was time for Trooper to show her what he could give in return.

And what a return he bestowed. As Trooper began his half jog along the narrow path that led to the sheep pasture, she felt on top of the world. The horse's ears pricked forward in eager anticipation, and his breath was quick. Annie knew he was as excited as she was. She bent over to stroke his neck. She wanted him to know that they were a team, going out on a grand adventure together.

The pasture was thick and tall with new grass, glistening

in the morning dew. There was no question that her sheep would dine well this spring and summer. It was one of the payoffs of surviving weeks of unrelenting rain and occasional snow over the past several months. It also was the reason Washington had earned its epithet as the Evergreen State.

The fence line predictably needed work. Blow downs from past winter storms had fallen across several fence posts, rendering the electric braid stretched below moot. Stray limbs were strewn everywhere, hazards to horses and sheep alike. Annie also noted a number of water pools inside the pasture, dangerous sump holes that contained filthy water and could break an animal's pastern with one misstep, or induce disease.

Annie had brought along a big red marker with her, which she now put to good use. She brought Trooper to a gentle halt to mark the fences that needed mending and the grassy areas that required repair. Not only would this make her first day working the land immeasurably easier, it was an excellent way to test Trooper's awareness of his rider. She could tell that, given his druthers, he would have cantered, no, galloped the short mile they now took at a leisurely pace. And if truth be told, Annie was just as game to fly past the posts to see what Trooper really had to give. But reason and experience told her that she had several hundred miles to put on Trooper's back before they were ready for the racetrack. Besides, by asking Trooper to stop every few dozen steps, she was reminding him that they were working together. If he obeyed her commands, she willingly gave him his head when they started again. It was a win-win situation that Trooper intuitively grasped. Annie marveled at the horse's intelligence. He'd been trained to run, and only run, yet he had a connection with her that was undeniably solid.

An hour later, they approached the north gate, where the

sheep would be unloaded in less than a week. Annie and her next-door neighbor, two miles away, shared an easement between the two properties. Annie used it for sheep loading and unloading; her neighbor used it to get to his private gun range down the road. Fortunately, the sound of shotgun and pistol practice was largely muffled by trees, and the sheep seemed oblivious to the noise each Sunday afternoon, the time her neighbor typically choose to exercise his Second Amendment rights.

She glanced up at the sky, looking at a sun that was gamely trying to shed warmth on a cold March morning, and stood up in her stirrups for a good long stretch. Trooper sniffed the three-bar aluminum gate, obviously curious about the new scent of eau de ovine. Annie reached down to test the latch. Sure enough, it ominously squeaked, unlike Hilda's worn-out gate. She wished she'd remembered to bring three-in-one oil with her and made a mental note to do so on her next trip out.

Annie decided to dismount and reward the bay with a ten-minute grass break. She had just swung one leg over the saddle when an unexpected blast from a shotgun rang out and something whistled disturbingly close past her ear.

With one foot still in the stirrup, Annie had to make a split-second decision. She watched Trooper's head rear up and felt his front feet lift off the ground. An eerie scream penetrated the air and for one heart-wrenching moment, Annie was afraid the bullet had pierced Trooper's skin. Then his front feet pounded to the ground and Annie hurled herself back onto the saddle, grasping the reins with both hands. Gone was the silent empathy that the two had enjoyed on the ride here; now Trooper was hell-bent to get back to safety. He pummeled his way down the fence line, with Annie hanging on for dear life. She knew better than to try to reel him in. She simply wanted to stay on his back and make sure the ride would end before they crashed into the tack room. For two unbroken minutes, all Annie heard and felt were the rapid-fire pounding of Trooper's hooves on the ground below. From her vantage point, Annie felt as if she were flying. If Trooper had been born with wings, they'd be airborne right now, she thought.

As the familiar round-pen and stable appeared in sight, Trooper eased his gait fractionally, and Annie tightened up on the reins. They were going to have to stop eventually, and she preferred that her dismount not be over the bay's head. She was sure her heart was beating as fast as Trooper's and prayed that she had enough good sense left to think for both of them. It had occurred to her midflight that Trooper could have mistaken the sound of the firearm as the cue to "go." After all, he had been trained as a racehorse. If that was the case, she was going to have to teach him that "stop" didn't always occur at the tape line.

She tugged on the reins hard and released, then tugged again. She had to make contact with Trooper's mouth, which at the moment appeared hard as granite. The horse simply wouldn't give. In one fluid motion, Annie slid her hand up her left rein and whipped it outward and around and planted it on her knee. Trooper's front hooves left the ground again, but he was forced to make a half circle. Annie kept her hand firmly planted on the rein touching her knee, which forced the horse to turn. But instead of stopping, Trooper kept turning in a dizzying circle, his head taut against the reins. Just when Annie was contemplating the possible injuries she might sustain by jumping off, Trooper abruptly stopped, and Annie instantly released the reins.

She never remembered dismounting. She only remembered sinking to the ground, her legs shaking uncontrollably, and feeling great relief that Trooper was content to remain where he was although he was shaking as much as she was. Annie caught her breath and grabbed the reins before Trooper could run off again. They both walked on trembling legs over to the round pen. Once inside and the gate firmly latched, she fumbled to remove Trooper's saddle and bridle. She glanced over to the horse pasture to see the rest of her herd cantering toward her, no doubt to investigate their mad-dash return. Setting down the saddle, Annie grabbed a stray lead rope and clicked for Trotter. Throwing the rope over the donkey, she walked him over to the round pen, which Trotter entered without fuss. Trooper was in the corner farthest south, agitatedly pawing the ground. Trotter placidly walked over to him and nuzzled the lowest portion of the bay's neck—the highest he could reach. After a few minutes, the bay began to nuzzle back.

If there was ever a time when Trooper needed a soothing companion, it was now. The trouble was, so did Annie. She knew the shot had not come from her neighbor. He might have a lifelong passion for collecting firearms, but he was scrupulously concerned about gun safety. Even if he'd just seen a cougar on his property, he never would have shot off a round without knowing where it would land. No, this was a bullet meant for her. Or Trooper. The knowledge was horrifying.

Annie would have liked to have taken to her bed with a bad case of the vapors, but she hadn't forgotten that her sheep were being sheared today. She resolved to buck up, but not without taking proper precautions. After thoroughly cleaning her Winchester, she restored it to the gun rack inside her truck and placed a full box of ammo in her glove compartment. Whistling for Wolf, whom she intended to have by her side from here on out, she climbed into her truck and set out for the Thompsons. There was no way to track the shooter unless she found a spent cartridge that fit a very rare gun. But she would be better prepared if there was a next time.

Annie wheeled into the Thompsons' and saw her flock crowded into Johan's front pasture, baaing and carrying on as if they were being asked to board the *Titanic* and already knew the advance headlines. Leif was kneeling in the middle, quickly and efficiently shearing a ewe that was putting up a pitiful wail against the sound of the electric shears. His cousin stood nearby, ready with the vaccinations that would come afterward. Johan stood beside him, clearly hoping to be called into service.

It was a relief to observe a traditional farm ritual after the trauma of the morning. Annie waited until Leif finished with the ewe, which trotted off baaing plaintively after being released from its undignified captivity. She watched Leif wipe his face and accept a glass of Hester's lemonade from Johan. Catching his eye, she walked over to where he was working.

"Leif! How's it going?"

"Not bad, Annie, not bad. I swear, your ewes grow more wool every year."

"Fabulous. More wool means more money from the co-op."

"Yeah, but it takes me twice as long as it did a few years ago. If you're going to keep treating them so well, I'm going to have to raise my rates."

Annie knew he was joking although he had a point. When she'd started her flock five years ago, she'd only had fifteen yearlings that had matured into adulthood remarkably quickly. After a few well-picked rams came to visit, motherhood soon followed, and now Annie was the proud owner of seventy-five fully developed and producing ewes. She'd learned to ignore the pointed suggestions from friends and neighbors that her babies would taste awfully good with a little rosemary and butter. Sheep growing was a smart move, for which Dan constantly demanded full credit, but she'd deliberately decided to breed them only for wool. Annie wasn't opposed to eating lamb. In fact, she was quite fond of it. She just pre-

ferred to partake of the shrink-wrapped variety she found at
her local grocery.

"Charge me whatever's fair, Leif. I trust you."

A flash from his eyes showed that he appreciated the gesture, which also meant that she'd forgiven him for his egre-
gious lapse in judgment at the accident site. Well, everyone
made mistakes, she thought, although when she might have
fallen short recently momentarily escaped her.

Annie didn't look forward to her next stop, but she refused to let herself back down. The truth was, she hated
meeting new people. She never quite knew what to say, and
she secretly believed her small circle of friends was already
sufficient to last her lifetime. It had taken all her courage to
accept Lavender's invitation to visit her new home yesterday although that had turned out to be surprisingly enjoyable. But Martha Sanderson's description of her closest
friends, the Truebloods, did little to inspire Annie's confidence. She realized she was meeting the Truebloods' offspring, but figured the genes had to be the same. Annie was
not a highbrow. She didn't listen to classical music, and her
trip to Travis Latham's house had proven that she knew
nothing about art. Yet she felt compelled to talk to the lumber barons. Just a few weeks ago, their fence line had been
the scene of horrible wreckage in which a man was killed.
She wondered what Dan had told them about the case since
then, if anything. She wondered what she might learn from
them today.

Yet, for once, Annie got the perfect opening line. As she
peeled off Highway 3 to turn into the Truebloods' driveway,
she noticed a chip blower off to one side, depositing mounds
of rich cedar chips onto the owner's garden beds. *What she
would do for that cedar,* she thought. The cost of buying
bags of cedar chips at the local Cenex for stall bedding was

significantly eating into her household budget. Perhaps she could hold the operator at gunpoint and demand that he dump some of the stuff at her barn.

Or perhaps she could just ask politely. She parked her truck at the foot of the driveway and walked up to the operator, who was oblivious to everything except the task at hand. The sound of the blower was overwhelming, and Annie could understand why he wore ear protection.

"Excuse me!" she yelled, standing to one side of the machine. The man looked up and turned off the machine, waiting patiently for her to explain why she had interrupted his work.

"I'm sorry to bother you, but I was on the way to see the Truebloods and noticed all that wonderful cedar that you were spreading. Any chance that we could talk later about the possibility of buying some of your chips?"

"That's up to your friends," was the blunt reply. "It's cedar from their sawmills. I just come over once a month to spread it on their landscaping. If they're willing to share it, I'm happy to spread it."

It turned out that Martha was right: the Truebloods must have been wonderful people, because at least one of their children certainly had married a warm and friendly host. Annie met Mary Trueblood coming out her home, obviously about to work in her garden, her hands swathed in green gloves and a tidy row of garden tools tucked into a skirt pocket. She was delighted to make Annie's acquaintance. Wasn't she that lovely woman who took in rescue horses? She was sure she'd read about her in the local newspaper before. And she was a friend of Martha Sanderson? Oh, my, she hadn't even realized that Martha was still alive. Wasn't that nice. She and her husband, Fred, had been such good friends of her husband's parents. Would she like to come inside for a glass of iced coffee? She could make fresh if that's what Annie preferred.

Annie was content with iced. And when she asked about purchasing cedar chips for her own use, Mary wouldn't hear of it.

"That sawmill produces more than we'll ever use," she told Annie. "We'd be delighted if you could take some off our hands. Cal's out at True Value, but I know he'll agree. Just give us your address and we'll make sure Ian—that's our man you saw coming in—drops off a load on a regular basis. We're just happy that someone else can put them to good use."

A great weight lifted off Annie's shoulders. She felt confident, then, to plunge into the primary reason that brought her to the Truebloods' door.

"You're too kind," she told Mary, meaning it. "You don't know how much this helps me out. You see, I've been taking care of the horse that was in that accident on the highway a few weeks ago, and it turns out he's allergic to straw bedding. It's been fine for my own horses, but Trooper gets a respiratory infection just by standing in it. I've had to change the bedding for all of them, and it's pretty expensive stuff."

"Oh my. So you were there that night. I didn't go out, but Cal did. He said the truck that was hauling the horse was horribly mangled."

"It wasn't very pretty although I was concentrating more on making sure the horse was safe. We were incredibly lucky that the trailer didn't flip. I guess we have your good fencing to thank for that."

"There are too many accidents on the road," Mary said emphatically. "People think a straight country road means they can go as fast as they want. They don't realize that we share it with deer and other wildlife. My own husband refuses to drive with me at night because I insist on going about twenty-five miles an hour just to avoid the deer."

"I hear you." Apparently, Dan hadn't informed the True-bloods that Wayne's crash wasn't caused by an animal trying to leap across the road. Well, why should he? That was protected police work, which only she was privy to.

Annie hesitated. "You know, I heard that there were some mysterious holes and tire tracks found on your property, close to where the rig crashed. Is that right, or is it just one of those rumors floating around?"

If Mary thought Annie's question improper, she didn't let on. She probably was too well-bred, Annie thought, unlike her, who popped off with whatever was on her mind.

"Cal did mention something about that. We thought perhaps the county had put up a sign there without getting our permission first—you know, one of the signs that tell people what the risk of fire is that day. But the fire department said they hadn't. Of course, they would have asked us first, and anyway, it was too early in the season. We still don't know what was there. It's a mystery. We don't recall ever seeing anything posted there before the accident, but then, we usually come in from the other side."

"I suppose the police came out and took photos and all."

"Well, I know they came out, but whether or not they took photos, I don't know. I do remember that Cal went down with them to take a look at the tire tracks. It must have been a four-by-four, or a truck with big tires. We had to haul at least a ton of gravel to fill in the holes that were made."

Annie's heart sank. "Do you have any idea how large the post holes were? I mean, how far apart?"

"I don't, but I'm sure Cal will remember. Why are you so interested in knowing?"

Ah. The question that was bound to come.

"No reason. It just seemed strange, that's all. I wondered if it had anything to do with the accident, I guess."

"Well, if it did, it escapes me. Can I refresh your glass, Annie?"

Before Annie made her exit, she steered the conversation clear of any controversial subjects and stuck to the tried and true: the Trueblood family. Mary was only too happy to tell Annie about her daughter Camilla's frequent successes as an environmental law attorney and her high-placed connections in the nation's capital, but the subject of children stopped there. If Annie hadn't already known, she would have assumed Camilla was an only child.

At 4:00 P.M., Annie said her good-byes, continuing to offer profuse thanks for the gift of cedar chips and promising to stay in touch. Climbing back into her truck, she noticed Wolf in the back, straining to get out of his crate.

"Sorry, buddy. I didn't realize I'd be gone so long." She opened the crate and waited for Wolf to take advantage of the nearest tree or jump into the front seat, his favored spot. Instead, Wolf bounded down the driveway, close to oncoming traffic.

"Wolf! Come, Wolf! Come!" Annie ran pell-mell down the asphalt. What was the dog doing? Honestly—first running after the Belgian puppies and now this. It was time for remedial dog training if Wolf didn't improve his response time to his mistress's commands.

She found him at the end of the driveway and grabbed his collar.

"Wolf! What were you thinking! Bad dog!"

Wolf ignored her. He was staring at a truck parked across the road, a black Ford pickup with dark tinted windows that nearly matched the color of the truck. Annie looked up, and saw a man, perhaps in his mid-thirties, emerging from the driveway on the other side of the road. He wore jeans and a stylish leather jacket. Annie watched as he walked around the back of the truck and opened the front passenger door. Wolf lunged forward and gave a low, menacing growl. Annie, whose hand hadn't moved from his collar, shook him to make him stop, but the sound had not escaped the man's notice. He turned and looked at Annie. He was not a big man, perhaps Annie's height, nor particularly well built. In fact, there was not a lot that distinguished him from the rest of the male population of Suwana County. Except for extremely bushy eyebrows that grew together in the middle.

"Dan, I'm telling you, I saw the guy who was in the steakhouse. He was right across the street from the Truebloods. I tried to get his plate, but by the time I got up to my own truck, he was gone."

Annie listened impatiently on her cell phone to Dan's response.

"Because if I didn't get Wolf back in the truck, he was going to break free and rip the man's head off, that's why. Wolf must have been watching him from the truck. Something set him off. But then, Wolf always could smell pure evil. It's why I keep him chained up when you come around."

Annie sighed as Dan broke in once more.

"I went to see if I could get cedar chips, that's why. Jeez, Dan, do I have to file a report every time I do something in this county? That's all. And if you don't like what I'm telling you, you can . . ."

Again Annie was talking to an empty line. She'd forgotten, or more precisely, hadn't had time to tell Dan about nearly being shot today. Well, no matter. There wasn't much he could have done about it, anyway. She'd tell him the next time their paths crossed.

Walking up from the stables to her farmhouse that night, Annie reflected that there was one more thing she had to check off before retiring that night and scotch, for once, would not help. But she would put it off as long as possible. She snuggled with the puppy, to Wolf's disgust, then washed and dried every dish in the kitchen from the previous week. Finally, there was nothing left to do but the thing she dreaded most.

Peering under her bed, she pulled out her shoebox amid the voluminous dust bunnies that had taken up residence there. She pulled the DVD out from the blank case, a deliberate act on Esther's part, and placed it in her antiquated CD player. Placing earphones on her head, she skipped through each track until she got to the proper place. Moments later, Marcus's voice filled her head.

"I will destroy you. You will be a dead woman before you know it. Consider yourself warned."

She put the DVD on pause and thought. It sounded like Marcus. According to Dan and the crime lab, it *was* Marcus. Even she had to concede that the tonal quality certainly matched the voice she'd heard for a few short days. But the cadence was off, and that was what bothered her. There was something about the rhythm of his speech that was off-putting. It sounded like Marcus's voice, but it didn't sound like the way he spoke. It wasn't the words. Annie already had difficulty believing that Marcus had uttered them, crime lab report or no. But it was the way they hung together that didn't ring true. Why was that? How could the message sound like Marcus yet not sound like Marcus?

Annie played the message again. And again. Finally, when she could recite the words and intonation by memory, she carefully put away the DVD and set the player and earphones aside.

She knew the answer. The problem was, she still didn't know who had done this to Marcus. And she had no idea how she was going to convince Dan that she was right.

CHAPTER 22

SUNDAY, MARCH 13TH

Normally, Annie loved Sundays. It was the only day of the week when she truly allowed herself to kick back, except for taking care of the horses, of course. Today, she longed to make a pot of tea, stretch out on her living room couch with a pile of old horse magazines, and enjoy the comfort and quiet of her home. Wolf, she noticed, was already sleeping by the sofa in anticipation of his mistress's imminent arrival.

What was more, this was the first Sunday in recent memory Annie had a chance of enjoying. Lavender had been doing her ridiculous smudging the previous week, and the week before that was the horrible day that Marcus had disappeared. And the Sunday before that . . . Annie searched her brain. Oh, of course. That was the Sunday that started all the upheaval in Annie's life. Technically, she'd been called out on the search and rescue of Trooper in the wee hours of Monday morning, but in Annie's mind, it remained Sunday night.

Annie put away her lunch dishes and took one last regretful look at her well-worn couch, sagging in all the places where she typically plopped. It appeared that this Sunday would be no different. Despite her flippant remarks to Dan, she was more disturbed than she'd let on by the appearance of the shaggy-eyebrowed-stranger outside the Truebloods' home. She trusted Wolf's instincts. And Millie had told her enough to convince her that it was this same stranger who'd spiked Wayne Johnston's diet Coke. Whether or not the stranger's malfeasance extended to shooting at Annie, killing Hilda, and kidnapping Marcus or worse, she didn't know. All she knew was that she didn't want to get in his crosshairs again, and she wanted to know his identity.

To solve that little mystery, she figured she had no farther to go than her local library, conveniently open to the reading public on Sunday afternoons. Annie sent up a silent prayer that her tax dollars allowed county residents this luxury. She knew that several of the libraries in nearby Seattle had far shorter hours of operation than her own rural branch.

After making sure the pup was settled and the woodstove stoked and set to simmer, she whistled for Wolf, who looked surprised and a little hurt at the change in plans. She stuffed a handful of dog treats in her jacket to help make his wait in the truck more palatable.

A helpful volunteer showed Annie where the old high school yearbooks were stored. It was in a seldom-used corner of the library; apparently not many borrowers wanted to go down memory lane and sneak another look at their photo on the track team. Annie hoped Mr. Bushy Brows, as she now called him, had attended one of the local high schools and his distinctive facial hair was evident in his adolescence. If not, she was out of luck.

She started her search with the 1993 Suwana High School yearbook, several years after her own graduation from Port Chester high. Annie had graduated in 1990, when hoodies, leg warmers, acid jeans, and Converse All Stars reigned. Only a few years later, the fashion trends that had filled her school halls had been replaced by branded clothes and a surprising number of visible tattoos adorning almost every part of adolescent bodies. How hideous, she thought, as she turned page after page in the class photos section. The kids looked so young. Were they really old enough to decide how and where to be permanently etched?

By the time she picked up the 1996 yearbook, her eyes were glazing over, and she worried that even if Mr. Bushy

Brows' photo was here, she wouldn't recognize him. This year, however, all the class photos switched from black-and-white to color, not just the senior section, which made them pop out on the page. Yawning, Annie began running her finger down the faces.

She found him toward at the end of the freshman section, sandwiched between Susan Trimble and Andrew Turler: Edwin Alford Trueblood. Eddie, as his family called him, had no hobbies and belonged to no clubs. He simply attended school. He was almost scowling in the picture, as if he resented having to pose at all or perhaps even participate in the public school system. But the scowl made his one-line eyebrows even more prominent. Annie guessed that he probably got teased for it. She could imagine the names: One Brow, Low Brow, Ape Man. Bushy Brows.

Well, might as well track his academic progress. The sophomore yearbook netted another picture, this one with Eddie in a Mohawk—although the eyebrows remained the same. The new fashion statement only him look more like the juvenile delinquent Martha had sadly told Annie he'd become. Annie wondered if there was a mug shot of him someplace— or did minors escape that part of the charging process?

Eddie was absent from the junior and senior yearbooks. Annie realized he may have transferred to another school, opted for Running Start, or, more likely, simply dropped out. But she had no interest in tracking him down further; that was Dan's job. She had what she'd come for: Bushy Brows' identity.

She made several copies of both photos on the library's one color copier machine, then made a pit stop before leaving the building. On the kiosk outside the bathroom, she noticed a flyer advertising a horseman's meeting at the Grange that evening—in fact, checking her watch, exactly one hour from now. *Damn.* Annie hated to go to the things. They were supposed to provide valuable information to horse owners in the valley, but Annie suspected they really were fairly transparent ways for local folk to get together and spin tales about their own lives. The speakers were often less than scintillating, and the social hour afterward, which consisted of weak coffee and store-bought cookies, often lasted longer than the presentations. Annie didn't socialize, not when she could help it. But as a staunch supporter and very active member of the search-and-rescue organization, she was obliged to attend at least a few of the meetings. Well, she was halfway to the Grange already. She might as well make an appearance.

She stopped for a greasy hamburger and shake at the closest drive-in, generously sharing her protein bounty with Wolf. What with the beef stew at Johan's, her faithful canine was almost getting spoiled. But she couldn't afford to be without his protection right now. The good news for the Blue Heeler was he was now regularly eating the tastiest cuisine of his entire dog life.

A dozen other pickups were already in the Grange parking lot when she pulled up. She recognized most of them; the good news about the county's horse owners was they were more than willing to help out the others in time of need, and most everyone had been to each other's ranch or farm several times. Short a half ton of hay at winter's end? Someone would surely sell you what they could spare until the first summer cutting, delivering it, too. Out of a probiotic for a colicky horse? Any horse owner with the stuff would rush to make sure you had what you needed in a crisis. Horse owners also were good about filling in when their neighbors were sick or called out of town. Annie pitched in and helped out as much as the next person, and actually enjoyed the interactions. It was the prescribed social activities that made her uncomfortable and long to be back to her solitary existence.

"Annie! Long time no see!"

A redheaded farmer in overalls ambled over, a cup of steaming coffee in his hand.

"CW, how are you?"

"Can't complain. Looking forward to tonight's talk. I've spotted two bears on the north side of my property in the past two weeks. I'd like to know how the state intends to let us deal with the problem. Right now, I've got my .12 gauge oiled and ready."

Bears? Annie thought she'd heard more local news than she ever wanted in the past few weeks, but apparently a key story had slid right by her.

"I didn't realize any bears had been seen in the valley," she admitted to her companion. "A bit early, isn't it?"

"And a bit out of their usual roaming range, I'd say. Bill over here says they got into his chicken coop just yesterday. Tore the head off a chicken and went after his turkeys."

Annie was dumbfounded. She was used to the predictable cougar alarms that sprang up every few years, when one or more was spotted in the area during cool autumn months. But bears? She thought they were all happily living in the Olympic National Forest, only a menace to campers who left their food or garbage out at night.

"Who's the speaker tonight?"

"Sergeant McCready. He's over there, talking to Lena."

Annie looked over CW's shoulder and saw the Fish and Wildlife agent chatting away with the club secretary. He seemed perfectly at ease.

"Well, maybe it's just a fluke. I sure hope so."

"You've got your ewes coming into your place pretty soon, don't you?"

"Yeah, but I've never seen a bear around the flock. The pasture is wired. And I put my donkey in for protection."

"Well, I sure hope you don't have any problems this spring. As I said, I'm armed and ready for any varmint that steps foot on my property. With or without the state's approval."

Having said his piece, CW nodded at Annie and went for a refill. Annie felt disgruntled. She really wasn't worried about any wildlife coming onto her ranch, but the idea of black bears in the vicinity still was cause for concern. A six-foot-tall bear wouldn't think twice about swiping a little Belgian Tervuren if it stood in the way of a food source.

The meeting got under way a few minutes later. Annie squeezed into a seat between two riding friends, Luann Schmidt and Jill Thayer, promising to catch up with them after the presentation. Sergeant McCready stood up and began to speak while the crowd was still talking among themselves.

"Most of you know me already, so I won't bother with a big introduction. I'm Doug McCready, and I've been with the Fish and Wildlife Department for the past eighteen years. Most of that time has been on the Peninsula. You got a problem with fish or wildlife, I'm your point man. I track all sightings, and I want to hear about them when they happen. That way, I can try to extinguish the problem before it gets out of control."

"Don't you mean exterminate?" The loud bellow came from the back of the room. Annie recognized CW's voice.

McCready ignored the interruption. "I'd planned on giving you an update on our cougar management removal program," he continued, "but since I've heard quite a few of you have spotted black bear on or around your properties, I'll switch gears and address that instead." The room quieted down.

"Every year, we get about sixty reports of black bear in our area. This year, we've already received reports of fifteen sightings. That's a substantial increase over past years. We don't know why we've had this surge, but there are a number of reasons why this could be occurring.

"As you know, our past two summers have been cooler than average. This means less food at higher elevations, where the bears typically spend their winters. Two, what with the economy the way it is, we had an actual decrease in hunters this past season. So there are more wildlife competing for less food.

"While I'm not happy knowing that bears are roaming our rural areas, I'm certainly not as concerned as when we had our cougar outbreak three years ago. Unlike cougars, black bears are essentially herbivores. Their primary diet is plants and berries. That being said, if you leave a half-eaten steak in your garbage pail at night, they still might go after it. Ditto for small domestic animals. Or chickens. So taking a bit of preventative care isn't a bad thing to do."

Annie began to zone out as McCready continued his discussion. It was all old news. She perked up again when he dragged out a life-sized cutout of a black bear cub.

"There was supposed to be an image of a female bear here, but it's gone missing," McCready said as he put the cub photo in full view of his audience. "Which is exactly what could happen in real life. You see one of these cute little fellows and decide you want a photo of him and your grandson together. Don't do it. You can be darn sure that mama bear is close behind and will attack on sight if she thinks someone is endangering her offspring."

As if she didn't know that, Annie thought sleepily, as McCready continued his discussion of black bear habits and ways of procuring food. Most of what he said was common knowledge to her, not to mention the rest of the people in the room. What they really wanted to know, she realized, is whether or not they had the state's permission to shoot any bears they saw on private land. She dozed off again until she realized McCready was nearing the end of his talk.

"In conclusion, I want to emphasize that there have been zero reports of any bears attacking a human. A little knowledge and common sense will keep it that way. Keep your small pets inside at night. Make sure your fence line is secure and hot-wired. Stow your garbage inside until you can put it in a safe receptacle off your property. And, please, if you see a bear, call me first. We're prepared to remove the bears if at all possible and restore them to their natural habitat. They probably don't like wandering around in your meadows any more than you like seeing them there. Now, I've left a number of cards on the table. Please help yourself and don't hesitate to call if you have any questions."

A thin smattering of applause filtered through the room. CW, however, wasn't ready to let the agent go.

"Can we kill them if we see them?"

McCready already was leaving the podium, but he stopped and addressed the farmer personally.

"CW, you know as well as I do that if a bear is attacking your livestock or other animals, you have every right to shoot. You're also required to report it immediately, I repeat, immediately, to the Fish and Wildlife Department so we can pick up the remains. But if you see a bear that's not acting aggressively toward your herd, all you can do right now is give me a call. There is no removal system in place that extends to private citizens at the moment, and quite frankly, that's how it's likely to remain, unless the number of bear spottings drastically rises."

He stepped down amid a number of other shouted-out questions. Apparently, CW had brought his bear-shooting fan club with him. Annie glanced over at her seated companions. They all rolled their eyes in unison.

An hour later, Annie emerged from the Grange, genuinely happy that she had attended. It had been good to catch up with her riding friends. And a few private words with Sergeant McCready had allayed the fears that good ol' CW had tried to fan. She unlocked Wolf's crate in her flatbed and whistled for him to join her in the front seat. It was only seven o'clock, but darkness had stolen over the mountains while she was inside. To her surprise, she was among the last to leave. Her horses would be anxious to be fed at this unconscionably late hour.

She turned on her headlights and started to back her car out of the parking lot. A moment later, she slammed on the brakes. Something had scurried behind the truck. It was too dark to see what it was, but she knew it wasn't a deer. Maybe a lost dog? Annie got out and told Wolf to stay. She rescinded her order a second later. This was not the time to be investigating in the dark by herself.

She stood still outside the passenger seat, trying to pierce the pitch-black night with her eyes. The county was notorious about putting in street lamps even in populated areas, and Annie cursed the government entity that had decreed the Grange had no need for overhead lighting. She turned and scrounged around inside the truck and retrieved an LED flashlight, mercifully still charged.

When she turned around again, she heard a small, breathless noise. It appeared to be coming from the bushes behind the Grange. She gave Wolf the signal to "find" and slowly stepped forward, her flashlight shining directly in front of her.

A whimper, undeniably human, emanated from the rear of the building.

"Who's there?" Annie's voice rang out in the cold night air. She sounded surprisingly authoritative.

Silence. Annie crept farther in, and Wolf began his signature long, slow growl. She poised herself on the south side of the building, flattening herself as much as she could, then thrust the flashlight around the corner.

"Who's there?"

"No shoot! No shoot!"

Annie deflected the light to the ground, to the place the words seemed to be coming from. Huddled in a worn jean jacket, a thin Hispanic man crouched on his knees, his hands held out in front of him in supplication.

"Juan! What are you doing here?"

At the change in her voice, Juan put trembling hands over his face. Annie crouched beside him, all trepidation gone.

"Juan, it's only me, Annie. Remember? I brought the horse to the ranch last month? Along with the donkey?"

Juan looked up, fear etched into his face. He was terrified at her presence, she realized. He hadn't understood a single word she'd said. She wasn't sure he even recognized her.

"Are you okay?"

It was perhaps the one American phrase Juan understood, and he nodded, although he looked anything but okay to Annie.

"Where have you been?"

She received a blank stare in return. Racking her brain, she tried again.

"*¿Dónde has estado?*"

But at this, Juan gave a sudden yelp, pulled his jacket tightly around him, and fled across the street, into the small community park across from the Grange.

Straightening her legs, Annie watched Juan flitter his way through the trees. She had no intention of following him. She motioned for Wolf to come and slowly walked back to her truck.

Against her better judgment, she called Dan after feeding the horses, none of whom appeared pleased to be dining at the same hour as their European counterparts. Pouring herself a scotch, she sat down at the kitchen table for what she hoped would be one phone conversation with Dan in which they both hung up at the same time.

For once, Dan didn't interrupt or berate her for giving her information about a case he was desperate to see the back of. He listened intently as she described how she discovered Eddie Trueblood's identity and her chance encounter with Juan just one hour ago.

"I'll send my boys out tonight to comb the park to see if we can reel in Juan. And good work on IDing the bushy-eyebrowed stranger. You've just saved me a pile of time. I'll pick up those color copies you made tomorrow morning and throw together a lineup. Looks like we've connected at least one piece of the puzzle concerning Wayne Johnston's wild ride."

"You mean, you think there's more to it?"

"I'm sure there is. I'll be bringing Mr. Trueblood in for questioning just as soon as I get Millie to make the ID. Tony and I aim to lean on him until he tells us who was involved in his little scheme."

"Do you think Eddie was involved in Hilda's death?"

"Could be, could be. I'm pulling Wayne's cell phone records as we speak. And I haven't ruled out Latham, either. What with Juan now within grasp, we just might be able to put *all* the pieces together before too long."

Including the mystery of what happened to Marcus, Annie thought. She realized that Dan had not once thrown in Marcus's assured culpability into the conversation. Perhaps he was finally seeing reason. But should she tell him what she suspected about the voice message? No. Not yet.

Still, heartened by their return to mutual civility, Annie decided to take the plunge and tell Dan about the shot that had whizzed by her just yesterday morning.

"I'm certain it wasn't from my neighbor," she told Dan. "Lord knows Chris loves to shoot off his guns, but I usually only hear him on Sunday afternoons, and he's a stickler for gun safety. Besides, he usually empties a clip at a time. This was a single shot."

The sheriff was uncharacteristically silent on the other line.

"Dan?"

"Annie, I want you to listen very carefully to me. I know you like to go off and do things your way, but until we know exactly what part Eddie Trueblood played in all these homicides, I want you to be extra careful, you hear me? Don't take any unnecessary chances."

Annie felt like Hannah after being told to be sure not to get stepped on by Bess's huge hooves. She bit her tongue.

"I am, Dan. I've got my Winchester and my dog by me at all times. And there's nothing more that I can do, anyway. I'm fresh out of clues."

"Keep it that way, Annie. I worry about you."

She was bone-tired, so tired, in fact, that it took all her energy to rummage around her bedroom to find an old manila envelope in which to place the yearbook photos of Eddie Trueblood. Her bedroom was beginning to resemble Lavender's before she left, Annie thought, but oh well. She shoved the yearbook photos inside the envelope, scrawled "Dan" on the outside, and set it outside by her kitchen door, underneath the eaves in case it rained.

She only saw the blinking red light on her answering machine when she picked up her empty glass of scotch to put it in the kitchen sink. She had two messages. The first was from James Fenton, telling her that he had received advanced notice that the court intended to make Hilda's will available to him early next week. He hoped that the contents would not have a bearing on the expected release of funds from Marcus's account. He would continue to keep her informed. The second phone call was from Todos, who respectfully asked if she would be available to come to the ranch tomorrow at ten, when insurance agents would be present to appraise the animals. If it was too much trouble, he would understand. But since she was the horses' executor, he knew she would want to know, and he would be grateful if she could find the time to be there.

Annie went to bed feeling more lighthearted than she had in days. She was frankly glad to hand over the case to Dan again. Her days of private investigation had brought out more questions than she had answers to, although she felt certain that ultimately Marcus would be cleared. She only hoped he would eventually be found.

In the meantime, she was content to return to doing what she loved most: being in the company of horses . . . even if it meant having to deal with the oh-so-mighty Todos. She pulled out the files she'd made of Hilda's pedigreed horses, pulled her coverlet over her knees, and began to read.

CHAPTER 23

WEE HOURS OF MONDAY, MARCH 14TH

For once, Annie had neglected to put her cell phone on vibrate before turning off the light. So when the shrill "brrring brrring" pierced her bedroom at 4:13 A.M., she yelped and jumped up as if she'd been stung by a wasp. She grabbed the phone and peered at the time illuminated on the screen. *What the hell? Not another horse accident, please dear God*. She jabbed the "answer" button and tried to speak as if she were awake.

312 *Leigh Hearon*

She soon was.

"Annie speaking."

"It's Tony."

"Another horse wreck?"

"Worse. Colbert Farm is going up in flames. Hilda's residence is nearly consumed and Leif's not sure he can contain it. We're getting outside help but even so . . ."

His unanswered sentence spoke volumes. Annie could think of only one thing.

"Tony, there are eighteen horses in those stables!"

"Don't I know it! They're already spooked and there's no place to put them."

Annie spoke without thinking.

"Yes, there is. The paddocks in the pastures. They all connect with each other and should be downwind from the fire. Open *all* the gates. I'm on my way."

She didn't wait for an answer before hanging up.

Annie later couldn't remember putting on her clothes. She only remembered shouting at Wolf to stay inside as she leapt into her truck and seeing him slither into the back cab. *Damn.* There was no time to entice him back into the house. There was no time at all.

Annie seldom exceeded the speed limit but tonight she tore through pitch darkness punctuated by roaming herds of fog as if it was the brightest day in June. She needn't have worried about being stopped by the State patrol; Sheriff County vehicles, fire trucks, and EMT vans zoomed by her as if she were standing still. She barely had time to move over to the shoulder of the road before the endless string of emergency vehicles disappeared from sight.

The flames appeared a half mile before the turnoff on Myrtle Road. They soared above the fir trees surrounding Hilda's house, and had turned the normally black sky into an eerie orange-red color that reminded her of a painting she'd seen in one of Travis Latham's art books—Edvard Munch's

The Scream. Which is exactly what she expected to hear upon her own arrival—the high-pitched hysterical screams of eighteen horses imprisoned in their stalls, smelling the smoke, feeling the fire, and mad with fear.

The electronic gate was wide open and Annie roared through before she heard the bullhorn behind her ordering her to halt. She stomped on her brake so abruptly that Wolf's body hurtled from one end of the cab to the other. Annie turned instantly to see what damage she had done to her dog but had no chance to investigate. A State trooper was beside her window, rapping loudly on the window. Annie rolled down the window and shouted out, "Annie Carson. Suwana County Horse Rescue Brigade. Here at Deputy Elizalde's request."

The trooper immediately pointed with one long arm to the arena-stable area, where she could see a bevy of fire-fighters quickly unwinding and spreading their hoses.

"Back up past the gate and leave your vehicle there. We don't know how far this will spread."

Annie nodded her understanding and put her truck in reverse, but not before telling Wolf to lie down. She was relieved to see him do so quickly and obediently. Once parked, she bolted from the cab and made no effort to keep him inside. Wolf had no business here, but there was no way in hell she was going to leave her dog in a locked vehicle in a roaring fire zone.

She ran up the hill and found Tony talking to Leif. As she'd predicted, the sounds of frantic whinnies and high-pitched squeals emanated from the stalls staggered around the arena. She rushed out and down to the pasture paddocks. She'd remembered how impressed she'd been on her first visit here by the interlocking paddocks weaving throughout the massive pasture, even as she bemoaned the fact that each horse was sequestered in its own private space.

Well, now the horses were going to get to know each other, she thought, like it or not. And Tony had done what she'd asked. Each paddock gate now was wide open, so that the horses had free range of the pasture.

She dashed up the hill and into the arena. Glancing around wildly, her eye fell on the storage room where all the Timothy hay was stacked. She'd been so impressed by this, as well. Now all she could think about was that once a traveling cinder alighted on a single bale, the whole room would turn into a blazing conflagration that would spread to the stalls in a nanosecond. Gauging from the smoke infiltrating the arena, it could happen any minute. Her throat already was raw. And the heat from the fire a quarter mile away was gaining. It was a slow, thick heat, the kind Annie imagined Dante describing in the seventh circle of hell. The time left for saving the horses was dwindling. It might already be gone.

She raced to the tack room, grabbing ropes wherever she saw them, then weaved her way through the dozens of firefighters who were expertly doing their jobs.

Approaching one, she shouted, "Sprinklers! The arena has a sprinkler system!" And was she seeing things? Juan, the missing Juan Salazar, was standing beside her.

"Juan!" she shouted. "Turn on the *agua!*" She thrust her arm toward the arena roof. "*Aquí!*"

Juan nodded and scurried off. *Thank God there was one man on the place who knew where the instrumentation was,* she thought. But where was Todos? He should have been loading the horses into Hilda's trailers long before she ever arrived. Had he been caught in the fire back at Hilda's? But why would he be there at all? Wasn't Hilda's residence off-limits to the staff?

Then it struck Annie. The hay. So much hay that it could, and probably would, turn the stables into a massive firestorm at any moment. The twelve-foot stacks had been there the day she'd discovered Hilda's body. *So why did Todos have to go to Eastern Washington to get more?*

She had no time to think about it. Wending her way through the crowd of firefighters, she saw Dan talking intensely with Harrison County's fire chief. Annie was sure Dan was glad for the help, but even in this worst of crises, territorial issues had obviously emerged.

"I'm telling you," said the chief, "It's impossible to isolate the fire at its place of origin. Whatever accelerant was used has caused a perfect storm."

"The Sam Hill it has!" Dan sputtered back. "Our boys extinguished the arc around the Colbert residence soon after their arrival. We expected you to clear out the remaining incendiary material. But it looks like whatever's left is now about to take over the barn."

"It's not our fault, Dan! There's a grove of fir trees lining the property line between house and stables. We can't account for every single cinder that's fueled by the debris on the ground. If you'd called us a half hour earlier . . ."

"I only found out about this fire a half hour ago. Now let's quit arguing and you go back and do whatever you can to keep this heat from the horses."

Turning aside, he saw Annie, and snapped, "What took you so long?"

Annie decided that at this moment in time she would be mature. It might be the only time in her life, but eighteen equine lives were at stake, and she didn't want to waste time badgering about irrelevant issues, such as how she felt she got here at warp speed. Still, curiosity couldn't keep her from asking a few questions now.

"So it's definitely arson?"

"Most definitely. Fire alarm in the residence and the barn dismantled, no sign of fire extinguishers in either place, which I know were here before, and clear signs of gasoline spread around the house. Can't get more obvious than that. As far as I'm concerned, we won't have need to call in Harrison County's fire scene investigator."

Suwana County had no such position. It was a sore point with Dan.

"Any suspects?"

Dan glared at Annie. "The usual. Everyone who's missing. Juan. Marcus. And now Todos. Haven't seen his hide since I got here. Now don't start looking at me like that, Annie. . . ."

"Juan's here."

"*What?* Juan? Here?"

"Yes, and he's just turned on the arena sprinkler system. So if all the fire alarm systems were turned off, how'd you even know about the fire?"

"Security system in Hilda's house. Operator on call alerted us. Now let's go fetch those horses. I hear you've got a mind to turn them out in the pastures."

"Don't see any other solution at this point. Trailers are parked behind the barn and probably about a thousand degrees inside by now. Our best chance is hauling them down to the paddocks and just praying that the fire doesn't get that far."

"Well, let's get to it."

Annie stood rooted to her spot. *So why didn't the security go off the day Hilda died? Or did it, and Dan just decided not to share this little fact with her?*

Dan strode over to the stall closest to the fire and yanked down the halter neatly hanging by the wooden door.

"No!" Annie screamed, suddenly back in the present. Dan turned to her with incomprehension on his face.

"Forget the halters! Nothing that has to be taken off! Nothing that can catch on fire." She thrust a lead rope in a bucket of water and then into his hand.

"Do this with every lead you use. Just sling it over the horse's head. I'll get the next one. We need someone down by the paddocks to let the horses know they can get into the adjoining paddocks."

Dan barked, "Tony!" into his squawk box.

"No!"

Dan again looked askance at Annie but kept his eyes locked on hers.

"We need Tony to help us move the horses. Anyone can open a gate. Is Deputy Lindquist here?"

Dan nodded abruptly, and issued the order.

"Lindquist, get down to the paddocks. We're bringing the horses down and need you to move them through. First two are on their way. Look for us coming down the hill."

Kim Williams had somehow materialized beside them. "I may not know horses, but I can take directions."

"Great," Annie said with relief. "They'll want to bolt. Just keep a wet lead rope over them and try to keep up with them. A contained canter is the goal. Not likely, but we can try. And let's keep them all within sight of each other. They need to know they're going as a herd."

Dan and Kim nodded dubiously. All around them, horses were rearing up, striking the stall walls with their hooves, and tossing their heads in fright.

"How the hell are we supposed to do this?" Dan asked with real fear in his voice, the first Annie had ever heard.

"Quickly." Tony and Annie spoke at once. Annie moved first. She opened the stall door a foot wide, threw the rope around a Palomino's neck, kicked the door open, and started moving. The Palomino took all her strength to control, straining to get loose and run as fast and as far as possible.

"Get going!" she yelled back to the others. "I can't do this alone!"

It was all Annie could do to keep upright as the Palomino ran down the hill. Lindquist was right where he should have been, holding the paddock door open with the door leading into the next paddock wide open as well. Annie ran to the second gate and released her hold.

"Shut the gate until the next one gets here!"

That was thirty seconds later, as Dan, slipping and sliding down the hill, frantically tried to keep his arms around the wildly twisting neck of the black stallion, the one Annie had seen off by himself in a nine-foot high gate. She glanced at the rest of the fencing. Six feet high at the most. Most of the horses were capable of jumping that high, especially in their current frenzied state. She prayed that they wouldn't, opting to stay with the rest of the herd than risk individual flight.

She passed Kim and Tony leading the next two horses. Predictably, Tony exercised the most control over any of the horses so far moved, although Kim's handling of the seventeen-hand Warmblood was impressive.

That woman doesn't know the meaning of fear, Annie thought. *And she's passing that onto the horse, whether or not she knows it.*

"Why can't we just let them all loose?" Dan panted as he reached the arena, his hands resting on his knees as he regained his breath.

"Half of 'em would just head back to the stables," was Tony's terse answer. "Let's go. Four down, fourteen to go."

"Why?" Kim whispered loudly to Annie as she accepted another lead rope.

"Home territory. Place where they always felt safe. Hanging out in one big paddock is a brand-new experience for them. But unless one of them jumps a fence, they should be safe."

Going into a stable with a crazed horse was sheer madness, Annie knew, but she knew of no other way to save them. There was no time to trailer them, and she had no idea if they would trailer easily or not in the midst of the pandemonium going on around them. The paddocks were not ideal—they, too, might be consumed by the fire, but there was no alternative space. By now, the sprinkler system was on full throttle, making the arena slushy, but it was reassuring to Annie.

"Spray the hay!" she screamed at a firefighter who was dousing the trees lining the northern-most door, the closest to Hilda's home. "And where's Juan?"

Juan, she was relieved to see, was now by the stables.

"I turn on the *agua*, Señora. Also in the *cabaña*."

"*Bueno*, Juan! Very good! Can you help us move the horses?"

Juan may not have understood her English, but he got the message. And Juan could not only move one, but two horses at once.

The horses trust Juan better than they probably trusted Hilda, Annie thought.

A minute later, an ominous crack thundered behind them, coming from the top of the arena, and Dan and Annie, both striding up the hill from their second transport, looked at each other. It had to be the sound of Hilda's roof beams collapsing. That meant cinders and flames were flying everywhere. It wouldn't be long before the arena, was also engulfed.

"How many more?" Dan yelled.

"Eight. Juan's handling two at once," Annie called back.

"Good man."

"Yup, and Todos is nowhere in sight. Any ideas?"

"Not a clue." He jerked open the stall door holding a massive Belgium, whose hooves looked as if they could knock off even Dan's immense head in one blow. He grimly swung the sopping lead rope around the Belgium's head and began the jerky run with the horse toward the open barn doors.

Annie looked after him, amazed at his ability to shed his initial fear so quickly. Crisis had a way of curtailing negative thoughts, she figured. But time was running out. Smoke was now surging into the arena at a rapid rate and she dared not look overhead to gauge the safety of the roof, even if she could have seen anything. The horse she now had to bring down was highly agitated and panicky. And who wouldn't be? She could barely see. She could barely breathe. Neither could the horse, and he didn't have the slightest idea why his safe environment had erupted into this nightmarish blend of heat, intense human activity, and worst of all, captivity.

This horse was much smaller, but no less out of control, rearing at the sight of her savior. Annie waited until the quarter horse's hooves hit the ground, then quickly slung the rope around his neck and started moving.

"Six more," she gasped to Juan, who was trudging up the hill. "Then we're done."

But Juan wasn't listening to Annie, and not just because he didn't understand her English. His gaze was on the top of the arena, the roof now undulating with fire passed on by the burning trees. He took off at a breakneck speed while Annie continued her slip-and-slide run down the hill.

When she'd safely passed the quarter horse to Deputy Lindquist, Annie took inventory of what the saved horses were doing. Most were racing along the fence line, still searching for a way out. Once more, Annie hoped that none would make a break for it. She could see a cascade of disappearing horses flying down the road and massive destruction ahead.

Back at the arena entrance, Kim, Tony, and Dan were donning smoke masks, handed out by Harrison County firefighters. The horses had no such luxury, but she knew they'd need them if they were to survive without injury to their lungs and eyes. And that wasn't all. The havoc inside the arena was increasing. The remaining horses would be skittering their way around hoses emitting water at a pressure that would knock any one of them on its side.

She thankfully accepted a smoke mask, then, as her colleagues looked on in astonishment, ripped off her sweatshirt, plunged it into a water bucket, and entered the next stall. This horse was an Andalusian, a magnificent Spanish

breed that usually was grace and beauty, but now appeared
every bit as crazed as the bay had been the night of his rescue. She stood poised by the door, ready to exit if the hooves
came close to striking her. The horse paused for one second,
just enough time for Annie to wrap her wet sweatshirt around
the horse's neck, covering the sides of its face to act as blind-
ers. She gave the horse's muzzle a quick stroke before lightly
flinging the lead rope around him. Their exit from the arena
was far removed from the ground manners Annie normally
demanded, but this was no normal day—which, she noticed
once outside, was fast approaching. It had seemed hours ago
that she'd been awakened by Tony's call. Now dawn was
breaking.

Annie ran with the Andalusian down the hill and into
Deputy Lindquist's now-experienced hands. He deftly directed the horse toward the next open paddock and then
quickly shut the gate.

Her team had taken the hint. The next three horses down
the hill all were swathed in wet outerwear, their eyes di-
verted from the havoc inside the arena.

"Should have thought of this before," Dan panted as he
came down the hill.

"Oh, bite me." Annie slowly trudged up the hill. Sixteen
down, two to go. The last two were in Juan's hands.

She saw him, holding two jittery horses that were testing
even his considerable handling skills. Annie took her sopping sweatshirt and wrapped it over one of the horses' head
and eyes. She gestured to Juan to give her the lead ropes. He
did, immediately ripped off his own shirt, immersed it in the
nearest bucket, and did the same. Each holding a lead rope,
they skirted their way past the firefighters and ran down to
the pasture. Annie's lead rope slipped off her horse moments before reaching the paddock but the horse's momen-
tum was so great that there was nowhere else to go but in.
Juan's horse followed by a nose.

Deputy Lindquist heaved the paddock gate shut and with trembling hands secured the bolt. The nightmare was over.

Only, it wasn't. It was just beginning, Annie realized, as she watched firefighters run from the arena and stand fifty yards back, still spraying their hoses at clearly a lost cause. Annie took one last look inside. Hilda's medals and photos had melted on the walls. All the accolades that had been bestowed on her had turned into grotesque art.

The arena rumbled as if it were part of an impending earthquake, followed by the sound of a colossal crack. Annie watched in horror as the green tin roof twisted and buckled. Within a half minute, the entire structure had collapsed in a heap of flames, smoke, and ash.

It was then that Annie remembered Wolf. She hadn't seen him since she'd fled from her truck. *Where was he?*

She ran around the arena and past the hay room that predictably had turned into a mass of white heat, flames shooting up twice the height of the original room. Hilda's perfectly planned, perfectly manicured empire had literally gone up in smoke. In a few hours, all that would remain would be a mound of smoldering ashes. The only assets left were her horses—which would need extensive PTSD therapy for years to come.

Annie turned from the heat and ran toward Hilda's shell of a home. Averting her glance from the pile of smoking wood on her left, she veered toward the right, past the bin in which she'd discovered the starving Belgian puppies, and toward the pathway in the back of the house. Perhaps Wolf had run up here to get away from the more immediate fire. She flung open the rusted gate leading to the path she and Marcus had taken weeks ago, which now seemed years. Again, there was no sound. *Why not? Annie wondered for the tenth time. There was nothing back here.*

The clues were coming fast and furious, but she had no time to assemble them. She had to find Wolf. She had to.

Instead, what she saw was a Jeep Cherokee bouncing up the road toward the back of Hilda's property. Who the hell was that?

Whoever it was, he or she was in an inordinate hurry. She saw a blur of black and gray fur racing alongside the Jeep. It was Wolf, and he was growling in his most aggressive manner.

Annie raced up the hill, picking up a rock. She heaved it at the Jeep. It cracked the front window, doing no harm to anyone, but it did stop the driver's flight. Annie ran forward, and with the Jeep's cessation of speed, she now recognized the driver. It was Todos, who turned and looked at her. Of all the humans on the Colbert property, he was the only one who was not covered in soot, white ash, and totally exhausted. In fact, Todos looked as if he was ready to take off on an enjoyable trip. His jeans were clean and creased and his cowboy shirt was the kind guys wore when they want to impress babes at the corner bar. A cowboy hat was set jauntily on his head.

Wolf continued to emit a low growl at the back of the Jeep. Still smiling at her, Todos put the car in reverse and shot backward a few feet. There was a sharp, sudden yelp.

He had run over her dog.

Annie rushed forward, ready to kill. Todos leisurely stepped out of the Jeep and waited for her arrival. When she raised her arm to smash his face in, Todos grabbed it with surprising strength. He immediately twisted it behind her back until Annie thought her arm was going to come out of her shoulder socket.

"You have been in my way far too long, Señora Carson," he hissed. A hoof pick appeared in his right hand and scraped across her neck. Annie twisted her neck as far as she could but the edge of the hoof pick was still firmly pressed against her jugular. She felt as if she was going to collapse, then rage took over and she continued to twist and turn and tried to scream. But all that came out were hoarse cries no one could possibly hear. Two hours immersed in an arson she was sure Todos had set had stripped her of her vocal cords. And now she was certain he was about to strip them, literally. She needed time. And help.

"Is this how you killed Hilda?" she managed to rasp.

"Of course. A pick is a most effective tool."

"Why?"

But Annie never heard his reply. Another large crack rang out into the open air—*not another structure falling,* Annie thought wildly—and Todos suddenly slumped, loosening his grip as he did so. As he slid to the ground, Annie saw Wolf leap onto her would-be killer, his jaws open and teeth barred. But the bullet that had struck Todos had done its work. Wolf pinned his paws on Todos's lifeless chest, lifted his muzzle, and uttered a deep, atavistic howl.

The last thing Annie remembered as her knees buckled beneath her was seeing Dan Stetson's meaty hands gently lowering her to the ground.

CHAPTER 24

MONDAY AFTERNOON, MARCH 14TH

If you tell anyone, I will have to kill you."

"What, me, the keeper of secrets? Perish the thought."

"Well, it's just that I've never fainted before."

"No one's ever tried to kill you before. To my knowledge, anyway."

Annie and Dan were standing by the electronic gate, watching a convoy of horse trailers rumble up the road and onto what was left of Hilda's property. It was late afternoon, and it had been an exhausting one. Wisps of smoke and ash still floated throughout the ranch and the smell in the air was positively acrid, but the fire was definitely out. The wreckage was overwhelming.

Wolf had a bruised paw from Todos's efforts to run him over, but nothing more. Annie was bone-weary. In fact, she couldn't remember ever being this tired. She, Juan, and Dan had spent the rest of the day helping Jessica and other local large-animal vets check out the horses. Thankfully, everyone seemed okay. One horse was on the verge of colicking, but now appeared to be past the danger zone. Jessica, after tubing the horse and giving him massive doses of probiotics, had trailered the pinto back to her clinic to make sure its recovery was complete by overnight.

The rest of the horses were about to be housed at the local fairgrounds in Port Chester, which had plenty of unused stalls kept for fairs and 4-H shows. The temporary accommodations were far less luxurious than Hilda's, but Annie doubted the horses would notice much, and the air at the fairgrounds certainly was cleaner. Several neighbors had come by, each offering to take a few of the horses in for the time being, but Annie had insisted that the herd remain together.

"They've had enough trauma for one day," she explained to the well-meaning Good Samaritans. "It's better that they can all still see, hear, and smell each other. They need reassurance that one thing hasn't changed in their lives today."

Juan already was at the fairgrounds, cleaning the stalls and setting up water and feed. It was a massive job, and Annie had politely suggested to the people who'd offered to house the horses that their efforts would be better served right now by helping the one surviving worker on Hilda's ranch.

Juan, she and Dan had learned, had merely been hiding out at a relative's home about ten miles away. He'd been scared away by Todos—that much Annie could gather from her pigeon Spanish—but beyond that, she was clueless.

"Let the guy go and get some rest," Dan told Annie as she struggled to understand the stream of Spanish pouring out of Juan, who, now that his enemy was dead, was eager to talk. "We know where to find him, and there's plenty of time to fill in the gaps."

Juan had offered to spend the night in one of the stalls, himself, to keep an eye on the *caballos*. Annie had given him a sleeping bag she always kept in her truck. As soon as the "all-clear" had sounded, Esther had driven in with a platter of homemade cookies. Hester Thompson arrived an hour later with a massive pot of homemade stew. Juan had left with copious amounts of both in his possession.

Just as the last horse was loaded, and to no one's surprise, the Harrison County fire inspector showed up. He now was peering and prodding around Hilda's home and appeared to have no intention of leaving anytime soon. Fortunately, Dan was spared much interaction with him.

"Might as well let him do his job," he'd grumbled to the core group that remained at Hilda's decimated ranch. "It doesn't take a rocket scientist to figure out what happened here."

Kim and Tony had both solemnly nodded their heads at Dan's acute sense for the obvious. Annie had not.

"But why, Dan? Why did Todos set the fire? And why try to kill me?"

"I don't know. But we know that he did. And you heard his confession about Hilda."

Yes, but she'd never heard his answer of *why* he'd committed the deed. While she and Dan had tended to the horses, Tony and Kim had immediately gone into investigation mode. Their efforts apparently had paid off. As she held the horses for the vets, she watched both Tony and Kim haul out several dozen sealed and taped evidence bags, and, she noticed, had rather smug looks on their faces. She could hardly stand not to know what they evidently did.

Now that the horses were safe and her job was done, Annie tried to wheedle it out of Dan. He was walking her to her truck, mercifully unscathed by the fire. Wolf was sleeping in the backseat. He was exhausted, and in his sleep mode no longer looked like the man-eating beast he'd been a few hours earlier.

"So why do you think it took Todos so long to skedaddle?"

Dan stopped and leaned on the side of Annie's truck, which was covered with ash. *He could hardly get any dirtier,* Annie thought. Fortunately, he didn't have the urge to race home and take a bath, as Annie did. Instead, he just felt like talking.

"My guess is that Todos planned to make his exit just at the crucial moment, when every hand was on deck, so to speak. Less likely that he'd be seen leaving the property. Besides, most arsonists like to hang around to see their handiwork. Todos probably was a quarter mile up the tree line from the house, watching us all work like crazy for nothing. We'll find out later tonight when the second team comes in to gather evidence."

Annie sighed. Her buddy was going to have a long night, and she was going home to a bath and Glenlivet. The horses had been fed—Luann Schmidt, her closest neighbor, had filled in when she realized she wasn't leaving Hilda's anytime soon. Jessica had already reported that Luann would again be on the job tonight. *Thank heaven for her few but steadfast friends.*

She realized Dan was still talking.

". . . even though his exit route was pretty well shielded. The security system—"

"What exit route?"

"There's a back road to the ranch that ends at the rear of Hilda's house. Todos was pulling out to get on it when you walked up. Perfect timing."

"That's one way to put it. Oh! That reminds me. Why didn't the security system go off the day Hilda was killed?"

"I wondered when you'd think of that. It didn't go off because it wasn't on. We realized that the day you found Hilda's body."

"So you assumed that Hilda knew her killer."

"Precisely. Which is why we were concentrating on Marcus, the only human being who apparently was allowed into her hallowed home. That, and the voice message."

Annie wondered if she should tell Dan now that she'd already figured out the voice mail. Naw, it would just rub salt into his wounds. He'd been so sure Marcus was the guy, and although the case was close to being solved, the primary perpetrator had come out of the blue.

"It's too bad a bear didn't eat Todos while he was hanging out, watching Hilda's place go up in flames."

Dan looked at Annie quizzically.

"That's exactly what we did find."

"A bear carcass?" Maybe those bear sightings everyone had talked about at the Grange were true.

"Not quite. It was a cutout of a bear, fastened to two poles, which I'll bet you dollars to doughnuts precisely fit those holes found just outside the Truebloods' fence line."

"No takers here. Sergeant McCready from Wildlife was looking for that cutout at our meeting last night. That was when I saw Juan, remember?"

"It's all coming together, Annie. All coming together."

"What? You don't believe *Juan* stole that bear cutout, do you?"

"No, it'd been stolen long before. And my hunch is that Eddie Trueblood had something to do with it. Tony's out looking for him now. It's his last job of the day."

"Hope it doesn't take all night."

"It won't. We know his watering holes. And Eddie's IQ. Which is disproportionate to his alcohol intake every day."

"Are you going to try to talk to him tonight?"

"Soon as I hear he's in custody. That is, if he hasn't lawyered up."

Annie decided to let Dan's usual barb against the criminal defense system go. *My goodness,* she realized, *she was getting more mature by the minute, and her birthday was still five months away.*

She looked up at her friend and said with true sincerity, "Thanks for saving my life today."

Dan shifted his feet and looked down.

"Well, looks like I almost could have saved the county a bullet. Last I saw, Wolf was more than ready to make sure Todos wasn't getting up again."

"He's not in trouble, is he?"

Dan knew she was referring to Wolf, not the dead man. There were laws in Washington State about vicious dogs.

"Nope. The shot from my Glock is what got him. Wolf was just coming to the defense of his owner, as far as I'm concerned. No law against that."

They both glanced at Wolf, sleeping peacefully in the backseat. He was getting a T-bone tonight, Annie decided, meat and all. Usually all he got was the bone after Annie had gnawed off half the marrow herself.

"You know, Dan, I think Todos is the most despicable, worthless person I've ever met. Imagine setting a fire knowing that eighteen horses were trapped in their stalls."

"Don't forget he managed to also kill two people. Almost three."

"And now, if you don't mind, I'm going home to six

equines who rank higher on the food chain than any person I know. 'Cept you, of course."

"Of course."

CHAPTER 25

TUESDAY EVENING, MARCH 15TH

"Well, Martha, don't mind if I do."

Dan extended his glass, which now held just a touch of amber liquid in the bottom. Martha Sanderson reached over and deftly poured a neat shot of Glenlivet into it. Placing the bottle back on Annie's table, she picked up her own glass and took a tiny, measured sip. The unspoken question among the crowd in Annie's kitchen was how such a petite, elderly woman could wield the bottle with such authority, not to mention consume the stuff with such savoir faire.

Lavender was the only one who felt compelled to ask the question out loud.

"Gee, Martha. I never would have suspected you as a single-malt drinker."

"Fred and I often enjoyed a highball on Saturday nights. And on our trip to Scotland in sixty-eight, we acquired a definite fondness for its authentic taste." Martha took another delicate sip.

"Wow." Lavender's eyes grew big, although it wasn't clear if it was because of Martha's declaration or because of the two glasses she'd already consumed herself.

"'O, wad some Power the giftie gie us, to see ourselves as others see us,'" Martha murmured as she set down her glass.

"Huh?"

"Nothing dear. Just a little Robert Burns. I thought it was appropriate."

Annie had trudged up the road to her house after turning out her horses that morning and straight back into bad déjà vu. She saw, to her astonishment, Lavender humming tunelessly in the kitchen, concocting an elaborate casserole that looked suspiciously devoid of meat.

"Oh, there you are, dear," said Martha, appearing around the corner. "You'd probably like a nice hot cup of coffee. I'm sure I can find one. Would you like a little toast to go with that?"

The news of the fire had spread as quickly as it had on Hilda's property, and Lavender and Martha had decided that morning to come over and see how they could help Annie, whom they were sure was still tired from yesterday's work. She was. In fact, every bone and muscle in Annie's body ached from exhaustion and she wanted nothing more than to go back to bed. Thanks to her two new caretakers, she could and did, but felt immeasurably relieved. If Martha had brought Lavender, she could take her away again, too.

Now, six hours later, there were more people in Annie's home that she could ever remember. It was truly a party, except that Annie could hardly be called the hostess. The other two women had taken over. Lavender and Martha had bustled around the kitchen all afternoon, and the entire house was redolent with good aromas. Wolf showed considerable interest in the oven, so Annie was hopeful that a bit of carrion had been added to the menu.

Dan appeared in the late afternoon, just as Annie had finished feeding the horses. He bore a gift of Glenlivet, and

Annie ushered him right in. Kim and Tony followed a few minutes later, and to her surprise, they had another guest with them—Travis Latham. As soon as Mr. Latham—who insisted everyone cut the bull and call him Travis—had been seated in Annie's one cushioned chair, Wolf had left Annie's side and settled comfortably by his feet. Travis tried not to show exactly how pleased he was by the dog's gesture. Annie again vowed then and there that the remaining Belgian, once trained, would find a home at the Latham residence.

The three officers were now sprawled in the remaining chairs around the small kitchen table. It was somehow disquieting to see them attired in civilian clothes. Kim's voluptuous figure was far more evident in skinny jeans and an off-the-shoulder sweater than it had ever appeared in uniform. Tony and Dan were practically unrecognizable in flannel shirts and corduroy jeans.

Annie was dying to ask Dan a million questions, but he obviously wanted to wait until he had his audience's full attention. He had it now.

"It's a complicated case. So let's start with the first murder—that of Wayne Johnston. We know from Annie's brilliant detecting work"—Annie couldn't help a small smirk— "that Eddie Trueblood was the guy who spiked Wayne Johnston's Coke. Millie the waitress has made a positive ID."

Tony broke in. "I picked up Eddie at the Roadside Tavern last night. Of course, he wouldn't say anything after I read him his rights—the guy knows his attorney's number by heart. But there's no doubt in my mind that Eddie drugged Wayne and is responsible for his murder."

"I'm also guessing he's responsible for taking a potshot at you, Annie," Dan added.

"I wouldn't be surprised," Annie replied. "But this obviously was a two-man job. You found the bear cutout back at Hilda's place. So while Eddie was busy drugging Wayne, Todos must have been setting up the scary bear."

"Yup. And calling Wayne a few minutes before he took the final pull from his Coke. Turns out that came from a bar within a few miles of Hilda's ranch. Had to be Todos, making a bogus phone call to distract Wayne so Eddie could do his part."

Martha held up her hand as if she was in school.

"Do you think Eddie was involved in Hilda's death, as well? I'd hate to think of him going to prison for life or worse because he'd been pulled into an evil scheme someone else had concocted. Besides, what was his motivation for helping Todos?" Of everyone in the room, Annie thought, only Martha would express concern for a man who had deliberately drugged and caused another man's death.

Travis now entered the conversation.

"Eddie's nose was out of joint because Hilda had outbid him for the property, just as she'd outbid me. I wasn't the only guy who felt cheated. Only, the stakes were higher for him than me. Everyone in the county knew that Eddie had already failed at two businesses. He probably figured this was his last chance to get Cal, his father, to ante up for a third try. I expect that Eddie was even more bitter about Hilda's ploy to get the property as I was."

Dan nodded his agreement. "Funny how all the correspondence from you and your Realtor was still in Hilda's office and Eddie's wasn't. Todos wanted *you* to be considered a suspect."

"But how did Eddie and Todos find each other?" Martha was intent on finding out the full extent of Eddie's involvement. After all, they were talking about the grandson of her very best friends.

"I'm guessing the two miscreants met up at some local dive and realized their common ground—pure hatred for Hilda.

"But, in answer to your original question, Martha, my gut tells me that killing Hilda was all Todos's work. It was personal with him. He wouldn't have wanted to share the pleasure with anyone else."

"But why *did* Todos kill Hilda?" This was from Lavender, eager to join in, and looking extremely pretty, Annie thought. Her brunette hair actually was very becoming and complemented cheeks rosy with excitement. Glancing at Tony, Annie noticed him watching Lavender out of the corner of his eye and wondered whether he found her half sister attractive. She'd warn him about Lavender later—Tony was a meat eater.

"I've been trying to figure it out, too," Annie said grudgingly. "I mean, did Todos mean to kill Wayne, the bay, or both? And if it was the bay, was it because the horse lived that Hilda had to die?"

"Brilliant." Kim was genuinely complimentary. "Dan, I think we should encourage Annie to apply for a job in the Sheriff's Office."

"Over my dead body," Dan said quickly.

And mine, thought Annie. "Well, here's all I know. Hilda was alive and well on Monday, and she was dead on Tuesday, the same day Todos was supposed to have gone off and gotten the hay, right? Which was totally unnecessary, since there was enough Timothy in that barn to last the winter."

"The elephant in the room we *all* missed," Tony said sourly.

"Well, we didn't know Hilda's stocking habits." Dan wasn't ready to make this concession. "And yes, Annie, Hilda was dead on Tuesday. But she'd been dead since Monday—as soon as Todos learned that the bay was still alive. We now believe she died sometime after you hung up the phone with her and before Todos came over to your place to scout out the bay."

"How do you know all this?" Annie was still skeptical.

"Well, I'm speculating now, but I think the facts will bear me out once I make a few phone calls," said the sheriff.

"And it shows just how cold-blooded Todos was, too. He'd planned the murder *and* his alibi right down to the minute.

"My guess is that after killing Hilda, he packed his truck with hay from Hilda's barn and parked it in the back of the party, the tail end of that path you started on, Annie. So after he returned from your place, all he had to do was drive to Pullman, check into a hotel, plant an empty six-pack, order and pay for a load of local hay to be delivered at some future date, and take off again. The entire trip wouldn't have taken more than eight hours instead of the twenty-four we assumed it had . . . and remember, no one else was allowed up in Hilda's ranch house, so Todos didn't risk anyone else finding the body. You actually upset his scheme, Annie, by showing up with the bay and insisting on finding Hilda. Remember how angry Todos was that day? He hadn't expected anyone to find the body for another day or so."

Annie shivered as she remembered about how she'd so brashly barged into Hilda's home that day. No wonder Todos had hated her. But enough to kill her? He must have thought she knew something she still did not. It was time to find out.

"So what did you haul off the property? Inquiring minds want to know."

"Well, as long as it doesn't go further than this room," the sheriff warned.

"To quote someone I know, perish the thought."

Dan noisily cleared his throat. "Because we'd dismissed Todos as a suspect, we, er, probably didn't do as thorough a job looking through his digs as we might have. He lived on the property, just a few hundred feet from the arena, but up the hill, so he could always see the horses."

"Well, that's refreshing." Annie couldn't help her sarcasm. "I never did understand why Hilda lived so far away from her horses. It's nice to know that she built a horse lookout for a guy who ultimately tried to kill them all."

"And her, Annie. You keep forgetting that Todos also killed human beings, which is a far greater crime in our great state."

Annie waved away this small distinction. "So what did you find?"

"Evidence of blackmail." Tony sounded grim. "Todos had been blackmailing Hilda from the time he stepped foot on the property—we'll probably find out it started even before that."

"What could Hilda possibly have been doing to inspire blackmailing?" Martha was aghast.

"Horse doping. She'd been doing it for years, to get peak performance from her show horses and she expected Todos to carry on the tradition."

Annie yelped. No wonder Hilda's horses had always seemed like they were tied up in knots. And no doubt she'd planned on doing it to the bay!

Tony glanced at Annie. He knew exactly how she felt. "He did her bidding, but made it clear that it came with a price. Over time, money payoffs weren't enough. He told her to change her will so that he would benefit from her death. He also wanted the bay. Hilda said she'd make him a beneficiary—easy enough to say. But she refused to give up Trooper. And when Todos realized he wasn't going to get his way, he tried to engineer the horse's death before it ever arrived."

Kim took up the story. "It took us all night, but Tony and I were able to download most of the incriminating letters and texts on what we hauled out of the caretaker's cabin. Up until now, Todos had had the upper hand. But after Wayne died, Todos realized he was boxed in. He knew Hilda would realize he'd staged the trailer accident and now had something on *him*. He really didn't have much of a choice but to get rid of her. Besides, then he'd inherit the ranch."

"Or so he thought." Dan gratefully accepted another half glass of whiskey from Martha. "Hilda was by no means stupid. I don't know what Hilda showed Todos, but there was no way he stood to inherit anything after her murder."

Another gasp went around the room. Dan smiled, enjoying the suspense he'd created.

"Hilda's will is going to be released next week, but Fenton gave me the rundown this afternoon. The ranch was in both Hilda's and Marcus's names. She didn't have the authority to deed it or any portion of it over to Todos. She may have dummied up something to placate him, but it never would have stood up in court. He died thinking he would inherit everything. In fact, everything in the will goes to Hilda's heirs . . . or Marcus, if he's still alive." Dan looked uncomfortable. Annie looked straight at him.

"You know, of course, that that voice message was a cut-and-paste job."

She stated it as a fact, not a question. Annie wanted Dan and in fact the entire Sheriff's Office to publicly admit to her that Todos had concocted the initially damning evidence and that Marcus was totally vindicated in the matter of Hilda's death.

"We do now," Tony admitted. "And it was pretty clever the way he did it. We know Hilda's voice mail password was weak, and I'm not surprised Todos was able to break it. He'd downloaded onto his laptop every voice message from Marcus to Hilda over a six-month period, right up to February 14, when he apparently got the best one to do the job. It would have been easy for him to forward the messages to his own phone, then transfer to his computer."

Tony pulled out a slip of paper from his shirt pocket. "I know you'd want to know what Marcus actually said, Annie, so here goes:

"'I will try to understand your needs, Hilda. But please

don't destroy this relationship now because we're fighting. It's not dead yet. You're a good woman, Hilda, and I love you. I'll be with you before you know it.' "

Annie sat, lost in thought. He really had loved Hilda. What was she thinking? Had she ever really had a chance? She looked up.

"How about the last sentence—the one about 'consider yourself warned'?"

Tony folded up the piece of paper and put it back in his pocket. "That was the easy one. Todos took that from a previous message, where Marcus actually said, 'Consider yourself warned.' But it was said in an entirely different light. Hilda had been urging Marcus to learn how to ride. He left her a message back in January where he told her he might do that. Those were his parting words."

"But Todos was even smarter than that," Dan added. "Remember, he'd planted Travis's correspondence in Hilda's desk. The words Todos chose to implicate Marcus had an eerie resemblance to one of Travis's last letters to Hilda. I guess Todos was hoping that we'd think Travis was a suspect in the case. Got to hand it to the guy. Most killers don't leave us with not one, but two false suspects to look at. Although it wasn't to rule out Travis once we'd interviewed him," Dan added hastily.

"I'm still happy to submit to a polygraph," Travis said drily, and everyone laughed.

Annie stood up. "One more question, Dan, and then I'll let Lavender serve dinner. I know everyone's hungry, and I'd sure hate for anyone to drive home now after all that scotch you've consumed."

"Ask away, Annie."

"Did you talk to Juan? And is he involved in any way?"

"Nearly forgot about him. Good question. We talked to him this morning. I've only had a chance to question him once with an interpreter, but it appears that Juan saw Todos hauling the bear cutout into the woods behind Hilda's place. It was all quite by accident, mind you, and, of course, Juan didn't have the foggiest idea what Todos was doing. But he could see that Todos was angry, and he decided not to stick around to see where that anger might get him. Who knows, Juan might have seen something else, too, that implicates Todos in Hilda's death and . . . um, well, Hilda's death."

Everyone was tiptoeing around the subject of Marcus. Annie found it infuriating. "Look, I know what you're all thinking—that Todos killed Marcus, too. It's okay. You may all be right. But until you find a body, I'm not going to give up on the idea that somehow he's still alive. We all know now that he's completely innocent. Maybe now he'll be found. I hope so." She said the last words almost to herself.

Travis walked over to Annie.

"I hope Marcus is still alive, too. But even if he is, I understand you have eighteen horses for sale. I've decided to look for another property for my project in Alex's memory. Can we talk in the days ahead?"

"Absolutely."

Annie suddenly felt ravenous, even for Lavender's cooking.

EPILOGUE

It was a glorious spring day—the kind that made people glad they lived in the great Northwest. The breeze was light, and the temperature hovered around sixty-five degrees, downright balmy for the Peninsula. Annie was astride her pinto, Sam, watching Johan Thompson load the last of her ewes into her now-thoroughly-habitable sheep pasture. The long line of woolly white ovines waddled in, baaing like fools, as if they'd never seen the place before even though it had just been six months since they'd last grazed here. The pregnant ewes looked immense, but they were all walking well, and, judging by the sounds of solid crunches on the wet green grass, none of their appetites had dampened yet. Annie knew that when the ewes began to eschew food, their lambs were soon to follow.

Thanking Johan, she secured the gate from Sam's back and checked to make sure the steady click-click of the electric charger was unobstructed by weeds or twigs. Satisfied, she turned toward home. Wolf trotted by Sam's side.

Two weeks had passed since her nightmare experience at Hilda's ranch. She'd survived the now-predictable rush of television and other media reporters quite nicely, mostly by spending her days working in the sheep field, making the acreage ready for her flock. For all intents and purposes, Annie simply was never home. She'd parked her truck at her neighbor Chris's place just to complete the deception. Apparently no one in the media realized that farmers and ranchers sometimes worked beyond the circumference of their homes. Well, that was their problem.

Eddie Trueblood had cracked. Against the advice of his attorney, but interestingly, at the urging of his parents, he'd told Dan all about Todos's scheme to kill the bay that Hilda had so thoughtlessly purchased, although Todos had never said anything to Eddie about killing Hilda, and Dan was inclined to believe him. Eddie was now looking at a single charge of Murder 1, which carried with it a twenty-year-to-life sentence, although with Eddie's complete cooperation and mental-health issues, Dan suspected Judy Evans would offer a plea that gave him far less time in prison. And, if the defense's psychologists were persuasive enough, perhaps a sentence served at Western State Hospital, where the criminally insane were housed. Dan was fairly confident the latter would never happen. He told Annie that the people of the great state of Washington tended to pooh-pooh insanity and diminished-capacity defenses.

Annie was just sorry that Eddie refused to admit shooting at her two days before she had her "tango with Todos" as she now lightly called it.

As Sam trotted up to the stable hitching post, Annie glanced over at her round pen, where her newest project was now awaiting its first lesson. She was a gorgeous Walker, 15.3 hands tall, jet-black, with a small white diamond in the middle of her forehead. At the moment, she was following Trotter around like a moonstruck teenager, yet another equine with flawless breeding who had fallen head-over-hooves in love with a donkey.

It was time to get the mail. Annie unsaddled Sam, rubbed him down, and let him loose in the pasture with a handful of carrots as thanks for assisting her that morning. She walked up the graveled driveway, cursing her boots, but too lazy to take them off for this small chore. Western boots were great for riding and looking good in cowboy bars; for all other purposes, they fell short.

She reached into the mailbox and pulled out an assortment of flyers and bills. Then she spotted a postcard. On it was a photo of two horses on a beach, galloping along the sand. Who among her small circle of friends had the time and money to take a vacation? No one. She turned it over. In Marcus's distinctive handwriting, it read:

> *Annie,*
> *I know you've been through hell and back since I*
> *disappeared. So have I, and the most frustrating part*

is that all the time I was only a few miles from your doorstep. I'll tell you everything over dinner. And this time, I promise not to be a no-show.

I'll be in touch, very soon.

That was it. But for the moment, it was enough.

Acknowledgments

A million thanks to Fern Michaels, who convinced me I had a sellable story and gave me the courage to submit my manuscript to Kensington. Another million go to Sandy Dengler, whose eagle-eye editing, suggestions on plot and character development, and advice on how to create a compelling mystery were essential to its creation. Everyone should have a writer friend like Sandy, and I'm glad she's one of mine. Ken Kagan made sure my interpretations of WA criminal law and courtroom procedures were accurate and plausible; if I screwed up,m it's not his fault. Robert Schwager made my first draft a whole lot better. My equine vet, Dr. Cary Hills, took time out of his busy schedule to make sure I got equine dentistry right. I am exceedingly grateful to both of them. I am not a horse trainer or member of a horse rescue team, but feel fortunate that I know many women who excel in these fields. I give special thanks and all my love to my husband, who encouraged me to write, read my work many, many times, and is my greatest cheerleader. He was a bit jealous of Marcus in the beginning, but should know by now his only real competition is grazing in our pasture.

Annie will return in . . .

SADDLE UP FOR MURDER
A Carson Stables Mystery

A Kensington mass-market and e-book on sale
November 2016!